O9-CFT-554

"I'm not leaving," Kat said. "One day I'll be able to clear my name."

Justin looked at her with the most intense gaze she'd ever encountered. Then he caught her wrist and gently pulled her toward him. Sheer surprise caused her to stiffen for a moment, then heat shot from where he touched her and every nerve in her body went on alert.

What was he doing?

His lips came down on hers, warm and gentle as a spring breeze. He couldn't possibly be kissing her—but he was. His moist, firm mouth demanded a response, and instinctively her body arched toward his. His lips parted just a little and she could taste mint on his breath. He nibbled on her lower lip, then sucked it into the heat of his mouth. It was a simple, almost playful gesture, but her toes curled in response and moisture invaded the lower reaches of her body.

He released her suddenly, but smoldering heat still fired his eyes as they met hers. With a cool smile, he murmured, "Stay out of trouble." Then he walked out the door.

Praise for the work of Meryl Sawyer

"Nail-biting suspense punctuates this
thrilling romantic adventure. The name
Meryl Sawyer is synonymous with
exceptional romantic suspense.
—*Romantic Times BOOKclub* on
Better Off Dead

"A riveting work of romantic suspense…
near perfection."
—*Publishers Weekly* on *Tempting Fate*

"Meryl Sawyer has become a brand name known for
taut, sexy and very intriguing romantic suspense."
—*Romantic Times BOOKclub* on
Closer Than She Thinks

"A page-turner…glamour, romance and
adventure on a grand scale."
—*Publishers Weekly* on *Promise Me Anything*

"A thrilling romantic intrigue that will fully
satiate romance readers."
—*Midwest Book Review* on *Half Moon Bay*

"Count on Meryl Sawyer to deliver a
fast-paced thriller filled with sizzling romance."
—Jill Marie Landis, author of *Heartbreak Hotel*

MERYL SAWYER

HALF PAST
DEAD

HQN™

If you purchased this book without a cover you should be aware
that this book is stolen property. It was reported as "unsold and
destroyed" to the publisher, and neither the author nor the
publisher has received any payment for this "stripped book."

ISBN 0-373-77063-4

HALF PAST DEAD

Copyright © 2006 by M. Sawyer-Unickel

All rights reserved. Except for use in any review, the reproduction or
utilization of this work in whole or in part in any form by any electronic,
mechanical or other means, now known or hereafter invented, including
xerography, photocopying and recording, or in any information storage
or retrieval system, is forbidden without the written permission of the
publisher, Harlequin Enterprises Limited, 225 Duncan Mill Road,
Don Mills, Ontario M3B 3K9, Canada.

All characters in this book have no existence outside the imagination of
the author and have no relation whatsoever to anyone bearing the same
name or names. They are not even distantly inspired by any individual
known or unknown to the author, and all incidents are pure invention.

This edition published by arrangement with Harlequin Books S.A.

® and TM are trademarks of the publisher. Trademarks indicated with
® are registered in the United States Patent and Trademark Office, the
Canadian Trade Marks Office and in other countries.

www.HQNBooks.com

Printed in U.S.A.

The best way to love anything is as if it might be lost.
—G. K. Chesterton

Also by Meryl Sawyer

Better Off Dead
Lady Killer
Tempting Fate
Every Waking Moment
Unforgettable
Closer Than She Thinks
Trust No One
Thunder Island
Half Moon Bay
The Hideaway

And coming in 2007 from HQN Books

Kiss of Death

Someone once said that a friend is a gift you give yourself. This book is dedicated to my good friend Kat Martin. I named the heroine after her and drew inspiration for her character from the real Kat. In appreciation for the years of friendship and for seeing me through the good times and bad— this one's for you, Kat.

PROLOGUE

"YOU'VE GOT TO KNOW when to hold 'em, know when to fold 'em. Above all, a killer instinct separates a winner from a loser."

Texas Hold-'Em was the man's favorite television show. If he wasn't home to see it, he recorded the program. Most contestants on the game were fair players. He would grant them that much. But if he'd been playing with them, the suckers would soon find out they didn't have killer instincts.

He knew he would never play Texas Hold-'Em on TV. His life was too important to devote so much time to the poker circuit. A pity. People had no clue what they were missing.

The man's attention was diverted from thoughts of poker by the task at hand. He trudged through Mississippi's waist-high underbrush in the dense forest of second-growth pine. He'd driven on one of the dozens of overgrown logging roads in the area, passing several hunting shacks hidden behind the dense brush. Like a carpet, cushy pine needles put a slight bounce in his step despite the slack load he lugged over one shoulder. The rank stench of the decomposing body made him breathe though his mouth.

He hadn't killed anyone in years, but he'd known this was inevitable. He accepted the risk the way he accepted a great many hazards. What else could be expected when he lived a double life? Risk brought a rush that ranked right up there with sex or money, and he'd come to crave it like a schedule two narcotic.

This snoop on his back had forced him to play his hand. A savage thrill coursed through him. Killing this blackmailer hadn't been as easy as he'd anticipated. She'd thrashed and moaned and bucked, but in the end her short, staccato breaths stopped and the life left her body like the air fizzling out of a party balloon.

His killer instinct had kicked in. Dump the body in the woods. By the time it was discovered, the advanced decomposition would give the authorities trouble identifying the corpse.

He pitched the woman into the thicket. Her carcass hit some branches and several snapped, a dry brittle sound in the darkness. A *whump* told him she'd landed on the ground, and he heaved a sigh of relief. Maggots and spring rain would take care of the trace evidence. What more could he want?

He turned to leave. But how could a man walk away from a fresh kill without admiring his handiwork? No way. He glanced over his shoulder. All he could see was her leg cocked at an odd angle in the underbrush.

Was he the best, or what?

He chuckled, the thick foliage muffling his laughter. The changing tides of destiny never failed to amuse him. Fate guided him and wouldn't ever desert him.

Some secrets should be carried to the grave. Dead men, dead women no longer have the opportunity to reveal your secrets. The power was his and always had been. This bitch couldn't be allowed to blackmail him and bring his life's work crashing down around him. Who was she? A nothing. He doubted anyone would report her missing.

CHAPTER ONE

Three months later

KAITLIN WELLS ONCE LOVED sunrise, a time of hope, promise. A new beginning. Kat hadn't seen the sun come up for four years, three months, and forty-two days. But she never missed a sunset.

She trained her gaze on the meadow in the distance. Buzzards spiraled on outstretched wings, circling lower and lower to feast on some creature she couldn't see. Probably a squirrel or rabbit in the last throes of death.

On the horizon the sun sulked in a spring sky that was a bleak shade of gray. Trees loomed like sentinels, guarding the top of the ridge, dark silhouettes backlit by a sun that would blister the earth in another month.

A sound behind Kat brought home to mind. She could almost hear children kicking cans and yelling at each other, almost smell chicken frying in cast iron pans. She could almost see the sidewalks banked by azalea bushes laden with pink blossoms.

Almost.

Back home in Twin Oaks, day drifted lazily into night. Here, darkness fell with eerie swiftness. The sun had dropped behind the ridge now, and less than half of the orb was still visible.

"Hey! What the hell do you think you're doin'?"

She ignored the guard's voice behind her and remained standing on the toilet and gazing out the window. The image of home slipped out of her mind like a fleeting dream. She trained her eyes on the horizon beyond the barred window. The light of the dying sun glinted off the razor wire capping the concrete wall, but Kat hardly noticed. She refused to miss the sunset. It was the only thing in her life with the power to lift her soul out of its dark spiral into hell.

Whack!

The guard's nightstick slammed against the back of her thighs. She'd been expecting the blow. The pain shooting down her legs didn't bother Kat. Nothing could hurt her now.

"I asked what you're doin'," the guard repeated.

"Watching the sunset."

"You've got company. A newbie."

She'd realized having the small cell to herself wouldn't last. Like all prisons, the Danville Federal Correctional Institution was overcrowded. There were at least two inmates in every cell and sometimes three or four.

With a metallic click, the cell door slammed shut, but Kat didn't bother to turn around. The sun had vanished, leaving spectral-gray twilight. Out of nowhere appeared a skull-like moon. Its pale light intensified with each passing second.

"Which bunk should I take?"

The timid voice grated on Kat's nerves like shards of glass. She jumped off the toilet and glared at the new arrival. Red hair flowed over her shoulders like molten lava. Well, prison shampoo would zap its shine. The woman was probably in her twenties, but didn't look much older than fifteen. Her brown eyes were bloodshot and puffy from crying.

"Use the top bunk."

The woman tossed her bag onto the upper bunk and stuck out her hand. "I'm Abby Lester."

She made no move to shake hands. "Kat Wells." She

dropped onto the lower bunk and picked up the book she'd checked out of the prison's library. It didn't pay to be friendly with the other inmates, especially a newbie. New arrivals were encouraged to snitch. They often made up things just to get a pack of cigarettes or a Hershey's bar. Kat had learned this the hard way and paid the price.

Ad seg—administrative segregation—was what the authorities called it. But prisoners didn't try to be politically correct. To them it was solitary, or "the hole." Kat had survived her time in the hole by mentally reviewing the new words she'd learned from *Building A Power Vocabulary.* She wasn't sure what she would do with words like *implausible* or *recuse,* but one day she would walk out of here. She wanted to be smarter than when she'd arrived.

"I shouldn't be locked up." Abby's voice was barely above a whisper.

Kat didn't take her eyes off the page. She knew Abby was going to insist she was innocent. That's what everyone in the joint claimed. If they confessed their guilt, there had been a really good reason why they'd committed a crime.

"I didn't know my boyfriend was going to rob the post office. He never said a thing about it. Honest. I was just waiting for him in the car."

Kat didn't respond. She tried to concentrate on Steinbeck's words. She'd read *Of Mice and Men* when she'd been preparing to go to college. She'd sobbed at the end, but this time she knew she wouldn't cry. Tears were a waste of time.

"My mother's using her retirement money to find me another attorney. He'll get me a new trial," Abby said, her voice choked with tears.

Abby's mother loved her.

Kat's lungs turned to stone, and the blood drained from her heart. She forced her eyes closed, then quickly opened them. Steinbeck's words were slightly blurred.

Thank God her father hadn't lived to see her in prison. Unlike her mother, he would have come to visit every chance he could. Her mother hadn't written even one letter. Other inmates received care packages from home, but Kat's mother and sister couldn't be bothered.

"THE COUNCIL HAS TO VOTE on appointing a new sheriff. We can't afford a special election. The council will go along with what I want."

Justin Radner nodded slightly at Tyson Peebles, mayor of Twin Oaks. He was the first black mayor of the small town where Justin had grown up. Although Peebles was seven years older, he and Justin had a lot in common. Both had been star players on the Harrington High football team. They'd each been offered a much-coveted scholarship to Ole Miss. Tyson had gone on to become one of the university's top stars. From there he'd been drafted by the Steelers and had played seven years in the NFL until a tackle after the whistle nearly paralyzed him.

Justin had refused the Ole Miss scholarship and accepted one from Duke instead. Ole Miss was THE football school in the South. Who in their right mind turned down Ole Miss? Occasionally Justin wondered how different his life might have been had he stayed in his home state.

"I never expected Sheriff Parker to have a heart attack. He'd been around forever. No one was prepared to hunt for a new sheriff." Filpo Johnson rocked back in his chair beside Justin and puffed on a Cuban cigar. "Thar's not much crime here, truth to tell. Kids 'n drugs mostly."

Even though he was black, Filpo loved to play the white cracker. Forget it. Justin wasn't fooled. Filpo headed the city council, and he had a mind as sharp as a new razor. Filpo had graduated from the school of hard knocks. He ran several successful businesses on the "north side" where most of the black people lived.

"The *Lucky Seven* docks at Tanner's Landing. It's in the unincorporated area where we have a contract to provide fire and law enforcement services." Peebles spread his hands wide and smiled. "The *Lucky Seven* has its own security. We don't have to worry about them."

The riverboat was owned by a syndicate rumored to be controlled by the Sartiano mob family from New Orleans. Twin Oaks had been a dying town until gambling hit the Mississippi. Justin bet half the town was employed at the floating casino or relied on it financially in some way. He got Mayor Peeble's message. Let the *Lucky Seven* handle its own problems.

"There are five of us on the council," Filpo drawled in a voice like warm honey. "Buck Mason will vote no."

For a gut-cramping second, the world froze.

Buck Mason on the city council? Since when? Filpo was right, no way in hell would Mason vote for him. Did it matter? Unless he missed his guess, the mayor and his buddy already had enough votes to have Justin confirmed as sheriff until the next election. It would be up to him to do a good enough job to convince the voters to elect him then—despite Buck Mason.

Filpo added, "Mason's got a hard-on for you big-time."

"Now you're scaring me."

Filpo chuckled, adding, "Just warning you, my man."

Justin shrugged, then stood up. "You have my cell number."

He strode out of city hall. Along the way Justin walked by the mayor's secretary. She quickly averted her head and pretended to study some papers on the desk. Once she'd been all over him, but that had been when he'd been a football star. And Verity had still been alive.

Justin walked into the morning sunlight. The town square, like so many others in the South, featured a bronze statue of a Confederate soldier with a musket. Massive pecan trees planted after the First World War shaded the square, and bright pink azalea bushes lined the walks, their blossoms swaying in a breeze scented with honeysuckle.

A vague memory invaded his thoughts as he gazed from the top of the city hall steps. He was a kid again, standing beside his mother. Men in white—some on horseback, others walking—paraded around the square. He clutched his mother's hand, asking, "Ghosts?" She'd hesitated a moment before responding that these were just men pretending to be ghosts—she'd marched him swiftly away from the square.

Years later, he learned he'd witnessed the last legally sanctioned KKK march in Twin Oaks. Times had changed, he decided, starting down the steps. In a town that had roughly the same number of blacks and whites, Twin Oaks now had a black mayor and a black president of the city council.

He seriously doubted that meant folks around here were any less prejudiced. They'd just learned to hide it better. Twin Oaks was half an hour and thirty years away from Natchez. Change came with agonizing slowness to small Southern towns.

Prejudice was something he would have to deal with when he became sheriff. Yessir. He'd be offered the job. He'd left Duke and enlisted in the army, where he'd become a Ranger. After the military, he'd joined the New Orleans Police Department. He would still be there if a drug bust hadn't gone bad and a bullet damn near killed him.

He'd returned fire and taken out Buster Albright, whose brother, Lucas, had sworn to get Justin. The court had sentenced Lucas to ten years in jail, but Justin knew Lucas wouldn't cool off in prison. One day the man would come gunning for him.

Why in hell had he returned home to seek the sheriff's job when he'd heard Parker had died? The answer was simple. Twin Oaks was in his blood. You could move, but you never really left the place behind. The town was small enough to have that old-fashioned feeling, even though it had grown in recent years, and everyone didn't know each other the way they had when he'd lived here.

He checked the rearview mirror for traffic and caught the reflection of his deep blue eyes. His dark hair was a bit long, he admitted. He would need to get it trimmed before meeting the rest of the city council—especially Buck Mason.

Justin revved the engine and headed out to Shady Acres Trailer Village. What a joke. Three dozen single-wides that had been there since the seventies did not make a village. It was a half step from living in your car.

The original owner had entertained grandiose ideas. A fancy wrought-iron archway typical of New Orleans had soared above the entrance. Now it had rusted and pieces had broken off or been scavenged. Several majestic oaks with swags of moss were clustered around the entry. Beyond the trees, he spotted three rusting Fords on cinder blocks that had been there for as long as he could remember. Muddy pickups and battered cars languished near ramshackle trailers.

"Here goes nothing," he muttered under his breath as he stopped near the single-wide he'd called home for the first seventeen years of his life. His mother had tried her damnedest to make the trailer look like a real home, but the white picket fence she'd painted every spring hadn't been touched since she'd died two years ago.

Justin stepped out of the Silverado. His boots hit the dirt with a thunk and dust billowed up to his ankles. Whoever was renting the trailer didn't appear to be home. Justin eased aside the gate dangling from one rusting hinge and walked up to the door. Wood slat steps with weeds jutting through the gaps between boards led up to the makeshift porch.

Justin could see himself sitting on the steps eating a mayo sandwich on white bread. His mother had never allowed weeds to sprout through the gaps, but even she couldn't keep out the snakes who liked the coolness during the ferocious summer heat. He'd dropped pebbles between the slats to see if any snakes were coiled below. A *plunk* told him he'd hit dirt, not a snake.

He shook off the memory and knocked. A Dixie Chicks tune blasted from the rear of the trailer park. With it came a gust of wind and the scent of rabbit stew. He wondered how many rabbits he'd shot and brought home for his mother to cook, when they hadn't had enough money to do more than pay the rent on the trailer.

No one came to the door. He tried the knob, but it was locked. He walked down the wooden steps and went around back where a propane tank supplied fuel to the trailer. The garden his mother had tended, even when she'd been so eaten up by cancer that she could barely walk, had been taken over by weeds and wild onions.

He didn't get it. He honestly didn't. From the moment he'd joined the Army and began making money, he'd tried to persuade his mother to move to a nicer place. To the end, she'd insisted this was her home.

"I'm glad you can't see it now, Ma," he whispered to himself. "The place is a disaster."

He saw a flash of red in the dense brush beyond the forsaken garden. What the hell? Wildlife thrived in the woods around Twin Oaks, but the only animal he could think of that color was a fox. The ones around here were gray, not red.

"I gots me a gun trained on yore back, sonny."

There was no mistaking the three-pack-a-day rasp. Cooter Hobbs should have died long before Justin's mother had, but the old cuss was too ornery to kick the bucket.

"It's me, Cooter," Justin said, turning slowly, his hands in the air.

Cooter stared at him from behind the barrel of a shotgun. He hadn't changed a bit since Justin had moved to Shady Acres as a child. His hair had been white then and shot skyward like a field of wheat. Beneath searching eyes worthy of a repo man were oysterlike bags.

"Whacha' doin' here, you?"

"Just checking out the old place."

"New feller in town lives here now. Works at the *Lucky Seven*. Janitor or some such." Cooter gestured at the single-wide with the weapon. "Don't keep up the place like yore ma. Stupid sumbitch."

Yore instead of *your* and *sumbitch*. No sir, time hadn't improved Cooter's vocabulary or mellowed him one bit.

"Movin' back, you?" Cooter hitched at his bib overalls with his thumb.

"Maybe."

"I knew you wouldn't amount to nuthin'. Shoulda gone to Ole Miss."

Justin bit back a smart-ass reply. He was going to get plenty of grief about Ole Miss when he moved home. There would be a lot of gossip about Verity, too, but no one would dare say anything about her death to his face.

Cooter raised the rifle and took aim at something in the bushes behind Justin.

"What are you doing?"

Cooter shook his head and lowered the shotgun. "Damn dog's too fast fer me."

"What dog?"

"The ole red mutt the Dickersons left behind."

Justin remembered the Dickerson's cute puppy. He'd played with Redd several times when he'd visited his mother. The pup had been tied in front of their trailer on the last morning Justin had come to see his mother. He'd taken her to the nearest hospital in Jackson, but by then it was too late to save her.

"Midnight movers," Cooter said with a huff of disgust.

People who didn't have rent money often moved in the middle of the night. If they didn't, Cooter would demand a television set or a gun as partial payment on the rent. Cooter didn't own Shady Acres but he managed it in return for free rent.

"Mutt's jist an egg suck dog."

"Redd's probably starving."

"Sumbitch's as good as dead." Cooter turned to leave. "Git outta here, you. Don't gots no vacancies. No one wants you here anyway."

Cooter shuffled off. Justin knew plenty of people, not just Cooter, would share this attitude. At least he had a year to prove himself before he would have to run for sheriff.

He shouldered his way through the brush and gave a low whistle. No sign of the red dog. He whistled, then called, "Here, boy. Here, Reddy."

A twig cracked and a black nose poked out. A head emerged just far enough so the dog could see Justin. The animal was as alert as a wolf. On guard. Set to hightail it.

"Reddy, remember me?" Justin squatted down so he was eye level with the dog, a trick he'd learned from the K-9 dog handlers in New Orleans. "It's okay, boy. It's okay."

The animal watched Justin but made no move to come closer. Justin noticed the dog's rib cage showing through his fur. There was game in the brush, mostly squirrels, rabbits, and nutria, but a dog raised as a pet wouldn't be much of a hunter.

"Come here, boy." Justin sat down on the carpet of pine needles. His cell phone vibrated in his pocket.

"Radner," he answered.

"You're in," Peebles told him. "Only Buck Mason didn't vote for you."

"Why am I not surprised?" He watched the dog creep forward a fraction of an inch. "When do you want me to start?"

"Tomorrow."

"I'll need a few days to clean up things in New Orleans and to find a place here."

"Make it fast. Kids hunting squirrels found a body in the unincorporated area. Dougherty says its been in the woods for some time, but you know he isn't up to a murder investigation."

Tom Dougherty had been a deputy sheriff for as long as Justin could remember. He was a nice guy, but he was about as bright as Alaska in winter.

"Any idea who the victim is?" Justin asked, kicking himself for the rush he felt. Someone was dead. He shouldn't be excited, but he was. He'd assumed returning to Twin Oaks would mean nothing but routine police work, and it would be hard to prove himself. If he solved this crime, he would certainly be elected sheriff.

"No. Dougherty says there aren't any missing person reports."

"He should check neighboring jurisdictions."

"From what Doughtery says we could have our first homicide in…what?…eleven years. Since what's-his-name shot his partner during an argument over their hogs."

"Maybe I'd better take a look before they contaminate the crime scene."

"Good idea. I'll call Dougherty and let him know you're coming."

Justin hung up, noticing Redd's curiosity had prompted him to slither forward a little more. The dog was peering at him, his head bowed slightly, his tail between his legs as if he expected to be kicked.

Justin wished he had food, but he didn't. He stuck out his hand. "Here, Reddy."

The dog ventured nearer, obviously responding to the sound of his name.

"Good boy. Good, Redd."

The dog slunk closer, and Justin patted his head. "Good boy. Looks like you've fallen on hard times."

Redd's tail swished just a little. Justin wouldn't call it a wag, but it was a start. The dog, a mix of golden retriever and coon hound, once had a silky coat the color of a new penny. It was matted and full of burrs. A tick bloated with blood hung below one eye.

"You could use a trip to the vet and a day at one of those fancy dog spas."

He stroked his head and fondled his ears. Redd licked his hand. Just his luck. The only one in town genuinely glad to see him was a dog.

CHAPTER TWO

"Ouch," Kat muttered under her breath. She'd nicked her knuckle with the carrot peeler for the third time. The dull blade could barely handle a carrot, but she was expected to peel beets from the prison garden with it.

"Hurry up," yelled the crew chief, a lifer from Baton Rouge who'd ruled the kitchen for twenty-three years.

Kat didn't respond. What difference did it make how well peeled the beets were? Few prisoners ate them. Most tucked them in their uniforms and took them back to their cells to make *pruno,* rotgut hootch.

She chipped away at a beet the size of a football. Whatever they were using to fertilize the garden really worked. Her hands were scarlet from beet juice that wouldn't wash away for days, but she kept scraping at it. This was better than her last assignment in the laundry.

Don't you dare hope, she told herself.

Still, she couldn't help fantasizing about being assigned to the garden. It was backbreaking work, but at least she'd be outside in the sunshine. The air would be fresh, the way it was in Twin Oaks. If she were home again, she wouldn't complain about the dank scent of the Big Muddy when the wind blew toward the town. Anything would be better than a jail rife with body odor that the most powerful disinfectant couldn't wash away.

"Yo, Wells!"

Kat kept her back to the male voice and furiously hacked

at the huge beet. Male guards sometimes singled out female prisoners to get them alone. They'd be pulled into storage closets while the other guards pretended not to notice.

"Hey! Bitch! I'm talkin' to ya."

Kat looked over her shoulder at the hulking guard, who was new. He glowered at her from the double doors that led into the kitchen area. Even though there were five women around Kat, an eerie stillness enveloped the room. She knew what they were thinking: the closet.

Kat was prepared with a shank hidden in her shoe. She was ready to use the makeshift knife even though it would mean solitary confinement. Then she would have to start over and be assigned to the latrines. It would take her two years to work up the job chain to the kitchen again. Extra time might be added to her sentence.

"Warden wants to see ya."

Yeah, sure, she thought. And pigs fly. Warden Bronson didn't want to see her. This was just an excuse to get her alone. She slowly washed her beet-stained hands in the large sink where the remaining beets were soaking off the dirt.

How exactly was she going to stop him? She didn't want to kill him—then she'd never get out of this hellhole—but she wasn't going to allow him to rape her. Sweat began to bead on her scalp. She took a deep breath, but it did nothing to calm her.

"Hop to. The warden doesn't like waitin'."

No one looked her in the eye as she crossed the large room. The guard moved aside, and she sized him up. He was a short man built like a coal furnace. A shank wound might just infuriate him, and he could use it as an excuse to beat her to death.

Under the glare of fluorescent lights, she walked at his side down the corridor. The concrete walls had once been painted gray, but they appeared to be molting now. There was a guard at the far end of the hallway, watching the women working in the laundry. Several storage closets lined the corridor. The guard marched her right by them.

"Yo, Hank. Hozit goin'?" he greeted the guard stationed at the laundry. "We're off to see the warden."

"Get out!" the guard replied as he gave Kat the once-over.

She had green eyes with long lashes and brownish blond hair. She'd come into prison chunky but hard work and prison food had left her slender. Once an ugly duckling, she realized she was somewhat attractive now. Once she would have welcomed the change, but in prison she knew this was bad news. She'd learned not to encourage guards by making eye contact.

The guard led her down the cement stairs to the first floor—the way to the administrative wing of the prison. A flicker of apprehension registered deep in her brain. She'd never actually known anyone who'd been taken to see the warden. Once a week, he came through the prison with the captain of the guards, looked around, and spoke in hushed tones with the captain, then left.

At the bottom of the stairs, the guard punched a code into the security panel at the steel door leading to the administrative wing. After a clicking sound the pneumatic door swung open, then closed behind them with a whoosh. They had to wait for the door to shut behind them and automatically re-lock before the second security door finally opened.

On the other side, the concrete gave way to industrial beige carpeting. The walls had fresh paint and travel posters mounted on them. It wasn't plush but compared to the other side of the door, it rated four stars.

Oh, my God, Kat thought, air suspended in her lungs. Maybe the warden did want to see her.

Why?

She followed the guard, unable to think of a reason. Her first parole hearing wasn't coming up for another year. She hadn't been in trouble for months. Even if she had done something wrong, the captain of the guards handled punishment, not the warden.

The guard walked into the reception area outside the warden's office. A secretary with hair like steel wool hovered over a computer terminal. She glanced up, saying, "Kaitlin Wells?"

"Yes," Kat replied, her voice tight.

"I'll let the warden know you're here." The secretary picked up the telephone and announced Kat's arrival.

A paralyzing numbness spread through her body, then subsided a bit, replaced by spasms in her gut. What now? Hadn't she been tortured enough for a crime she didn't commit?

Warden Bronson opened the door to the inner office. His gray hair was cut ruthlessly short, which made his forehead seem higher than normal. Probing brown eyes stared at her while he spoke to the guard.

"Wait here for Ms. Wells." To the secretary, he said, "Hold all my calls."

He stepped aside and motioned for her to come into his office. Uneasy, Kat stepped in and froze. Her breath came in short, shallow bursts, making it difficult to think. Harlan Westcott, the federal prosecutor responsible for her robbery conviction, sat in a chair in front of the warden's desk.

A charged silence like the air before a summer storm filled the room. Lightning was about to strike, she decided, and it was going to electrocute her. The warden closed the door with a clank that seemed more ominous than the way guards slammed shut the steel cell doors.

"Hello, Kat," Harlan said casually as if they were old friends.

Kat nodded at him but didn't trust herself to speak. At the trial, the prosecutor had been hateful—no match for her public defender. The memory triggered a raw, bitter ache underscored with anger.

Warden Bronson told her to sit down as he sat behind his

desk. The only chair was next to Harlan Westcott. She walked over and lowered herself into the seat without looking at the prosecutor. Her hands were still red from beet juice, but she didn't care what Harlan or the warden thought.

"I have a proposition for you," Harlan said.

Those who hadn't seen him in the courtroom might have mistaken the curl of his lips for a smile. Kat didn't respond. What was going on? What kind of proposition could Harlan Westcott have for her?

"Do you want to go home?" asked the warden.

Her heart lurched at the word *home*. Why were they jerking her chain?

"You can walk out of here tomorrow," Harlan told her. "If…"

If. The big if. The catch was coming. She could see it in Harlan's ice-blue eyes—the same eyes that had relentlessly accused her of taking money from the bank's vault.

"If you help us catch the people who really took the money from Mercury National Bank, you may go home."

Her world slammed to an abrupt stop, and her breath stalled in her lungs. Sound in the room ceased. She was conscious of Harlan's lips moving, but she didn't hear the words. Had he really said he knew she wasn't guilty?

"We know you didn't take the money," the warden said.

A surge of white-hot, primitive anger hit her like a sucker punch to the gut. She wanted to smash her fist into Harlan's smug face. Rage throbbed inside her, more intense than anything she'd ever experienced. It was a full minute before she could speak.

"Then why on earth am I still in this hellhole?"

"I can't reveal my source," Harlan replied. "We uncovered the information as part of an ongoing investigation."

She clamped down on her jaw and battled the nearly uncontrollable urge to call him a son of a bitch, but she refused to give him the satisfaction of seeing her lose it. "Then I'm free."

The warden spread his hands wide and the ring on his pinkie caught the light. "No, you're not."

If they knew she was innocent, why wouldn't she go free? How could this be justice in America? She'd spent over three miserable years in prison.

"It's complicated, but I think Harlan has the solution."

"I'll just bet he does." A bitter edge crept into her voice despite her best efforts to conceal her emotions.

Harlan Westcott adjusted his perfectly knotted rep tie, and a whipcord thin muscle in his neck pulsed. "We can't just release you without explaining why. At this point it would jeopardize this undercover investigation, but if you agree to help us…" He paused. "You can leave tomorrow."

Tomorrow. She could be free. She would be able to raise her face to the sun and smell the flowers and enjoy fresh air. She would do just about anything to get out of here.

"If I don't help him, then I can't leave?" she again asked the warden, unable to believe they could refuse to release her.

"I'm afraid not." His voice deepened with concern. "I'm legally bound to keep you incarcerated until what Harlan has discovered becomes public record."

"When will that be?"

"Who knows? It's a large-scale investigation. It could go on for a year or two." Harlan's shrug said: Who cares?

They'd discovered she was innocent but weren't going to make the facts public. Betrayal whiplashed through her. She should be allowed to leave. She hadn't planned on returning to Twin Oaks. Why would she? Her own mother and sister had turned their backs on her. She intended to go to Miami and start over.

"I want a lawyer." She ground out the words, hardly able to keep from shouting. "You're violating my civil rights."

"Do you have the money for an attorney?" Harlan asked in a snide tone.

Kat didn't bother to respond. They both knew she didn't have a cent.

The warden cleared his throat. "It could be months before a PD could find the time to handle this."

PD. Public defender. She'd been forced to use one at her trial. The guy had been nothing but an empty suit. She refused to trust her fate again to one of those jerks. If you were rich enough to afford a first-rate lawyer in America, you could get away with just about anything. Everyone else did time. "What would I have to do?"

"For good behavior, you'd be released on a work furlough program," Harlan explained. "That's what we would tell people. You would return to Twin Oaks and work at the *Tribune*."

"Doing what?"

"You'll be assistant to the editor, David Noyes. No one will know about your connection to the bureau."

"Bureau? Like the FBI?"

"The Mississippi Bureau of Investigation."

This wasn't logical. Not at all. Why would the bureau need her? "What will I be doing for them?"

He gazed at her with the haughty superior stare she recognized from the courtroom. "We believe someone will contact you about the robbery. Not all of the missing money was recovered. We believe they'll double-check to see if you have it or know where it is."

"What am I supposed to do if they contact me?"

"We'll give you a number to call. We just need to know the identity of the caller." He said each word slowly and deliberately as if he was trying to have an intellectual conversation with a toddler. "It's possible this is part of a larger money laundering scheme."

This must be a bigger operation. That's why the MBI was involved. She was being used as bait in what was probably a dangerous situation.

"If I refuse to do this—"

"You'll remain in jail until you come up for parole next year." Triumph crackled in Harlan's voice. "Your mother might die before then."

She gasped, shock seeping through every pore and spreading through her body with a mind-numbing speed. "Is my mother ill?"

Harlan glanced at the warden with a frown, then turned to Kat. "Your mother didn't tell you she has ovarian cancer?"

Kat shook her head. She didn't bother mentioning she hadn't heard anything from her mother and sister since she was arrested. How could Tori not have at least dropped her a note about their mother?

Cancer.

Her mother was dying. The revelation hit a target she hadn't realized still existed—the hollow spot that had once been her heart. The news resurrected old demons, feelings she'd believed had died here in prison.

Kat had convinced herself that she no longer cared about her mother. She hated her mother for deserting Kat when she'd most needed her. Her feelings toward Tori were more ambivalent. No, Tori hadn't come to her aid either, but there had been times, when they'd been growing up, that Tori had tried to help Kat. Above all, Tori never tattled. If Kat slipped out to visit her friend in the trailer park, Tori kept her mouth shut.

"Work with us and you can go home and see your mother," Harlan said.

"Okay," she replied. She didn't have a choice, and both men knew it.

"You'll be undercover. Only you and your contact will know the truth. Don't tell anyone—not even your mother."

She would be free but everyone in Twin Oaks would still think she was a criminal and treat her like one. This just kept getting better and better. It didn't matter, she decided. Anything was better than being in prison.

"The field agent who will handle you is with the bureau's office in Jackson. Contact him if you have anything to report. He'll give you another number. It belongs to an agent who's been working undercover in Twin Oaks. Don't call it unless there's an emergency."

"Tell me what's really going on," she demanded. "Will I be in danger?"

Harlan lifted his briefcase off the floor and stood up. "I don't have the details. I'm sure the agent who picks you up tomorrow will brief you."

KAT NEVER RETURNED to the kitchen. Instead she went to her cell and stretched out on her bunk. The paperwork was complete, and she would be released first thing in the morning. The agent from the Mississippi Bureau of Investigation office in Jackson was scheduled to drive her to Twin Oaks. He would get her a car and arrange for a place for her to live.

Her mother had ovarian cancer. Unbelievable. How long did she have to live? Would her mother want to see her? Kat thought about it and couldn't decide.

Her mother had barely tolerated Kat when she'd been growing up. She'd often wondered why her mother loved Tori but not her. She'd asked her father. He'd solemnly told her that it was his fault. Loretta Wells still loved Tori's father.

Being near death changed people, or so Kat had heard. Despite the way her mother deserted her, despite Kat's vow to never see her again. Kat knew she had to say goodbye.

"Hi," Abby said when the guard opened the cell door for the redhead. "I've been assigned to latrine duty."

"Newbies always get latrine duty. It makes everything after that look good."

"Where are the latrines? We have our own john in here."

"There are toilets by the showers, near the exercise yard, and at the guard station. They're the worst. Most of the guards are men with lousy aim."

"Oh, yuck!" Abby climbed up to her bunk.

"Get to know Etta. She's one of the guards. Black hair in a long ponytail. She's in charge of job assignments."

"I—I'm innocent. I shouldn't be here. You don't know what it's like to—"

"It doesn't matter. It is what it is—and then you deal with it. You have to learn to get along here. Even if you're innocent, it's going to take time to arrange for a new trial."

Abby sniffled. "I'm scared. Really scared."

Something about Abby's tone struck a chord in Kat. With a pang deep in her chest, she realized she'd been Abby once—a green newbie at the mercy of a cruel system. No one had clued her into the unspoken rules that inmates in the Graybar Hilton lived by. She'd had to learn the bitter lessons on her own.

Once the guards had it in for you, it was a one-way ticket to hell. It didn't take much to anger them. Kat had turned them against her when she complained about a guard fondling her breasts while supposedly searching for drugs.

"Weren't you frightened when you first arrived?" Abby asked.

"I'm still frightened. Everyone here is. They're lying if they say they're not."

"You get used to prison. It gets better, right? This is a federal prison, not a jail loaded with killers."

Kat couldn't bring herself to lie. "No. It doesn't get better. Don't kid yourself. Danville has just as many hardened criminals as other prisons."

"I don't know what I'll do if my mother can't get me a new trial."

Kat detected the threat of tears in Abby's voice. "How long is your sentence?"

The words hung in the air like a noxious cloud. Kat

couldn't see Abby in the bunk above her, but she suspected the girl was crying.

Finally, Abby said, a quaver in her voice, "Fifty years."

"What? Fifty years for robbing the post office?" Kat jumped to her feet so she could look up at the girl.

Abby let out a gulping sob, "Travis shot a customer who tried to stop him."

"That explains it." She could be wrong, but Kat thought the possibility of another trial was remote. Even if Harlan Westcott hadn't discovered the truth, Kat would have been up for parole next year. This poor kid would be a shriveled-up old crone by the time she came up for parole, her life over. Spent in hell on earth.

"I'm sure your mother will get you a new trial, but you're here until she does. I'm leaving in the morning."

"How?" Abby sat bolt upright and swung around so her legs were dangling over the side of the bunk.

"I'm getting out on a work furlough for good behavior."

Tears trickled down Abby's cheeks. "Th-that's great."

"Come down here." Kat sat on her bunk. "There are a few things I need to explain to you."

CHAPTER THREE

JUSTIN STUDIED the coroner's report on the body that had been discovered in the woods. Like many small towns, Twin Oaks did not have a full-time coroner. Autopsies were seldom necessary. When they were, a local mortician performed them. This autopsy did not reveal a cause of death.

Justin had arrived at the scene just before the woman's body had been removed. It was obvious the victim had been dumped in the heavy underbrush. She hadn't simply wandered off and died. It was murder. But what had killed her?

He'd instructed the coroner to take extensive photos and collect tissue samples. Now it was time to call in a favor. He phoned a guy in the New Orleans coroner's office.

By noon the samples and the body were being driven to New Orleans by one of his deputies. There was little else Justin could do for now. There had been nothing at the crime scene. Spring rains had washed away what trace evidence there might have been.

"Come on, boy," he said to Redd.

The dog cautiously popped his head out from under the big wood desk that had belonged to Sheriff Parker for over thirty years. Redd had spent last night at the vet's and this morning at the Dog Spaw. Nothing could be done to save his fur. Redd's coat had been given a boot-camp cut. The groomer had been able to trim his ears so they were still a little fluffy, but his tail had to be shaved, too.

"You're a sight." Justin stroked the dog's head, and Redd wagged his tail. "Come on. We're outta here."

Redd trotted at his heels. He seemed to sense he was Justin's dog now.

"If you need me, call me on my cell," he told Nora Adams.

"Yes, indeedy," she replied.

Nora was older than the pharaohs and looked like one. She had dyed black hair pulled straight back into a golf-ball-sized bun that emphasized her thin face and taut skin. She'd been the receptionist/dispatcher since Justin had been a child.

With little crime and five deputies who did their best to raise revenue by catching speeders and writing up DUIs, Justin figured Nora pretty much ran the place. Well, hell, that was about to change. But he wasn't rattling her cage until he'd settled in.

"Do you want me to have Sheriff Parker's cruiser tuned up for you?"

"Good idea," Justin said, and waved as he walked out the station's door.

He didn't plan to use the cruiser, but it wouldn't hurt to have another car in good repair. Something was always going wrong with patrol cars, and with the budget crunch in Twin Oaks, he wasn't likely to get any new equipment.

He opened the door to his pickup, saying, "Get in."

Redd hopped in the passenger side. Justin walked around, opened his door, and lowered the window for Redd before he climbed in. Like all dogs, Redd loved to hang out the window, nose to the breeze.

He pulled out of the space marked Sheriff Parker. "I guess we'll have to find a house with a fenced yard for you." He thought about it for a moment. He didn't like leaving a dog alone in a yard all day. There wasn't any reason he couldn't take Redd with him most of the time. "Deputy Dawg," he told Redd, but the dog was too busy sniffing the fragrant honeysuckle in the air to pay attention.

Justin's cell rang. It was Mayor Peebles.

"Any news on the homicide?"

"No. I've sent the tissue samples and photographs to New Orleans along with the body. A friend owes me a favor."

Peebles was uncharacteristically silent for a moment. Justin knew what he was thinking. The evidence was going to another state.

"He's going to rush it for me. You know the state crime lab takes forever." Justin didn't add anything about how sloppy their work was.

"Have you ID'd her?"

"Not yet. The coroner thinks she was Hispanic. We'll see if my friend agrees."

"We've got a lot of illegals these days that spilled out of Texas. Most of them work at the casino."

"I'll ask around out there."

"Okay. I called to give you a heads-up. David Noyes wants to interview you about the case and your new job."

"He's a reporter at the *Trib?*"

"Nope. He's the new editor. Came here about a year ago from Boston. He won two Pulitzers while he was there."

"You're saying Noyes will ask tough questions."

"He could put on the heat. He did a whole series on how the casino was polluting the river. Stirred up a whole lot of folks around here. I don't want everyone going ballistic, thinking there's a killer on the loose."

Justin smiled inwardly. Politicians. Weren't they a trip? "What are they supposed to think? A woman was murdered."

"I'm guessing a transient or a tourist at the casino committed the crime. Someone long gone."

"It's possible." Justin got the message. He was supposed to tell Noyes this was his theory so it would appear in the paper and calm Twin Oaks.

"One other thing," Peebles added. "Judge Kincaid wants to see you."

"About what?"

"Didn't say, but he's not happy you're sheriff. He wants to have a special election now. I told him, no way. The city is too broke. You're acting sheriff until the next election."

"What did he say?"

"He understood my reasons, but the judge is one tough dude. Don't rile him. You hear me, Radner?"

Cross my heart and hope to die.

Justin snapped his cell phone shut. Judge Kincaid was Buck Mason's best friend. Might as well take the bull by the horns, he decided.

Turner Kincaid like Buck Mason had old money, which in this neck of the woods meant their families had been plantation owners at one time. They socialized together and married each other. Even those who'd lost their money along the way were still part of the group. Ancestors were what mattered, what made you important and acceptable. In their eyes, he was poor white trash from the trailer park—and always would be.

Judge Kincaid's law offices were on Acorn Street just off the town square. Technically, a judge wasn't supposed to practice law when he had a position on the bench. Kincaid claimed his son did all the work, but everyone knew the judge still worked for friends.

Justin parked his Silverado in the shade and walked past Kincaid's black Cadillac. Every year Kincaid purchased a new Caddy from the dealership in Jackson. He looked down on foreign cars and made it a point to tell everyone his opinion. Justin doubted Kincaid did this out of patriotism. More likely, Kincaid thought this would enhance his political career. It was an open secret Judge Kincaid intended to run for Senator Foster's seat when the senator retired next year.

He walked into the oak-paneled office. Classical music

played softly from speakers Justin couldn't see. Pictures of Kincaid with every political figure in the state and several past presidents paraded across the walls in silver frames.

He quickly glanced around. There wasn't a single photograph of Clay Kincaid. Go figure. The judge just had one child. You'd think there would be at least one picture, but you'd be wrong.

"Chief Radner to see the judge," he informed a blond receptionist with Texas hair and enough makeup for a dozen porn stars. "I've got about two minutes for him."

"I'll let him know." The woman teetered off on spiked heels that matched her screaming red lipstick.

He wondered how much work the woman actually did. Kincaid's wife, May Ellen, had a reputation for popping pills and drinking too much. Rumor had it the judge kept a mistress in Jackson. Justin wondered if he even bothered to go that far.

The receptionist reappeared. "You may go in now. The door at the end of the hall."

Justin walked down the hall, rapped his knuckles on the door, then opened it without waiting to be invited in. Kincaid was seated behind a desk the size of an aircraft carrier, with more pictures of himself with dignitaries on the wall behind him. Tall and patrician with a thick head of silver hair, Turner Kincaid looked like central casting's version of a judge—or a senator.

"I hear you're looking for me, Turner." Justin deliberately used the judge's first name. He knew Kincaid liked everyone to call him "judge."

"What in hell do you think you're doing by coming back to my town?"

"Last I heard it was still Twin Oaks, not Kincaidville. You may be a judge, but this town belongs to a whole lot of folks."

"You were always a smart-ass. Clay said so way back."

Justin had gone to school with Clay, the judge's son. He'd beaten him out for the quarterback position in junior high and Clay had never forgiven him. Not that he gave a rat's ass. He'd always found Clay to be a sneaky, self-centered rich kid.

"Get out of town."

"Is that a threat?"

"It's a promise."

Justin manufactured a smile. "And if I don't?"

"You're as good as dead."

Justin pulled a miniature tape recorder out of his pocket. He'd used it when he'd been on the force in New Orleans. "I've recorded every word you said. I'm meeting with David Noyes. I'm sure the *Tribune* will be interested to hear your threats. It'll do wonders for your political career."

Color leached from Kincaid's face, then it suddenly flushed plum-red. "You son of a bitch."

Justin jammed the recorder into his pocket, then leaned across the desk and grabbed the prick by his gray silk tie. "Anything happens to me—*anything*—the press gets this."

"I—I didn't mean I was going to kill you—"

"Save it. The recorder's off. Just be sure you and Buck and all of your buddies stay away from me." He released the tie and left, slamming the door behind him so hard that one of the pictures fell off the wall. He could hear the glass shattering on the gleaming oak floor.

He was back in his car with Redd when his cell phone rang. It was Nora.

"An agent from the Mississippi Bureau of Investigation wants you to call him back on a secure line."

He wrote down the number and hung up. What in hell could the bureau want? Maybe they'd ID'd the murder victim, but he doubted it. That wouldn't require a secure line.

He stopped at the Shop 'N Go and took Redd with him

while he used a pay phone. An agent answered on the second ring, and Justin identified himself.

"The bureau is letting you know you're getting a felon on a work furlough at the local newspaper."

"Okay," Justin responded, not surprised. Work furloughs used to be rare, but now prisons were packed. With one in every one hundred and fifty people in the country behind bars, furloughs were becoming more common every day to make space. "What's his name?"

"Her. It's Kaitlin Wells. She stole money from the Mercury National Bank."

He vaguely recalled his mother telling him about the case. "When's she coming?"

"She's on the way. We've arranged for housing, a job, a car. She'll report to us, of course, but keep an eye on her. If you spot anything strange, call me on a secure line."

THE BELL ON Crestwood Realty's door jingled, and Tori Wells looked up to see a hunk with long, khaki-clad legs, shoulders like a college jock, and killer blue eyes walk into the office. At his side was a copper-colored dog. The animal's coat appeared to have been shaved, making it look very funky. The guy seemed vaguely familiar, but she couldn't quite place him.

"Hi." Tori flashed her megawatt smile. "May I help you?"

He held out his hand, and she reached for it. "Justin Radner."

Tori felt her eyes widen as he clasped her hand in a death grip. Not Justin Radner. He'd been the star of Harrington High's football team, and he'd dated Verity Mason. Why would he be back here?

"I remember you from high school," she said smoothly, gesturing toward the chair in front of her desk for him to sit. "I'm Victoria Wells. My friends call me Tori. I'm sure you don't remember me. I was two years younger."

Justin nodded, but Tori couldn't tell if he was admitting he didn't remember her or that he did. She'd expected him to say he knew her. Tori had always been beautiful, with the kind of body men didn't ever forget.

"What brings you back here?" she asked, sitting down.

"I've been hired as sheriff."

Tori forced herself not to gasp. The judge would have a conniption. He and Buck Mason were tighter than ticks. Buck hated Justin with a passion Tori found bizarre.

"I'd like to rent or lease a house—" he stroked the dog's head "—with a yard."

"You've come to the right place," Tori said in her cheeriest voice. "Crestwood Realty is Twin Oaks' leading realty." She didn't add she was the top agent in town. Justin must have asked. That's why he'd come here.

"I'll need at least two bedrooms."

Tori nodded, waiting for him to say more. She sneaked a quick glance at his left hand. No ring. That didn't necessarily mean he wasn't married.

When he didn't add another request, she said, "I have several properties that would be perfect for you. Let's do a virtual tour to eliminate some."

Usually she would take the time to show a hunk like this each property, but she was having dinner with the Kincaids tonight. She wanted to get home and have plenty of time to shower, change and do her hair before Clay picked her up. After years of being together, he'd promised to announce their engagement tonight.

Tori clicked on her computer, then turned the monitor toward Justin. She let her long eyelashes flutter just slightly. The gesture always captivated men, but Justin didn't seem to notice. She took him for a virtual tour of several homes. He watched but didn't comment.

Tori suddenly had one of her brilliant ideas. There was a home in the unincorporated area that she'd been trying to lease for an absentee owner for over two years. Locals knew better than to take it. The next-door neighbors were notorious for their domestic fights and loud parties. The judge would hoot with laughter if she could pawn off the place on Justin.

"Here's a furnished home that's perfect for you." She pulled up the listing. "The yard has nice shade trees for your dog."

"Hey, Redd. That looks like a good yard for you." He leveled his striking blue eyes on her. "Let's see the inside."

Tori raved about the three-bedroom ranch-style home and the tacky furniture. She had to admit it was a good deal. If it weren't for the neighbors, it would have been snapped up long ago.

Justin nodded approvingly. "Will the owner mind if I install a dog door?"

"Not a problem," she assured him. The owner would be overjoyed to get anything out of this. "He wants a year's lease, first and last month's rent, and a security deposit." She pretended to think for a moment, making everything up as she went. "He may ask for a little extra in the security deposit because of the dog."

"Seems fair," he replied. "Let's go see it."

She grabbed her purse from the drawer, deliberately bending over so that he could catch a glimpse of her impressive cleavage. Just because she'd tricked Justin didn't mean she couldn't flirt with him. It would be fun, and it would make Clay jealous. He'd always hated Justin Radner. No telling what Clay would do.

CHAPTER FOUR

KAT GLANCED AROUND her new studio apartment over a beauty parlor. It was one large room with a kitchenette off to the side. Scuffed linoleum that might once have been yellow covered the floor. It was furnished with a small Formica kitchen table and two mismatched chairs. In a small alcove stood a faded green convertible sofa pocked with cigarette burns. A battered brown trunk served as a coffee table. The stale odor of cigarette smoke filled the small studio. It wasn't much, but to her, it was heaven.

She now had a home, a car and a job. It was clear Harlan Westcott had known she would agree to his proposition. They'd rented this place, bought a junker car, and arranged for a job, all of which had taken time and planning.

She'd tried her best to pry the truth about her mission out of Special Agent Wilson, the man assigned to be her handler. He hadn't told her any more than Harlan had. She was to call Wilson immediately if anyone contacted her about the funds missing from the bank. If she sensed imminent danger, she had the local number of some mysterious undercover agent who could immediately come to her aid. The presence of this undercover guy made her even more suspicious. What would someone be investigating in Twin Oaks that required deep cover?

The only thing she could think of was the riverboat casino docked just outside of town. She had no idea how she fit into any of this, but not knowing gave her a deep sense of dread she couldn't shake.

She walked into the bathroom and gazed at her reflection in the medicine cabinet mirror. Tori stared back at her. Losing weight had changed her face. Now she had Tori's green eyes and high cheekbones. Her hair was dishwater brown, though, while Tori's must still be vibrant blond.

In prison she'd noticed how her face had changed, but hadn't thought about what it would mean when she came home. She didn't want anyone—especially Tori and her mother—to think she was copying Tori. She wondered if the salon downstairs could help her. Special Agent Wilson had stopped in Jackson where she'd purchased clothes. He'd given her money to tide her over until her first paycheck. She hadn't ventured out into the town yet.

"Get over it," she told her reflection. She grabbed her purse and headed downstairs.

The wooden slats creaked beneath her feet. She stopped and lifted her face to the sun with a smile. She remembered how the world had shut down around her when she'd been sent to prison. The walls closed in and it hurt to breathe the tainted air. She was finally free to smell fresh air with a hint of honeysuckle and to enjoy sunshine on her face.

She took the long way around the building to the salon. She walked slowly, admiring the dogwood trees lining the street. Their white blossoms swayed slightly in the breeze. After dark, she would pick a few to brighten up her place.

A hummingbird caught her eye as it flitted from flower to flower in the clay pots outside Petrie's Hardware. It stretched its tiny neck out, wings aflutter, and sipped nectar from each blossom. The bird was so beautiful and graceful that watching it warmed her heart. Nothing in over three years had soothed her like this.

She thought about her mother. In a small town, news spread quickly. Soon Loretta Wells would know Kat was home. Would she come to see Kat? Would Tori?

A permanent sorrow weighed her down when she thought about her family. They'd deserted her when she'd needed them the most. She gazed at the industrious hummingbird and reminded herself that she was free. Enjoy it.

Kat entered All Washed Up just as a woman about her age was putting an elderly lady in perm rollers under the dryer. It took a second for Kat to recognize Lola Rae Phillips. They had gone to school together since kindergarten, but they'd never been friends. Lola Rae had entered beauty school in Natchez just about the time Kat had gone to work at the bank.

Lola Rae walked away from the dryer, staring at Kat. She stopped, wiped her hands on her apron, saying, "Kat? Is that you?"

"Yes. It's me," Kat replied, trying for a smile.

With a wide, toothy grin, Lola Rae dashed across the room. She threw her arms around Kat and bear-hugged her. "Sweetie, it's so good to see you. Know what I mean?"

Kat had no idea what she meant, but she was more than a little touched by Lola Rae's response, yet tried not to show it. Lola Rae had always been a warm, outgoing person. She wasn't exactly pretty but her honey-brown eyes and ready smile had made her popular with other students. Lola Rae had been Kat's exact opposite. Introverted and embarrassed by her weight, Kat barely spoke to anyone and had few friends.

Lola Rae asked, "When did you get out?"

"Yesterday. I'm on a work furlough program for good behavior. I'm renting the apartment above your shop."

"Awesome! Totally awesome." She gave Kat a one-armed hug. "Come down for coffee in the morning. I'm here by seven. Hear what I'm sayin'?"

"Thanks," Kat replied, a note of wonder in her voice. She'd been lonely and cut off for so many years. She had no clue how to react to Lola Rae's kindness. She needed to respond with more than a "thanks" but what in the world could she say?

"Sugar, can I do something for you?"

Kat lifted a strand of limp hair. "I need help."

Lola Rae inspected the hair that had been stripped nearly lifeless by the harsh prison shampoo. "Let's get the dead ends off and style it. Color would help. Know what I mean?"

"How much?" Kat asked. She had been given some money but it had to last her until payday.

"Look, pay me when you get a job." She gave her an affectionate pat on the shoulder. "It isn't like I don't know where to find you."

"I appreciate it, but I want to give you at least part of it today. I have a job at the newspaper, but I won't get paid for a month."

"Good enough," Lola Rae replied. "Let's get started."

Lola Rae went into the back room and brought out a Hispanic woman with a slender build and large dark eyes. "This is Maria. She's my assistant, and she will shampoo you. She doesn't speak much English yet, but we're working on it. Right, Maria?"

"Right," Maria said in a soft voice.

"She cooks Mexican food to die for," Lola Rae added. "I'll have her make you a few tamales."

Kat stopped herself from saying she wasn't eating anything fattening. She didn't want to chance hurting Lola Rae's feelings. Kat could never have predicted someone would be thrilled to see her. And she hadn't realized how much she wanted a friend.

"Okay, I'm going to show you a few pictures, then some color swatches," said Lola Rae after Maria had shampooed her hair. "I think you'd be dynamite with lighter blond hair. I could weave several shades—"

"I don't want to look anything like Tori."

Lola Rae put her hand on Kat's shoulder. "Of course. I didn't think. Tori and your ma up and bailed on you when you were arrested."

Kat nodded, not trusting her voice. Those first days had been overwhelming, and to know her family didn't care had been crushing.

"Well, Tori doesn't get her hair done in town. Since she's made so much money in real estate, she's too good for us. Know what I mean? 'Course she's still chasing after Clay Kincaid."

Of course, Kat thought. Some things never change. Tori had been crazy about Clay since high school. She'd followed him to Ole Miss and worked part-time just to be near him.

"Tori drives into Jackson for her hair and clothes, but I see her around. She's wearing her hair past her shoulders, and it's platinum-blond."

"Make mine shorter and darker."

"Know what I think would be great on you?" Lola Rae didn't wait for an answer. "A light brown with reddish-gold highlights. We'll cut it chin-length and flip it a little."

"Go for it."

"We'll cut it first, then put on the color." Lola Rae snipped quickly, letting hanks of Kat's hair drop to the floor. "Can I ask you something?"

Kat was pretty sure she knew what Lola Rae planned to ask. "Sure."

"What was it like in prison?"

"Hell on earth. Don't ever commit a crime."

A timer went off. "Oops! Mrs. Avery's perm is done. Let me comb her out and style her. Just sit here and read a magazine."

"Do you happen to have a copy of the paper?"

"You betcha. It's behind the counter."

Kat walked over and found the paper. She was curious about how the *Tribune* looked these days. Special Agent Wilson had told her she would be working with the new managing editor, David Noyes. She took the paper and sat back down in the chair next to the older woman Lola Rae was working on.

Mrs. Avery had been the local librarian and a Sunday-school teacher until she'd retired the last year Kat was in school. Their eyes met in the mirror, and Mrs. Avery scowled.

"What are you doing here?" she demanded.

"Getting my hair cut and colored."

She whirled in her chair and faced Lola Rae. "You're not doing her hair, are you?"

Lola Rae beamed. "Yes, I am."

"She's a criminal."

"Kat has served her time. Know what I mean? Everybody deserves a second chance. Isn't that what God teaches us?"

"Ha!" She faced the mirror, her back ramrod-straight.

Kat concentrated on the newspaper. The headline screamed: BODY STILL UNIDENTIFIED. *Wow*. She could recall just one murder in all the years she'd lived here. A farmer had shot his partner over some dispute about chickens or pigs or something.

She read the account of the murdered woman carefully. Apparently she'd been dead for some time. Sheriff Radner refused to discuss what leads—if any—he had in the case.

Justin Radner. Tall and lanky with jet-black hair and piercing blue eyes, Justin had been the star of the football team. He'd been four years older than Kat so she had never been in class with him, but she'd dreamed about him at night sometimes. So had every girl in school except Tori, who thought Clay Kincaid hung the moon.

At one point Kat had a friend who lived in the Shady Acres trailer park near Justin. Kat's mother was phobic about her girls associating with white trash and insisted Kat have nothing to do with her friend, but Kat would sneak over to Shady Acres to play. She often watched Justin from afar.

She'd wondered what it would be like to go out on a date with him. How did Verity Mason feel when she was at his side, when he held her in his arms? Just thinking about it had made Kat all breathless and fluttery.

Her thoughts shifted to her mother and sister. Loretta Wells had always adored Tori. Kat's half sister was the product of her mother's marriage to the love of her life. When he'd been killed in an auto accident, Loretta had remarried Kat's father. From as far back as she could remember her mother had made it clear that Tori was her favorite.

No wonder. Tori was stunningly beautiful. She'd never gone through that gawky phase like most teenagers. Of course, Kat hadn't experienced that phase either. She'd been a plump child who became a fat teenager. The only thing Kat could say for herself was that she had brains.

What shocked her was how much it hurt not to have been told about her mother's cancer. How could they still have that power? Through the hell of prison, she'd told herself she didn't care, but despite her best efforts something deep inside her ached.

She forced herself to concentrate on the newspaper. She would deal with her mother and sister soon enough. The paper seemed to have more ads than she'd remembered. There were lots of articles about the local teams and reports of church services.

It intimidated Kat a little to be going to work at a newspaper. She wished she had more education. Her father—bless him—had wanted her to go to college. He told her he'd set aside money for both Tori and Kat to go to a state school. They would have to work while they were there, but the money was in a special account for their education. It had mysteriously vanished after his death.

Tori had been in Oxford, taking extension classes at Ole Miss and working at an expensive boutique. In the months immediately following her father's heart attack, Kat had expected her mother to try to get Tori into Ole Miss full-time.

It hadn't happened. Tori was still attending part-time when Kat had been arrested. Kat had called her mother from jail. She'd hung up on Kat.

IT WAS AFTER EIGHT O'CLOCK by the time Kat's hair was done and she'd gone to the supermarket for food. She'd stocked her small fridge with low-fat, low-carb goodies. She was better-looking, thanks to Lola Rae. The warm brown hair with red highlights in a bouncy flip made her eyes seem greener and her skin less sallow from the years in prison.

Lola Rae had shown her a few tricks with mascara and a hint of eye shadow. She'd applied a light sheen of foundation with a sponge and dusted Kat's cheekbones with a soft coral blush. All of the cosmetics went onto Kat's tab. She hoped she could duplicate Lola Rae's efforts on Monday before she went to work.

Her stomach rumbled, reminding her she hadn't eaten since Special Agent Wilson had bought her a salad at noon. She should stay home and study the paper more closely so she would be familiar with the layout, but she'd been dreaming about Jo Mama's Ribs for years. Surely her first night of freedom called for a small celebration.

She drove her Toyota over to the north side, where Jo Mama's Ribs had been located for nearly forty years. Jo Johnson had opened the place back when her husband became one of the first black pilots in the Tuskegee Air Squadron during the Second World War. He'd been killed early on, and a foul-up had deprived Jo of his pension for years. She supported their five children by making the best ribs in this part of Mississippi.

Abe Johnson had taken over when his mother's health began to fail. A mountain of a man with a huge smile, Abe had inherited his mother's talent for cooking. Big Abe's ribs had been her father's favorite, and he brought her to Jo

Mama's at least twice a month when he'd been alive. Her mother and Tori never came, her mother insisting no self-respecting white person would be seen in the "north side."

Kat parked and walked up to the outside takeout window. Being Friday night, the place was packed, and there was a long line waiting to get in. More than half of the people appeared to be white. Just like her father had always said, "Good people know good food, and good people don't care about the color of your skin."

She waited behind a man who could no longer see his shoes, and his wife, who shuffled along beside him in what appeared to be a housecoat. Kat promised herself she would limit Big Abe's ribs to special occasions.

The couple put in their order and stepped aside. Kat moved up to the window. Big Abe's daughter DeShawnna took Kat's order for baby back ribs and coleslaw—no fries, onion rings, or barbecued beans.

DeShawnna hesitated a moment, pencil poised in the air and asked, "Don't I know you?"

She paused, reluctant to say her name. What if they refused to serve her? *Get over it,* she told herself. "Kat Wells."

"Kat? Well, I'll be jiggered. You're beautiful." She peered out the service window at Kat who was still wearing the white capris and red blouse knotted at the waist that she'd worn to have her hair done. "Girl, how did you get so skinny?"

Heat flushed the back of Kat's neck. No one had ever called her beautiful. She knew she was thinner and vastly improved but "beautiful" was a stretch.

"Daddy, git out here. You gotta see this."

A few seconds later Big Abe poked his head through the window. Kat smiled at him, remembering how kind he'd been to attend her father's funeral. It had enraged her mother, of course, but Kat believed her daddy was with the angels and would be thrilled to see Big Abe at the service.

"Is that you, Kat?"

"Yeah. I'm out for good behavior. This is my first night home. I've been dreaming about your ribs for years."

Abe's smile was startlingly white in his dark face. "Hold on."

A minute later he was outside, hugging her. "Glad to see you, honey. You're looking mighty fine. Come on inside. We'll get you a table. A first night of freedom calls for a party."

"Oh, no, Big Abe. It's just me. I don't want to take a whole table on a busy evening."

"Don't matter. They'll wait. I take care of my friends."

He escorted her past the line at the door. She didn't recognize any of the people. Inside a huge ceiling fan substituted for air-conditioning, stirring the delicious smell of barbecued ribs through the café. Wooden tables were covered with red-and-white gingham paper cloths. All the food was served on paper plates and the entire mess was bundled up and thrown away after each patron.

"Sit yourself down right here," Big Abe told her as a table for two was being reset. "Baby backs, my special slaw, and onion rings, right?"

"Right," she replied although she wouldn't have ordered the onion rings if Abe hadn't been so genuinely glad to see her. She sat down, her back to the wall, facing the crowded room.

Big Abe bent low and whispered in her ear. "Your pappy would be right proud of you. You're his girl…and never forget it."

Big Abe trundled off toward the kitchen. "His girl" echoed in her ears. Big Abe was right, she decided. Kat might look like Tori a little, but Tori was Loretta Wells' child through and through. Kat was like her father—quieter, more studious, and uninterested in "society."

A waitress brought her an iced tea with two springs of mint. Kat couldn't help smiling. Big Abe remembered everything.

Kat glanced around the room, checking to see if anything had changed. She didn't allow her eyes to linger too long, not wanting to make eye contact. Her first day home hadn't been as stressful as she'd expected. Lola Rae had shut up Mrs. Avery, but Kat knew there would be others who wouldn't be easily cowed.

Jo Mama's hadn't changed much since the last time she'd been here with her father. They'd discussed her application to Ole Miss. He'd been proud of her early acceptance. Neither of them mentioned Tori, who had been rejected by the school two years earlier.

Three weeks later, her father had slumped over at his desk at Twin Oaks Power and Gas. Parker Wells had been pronounced dead when the paramedics arrived. Kat was thankful he hadn't suffered, but she wished she could have seen him one last time.

She would have told him, "I am what I am because you loved me." It was true. In her father's eyes she wasn't a fat little girl with no potential. She was a princess who received good grades and could be anything she wished to be.

Lost in memories, it took Kat a moment to realize the din in the room had dulled to hushed whispers, and people were staring at her. She added low calorie sweetener to her iced tea, even though she never used it, and busied herself stirring her drink.

She glanced up to see a hulking man weaving between the tightly spaced tables, heading toward her. Hank Bullock. In high school, Tori had gone out with the tackle a few times but dropped him when Clay started calling. Hank had never gotten over Tori and he'd never missed an opportunity to tease Kat, telling her Tori had the looks in the family.

"Well, call me a dog if the jailbird ain't back in town." He leaned close, his breath rank with whiskey and onions. "You're lookin' better, piggy. I guess prison got rid of that fat ass."

Kat made herself smile as if she'd received a supreme

compliment. She poked the belly that slopped over his belt. "My loss. Your gain."

It took a second for the insult to register in his inebriated brain. The old Kat would have cowered, but she wasn't giving an inch.

"You bitch! This here's a hard body."

Kat could see the bully was going to make trouble. She refused to let a lowlife like Hank make a scene that might ruin Big Abe's Friday night profits. The man's friendship meant too much to Kat for her to allow it to happen.

Another thought hit her. She'd been warned that any brush with the law—no matter how minor—and she could end up in prison again. She knew how to take care of this bum, but she couldn't do it in front of witnesses. She attempted a coy smile. "Let's go outside."

Hank's conceited smirk made her want to slap him. He didn't get it—at all. He turned toward a table across the room where his buddies were watching. They gave him the thumbs-up.

Kat led him by the line outside the door and around the bend into the parking lot. She stopped near her Toyota and looked up at the sky. A star winked at her. It was the first time she'd seen the stars as a free woman. A scumbag like Hank Bullock wasn't going to ruin her second chance.

Hank stumbled up behind her. "In jail too long, huh? Need a good fuckin' bad? Real bad."

Kat almost laughed. She wasn't a virgin, but the thought of Hank touching her made her stomach churn. Hank grabbed his crotch and fondled himself through his jeans.

"Look, you jerk! Stay away from me."

Hank reached over and mauled her breasts. His meat-hook hands were hot and sweaty. "Get a load of your rack. You were so fat. Who knew you had tits like this?"

Kat shoved him away. "I'm warning you. Leave me alone."

"I'll leave you alone after I fuck your brains out. Tori

thinks she's too high and mighty for me, but you." His hand clamped around her wrist and twisted. "You're just a loser jailbird. Who's gonna care if I rape you? Who are they gonna believe—you or me?"

Kat didn't hesitate. She lunged at him and kicked him square in the groin. He dropped to his knees, doubled over in pain. She let him whimper for a few seconds before moving closer. She clutched his neck, gripping his windpipe and pressing down on his carotid artery. The takedown was a favorite of the guards. A prisoner would pass out and there wouldn't be a telltale mark on the neck.

"Don't you dare touch me or come near me again."

Hank's head bobbled. She took that for a yes and released him.

"Ah-ah," sputtered Hank, gasping for breath and clutching his crotch. He looked beyond her with glazed eyes. "Sheriff, arrest her! She tried to kill me."

Kat turned and found herself nose-to-nose with Justin Radner.

CHAPTER FIVE

KAT GAZED into the most intense blue eyes she'd ever seen. Even in the dim light of the parking lot, she could feel their heat. Justin Radner was taller than she remembered. The planes of his face had become more angular and small lines fanned out from the corners of his eyes. He still had an athlete's hard body with broad shoulders, well-defined muscles, and a trim waist. He was a man now, not a boy.

And he was the law.

She muttered a silent prayer. This man had the power to send her straight back to prison before she'd spent one night in her new home. If he charged her with any crime, her furlough would be revoked. Don't allow yourself to remember how attracted to him you were in high school, cautioned the rational part of her brain.

Still, being this close to him made her pulse pound in her temples the way it had when she'd secretly watched him at the trailer park years ago. Kat reminded herself that times had changed and so had she. But still, there was *something* about him that called to her and always had.

She'd forgotten how powerful and confident he'd always been. Without even knowing she existed, he'd overwhelmed her as a teen. That was then; this was now. The last thing she needed was the attention of a sheriff whose virile good looks she'd always found disturbingly appealing.

The way he stared at her seemed impudently familiar. His

eyes roamed over her in silent appraisal, tracing the curve of her cheeks and dropping to the swell of her breasts, then roving lower to her hips, then thighs until he reached her toes. She wondered if he was recalling her fat years. No, she decided. He'd never noticed her then, and he wasn't interested in her now. She found him sexy, but his expression said he was so bored that nothing short of a terrorist attack would move him.

Hank lurched to his feet. "You saw what the bitch did. Arrest her!"

"I was defending myself. He was trying to rape me."

Kat watched Justin study them both for a moment. "I was right over there." His voice was deep and husky as he inclined his head toward a nearby black pickup where a hound of some kind was leaning out the window. "I saw your hands all over her, and I heard you threaten her."

"I was just joshin', that's all." Apparently, Hank was still sober enough to know not to cross a man like Justin.

"I could haul your sorry ass to jail, but I'm letting you go with a warning. Don't come near this woman." He pointed his finger at Hank. "And get someone to drive you home. You don't need another DUI."

Hank weaved his way toward a battered car with duct tape holding a taillight in place. He yanked open the rear door and threw himself onto the backseat, where Kat assumed he was going to sleep it off.

"Thanks for helping me."

"Don't thank me," he said, a threatening undertone in his voice, and something clenched in her stomach. "I've seen you in action."

"In action?" Droplets of sweat blossomed across the back of her neck.

"You used unnecessary force on Hank. Kicking him in the balls would have been enough," he said in an emotionless, de-

tached voice. "Must have learned the takedown maneuver behind bars."

"If I hadn't taught him a lesson, Hank would have come
after me later." She paused, trying her best to make her case
and not anger this man. "I needed to show him that I can take
care of myself."

"I'll just bet."

His voice could freeze vodka. She couldn't afford to alienate
the sheriff. She might be innocent, but only a few people knew
the truth. A deep anger born of frustration welled up inside her.

She looked away from him and thought about the hummingbird for a second. Her heart was thumping painfully
against her ribs. It eased a bit when she pictured the dainty
bird. She reminded herself that she'd been through worse
than this and survived. The way to handle Justin Radner was
not to get angry and not to give him any reason to arrest her.

"My dinner's probably been served," she told him.

He followed her. "I'm going to talk to you while you eat.
There are a few things we need to get straight."

Inwardly she was still trembling from her encounter with
Hank, but before she could adjust, she had to deal with this
man. No doubt he was going to lecture her about toeing the
line while she was on furlough. She'd be forced to sit through
it—and smile.

A mountain of baby backs was waiting for her. The aroma
of barbecue sauce made her stomach growl and brought back
fond memories of times with her father. She took her seat and
Justin sat opposite her. He leaned forward across the small
table. Too, too close.

The crowded room was almost silent. Only the slight whir
of the ceiling fan and the muffled clatter from the kitchen filled
the air. Everyone was watching and waiting for them to talk.

Big Abe lumbered out, slapped Justin on the back, and
asked, "What can I get for you?"

"Nothing tonight, Big Abe. I'm just keeping Kat company."

Justin sounded as if they were old friends. Big Abe smiled and winked at Kat. He turned to the silent room. "Now you folks finish up so those in line can get in. Kat Wells is back in town. She's out for good behavior, and we're going to see she gets the second chance she deserves."

"Yeah, right," said a male voice with a pronounced twang.

Justin surged to his feet. Every eye swung to his towering frame. The confidence he'd exhibited as a youth had become an aura of power. "Don't let me catch any of you giving this woman trouble."

"Iffin' you do," Big Abe chimed in, "don't come to Jo Mama's. Get your ribs over in Jackson."

Justin sat down and Big Abe clambered into the kitchen. Kat picked up a rib and took a small bite. The tender meat with the special barbecue sauce brought the sting of tears to her eyes. This one's for you, Daddy, she said to herself.

A few minutes later the noise level in the room returned to normal, and Justin said, "I was just notified this afternoon that you're here on a work furlough. I'll be keeping my eye on every step you take."

"Why? Don't you have a murder to solve? Isn't your time better spent on that?"

Something flared in the depths of his eyes, and she regretted not keeping her mouth shut. *Don't turn this man into another enemy.*

"You're a real smart-ass, aren't you?"

Kat wiped her hands on her napkin. Once having a man talk to her in that tone and using those words would have shocked her, but prison had transformed her in ways she was just now realizing. "Let's just say being convicted of a crime I didn't commit and serving time for it has changed my outlook on life. I'm not letting people push me around."

Justin lofted his dark brows, obviously not believing one

word. Then his lips curved into a suggestion of a smile, reminding her of how attractive he could be when he wasn't being a total jerk. His smile evaporated as if it never existed. "I'm not pushing. I'm the law. It's my duty to make sure you don't return to a life of crime."

Anger simmered inside her, but Kat picked up another rib and decided not to argue her innocence. Until the truth came out, most people would assume her to be guilty the way Justin did.

"You don't have to watch me too closely. I'll be working—"

"For David Noyes at the paper. I know all about it."

"Then what's your problem? You can check on me without watching every step I take."

He leaned back in his chair and rocked it slightly while he gazed at her with an intensity that made her uncomfortable. A brief, bristling silence followed. "I'm going to keep close tabs on you. Tell you why. Most people don't just suddenly commit a crime. It's a gradual thing. Filching money from their mother's purse. Pocketing pens and pencils when the teacher isn't looking. Then it escalates to petty shoplifting."

Kat kept stuffing rib meat in her mouth to keep from saying something she would regret. What an arrogant jerk! What happened to the boy who'd seemed so nice in high school?

"When all this goes unnoticed or they lie their way out of being punished, criminals move onto bigger things like you did."

Kat started on Big Abe's slaw. It was loaded with fresh cabbage and finely shredded carrots with a hint of horseradish. Everyone loved it, and no one could sweet talk Big Abe out of the recipe. She refused to allow Justin Radner to ruin a meal she'd been dreaming about for years. Let him think whatever he wanted.

"Then they're caught and convicted. In prison they learn tricks like the take-down hold and new ways to break the law.

They get out, thinking they're smarter now and can get away with crime."

Kat finally lost it completely. "Is there a point to this?"

He let his chair legs down and again leaned toward her. He reached across the small space and seized her hand. Kat's pulse skittered alarmingly. She had to remember this man was the enemy. She tried to pull her hand away, but his grip tightened.

"Over ninety percent of parolees return to prison within two years."

"I know. It's called recidivism."

"I'm going with the odds." His voice was low but had a lethal charge to it. "You'll break the law again."

"You're wrong. I've never broken the law, and I won't now."

His jaw flexed, and she expected him to make some scathing comment. Instead, he stood up and left without another word.

JUSTIN WAITED down the road in his pickup until Kat's car rolled out of Jo Mama's parking lot.

"That woman's something else," he muttered to Redd as he scratched the dog's chest. Redd leaned into his hand as if to agree. She was one hot babe. He wasn't usually attracted to brunettes, but Kat was an exception.

After Justin had received the call from the Mississippi Bureau field office, he'd phoned Warden Bronson at Danville Federal Correctional Facility. According to the warden, Kaitlin "Kat" Wells had been a model prisoner and had an excellent chance of being rehabilitated.

Justin wished he had the faith he'd heard in the warden's voice. He knew the odds. Most criminals became repeat offenders. Crime was the only life they knew.

The system had been set up to promote rehabilitation. The reality was a damn sight different. First-time offenders came out hardened cons. The system worked against them, not for them. Justin hadn't a clue how things could be changed, but something had to be done.

Kat had come out a hard case, all right. Not that he blamed her for defending herself against Hank, but using the take-down on him had proven how tough she'd become. Tough and beautiful. And sexy as hell.

Justin had spent part of the afternoon with Tori. Kat's older sister was a flirt with a polished veneer that reminded Justin of the society wannabes in New Orleans. Those women were after one thing—money. Kat was different. He wasn't sure how exactly, but he could sense it. She didn't try to flirt with him or manipulate him the way Tori had.

He'd remembered Tori from high school. Who wouldn't? She'd been every horny guy's wet dream, but all she'd cared about was Clay Kincaid. He didn't remember Kat at all. She was several years younger and back then kids more than a year behind you were babies. You wouldn't be caught dead near them. Even if she hadn't been in any of his classes, he should have remembered her from around town. He'd thought about it and had drawn a blank.

Tori hadn't mentioned Kat was out on furlough. He suspected she didn't know. He recalled his mother telling him how Kat's family had turned their backs on her when she was arrested.

He kept his lights off and followed Kat's Toyota at a distance. "Claims she's innocent," he said to Redd. As usual when the car was moving, the dog had his head out the window and wasn't paying any attention.

A few cars joined him on the road behind Kat, and he turned on his headlights. A group of teenage boys sped past him, hanging out the windows of a battered SUV. They flipped him off as they drove by and yelled, "Muthafucka!"

He could have slapped the portable flasher on the roof and

triggered the siren, but he'd long ago learned an unwritten law enforcement rule: Don't sweat the small stuff. He'd been young once. Friday nights in Twin Oaks didn't provide many diversions.

He followed Kat into the downtown area. Fewer cars came this direction. Like the center of most towns, Twin Oaks had little going on there at night. It was almost nine and the No Latte Café was shutting down. Ragin' Cajun Tavern would be open until two, an illegal poker game going on in the backroom.

Kat pulled into the alley behind All Washed Up. He waited, idling with his lights out. A few minutes later, he saw her sexy silhouette against the shade upstairs.

She'd taken him by surprise. Totally. In spite of everything, he found himself liking her. He didn't know if prison had taught her that take-no-crap attitude or if she'd been that way when she'd lived here, but he liked it. He'd never gone for women who clung to men. Verity Mason had taught him how treacherous they could be.

Far too many women had paraded through his life after Verity, but he'd kept his relationships—if you could call them that—brief and with no commitment on his part. What would Kat be like, he wondered? There was a very compelling quality about her. He kept thinking of her soft mouth with its full lower lip and his pulse kicked up a notch.

She had the damnedest eyes, cat-green and fringed with long lashes. Alluring. Sexy as hell. An image kept recurring in his mind. The ceiling fan in Jo Mama's had stirred the wispy hair at Kat's temples in a way that he found extremely provocative. Okay, okay—arousing.

She had a temper like a tightly coiled spring. Defiance and anger had flared in her eyes more than once. He'd been brutally direct, because he wanted her to change her behavior patterns. He intended to watch her very closely. With him dogging her all the time, she might just beat the odds and turn her life around.

Beneath her anger, he detected sadness and something else—a loneliness he intuitively recognized. It was a self-protective maneuver. Prison could do that to a person. So could a stint in the service with special forces followed by a career in law enforcement.

Kat Wells was a troubled woman, he decided. She was incredibly intense, and it was clear her anger had been pent up for a long time. She'd kept herself in check but only with difficulty. She must have been warned that one brush with the law and her cute butt would land back in prison.

He drove to the station and brought Redd inside with him. He wanted to check Kat's file. He'd been too busy earlier to rummage through the inactive files stored in the basement.

"Anything going on?" he asked the night duty deputy who was working dispatch.

Until the murder, not much had happened around here. The deputies justified their paychecks by zealously pursuing vandalism cases. Bashing mailboxes with a baseball bat was a local sport. Now things had changed. Despite what Mayor Peebles wanted the citizens to think, there was a killer out there.

"The usual stuff," responded the deputy over a burst of static from the two-way radio. "A couple of drunk drivers and a report of gunshots on the north side."

"I'll be downstairs if you need me."

The sheriff's station wasn't large. The brick building had a small reception area with a booking desk off to one side that doubled as the dispatcher's station. Behind double doors was the squad room. A small briefing room also served as an interrogation room and had a one-way mirror.

He could see into the interrogation room from his corner office with walls that were glass halfway down. The glass was covered by shades. Nora had told him Sheriff Parker *never* left the blinds open or the door to his office. Justin had the blinds up and his door open. He wanted to be accessible to his staff and the community.

Behind the offices were three holding cells, two for men and one for women. Few women were arrested and most of the men were DUIs who were locked up to sleep it off. He wondered where Kat had been held. She'd probably been sent straight to Jackson. Since bank robbery was a federal crime, she must have been tried in the state capital. Still, there would have been at least the original robbery report and the record of her arrest.

He headed down the narrow stairs at the back of the building. Justin flicked on the lights in the basement. It was one huge room heaped full of outmoded equipment: black rotary phones, a ditto machine, an old radio set with broken earphones. Bins with old evidence lined the walls, a legal disaster waiting to happen should a case need to be retried.

He'd have to get someone to sort through this mess. The stuff had been commandeered by spiders. Everything was festooned with cobwebs.

The old case files were stored in surprisingly good order. Nora's work, no doubt. He found the box with the year Kat Wells had been tried. None of the files had her name on it. There wasn't a file with Mercury National Bank on it either.

Weird. Friggin' weird.

He checked the boxes for the year before and after, thinking it had been misfiled. Nothing. He rummaged through all of the boxes, which went back fourteen years. There would have been more, but a broken pipe had flooded the basement fifteen years ago and destroyed the other files.

What in hell had happened to the damn file?

CHAPTER SIX

HE HATED BEING OUT OF THE LOOP. He liked to know things before the others did. Not after. Something was going on. He felt it deep in his bones, an inner rumble of suspicion. Fate hinged on the smallest—often unnoticed—details.

Justin Radner and Kat Wells were back in town. He wasn't sure why this bothered him, yet it did. The news made something niggle at the back of his brain, warning him.

Worse, the body he thought wouldn't turn up for another few months had been discovered by some no-account kids nosing around in the woods. Had all the trace evidence been washed away by the spring rains?

He'd seen *CSI* only once but he was familiar with how seemingly insignificant fibers or some stray mark could snare a killer. If the autopsy results from Benton at Gaylord's Mortuary had been accepted, he wouldn't have been concerned. But that prick Radner had sent the body to New Orleans where it would receive a much more sophisticated analysis.

He might have to get rid of Justin Radner. He considered the situation for a minute. Kat Wells could present a problem also. She'd been framed for the money missing from the bank's vault. What if she investigated what had really happened?

Again, he wouldn't have worried about it, but Kat was going to work at the newspaper. David Noyes was a top-flight investigative reporter with two Pulitzers to his credit. He might help Kat unearth some damning evidence.

"Settle down," he said out loud. He needed to wait to see what happened and keep the others calm.

After all, he had his standards. He didn't go off half-cocked. He planned and paid strict attention to details. Above all, he didn't make stupid mistakes.

TORI WAITED until dessert was served to spring her news. Since they hadn't sat down to dinner until nine and it was now almost ten, Clay's mother was soused. Not that Tori cared. It was the judge she wanted to impress.

The whole town knew May Ellen popped pills and drank too much alcohol, but she was a Hutton and could trace her ancestors back to the earliest plantation owners. People looked the other way and pretended nothing was wrong.

Tori was always very polite to May Ellen, but Tori knew the truth. A Hutton or not, the woman was a political liability. The judge would never divorce her. He was a man to whom family values meant everything. Clay had told her the judge intended to make moral values part of his platform when he ran for senate.

Politics. Yuck. Tori hated the thought of boring bills and tedious legislation. Who cared?

When he won, Tori was positive the judge would find a reason to leave May Ellen in Twin Oaks. That was okay with Tori. Having the judge in Washington and May Ellen boozed-up, Tori would have Clay to herself—finally.

"I leased a house today," Tori announced. "The Atherton place."

"Next to the guy who's always having wild parties and beats up his wife?" Clay asked.

"Yes, the Randolphs." Tori tried to keep the excitement out of her voice.

The judge studied her with interest. "Who'd be fool enough to take it?"

Tori took a sip of her wine to let the drama build. "Justin Radner."

"Radner?" The word exploded out of Clay, and Tori smothered a smile.

"The white trash kid who stole your place on the football team?" asked May Ellen.

"Yes," Tori informed her. "He's been appointed sheriff."

"How in hell could that happen?" Clay asked his father. "Doesn't there have to be a special election?"

"Not according to the county charter," Tori informed him. "The mayor with council approval can appoint a sheriff and wait for the next regular election."

"This sucks." Clay kicked back the dregs of his whiskey.

"Watch your mouth," May Ellen said.

Tori had long ago noted that May Ellen stayed tuned to conversations even when she was tipsy. Very little got by the woman. She was devious and deceitful. Not to mention self-absorbed. She knew Tori's mother had cancer, but May Ellen never asked how she was doing.

"The city council had to approve Peebles' choice," the judge added. "The vote was five to one. Only Buck opposed it. Guess we know that's what happens when…undesirables take over the city government."

Tori smiled at the judge. "So true. Well, I got even a little by pawning off that dump on Justin."

"You were with Radner?" Clay asked. "Showing him houses?"

"Not really," Tori said, thrilled to hear the note of jealousy in his voice. "I did a virtual tour, pushing the Atherton property. When Justin went for it, I had to show it to him. I just took him to the Atherton place."

Clay didn't say anything, but the fire in his eyes told her that she would hear more about it later. Fine. She knew how to handle Clay. His father was another matter. The judge wasn't nearly as impressed with her accomplishment as she'd hoped he would be nor did he compliment her on knowing about the city charter.

"I fail to see how foisting off that property helps." Clay's mother glared at her. "Now we're stuck with that piece of trash."

"There are ways of getting rid of him," the judge assured his wife. "I think Tori did us a service. You never know. Radner might get killed if he tries to stop one of the Randolphs' wild parties."

"Yeah," Clay agreed. "Randolph goes ballistic when he's drunk. He's beat his wife within an inch of her life several times."

Tori seriously doubted anyone was beating up Justin Radner. It would take a lot more to kill him.

The judge said, "There was another interesting development today."

"What was that?" Clay asked.

The judge took a swig of the Johnnie Walker Blue Label he always drank, savoring the expensive whiskey before responding. "Your sister has been released on a work furlough."

Tori couldn't stifle a gasp. Kat was home? Why? *Why?* Why now when Clay was set to announce their engagement? May Ellen was pathologically obsessed with society. Having a felon in the family would set her off like nothing else.

May Ellen stared at Tori, slack-jawed. "Your sister is back? How will you be able to hold up your head?"

"Why?" she practically screamed at the old souse. "I haven't done anything. I've made something of myself. I'm the most successful real estate agent in this town. I'm not responsible for what—"

"She'll be working at the paper," the judge informed them.

"I didn't think she was up for parole yet," Clay said.

The judge shrugged. "Prisons are horribly overcrowded. Like a lot of convicts, she's out for good behavior."

"She'll steal again," Clay's mother said. "Mark my words."

Tori had felt sorry for the ugly duckling when they'd been growing up. Her sympathy vanished when she'd received the call from her mother saying Kat had been arrested. They'd immediately decided to distance themselves. Why ruin their reputations in a small town where family counted for so much?

Tori had believed Kat would be paroled and disappear from their lives. Tori had worked long, brutal hours to make something of herself. Now, on the very evening Clay was going to tell his parents they were getting married, her deadbeat sister reappeared to ruin it all. Like a grenade in the pit of her stomach, her anger was primed to explode.

"Well, we'd better go," Clay said, abruptly. "I have to be in court in Jackson first thing in the morning."

"LOOKS LIKE Mayor Peebles is having a party," Tori commented as they drove away from the Kincaid estate.

Clay's family's home was hidden by tall trees and a stately hedge. It was the epitome of class consciousness. Tori's mother had explained this when she had been just a little girl. "Quality people" didn't flaunt their money. That would be in bad taste.

Tyson Peebles' mansion wasn't hidden from view. He'd cut down the hedge shortly after buying it. Like a preening swan, the antebellum home sat atop a rise surrounded by acres of lawn that put the country club's golf course to shame. A sweeping cobblestone drive led up to the front door and swung around a fountain Tyson's landscape architect from Atlanta had commissioned. A trio of enormous marble lions spouted water from their mouths into the reflection pool surrounding their huge paws. Totally tasteless, but what could you expect from a black football player?

Tori never mentioned it, but she thought it was a hoot that Tyson Peebles had bought the house next door to the Kincaids.

Every day, the judge and May Ellen had to drive past Peebles' in-your-face mansion. Served both of them right. They thought they were so perfect.

"What are you going to do about your sister?" Clay asked.

Tori knew that tone of voice. She'd been in love with Clay since she was sixteen. She was pushing thirty-four now. Clay was upset—with her, with Justin Radner, with Kat. The only thing to do was placate him and wait it out.

"What can I do? If Kat's out on some type of work program, how can I get rid of her?"

He hitched his shoulders and kept driving. Tori glanced out the window at the mini-Taras in the middle-class section of Twin Oaks. They were squeezed onto lots the size of Tyler Peebles' fountain. "Aping their betters," Tori's mother often said.

Tori's condominium was in a discreet building hidden behind a row of stately cypress trees. It was the nicest complex in town, and Tori prided herself on the way she'd decorated it with beautiful antiques and fine fabrics. She'd invited the Kincaids for dinner once, and May Ellen actually complimented her decorating, but they'd never accepted another invitation.

Clay pulled his sleek silver Porsche to a stop in front of her condo. She gazed at him, willing the Clay she knew and loved so much to resurface. A hard silence engulfed them. Tori waited, not quite holding her breath.

"There's no 'us' if you can't get rid of your sister. My father's seriously gearing up to run for the senate. We can't afford to have criminals in the family."

"What can I possibly do?"

He turned to her, and in the dim light, she saw eyes as hard and cold as a knife blade. Clay's were usually bluer and sparkled with humor. "You'd better think of something."

She reached for the door handle.

Clay put his hand on her arm, stopping her. "You know I love you."

Tori's heart seized up, and she gazed at him. She'd loved him for so long. She couldn't remember caring one whit about another man. She would do anything for him. She'd already proven that.

"My father wants me married by the time the campaign starts. I'll stump the state with him. He thinks it would be helpful if my wife were pregnant."

The shock of the revelation almost brought her to her knees in utter defeat. She knew what he was really saying. If she didn't get rid of her sister, Clay would have to marry someone else.

Tori couldn't muster the breath to say good-night. She climbed out of the car and he roared away before she reached her porch. Somehow she managed to unlock her door. She stumbled to the sofa and sat there in the dark. What was she going to do?

She couldn't imagine who the judge would want Clay to marry. The girls from the "good" families were already married. Once the judge and Buck Mason had wanted Verity and Clay to wed. Then Verity had taken up with Justin Radner.

When Justin dumped Verity and left for Duke, everyone assumed Clay and Verity would get together at Ole Miss. They'd dated, but Tori had been there and Clay loved her. Soon Verity was out of the picture forever.

Tori had been through so much with Clay for so long. She couldn't give up now. Even though it was almost midnight, she decided to go see her mother. She was in so much pain these days that her mother rarely slept except right after the nurse had given her an injection. Even then it was only for an hour or so.

She drove up to the condo Loretta Wells had bought after her second husband—Kat's father—had died. It was in a better neighborhood than the small house Parker Wells had purchased after they'd married. The home where Tori had grown up had been near winding Tuttle Creek. It was known in the area as "the crick," and on the other side of it white trash lived in homes that squatted on concrete blocks. Pickups were parked on lawns that were nothing more than weed patches. Tori's mother had wanted to distance herself from "those people" as much as possible.

When her mother had fallen ill with ovarian cancer, Tori had been going through her things to help and discovered her mother had taken the money Parker Wells had set aside to send Tori and Kat to college. She'd bought the condo with it.

Tori had been angry with her mother for about two seconds. Then she decided her mother had done the right thing. Tori hadn't wanted to go to Ole Miss full time. She'd taken extension classes there to be close to Clay so Verity wouldn't steal him away.

Her mother had moved to a much more respectable area— a fact not lost on the Kincaids. What did make her angry was May Ellen Kincaid's attitude. Even though her only child had dated Tori for years, May Ellen had never once invited her mother to her home.

Loretta Wells never mentioned this slight. Getting Tori married to Clay had been a religious crusade for her mother. Tori would love to make her mother's dream come true before cancer claimed her life.

The light in the living room of her mother's small condo was on, and Tori could see the blue-white flicker of the television. Tori parked her car in the space in front of her mother's condo and got out. She wearily walked up to the door. She hated dumping this news on her mother.

Tori let herself in with her key. Her mother's eyes were wide open, and she was staring at the television, but Tori doubted she was actually paying attention.

"Mom, how are you doing?"

"My stars, don't you look beautiful!"

Tori tried for a smile. Since she could remember, people had told her how beautiful she was. What good was beauty if you couldn't marry the man you loved?

She sat beside her mother on the yellow chintz sofa Tori had bought when she'd redecorated her mother's condo. The green eyes Tori had inherited gazed lovingly at Tori. Since the chemo, their vibrant color had dulled, and her gaunt face had cavernous hollows beneath the cheekbones. She was so thin that her housecoat hung on her like clothes on a scarecrow. Short, ropy strings of gray hair stuck out from her head.

Tori asked, "How are you feeling?"

"'Bout the same. Pain's everywhere now."

"I wish there were something I could do." Tori had taken her to specialists, brought in the best food, arranged for a nurse to come in three times a day, but nothing in Tori's power was going to stop the cancer. With it came pain that pills and injections muted but couldn't make go away.

"I would feel better if you married Clay before I'm gone to glory."

Tori nodded, afraid to trust her voice.

"What's wrong?" Her mother fired the question at her the way she would have when she'd been well.

Tori had never been able to lie to her mother. She read every gesture, every expression with startling accuracy. She had an uncanny perceptiveness where Tori was concerned.

"Kat's back in town. She's out early for good behavior."

Her mother slumped back against the cushions, her eyeballs rolling heavenward. "Lord Almighty, this could finish me."

Tori waited, afraid to say more, until her mother's breathing became more normal, and she looked at Tori. It took a few minutes to explain about the Kincaids' reaction to the news, and Clay's need to be married before his father started campaigning.

Her mother stared at the TV for a moment, thinking. Then

she asked, "If she's out on parole, couldn't she be sent back for a violation or something?"

"Maybe. I should ask Justin Radner. He'll know."

"Radner? That no-good from the trailer park? Is he back, too?"

Sometimes it amazed Tori how like May Ellen her mother could be. She told her all about Justin and how she'd pawned off the Atherton place on him. Her mother rewarded Tori with a smile.

"I'm sure Justin will help me."

Desperation glinted in her mother's eyes. "If not, there are other ways."

CHAPTER SEVEN

DAVID NOYES LET HIMSELF into the *Tribune's* offices just after dawn. The red brick building with white Corinthian pillars was classically southern. It was a throwback to an era David recalled fondly from his youth. All of Twin Oaks was in a time warp. He'd come here because he'd had no alternative. It had taken him over a year to recuperate from an automobile accident that had almost killed him. While he was recovering, the *Boston Globe* had replaced him with a young hotshot investigative reporter.

Even with David's credentials—two Pulitzers and sterling recommendations—no one wanted to employ a sixty-seven-year-old man with a bad back. His roommate from Harvard, Silas Beaucannon, had founded AmeriNews, which owned small-town newspapers across the country. Silas had given him a job. The *Trib* wasn't a run-and-gun outfit like the *Globe*, but David discovered he really liked it here. The small-town atmosphere reminded him of rural Virginia where he'd grown up. Best of all, as executive editor and publisher, David was his own boss for a change.

What he didn't like was Beaucannon forcing a convict on him. He had no idea what he was going to do with the woman. He had a reporter who covered local sporting events, and a lady who wrote the society page. Folks around here bought the paper to see their names in it.

What generated revenue was advertising. He was lucky to

have Ace Holmes to do that job. Ace was a good old boy through and through. He knew everyone in town, especially the business people. Ace had no problem calling up businesses to remind them that special sales and coupons meant increased profits. Maybe Ace could put the woman to work.

He turned on the lights in his office and inhaled deeply. There was always a trace of printer's ink in the air. Old-fashioned presses in the back of the building produced the newspaper. Big-city papers had turned to computers, but the *Trib* still used a typesetter and a printing press. The smell never failed to bring back the old days when he'd been a cub reporter in Chicago.

Where had the time gone?

Reporting had been his life. Although he'd come close twice, he'd never married. Now he wondered if he'd made a mistake. A pang of loneliness hit. When had his life become so stagnant? He purged his regrets from his thoughts and concentrated on his notes about the murdered woman. He had one worthless field reporter who phoned in most of his news. David did the investigative reporting—not that there had been much to investigate until this murder. He'd covered every angle of the crime he could think of and come up with nothing.

Someone had to have known her, but in the hours he'd spent interviewing people, no one had a clue who she was. The sheriff hadn't had any better luck—or so he claimed. David had interviewed Justin Radner and was impressed with him, but David couldn't help suspecting Radner was holding something back. His sixth sense had paid off in the past.

He needed to develop a source inside the sheriff's station. It hadn't seemed necessary before because serious crime was rare in Twin Oaks, only one murder years ago and the robbery at the bank. He glanced at his watch. Kaitlin Wells should arrive in another two hours.

David concentrated on the front page articles. Most would be pickups from the wire services. He decided to move the murdered woman's story from the prime spot above the fold to below the fold. As long as the woman remained unidentified and the cause of death unknown, he doubted the readers would be interested in another rehash of what little facts were known.

He scanned the wire services for possible stories. People drifted into the city room's cube farm, and he waved from behind the glass that formed the top half of the wall enclosing his corner office but kept working. As soon as he had the Wells woman settled with Ace, he wanted to go over to the sheriff's station and see if he could pry some new information out of one of the deputies about the murdered woman.

David heard a knock on the open door to his office and looked up. Connie Proctor was leaning against the doorjamb. An imposing widow with blond hair bleached almost white, Connie was a workhorse who served as the copy editor and wrote the obituaries. She was also in charge of death notices, which usually ran with a picture of the deceased and were paid for by the family. It had proven to be a lucrative source of revenue for the paper.

In his experience, every office had someone like Connie—a stellar employee but a person who enjoyed bad news and put a negative spin on anything she could. With David, she was friendly—almost too friendly. He couldn't decide if this was her way of getting on the good side of her boss or if she was flirting with him. He handled her behavior by keeping strictly to business.

"Kaitlin Wells is here," Connie informed him, rolling her eyes as if the devil himself had arrived.

"Have her come in." David selected the final article for the front page from UPI and pressed his computer's save button. When he spun around in his chair, an attractive brunette in a blue suit with a short skirt that showed off her slim legs was standing in front of him.

"Mr. Noyes," she said in a soft voice. "I'm Kaitlin Wells. I want to thank you for giving me the opportunity to work here."

"You're welcome." He gestured for her to sit in the chair in front of his desk, thinking she didn't look anything like the picture he'd seen in the *Trib*'s archives. "Kaitlin, I want to discuss some of the terms I have for employing you."

"All right." She gazed at him with arresting green eyes. If she had long blond hair, she would be a dead ringer for her sister, Tori. "Everyone calls me Kat."

"Okay, Kat it is." He decided she seemed to be more assertive than he'd been led to expect when he'd told the staff she would be at the *Trib* on a work furlough. He'd envisioned a plump woman in plain clothes, hunched shoulders, and world-weary eyes from being incarcerated. If he'd seen Kat on the street, he would never have imagined she was a felon.

"I want you to be on time. Come in at eight and you may leave at five. You'll have one hour for lunch. We have a break room with a refrigerator and microwave, in case you want to bring your lunch. No eating or smoking at your desk."

"Where is my desk?"

"Out there in the city room. That's what we call the room where our reporters work. I'm going to give you a few different assignments until I decide what suits you best."

"I notice the paper seems to have more ads than when I lived here."

David smiled inwardly. She'd taken the trouble to look over the paper. A good sign. "AmeriNews bought the paper five years ago. They own over two thousand papers in small towns. Advertising is what makes any paper profitable. I think I'll start you off working with Ace Holmes. He's in charge of advertising."

A beat of silence. "Will I have a chance to do any reporting?"

He was momentarily speechless with surprise. "I'd have you help me with a murder case that—"

"The woman found in the brush out in the unincorporated area. I read the article in Saturday's paper."

He really didn't have time to teach her reporting. It would be better to assign her to Ace, but he found himself saying, "I think the sheriff knows more than he's telling us. Any ideas on how to find out?"

She looked at him with wide green eyes. He doubted she had what it took to become a reporter, and he mentally kicked himself for asking.

"I have an idea. If you take me to my desk, I'll make a call."

He hesitated, measuring her for a second before asking, "Why don't you tell me what you're going to do?"

She leaned forward slightly, excitement lighting her face. "Women talk. I have a friend who's a hairdresser. There are only two beauty shops in town. I'll bet Lola Rae styles a deputy's wife or someone at the station."

He hated to admit it, but this wasn't a half-bad idea. Women gossiped, and they had been reliable sources in the past. "Call her from the second desk, the one with the *National Geographic* calendar on the wall."

David watched Kat walk out to her desk in the cube farm. When he'd heard she was coming, David had gone to the newspaper's morgue where all the previous issues of the paper were stored. He'd read about her being caught by the president of the bank with money missing from the vault. The evidence seemed irrefutable.

Because it was a federal crime, the trial had been held in Jackson, the capital. The *Trib* had sent a reporter, and the paper had printed detailed articles. The reporter had left the *Trib* shortly after the trial, but reading between the lines, David decided Kat's public defender had done little to help her case.

A few minutes later, David looked up and Kat was standing at the entrance to his office, grinning. "I was right. Lola Rae does a deputy's wife's hair. The woman told her that the sheriff didn't have much faith in the local coroner."

"He's just a mortician. There isn't enough call for autopsies to justify a full-time coroner."

"Sheriff Radner sent tissue samples and the body of the victim to New Orleans."

David frowned. "New Orleans? Why not the state crime lab?"

"The woman said the sheriff thinks they're slow and sloppy."

He considered this information. "I haven't had any experience with the state lab, but Radner would be in a position to know."

"The results are supposed to be back today."

Interesting, he thought. New Orleans was practically murder capital U.S.A. It wasn't as big as L.A. or New York, but for its size, the city had an alarming number of homicides. No doubt, the coroner's office there could analyze the information even better than the state crime lab.

"Okay," he told her. "Here's what a reporter does."

"Verifies the information with a reliable person. We don't want to print rumors," she said quickly. "I read a book on newspapers from the library over the weekend."

David couldn't help smiling. Despite his earlier reservations, he liked Kat Wells. He just hoped she didn't make him regret helping her. "We need to talk to the sheriff and ask him if it's true."

"But protect our source, right?"

"Let's go over to the station now." He stood up.

"What if the sheriff isn't in?"

"Ask a deputy to confirm or deny."

JUSTIN RADNER GAZED across his desk at Tori Wells. She'd sashayed into the station slightly after ten o'clock. He'd been sorting through the load of paperwork that had accumulated between Sheriff Parker's death and Justin being hired.

"Run that by me again," Justin said as if he didn't understand her.

Tori flitted her eyelashes. Either she thought that worked with men or she had an eye problem.

"I want to know what would terminate my sister's work furlough."

"You mean get her sent back to prison?"

"Absolutely. That's where she belongs."

"Hard to say," he hedged. He took a sip of the sludgy brown liquid that Nora claimed was coffee, then reached under his desk to pet Redd. "Work furloughs are just coming into use with the severe prison overcrowding. I've never been involved with one before."

Tori leaned forward, treating him to a cleavage shot. "My mother's very ill. Dying, actually. It's very distressing to her to have Kat around."

"Get a restraining order. You know Judge Kincaid well enough to get one by noon."

An odd gleam came into her eyes. Uh-oh! Now he got it. Tori's about-to-depart-this-earth mother wasn't her primary concern. The Kincaids were upset to have their son involved with the sister of a con. A tragedy, sure, but Turner Kincaid had political ambitions.

"I hate to bother the judge." She did the eyelash thing again. "Could you find out what it would take to get her sent back?"

He battled the urge to leap over the desk and strangle her. What kind of woman would want her sister in prison? He might have been brought up in a run-down trailer park, but his mother had loved him. No matter what he might have done, she would have stuck by him.

"Short of murdering someone, I doubt Kat's furlough can be revoked." This was a bald-faced lie. A jaywalking ticket could get her furlough canceled, but he wasn't about to divulge the truth to this scheming bitch.

TORI PARKED her Lincoln LS in her mother's parking space. She wondered if Justin Radner was gay. He didn't look it, but these days it was hard to tell. When she turned on the charm most men did what she wanted. Well, not all the time. Clay certainly had been ice-cold last night.

Didn't he appreciate all the things she'd done for him?

Of course not. In many ways, Clay was spoiled and pampered. But still, she loved him, and she intended to be his wife. Even though she despised politics, Tori put a positive spin on the situation. When the judge went to Washington, they would be invited to all sorts of events. That would compensate for the utter boredom of politics. She wasn't letting an ugly duckling half sister who'd committed a crime ruin her plans.

She got out of the car and walked up to her mother's condo. Drops of perspiration spread across the back of her neck. She fluffed her long hair, thinking in another few weeks the heat and humidity would be suffocating. In Washington, it would still be hot and sticky, but at least there would be exciting things to do. Parties with glamorous, powerful people.

She found her mother exactly where she'd left her last night—on the sofa staring vacantly at the television. Some talk show was on. "Ma? You okay?"

Her mother nodded. "The nurse gave me a shot."

Morphine. Her mother would be groggy, not fit to discuss the situation intelligently. "I spoke to the sheriff. He says unless Kat commits a major crime like murder, her furlough won't be revoked."

Her mother gazed blankly at her, then the words finally reached her morphine-numbed brain. "I don't have much time."

Tori collapsed on the sofa beside her mother. "I know. I want to at least be engaged to Clay before…"

A burst of laughter erupted from the television.

"I'm dying, Tori. I know it. You know it. I'm just hanging on to see you and Clay married."

She shuddered inwardly at the thought of not having Loretta. Tori loved her mother. They'd always been close. If she could just wrangle an engagement ring out of Clay, her mother could die in peace.

"I'm going to ask Clay what he thinks. Maybe he knows someone who could help."

There had always been a dark side to Clay. He gambled and hung out at the casino. It was common knowledge New Orleans mobsters owned the riverboat. Maybe one of them could help scare Kat into leaving town.

CHAPTER EIGHT

NORA KNOCKED on Justin's office door shortly after Tori left. He'd asked her about the missing file on Kat, but Nora seemed shocked that it wasn't downstairs. As he'd suspected, she'd kept those files in order. "David Noyes is here to see you."

What did Noyes want? Justin liked the old guy, but he'd already given him an interview about the murder. He had a load of paperwork to finish before he received the coroner's report from New Orleans. Then, with luck, he'd have a lead or two to investigate.

"Did he say what this is about?"

"No but he has the woman who robbed the bank with him."

Kat Wells? She'd just missed her conniving sister by minutes. That would have been some scene. Justin wondered if he should warn Kat. He thought about it, then told himself to mind his own business.

"Send them in."

"Yes, indeedy."

To avoid staring at Kat, Justin kept his eyes on Noyes as they walked into his office. Noyes wore a charcoal-gray suit a shade darker than his short-cropped gray hair and a blue tie. He was tall but slightly stooped with age.

Kat strode in beside him, attitude oozing from every pore. She was dynamite in an outfit that emphasized high, full breasts without revealing them and showed off sculpted, showgirl legs. Tori overdid it when she tried to be sexy. Kat was hot without even trying.

"This is a surprise." Justin stood and shook Noyes' hand, then reached for Kat's. He looked directly into her smoldering green eyes, and unexpectedly had an image of her in his bed, her hair fanned across his pillow—those compelling eyes wide with desire.

"We've received some information," Noyes said.

"We'd like a confirmation from you before we go to press," Kat added, dropping his hand the instant their fingers touched.

Deafening alarm bells chimed in his head, blocking out the image of Kat. Now what? Redd chose that moment to scratch himself, and the desk began to shake. "My dog's under there."

"Really?" Kat's expression softened but she stopped short of a smile.

Evidently she liked dogs. A point in her favor. He reminded himself Kat Wells was a felon. *Don't start liking her,* he warned himself. "I rescued Redd. He'd been abandoned and was living in the woods. He's still a bit shy."

Kat rewarded him with a real smile. A gorgeous smile.

"What would you like me to verify?"

Noyes glanced at Kat, obviously letting her handle this. It was surprising they were getting along so well so fast. Go figure.

"Is it true that you sent the murdered woman's body to the New Orleans coroner?"

How in hell had they heard about it? Justin had told everyone at the station to keep quiet. Then he remembered neglecting to warn Mayor Peebles. The leak must have come from there.

Justin tried to sound shocked. "Send the body out of state?"

Kat stared at him with a look that said she'd read his mind and knew he was bluffing. "A reliable source claims you did."

Justin quickly weighed his options. He did not want this in the paper. It would just be ammunition for Judge Kincaid and Buck Mason to use against him. In a year, Justin would have to stand for election. Mason and Kincaid would back some other candidate and fling around crap about Justin.

"This is off the record." Justin waited. He knew Noyes would realize he couldn't print the information, but Kat might not.

"All right," Noyes said reluctantly. He turned to Kat. "That means—"

"We can't print it." She glared at Justin with burning reproachful eyes. "Don't the people have a right to know? There's a killer out there. Others could be in danger."

"Not necessarily. Some folks think a tourist visiting the casino committed the crime. You know, someone passing through. The woman died months ago, and no one else has been killed."

"Is that your theory?" Kat inquired in a voice that was just a touch too sweet for the look in her eyes.

Hey, she could be tough. He hated to admit it but she already read him like no one else could. Justin saw Noyes smile slightly. No doubt, he would have asked the same question.

"I don't jump to conclusions when I'm working a case. I deal in facts. Theories make you miss things."

"Okay," Noyes said. "What were you going to tell us that's off the record?"

"I did send the body to New Orleans. I wanted as fast a turnaround as I could get. I should have the test results today."

Kat put her hands on her hips. "This is too small of a town to keep this a secret."

"True, but I'd rather not have people yelling at me. I have a few enemies in this town that I don't need to hear from just after I've been hired. With a little luck, I might discover who the murdered woman is and crack the case before word gets out."

"Enemies?" Noyes asked. "You've been away for years."

"Buck Mason and Judge Kincaid," Kat said.

Noyes whistled and shook his head. "Two guys with a lot of clout around here."

"Yeah, tell me about it."

Noyes studied him with shrewd eyes. "What can you give us that's new?"

"There's nothing new on the case."

Kat's lips curved into a smile that lacked a trace of warmth or humor. "There may be new information when you receive the report."

Justin shrugged. "Maybe, maybe not. What you could print is a plea for someone to step forward and ID the woman."

"We've already done that," Noyes pointed out.

Kat raised her hand, the other hand still on her hip. Sexy as hell. "You thought she might be Hispanic."

"That's what the mortician who performed the autopsy here said. I sent a hair sample to New Orleans. They'll run a DNA profile on it and let me know."

"Well, did you question Hispanics in town or just out at the casino?"

Prison certainly had changed her. She wasn't shy the way he'd been led to believe by Nora who'd known Kat for years. She didn't hesitate to ask probing questions. "I have a deputy who speaks some Spanish. He asked everyone he could find."

"If they're undocumented, they might not be willing to tell what they know," she said. "They could be deported."

Justin had come to the same conclusion, but he didn't mention it.

"I bet I know a woman your deputy missed."

"Who is it? I'll interview her."

Kat shook her head, and her gleaming brown hair bounced alluringly against her cheek. "Let me talk to her—"

"You speak Spanish?"

"A little. I studied it in high school and again in prison."

She said this matter-of-factly, obviously not too embarrassed about doing time. "I think she might open up to me while a law officer is liable to frighten her."

"I agree, but this is law enforcement work—"

"What can it hurt?" Noyes asked.

Justin shrugged, thinking that the deputy who spoke some Spanish had left yesterday for a two-week vacation. His own grasp of Spanish was limited to *cerveza* and the word for beer wasn't likely to get him far. Besides, many Hispanics *were* here illegally and were afraid to talk to the police. The woman just might talk to Kat.

"Okay, question the woman," he told Kat. "If you find out anything that could possibly help with this crime, I want you to bring the information to me immediately."

IT WAS NOON by the time Kat parked in front of All Washed Up. Waves of heat and humidity surfed upward from the asphalt. The scent of wild honeysuckle drifted through the heavy air. It was only May, but summer seemed to be coming early. Her hair had been bouncy this morning, but it was limp and damp around her neck and face. Naturally, the Toyota they'd provided had no air-conditioning.

She left the car clutching the notebook and pen David had given her. She liked David Noyes. At first she thought he was going to assign her to some menial task just to get her out of the way, but he hadn't. Calling Lola Rae had been a good idea that had paid off and had validated his confidence in her. Questioning Maria probably wouldn't be as helpful, but as David said—a good reporter checked all possible leads.

She smiled to herself for—what?—the hundredth time today. Not only was David Noyes training her to be a reporter, he trusted her to do her very first interview on her own. Pretty amazing. Even more amazing was that the sheriff had allowed her to question Maria. He probably knew it was a dead end, but he seemed nicer today than he had last night. David's influence, she decided.

She remembered standing in front of Justin's desk. He hadn't been wearing a uniform. His blue polo shirt gaped open at the neck and revealed a tuft of dark hair. He'd insolently scanned her body, finally meeting her eyes with a smile that would test a nun's vows. When he spoke, she felt his deep voice inside her chest, and a warm glow flared into something more when she gazed into his eyes.

Just thinking about him did ridiculous things to her pulse. No matter how attractive she found him, Justin wasn't on her side. He was looking for an excuse to send her back to prison. *Never forget it.*

She opened the salon's door and a whoosh of blessedly cool air greeted her. She stepped inside and quickly shut the door behind her. Lola Rae was cutting an older woman's hair.

The line of the woman's jaw reminded Kat of her mother. Surely by now, her mother knew she was back in town. Kat hoped she would come to see her, but doubted this would happen. An ache too deep for tears assailed her. She managed to tamp it down and told herself that she would have to go see her mother herself.

Lola Rae glanced up and her deep brown eyes widened. "What happened to you?"

"A car with no air."

"Well, sit down and I'll fix you in a minute. Know what I mean?"

Kat waved her off. "Thanks, but I haven't got time. I just dropped by to see Maria."

Lola Rae's expression was questioning, but Kat didn't explain. "She's in the back."

Kat found Maria in the storage room, cleaning brushes. It took Kat a few minutes and lots of hand gestures to make

Maria understand what she was asking. Kat could see the young woman was fearful.

NORA RAPPED SOFTLY on Justin's doorjamb. Her blouse had smudges of dust from moving around junk in the basement. He would have had one of his deputies do it, but they were down at the river where the noodling contest was in the preliminary stages. This was the only county in a three-state area where noodling was legal and it drew a big crowd.

Why anyone would want to catch catfish with their bare hands defied all logic, but noodling was a big sport in the area. A lot of drinking went on between rounds and that meant fights. He'd given Nora instructions to come get him to lift anything heavy.

"Need my help?" he asked.

"No. Kat Wells is here to see you…again."

He was momentarily speechless. If she was back so soon, she must have found out something. I'll be damned, he thought. "Send her in."

Kat walked into his office as fast as her shapely legs could bring her. By the eager look on her face, he could see that she had information. Well, so had he. The state crime lab might not know jack shit, but the coroner in New Orleans was first rate.

She sat down in the chair in front of his desk and leaned forward. "I have some information…off the record, of course."

He couldn't believe her nerve. It almost—almost—gave him hope that she might make it. But the odds were against her. She was more likely to end up in prison again than to lead a normal life.

"Why is this off the record? Law enforcement doesn't do off the record. That's media stuff."

Her lips twisted into a grim smile. "Do I look stupid?"

"Well, now that you mention it."

"Very funny," she shot back, standing up. "Obviously you don't want to solve this case. I'm outta here."

"Sit down, sit down."

She lowered herself into her chair. It was a simple movement, but he found it very provocative. Well, hell. He'd found her sexy from the get-go, but the more he was around her, the more intense the attraction became. He had to keep reminding himself who she was—*what* she was.

"Okay," he said reluctantly. "Off the record."

"Maria Sanchez told me that she thinks the murdered woman is Pequita Romero, an illegal alien who worked somewhere deep in the woods."

"What makes her think the victim is the Romero woman?"

"The Hispanics in the area get together every Sunday. One guy was once a priest. He performs a short service, then they have a potluck. Pequita hasn't been around for some time. A man who worked with her claims she went back to Mexico. Maria doesn't buy it. She says Pequita is smart and aggressive and determined to make money quickly in the States."

Interesting. None of the Hispanics his deputy had interviewed had mentioned a weekly get-together. He'd been right to let Kat question the woman. She'd had better results than his deputy.

"Where was this woman working?"

"She remembers Pequita telling her she worked near the river off Shady Hook Road. They were cooking stuff in big vats, according to Maria. I can't imagine what they would prepare way out in the boonies, then haul into town."

Big vats. Something clicked in his brain. Kat had stumbled across some very useful information. "It might make perfect sense, if she worked at a meth lab."

"Meth? There were a couple of tweakers in prison." She wrinkled her nose. "You'd be amazed what can be smuggled into jail."

"No, I wouldn't. Short of an elephant, I know prisoners can get just about anything."

"True, but crystal meth is easy because it's a powder. Those gals were paranoid, delusional half the time, and concentration camp skinny," she said, genuine sadness in her tone, as if she wished she could have helped them. She wasn't as tough as she acted.

"Ever try it?"

"Never," she replied emphatically. "I've never touched any drugs. Actually, there weren't many around when I was in school. A little marijuana, but that's it."

"Times have changed. Meth is now the numero uno drug in rural America because it's a no-brainer to produce."

"I know," she snapped back. "Mix cold tablets, drain cleaner, and a few other things together, then heat it up on top of a stove."

"Most outfits are mom-and-pop operations, making a modern-day version of moonshine but much more deadly."

"Vats doesn't seem like a small-time operation to me."

Not only was Kat sexy, she was sharp, far sharper than he'd expected. She kept surprising him. He liked a challenging woman. Most were transparent, exactly what they seemed—but not Kat. He couldn't help staring at her lips, spellbound by their seductive movements as she spoke. Her voice was soft, but sensuously rough, like the rasp of a cat's tongue.

"You're right. This sounds like a bigger operation. Meth can be smoked, snorted or injected, but I'm betting they're reducing it to crystal meth—poor man's cocaine. A powder is lighter, easier to transport."

Redd wriggled out from under the desk. Justin watched the dog slink around the side and peer cautiously at Kat.

She lowered her thick dark lashes and studied the dog. "Hello. What's your name?"

"Redd with two *d*s."

She reached out her hand. "Here, Redd. Here, boy."

The dog gingerly stepped forward, but not close enough for her to pet him. Still, Justin was surprised. Redd hadn't shown any interest in other people who'd come into his office.

"Redd, what happened to your fur?"

"It was so matted and full of thorns that it had to be shaved. The family who owned him left Redd in the woods to fend for himself when they moved. He was slowly starving to death."

Her eyes had been on the dog, but now she looked up at him. Respect stole into her expression. For reasons he couldn't articulate, he wanted her to see him as something more than the law. She flashed him a smile that could light up hell.

"Here, boy." She reached out to Redd. "I won't hurt you."

The dog inched forward, and she let him sniff her extended hand. Apparently he liked what he smelled. Justin had already caught a trace of a floral scent when she'd first walked in. Redd edged close enough for her to touch him. She stroked his head and fondled his ears.

"What a good boy you are."

Justin imagined those hands on his body and heat pooled in his groin. Don't go there, he told himself. Don't get involved with a woman who's going back to jail. But his body had other ideas. The iron heat of his sex pressed against the fly of his khakis. Holy shit! How could she get to him so easily?

He was horny—plain and simple. He hadn't had sex in—what?—a month or so. He couldn't remember exactly. That had to explain his intense reaction.

"How do you think Pequita figured in?" she asked as she continued to pet Redd.

It didn't take him a second to answer. "She worked there. Cheap labor."

"Why would they kill her, I wonder?"

Justin wasn't sure they had. Drug dealers liked to kill people execution style. This victim hadn't died that way. That's what kept bothering him. Something was off here.

Kat surprised him by asking, "Did you get the report?"

He nodded, not sure how much he wanted the press to know.

"Did it pinpoint the cause of death?"

He quickly went through his mental file of reasons for withholding the information, then he decided to give her a break. After all, she'd already helped him with the case. An article in the paper might flush out more info from someone out there.

"The victim was poisoned with a very deadly substance. Fluoroacetate is the lethal ingredient in rat poison. A drop will kill a person in a few hours."

"Is this on the record?"

He winked at her. "Yes, I didn't bother to check with manufacturers of rodent killers. Anyone with an average knowledge of chemistry could produce a batch of fluoroacetate."

"Is it an ingredient in crystal meth?"

Justin shook his head.

"Why go to such lengths to kill someone?"

"Good question."

CHAPTER NINE

A LITTLE AFTER TWO that afternoon, Kat parked her Toyota in the *Trib*'s parking lot. Droplets of perspiration would soon drench her. She could get a fan for her studio, but how was she going to handle driving this car all summer? She'd constantly look like a wet rag.

Kat stepped out of the car and stamped her feet to unglue her skirt from the back of her legs. She could hardly wait to see David. Her very first scoop! On her first day at work, no less.

She heard a motor running and glanced over at a blue Lincoln LS with tinted windows. Nice car, she thought. Some day. *Be thankful for what you have,* she reminded herself. She gazed heavenward where drifting clouds painted the sky. She was free. That should be enough.

The motor shut off and the car door opened. A stunning blonde in a pale-yellow linen dress stepped out. *Oh my God.* Tori.

"I've been waiting for you," Tori said.

Her voice hadn't changed one bit. It was still like warm honey. Tori looked more mature, even more beautiful than Kat remembered. She'd always had style, but now she obviously had money. Her long hair was flawlessly cut and woven several different shades of blond.

"I'm back," Kat said, dismayed to hear her voice crack.

"So I see." She smiled fondly at Kat.

Kat felt herself responding to her sister's smile. She hated herself for it, for the childhood memories it evoked. Nostalgia welled up inside her. She could almost see herself as a child. Her father was telling a story to them. Tori was gazing up at him with the same irresistible smile.

"It's hot out here. Let's talk in my car."

Kat followed her half sister to the car. *Talk about what? Why you never wrote, never came to see me?* She told herself to remain detached, emotionless, but it was impossible. A bitter ache filled her, black and all-consuming.

Inside the car, Tori turned on the air. It was so frigid it gave Kat a chill, but it didn't take her mind off the situation. She might still be Tori's little sister, but she wasn't an awestruck, obedient child any longer.

She'd counted on her father's love as a child. She'd been too fat, too shy to assert herself. As absurd as it sounded, prison had been good for her in one way. Jail had been the school of hard knocks.

Only the strong survived.

"Why didn't you let me know Mother has cancer?"

Tori turned to Kat, a spark of some indefinable emotion in her green eyes. "I thought you had your own troubles. Why bother you with anything else?"

Tori sounded sympathetic, as if she genuinely hadn't wanted to cause more grief for Kat. She felt her throat constrict slightly, but she refused to cut her sister any slack.

"I had a right to know. She's my mother, too."

Tori met Kat's accusing eyes with a contrite expression. "I wanted to call, but I was embarrassed because it had been so long since we'd spoken. When you were arrested, I was in Oxford. Mother said to distance ourselves. You know how she is. I should have come home and seen if I could help somehow."

Her confession tore at something inside Kat. Her stomach rose, then fell with a sickening lurch. No matter what Tori said now—it still hurt. Being falsely accused of a crime and deserted by her family wasn't something she could easily forgive.

"It would have been nice if you had tried to help me. Between Mother and the Kincaids, I guess you didn't have much choice." The bitterness in her voice made Kat angry with herself. She didn't want her mother or sister to know how emotionally crippling the pain of their betrayal had been.

"I know you're angry with me," Tori said, her voice low and apologetic. "I don't blame you."

Get over it, Kat told herself. You can't change the past. It is what it is, then you deal with it. "How is Mother?"

"Dying. She's on morphine constantly now."

Her sister's words breached the hairline fracture in her composure and a soft gasp came from her lips. She'd known her mother was dying, but hearing her sister say it made the situation frighteningly real. Even if they hadn't really gotten along, Loretta Wells was still her mother. It was impossible to imagine a world without her. "I should go see her."

Tori shook her head. "You'll only upset her. You know how Mother is. Appearances are everything. She's mortified that you're back in town."

The truth ripped at Kat like a serrated blade and anger mushroomed inside her. "Did it ever occur to either of you that I didn't take the money?"

Tori gave Kat's hand a quick, reassuring squeeze. "I never ever believed you stole the money. It isn't in your nature to lie or steal."

"What does Mother think?"

Tori hesitated a moment. "It doesn't matter what she believes. In her eyes, you humiliated her, disgraced our good name."

"I see," Kat said, although her tone indicated she didn't understand at all.

Loretta Wells had been socially ambitious for her daughters. She'd insisted they associate with the "right" people. Being poor was a cardinal sin. But no matter how repugnant Kat found her attitude, Loretta was her mother, and she was near death.

"How long does Mother have to live?"

"It's hard to say." A single tear like a small diamond sparkled on Tori's eyelashes. "Weeks or months, but not much longer. I see her every day. She doesn't always know I'm there."

Tori and Mother had always been very close. This had to be heartbreaking for Tori. Until now, Kat had thought only about herself. While Kat had been in prison, Tori had been taking care of their mother. Facing the death of someone you loved dearly had to be a nightmare that ranked right up there with going to jail. It might even be worse. Freedom came at the end of a prison sentence. Death was final.

"Is there anything I can do?" Kat asked.

An uneasy silence filled the car. Uh-oh. Here it comes.

"You know Mother has always wanted me to marry Clay Kincaid."

True. Their mother worshiped the Kincaids because they were "quality" people who could trace their ancestors back to plantation days. Since high school, her heart had been set on Tori marrying Clay.

His family had pushed Clay to marry Verity Mason. They'd dated for a time their junior year in high school, then Verity had fallen for Justin. Clay and Tori hooked up, and when he went off to Ole Miss, Loretta had supported Tori's move to Oxford. Neither one of them wanted to chance Clay falling for someone else.

"Clay's ready to give me a ring and set the date," Tori said with pride.

"Great! It's about time. You two have been together for years."

"There's just one problem." Kat detected the snick of barely concealed anger in her sister's voice. "You."

"Me? I don't expect to be invited to the wedding," she said, hoping she sounded indifferent. "Just go on with your plans and forget about me."

Tori drummed perfectly manicured pink fingernails on the steering wheel. "I wish it were that simple. The judge is going to run for senate next year. They don't want a felon in the family."

"What am I supposed to do?"

"I'll give you money to move away. Get out of the state so you can't be interviewed. Out of sight, out of mind."

Anger arced through her with the force of an electrical charge. So this was why Tori had come to see her. Her sister might not have been mean to her when they were growing up, but Tori's world had always revolved around her own interests. Evidently she had a gene that rendered her unable to concentrate for more than a few minutes on anything but herself.

"You're pretty now, Kat, and slim. You could start over somewhere else."

"I'm not free to leave," she snapped. "I have to stay here until they release me."

"When will that be?" Impatience underscored every syllable.

"I'll be up for review next year."

"That's too late. I need you to go away now."

Kat yanked the door open and jumped out of the car without another word. She didn't trust herself not to lash out at her sister. What good would it do? Tori peeled out of the parking lot, leaving the smell of burning rubber in her wake.

For a minute there, Tori had her believing she regretted the way she'd treated Kat. What about this don't you understand? Kat asked herself. Some things never change. Her family was one of them. Her father had loved her, Tori tolerated her when it was convenient, but her mother had never cared.

"Hey, it can't be that bad," David Noyes said as she walked into the *Trib* building. He was working with Connie Proctor, the copy editor.

She mustered a smile. Fifteen minutes ago, she'd been so happy. Now she was as depressed as she'd been in prison.

Even though she was dying, her own mother didn't want to see her, and her sister was so desperate to get rid of her that she'd offered her money to leave.

"I have a scoop," she announced.

Connie's brow furrowed into a tight frown. "We've put the paper to bed."

"That means we've formatted it and it's in the back of the building ready to be printed," he explained. "What've you got?"

She told them about the lethal poison that killed the woman. "Justin says when we print the story, we should ask people to call him if they know someone who has a lab or has been tinkering with solutions. Fluoroacetate has to be made somewhere. You can't easily buy it because it's illegal. Someone has to know something."

"This can wait for tomorrow's edition," Connie said with a look that told Kat how little she thought of her scoop.

"No, it can't." David picked up the telephone and punched a button. "Hold the press. We're reformatting the front page." He hung up with a broad smile. "I've been dying to say 'hold the press' for years."

Connie groaned. "You've got to fit the story into the news hole."

"You work on the head. I'll fill the hole." To Kat he said, "Come with me. We're in a rush, otherwise I'd let you write the article. You need to learn the lingo. Heads mean headlines. Copy editors write them because reporters are notorious for being late to meet deadlines."

Connie glared at Kat as they headed for David's office. It was clear she didn't appreciate being overridden, but Kat suspected the older woman would blame her. Connie knew David was in charge and would forgive him for the extra work this would mean.

"News hole refers to the space remaining for articles after the ads are inserted. Ads are placed first. It's our bread and butter. We fit the news around them."

"But there aren't ads on the front page."

David smiled at her and once again, Kat thought how much she liked him. "We still call them news holes. In this case the paper is ready to print. We'll have to fit your scoop into the space where we inserted a pickup article from UPI."

She followed him into his office, saying, "The woman I interviewed may know the name of the victim. Justin wants us to withhold that info until he checks it out. We might be able to use it tomorrow or the next day."

David spun around, clearly astonished. "Your source knew something *and* you convinced Radner to share the report with you?"

"I just got lucky. The only two people I've spent time with since returning were helpful."

"No. *I* got lucky when they sent you here on furlough."

She'd been so alone for so long. It had been years since anyone was actually glad to have her around. Before she could stop herself, she blurted out, "I want you to know that I did not steal the money."

Between level brows, David studied her for a moment. "What happened?"

How could Kat explain? She almost wished she hadn't brought it up. She couldn't tell him she was here undercover. "I don't know what happened. Suddenly, the sheriff was at the bank, claiming money had been found in my purse." She shrugged weakly. "I have no idea how it got there."

"No idea?" David's gaze was sharp now.

"Someone at the bank must have framed me."

"I see," David said softly. "Why?"

"I wish I knew." She told him the truth even though she'd

never uttered the words to anyone else. "I asked myself that question a hundred times a day for over four years."

He reached out and touched her arm. Kat had to fight back tears.

IT WAS NINE O'CLOCK by the time Kat got home. After David had written the story and delivered it to the press room, he'd spent hours with her while she practiced writing articles. He'd ordered a pizza, and they'd eaten it at her desk as she wrote. It had taken all her willpower to restrict herself to one piece.

When she'd been furloughed, the future had shimmered like a mirage, out of focus, out of reach. Now she knew what she wanted to do. She would be a reporter. She loved it. She honestly loved it.

Kat changed clothes and walked barefoot across her studio, the worn linoleum cool beneath her feet. She pivoted and returned to where she'd begun. It had been years since she'd gone barefoot. As a kid, she'd spent the entire summer not wearing shoes except to church. But the rough concrete floors in prison were mopped every day with an antiseptic that made your feet stink.

Life was full of small pleasures, she decided. Going barefoot was one of them. Watching the hummingbirds was another. Just being able to walk out the door on your own ranked right up there.

People were at the top of her list, too. David treated her with respect and his lead meant the rest of the staff did, too. Well, Connie was a little snippy, but Kat could handle her. Lola Rae had left a fan on her doorstep with a note, saying it had been sitting in her garage. Now the small studio was much cooler than it had been when she'd come home. Beside the fan had been a foil tray with a stack of tamales from Maria.

How could some folks be so kind and others so selfish?

Forget about Tori. Forget about your mother. There's nothing you can do to change them. Nothing.

She'd told David she was innocent, and he'd believed her without even questioning her. One day the truth would come out, but there might be something she could do to make it happen sooner. David was teaching her to be an investigative reporter. She planned to work on her own case.

Someone in the bank took the money or knew who did. Cloris Howard was still president of the bank. Kat had seen her name in one of the articles in the *Trib*. Elmer Bitner was probably still the VP. There had been three other tellers present the day the money disappeared. They might have left for better-paying jobs. Someone had put the money in her purse and taken off with the rest.

At least that's what she'd always thought. Now, though, being used in a sting made her believe something else entirely might have happened. Why else would the authorities think she would be contacted? So far there'd been nothing. But she hadn't been home long. It would take a little time before everyone in town heard she had returned.

A knock at her door startled Kat. She peeped through the frayed curtains on the door's small window and saw Justin standing there, Redd at his side. The yellow bug light gave his dark hair a warm glow. He flashed her an irreverent grin that showed his white teeth and accentuated his heart-stopping good looks.

"Open up. It's hot out here."

She turned the knob and the door creaked open. "What do you want?"

He barged in. "Just checking on you." He looked around. "The state didn't provide much, did they?"

She bent over and petted Redd. "No, but it's better than a prison cell."

His smoky blue-gray eyes roved over her body. She'd changed into a lavender T-shirt and white shorts that hung low on her hips, revealing her midriff. The way he was looking at her made her feel as if she was standing here in her undies. His expression was so galvanizing a tremor went through her.

"Did you get the article written?" he asked.

"Yes. David wrote it, but he insisted on putting my name on the byline. You'll see it front and center in tomorrow's paper. He made you sound brilliant for getting the results so quickly."

"It wasn't any big deal."

She reminded him, "You have enemies, and you'll have to run for sheriff next year."

"I drove out to the Shady Hook area. I didn't find anything but fishing shacks. I'm going to try again tomorrow. Any chance you can find out from Maria the name of the guy who worked with this Romero woman?"

"Sure. I'll ask her first thing in the morning. She comes to the shop early to set up."

He studied her a minute with an unreadable expression. "Your sister came to see me this morning."

She stopped petting Redd, her apprehension mounting. "What did she want?"

"For me to get rid of you."

Kat wasn't surprised. Tori had no trouble wrapping men around her little finger. Justin Radner wouldn't be immune to her charms.

"I didn't tell her that you could be sent back for any minor offense."

"What did you say?"

He sat down on her sofa and patted the space next to him. "Nothing."

"Thanks." Kat sat beside him and began stroking Redd again. She was totally aware of Justin's nearness. His polo shirt outlined the hard planes of his powerful chest and impressive biceps. She allowed her eyes to stray lower for a second. He had powerful thighs and between them—she didn't want to think about the masculine bulge behind his fly.

He crossed his long legs, and she saw he was wearing an ankle holster with a pistol in it. He might not wear a uniform or drive a patrol car, but he was armed.

"I don't much like your sister. She's conniving. Watch your back around her."

It touched her that he seemed concerned. He'd come on like a Nazi when they'd first met, but evidently her work today had changed his negative opinion of her a little.

"Tori came to see me this afternoon and offered me money to leave town."

He arched one eyebrow, a gesture she found very boyish. And adorable. "You refused."

"I'm not leaving. One day I'll be able to clear my name."

His eyes became sharper, more focused. "I tried to look up your case, but the file was missing."

"Really?" Kat tried to sound surprised. She was pretty sure the authorities had lifted the file as part of the ongoing investigation. If they hadn't, the person they had working here undercover might have taken it.

He looked at her with the most intense gaze she'd ever encountered. She could almost hear the click, click, click of his brain. He probably suspected she knew more than she was telling. He was suspicious of her already, and this wasn't helping.

"Watch out for Tori," he said, rising. "She won't give up easily."

She walked him to the door and reached for the knob. He caught her wrist and gently pulled her toward him. Her breath came out in a startled gasp. He released her wrist and took her face in his big hands. Sheer surprise caused her to stiffen for a moment, then heat shot from where he touched her and every single nerve in her body went on alert.

What was he doing?

His lips came down on hers, warm and as gentle as a spring breeze. He couldn't possibly be kissing her—but he was. His moist, firm mouth demanded a response. Instinctively, her body arched toward his. She couldn't help reveling in the sweet sensations assailing her body.

His lips parted just a little and she could taste mint on his breath. She managed to keep herself from nudging her tongue between her lips to greet his. He nibbled at her lower lip, then sucked it into the heat of his mouth. It was a simple, almost playful gesture, but her toes curled in response and moisture invaded the lower reaches of her body.

Surely, he had to be experiencing the same mind-blowing explosion of passion. If so, he wasn't doing anything to indicate it, cautioned the one cell in her brain that was still rational. He's too experienced, she warned herself. This was just another kiss to him. He had to be toying with her.

Even knowing this, she couldn't stop her arms from sliding upward a scant inch at a time. Finally, one arm hooked around his neck and explored the soft hair at the base of his skull while the other arm circled his shoulders. Their bodies were one now. Every well-defined muscle and powerful bone pressed against her. Mounded to the firm wall of his chest, her breasts felt tight and warm and ached for his touch.

Her heartbeat skyrocketed as his tongue leisurely edged between her lips and brushed against hers. The kiss assumed a life of its own, and she responded with reckless abandon.

He unexpectedly released her, and she dropped her arms. Why had he stopped? Scorching heat flooded her cheeks. Her whole body was quivering with desire. She felt weak and confused. Was she pathetic or what?

Smoldering heat fired his eyes as they met hers, but his voice was cool. "Stay out of trouble." He opened the door and Redd trotted out ahead of him. "Check with me tomorrow afternoon and I'll let you know what the search found." He handed her a business card. "Here's my cell number, in case you find out the man's name."

He left and she collapsed onto the sofa, clutching the card. Justin Radner had kissed her! Why? Surely, he had a girl-friend. Several, probably. Why was he jerking her chain?

The last time she'd been kissed was during a brief, disastrous affair she'd had while working at the bank. She put her fingers to her moist lips. This had been much more erotic—from the last man she should be involved with. She reminded herself Justin could send her back to prison. She should distance herself. But she knew she couldn't.

CHAPTER TEN

HE WAS WALKING down the street, enjoying his morning, when the *Trib*'s headline jumped out at him from a rack of newspapers. He stopped abruptly and stared in utter disbelief. DEADLY POISON KILLED WOMAN. He rarely read the newspaper—it was always old news. He watched television news instead.

He dropped fifty cents in the slot, lifted the lid, and grabbed a paper. He scanned the article. "Shit."

Justin Radner had managed to discover he'd used fluoroacetate to kill the bitch. He'd known the smart-ass sheriff had sent the body to New Orleans, but the poison was supposed to be nearly impossible to trace. All it took to kill was a drop the size of a baby's tear.

He read on and saw the sheriff was requesting people report anyone they'd seen mixing chemicals. Radner could ask people to snitch all he wanted. No one—not even his partners—knew about the deadly poison or where he'd concocted it. He'd made just enough, then destroyed all the equipment. He had a small vial of the lethal stuff stashed where no one would find it. Who knew? He might need it again.

He slowly reread the article. By Kaitlin Wells, *Tribune* staff reporter. He cursed under his breath. Fuckin' A! What was Kat Wells—an ex-con—doing writing front-page articles? She must have been trained in the slammer. A waste of taxpayer dollars.

He'd have to keep his eye on her. He might be dealing with another nosy bitch, he thought, crumpling the newsprint in his fists. He saw red for a moment, but reined himself in.

Be calm, controlled. He could handle this. He pitched the paper into the trash can at the corner. So what if they knew about the poison? They didn't know who the bitch was or where she worked. Radner was spinning his wheels.

THE CELL PHONE in Justin's jeans pocket vibrated, and he pulled it out. "Radner."

"I have the name of the man who worked with Pequita Romero." It was Kat. "Tony Mendoza is working at the riverboat now."

"Great. I'll go talk to him."

"Justin, listen. Do *not* mention Maria's name. She's terrified of this man."

Justin gazed up through the canopy of trees between Shady Hook Road and the river where he and a deputy were searching for the meth lab along the levee roads and cane breaks. Dense pines hung low and heavy with oozing tar. It was barely nine o'clock, but the sun was burning white-hot, blistering the blue out of the sky barely visible between the treetops.

"Why is Maria frightened?"

"My Spanish isn't so good that I get every detail. From what I gather, the Hispanics are a pretty close-knit group. She doesn't want to upset them or cause trouble."

Justin understood. It was risky for them not to stick together. They got each other jobs and shared housing. Ratting on someone would mean big-time trouble. He was surprised Maria had done it, putting herself at risk needlessly. Maybe she wanted to curry favor in case she ran into trouble with the law.

"Not a problem. I won't mention Maria's name. I—"

"Sheriff, looky here," called his deputy from up ahead in a thicket of bushes.

"Gotta go. We may have found something."

"You promised to let me know what's happening—"

Justin clicked the cell phone shut and headed toward the spot where his deputy had disappeared into the underbrush beneath "blackjack"—scrub oak. Redd trotted along beside him. Justin could no longer deny the truth. He wasn't just attracted to Kat. He wanted her with a need so fierce it overwhelmed common sense. He shouldn't have gone to see her last night, and he certainly had no business kissing her.

But she'd felt so good. He recalled the texture of her skin. Invitingly soft and smooth. Lips a glossy peach color. Begging to be kissed.

It had taken all his willpower to pull away. He'd locked his jaw and ground his teeth to regain his self-control as she'd gazed up at him. Wanting him to keep kissing her.

Honest to God, what was he doing? Thinking with his pecker. He had to remember this woman was nothing but trouble. A convict. She would be heading back to prison in no time. Don't get involved with her.

"Look, Tony. I'm not going to bust you if you tell me the truth." Justin spoke slowly. Tony Mendoza knew English fairly well, but from Justin's experience overseas, when people spoke a foreign language rapidly, it became difficult to comprehend what they were saying.

"Dunno nothin'."

They were standing on the stern of the paddle wheeler. It was nearly two-thirty in the afternoon. In another few hours, the *Lucky Seven* would cast off and troll along the river so customers could gamble. Justin cuffed the sweat off his brow with the back of his hand and decided to get tough.

Mendoza was short with a wiry build. He had a slightly dazed look like someone who'd just dodged a bullet and still expected to be shot. Justin tried to read Mendoza and wondered what his silence meant. He'd checked with management. Mendoza had his green card so the busboy couldn't be worried about being deported.

"Several people told me you worked with Pequita Romero."

Tony's dark eyes darted from side to side as he shook his head.

"We raided a shack out by Shady Hook Road. An abandoned meth lab." He grabbed Tony's hand. "Your fingerprints are going to be all over that place, aren't they?"

Tony sucked in a harsh breath. Justin could see he'd intimidated Mendoza but the man still wasn't talking.

"Unless I get the truth, I'm taking you to the station to fingerprint you. Know how many years you'll get for making meth?" Justin was betting Tony didn't know that it was almost impossible to prosecute anyone for making meth unless you caught them in the act.

"In prison, Tony, you'll meet up with the boys from the Aryan Nation."

The color drained from Tony's tan face. If Tony had been facing prison in Texas or California, he'd have the Mexican gangs to protect him. But there weren't enough Hispanics in the Mississippi system to help him. At the rate things were going, that would change, but for now, Tony was terrified of being in jail with the skinheads.

"This is the last time I'm going to ask you. Did you know Pequita Romero?"

He hesitated, then out came a tight, "Yes."

"Did you work with her out by the river?"

"Yes."

When you got right down to it, this guy was just dying to help. Justin tried another tack. "I'm not going to do anything about the meth lab. It's clear it's no longer in use. What I'm interested in is what happened to Pequita. When did you last see her?"

Tony strangled out the answer. "A-a-ah…two month."

"She disappeared and they shut down the lab, right?"

"*Si, si.*"

Justin thought he detected a look of sadness in Tony's eyes. The illegals endured a hard life, far from home and family. He wondered if the guy had been involved with Pequita. Probably. Her death must have hurt him, but Justin knew Tony would be afraid to tell him any more.

DAVID NOYES LOOKED THROUGH the glass partition surrounding his office and saw Justin Radner walking into the building. He hoped Justin didn't have important information to give them. Connie would have a fit. It was nearly five o'clock, and the presses were churning out tomorrow's edition.

David waved for Justin to come into the office. Unlike the other times when David had seen Justin in khakis and polo shirts, today he was wearing dusty jeans and a blue chambray shirt with smudges of dirt or grease on it. At his heels was a skinny cinnamon-colored dog with a shaved coat.

"Where's Kat?" Justin asked. "I could use her help."

"She went to interview Mayor Peebles and Filpo Johnson to see what they think about the poisoning." David didn't add that they intended to put a positive spin on Justin's decision to send the body out-of-state. "She should be here in a minute. Have a seat."

Justin sank into the chair opposite David's desk, and the dog curled up at his feet. David wondered if he should get a dog. Twin Oaks was pretty laid-back. He could bring a pet to work like Justin. At night, David wouldn't be the only one kicking around an old house. He didn't even have a plant. He thought about the absolute, total silence in the home he'd bought. It was broken only by the creaking of the stairs when he walked up them. The omnipresent ache of loneliness had edged closer to the surface now that he was living in Twin Oaks.

"Let's talk off the record," Justin said, taking him by surprise.

"Okay. What's up?"

"All the documents on Kat's arrest are missing from our files."

"Interesting. What do you suppose happened to them?"

"Damned if I know." Justin shook his head. "Since bank robbery is a federal crime, copies of the investigation records were sent to Jackson."

"You called the capital."

"Yeah. The file is sealed."

"Sealed?" The only times David had encountered sealed files the cases had involved witness protection or an ongoing investigation.

"I gather there's some aspect of the case still under investigation," Justin told him. "Do you have copies of the stories the *Trib* ran about the robbery?"

David chuckled. "Great minds think alike." He slid open the bottom drawer in his desk and pulled out a sheaf of papers. "I took these from the morgue—that's our file of previous papers—yesterday. We run two copies of each edition on acid-free paper so it doesn't yellow over time."

"Why did you pull them?"

"Kat told me she was innocent."

Justin's expression was openly skeptical. "You believed her?"

"The way she said it, the look on her face. My gut said she was telling the truth."

Justin nodded slowly. It was hard to judge what he was thinking, but David had already picked up on the sheriff's interest in Kat. Who could blame him? Hell, if he were thirty years younger…well, he wasn't.

"She's a con. You know what that means. Most of them are sent back to prison."

"But not all of them. Some make it. Why don't you take these and read them?" David asked, handing him the issues that covered Kat's case. "I have another set."

"Good idea."

"Let me put them in a folder." David opened a drawer and pulled out an accordion folder.

"What did you think when you read the articles?"

"A rush to judgment," David replied as he slipped the papers into the file and handed it to Justin. "It would have been helpful to read the reporter's notes, but the man's long gone. I've tried e-mailing him. He's no longer on AOL."

"Why do you want to read his notes?"

"Often reporters write down rumors or things they can't verify. That information doesn't make it into print."

"I get the idea."

"What about the deputies? Did any of them help with the investigation?"

"I've asked, but they said Sheriff Parker handled everything himself."

David frowned. "That in and of itself is suspicious. I knew the sheriff. He was a fat, lazy blowhard. I can't see him doing all the work."

Justin nodding, thinking he would need to investigate this. Maybe Nora knew something. She was sharp and had been around for a long time. He glanced over his shoulder to be sure no one else was nearby. He pulled the tape of his conversation with Judge Kincaid out of his pocket.

"Do you have a safe?" he asked David.

"There's a safe over in that closet."

"Would you store this tape for me? If anything happens to me, play it."

David took the tape and walked over to the closet. Inside was a big old-fashioned safe. "Are you expecting trouble?"

"It's a possibility. When I was on the force in New Orleans, I killed a man during a drug raid. Lucas Albright's in jail, but he swore he would get me."

"Is this tape about that case?"

Justin gave David credit. The guy was sharp. "No, Judge Kincaid and Buck Mason hate me. That's what's on the tape."

David nodded. "Kat told me the story. It seems ridiculous that they blame you for Verity Mason's death."

"She killed herself months after we broke up, but Buck contends it was because she was still in love with me."

"She sounds a little…unbalanced."

"I suppose she was. I was too young to notice. I just thought she was too clingy, too needy. Buck spoiled her. He gave her everything she wanted. She had trouble accepting our relationship was over."

JUSTIN HAD FINISHED READING most of the articles on Kat's arrest when she returned to the *Trib*. He quickly stashed the papers in the folder. He was sitting in David's office as she sailed in. A vaguely sensuous current passed between them.

Her sassy hairstyle had gone limp, a victim of humidity. Nevertheless she was still incredibly appealing. He held back, steeling himself against his almost primal reaction to her.

"Your information paid off," he told her, and David motioned for her to take the chair beside Justin. "Tony Mendoza did work with Pequita Romero."

Her lips edged into a rare—genuine—smile. "At a meth lab?"

"It was more like a meth shack. A lean-to with a propane stove. They'd abandoned it, but the shack was still rank with ether fumes. The smell gets into the wood and the heat and humidity bring it out."

"Did Tony say who was running the operation?" she asked.

"He claims he never met the ringleader. An acquaintance in Natchez told him about the job. The supplies were left for them. Their pay was there every Friday when they came to work."

"Do you buy that?" Kat asked, and Justin noted David's approving smile.

"I'm not sure," he conceded. "It's possible. When I was in New Orleans, we encountered a lot of double-blind operators."

Kat's look was puzzled. "What's double-blind?"

"A dealer gets his drugs from someone else. That person picks them up from a drop-off point. Neither of them know the name of the actual dealer."

"That makes dealers difficult to catch," Kat said.

"From the size of the drum barrel vats they left behind, they were producing humongous amounts of meth."

"Wouldn't it take a lot of cold medicine to produce that much meth?" David asked.

"You bet. These days pharmacies limit the number of packages one person can buy. This much meth took a boatload of cold tablets—"

"Boatload," Kat interrupted. "Doesn't the *Lucky Seven* paddle-wheel down to New Orleans and back? Could they be bringing cold tablets by the boxful disguised as food or something for the casino?"

"Good thinking," he said, and found that he meant it. Kat had a power and depth to her that went beyond merely being attractive. She was more intelligent than most women he'd met. *Never mind. Don't trust her until she proves herself.*

David might believe her sob story, but Justin had his doubts. His experience with Verity had taught him a bitter, painful lesson.

"I did a series on the riverboat," David told them. "They're major polluters, but nobody wants to do anything about it. And there's something fishy going on out there."

Kat looked at David. "Did you try to find a source at the casino?"

"Yes, but no one was willing to talk to me. My reports came from public records on testing done by the Army Corps of Engineers on pollution in the Mississippi." David hitched up his shoulders in an exaggerated shrug. "I have a source out there now. I've asked for detailed information about who comes and goes and when. Over the years, I've found that's the best place to start."

Justin nodded his agreement. "That's how I was trained to investigate a crime. Know who the players are. And I don't think we're looking at a couple of scared illegals."

CHAPTER ELEVEN

"ANY OTHER IDEAS?" Tori asked Clay.

Clay took a swig of Johnnie Walker Blue Label. He savored the premium scotch for a moment before swallowing. "Not really. I thought offering your sister money would work."

They were sitting in the dining room of the Twin Oaks Country Club. They ate there several times a week. There were better restaurants in Jackson, and they often went there, but Clay preferred his club to anyplace in town. When she married Clay, she intended to be like May Ellen and have a cook. Then they would eat at home—just the two of them.

"She could take the money and disappear—if she wanted to." Tori swirled the chardonnay in her wineglass but didn't take a sip.

This woman who'd emerged from prison wasn't the sister she'd been expecting. Several people had told her Kat had lost weight and was pretty. What an understatement! No one mentioned how assertive and downright hostile Kat had become. Tori had explained to her mother that there would be no manipulating Kat. Her mother had sat grim-faced and with unfocused eyes staring at some soap opera on the television. She'd replied "okay" in a weak, emotionless voice. Tori had never heard her mother sound so miserable. The end might be nearer than Tori thought.

"What are we going to do?"

Clay shrugged, his broad shoulders lifting the blue blazer he was wearing. "We'll think of something. We always have."

"True," Tori replied, cheered by Clay's attitude. Lately, he'd been cold, distant. If she could no longer count on her mother, at least Clay was at her side.

"Don't look now, but here comes Buck Mason."

Tori groaned quietly. Buck Mason resented Tori. He'd planned for his daughter Verity to marry Clay before she'd unexpectedly killed herself.

"Hey, Clay. How are you doing?" Buck asked.

"Same old, same old."

Buck, the epitome of the Southern gentleman, nodded politely at Tori with the same cool blue eyes that had given Verity a reputation as an ice princess. Tori knew Buck would make no attempt to draw her into the conversation. He never did.

Buck was over six feet and still had the linebacker's build that had propelled him into Ole Miss's Hall of Fame. He kept himself fit by working out at the gym Tori used. A Friar Tuck fringe of ash-colored hair rimmed his head. The few wispy curls that survived were standing straight up tonight. His eyes were even more sunken into the fleshy folds of his face than usual.

Buck's wife had died shortly after Verity was born. He'd never remarried. A pharmacist, he'd devoted himself to raising Verity and running Mason's Drugs and Gifts. His daughter's death had crushed him.

"I need some advice." Buck's voice had a raspy edge to it.

Clay had no choice but to invite the older man to sit down. As Buck pulled out the chair, Clay rolled his eyes at Tori.

"What's the problem?" Clay asked.

Tori prepared herself to hear some legal issue. People were unbelievably cheap. Instead of making an appointment to see Clay at his law office, they waylaid him at dinner or at parties.

"Justin Radner's back in town. Peebles made him the sheriff."

The venom in Buck's voice could have backed down a pit bull. It reminded her of unstable guys who suddenly went postal. Tori had heard Buck rant about Justin ruining Verity's life numerous times but tonight he sounded lunatic furious.

"Peebles should have called an election," Clay said.

"How am I going to get rid of him?" Buck's voice ticked up a notch.

Clay considered the question a moment. "Find a candidate to run against him next year. I'll help you do a smear campaign on Radner. Sending evidence out-of-state is a start."

"I'm not having him in my town a whole year. I want him gone now!"

Buck had raised his voice so much that several diners turned to stare at him. Southern gentlemen did not yell especially in country clubs.

"Buck, get a grip," Clay said, his voice pitched low.

The older man racked his fingers through the wispy tuft of hair on top of his head. "You don't know what it's like to have your little girl taken away because of a white-trash scumbag like Radner."

To Tori's way of thinking, this was convoluted logic. Justin had broken up with Verity in the middle of the summer after their senior year. He'd gone off to Duke while Verity had attended Ole Miss. Verity didn't die until a few days before Thanksgiving. At the time she'd been dating Clay.

Tori shuddered inwardly. She'd been living in Oxford back then. Tori had nearly lost Clay. It had been a close call, but in the end, they were together again.

"I know how you feel," Clay told Buck. "Radner's a worthless piece of—"

Tori almost laughed. Had they been alone, Clay would have said "shit." But Buck was from the old school, and like the judge, he didn't condone cursing around ladies.

"Your father won't do anything." Buck spit out the words—

an accusation more than a statement of fact. "He says to let Radner alone. Wait for the election. I thought he was a better friend than that."

Wow! How had Justin Radner managed to come between two men who had been best friends for over half a century? Tori had been certain the judge would be dying to get rid of Justin. Turner Kincaid must have political reasons for staying out of this, she decided.

"I thought you might know someone out at the *Lucky Seven* who could help me," Buck said.

The consortium backing the riverboat casino was rumored to be linked to a New Orleans crime family. Tori knew Clay went out there to play poker, but he'd never mentioned that any of the men were actually mobsters.

"I can sniff around," Clay replied. "I'll tell them to contact you directly."

"I appreciate it." Buck slowly pushed up from the table.

After Buck had left the dining room, Tori asked, "Can you help him?"

Clay shrugged. "I can put out the word at the casino. That's all I'm going to do. Radner's a world-class asshole, but I have to think about my father's political career. I can't be directly involved in this."

Once again politics had invaded her life. Last week, Clay wouldn't have used his father's political ambitions as a reason for not helping Buck. The realm of politics was a large, ugly world full of people beyond her control.

An idea occurred to Tori. "Can you ask around at the riverboat and see if someone will talk to Kat? Scare her a little. Then she'll leave."

"I can ask," he shrugged, "but I'm not sure I'll find anyone."

"Maybe I'll come up with something. I talked to Justin about getting her furlough revoked. He wasn't very helpful."

"Stay away from Radner," Clay warned.

"THEY ALL SHOULD BE HOME by now," Justin told Kat.

They were on the outer fringe of the "north side" in Justin's pickup. Tony Mendoza told Justin that Pequita had lived in this one bedroom shanty with five other women. Since none of them spoke English, Kat had agreed to interview them to confirm what Tony had told Justin.

Kat nodded, gave Redd's nose a pat, and hopped out of Justin's pickup. She walked up to the wooden shack that hadn't seen a paintbrush in years. The front door was open and the screen door had several holes in it. The radio inside was tuned to a Spanish language station. The delicious aroma of *carne asada* made Kat's stomach rumble. It was after eight, and she hadn't had a thing since eating a yogurt at noon.

She'd gone about her business, doing the interviews David had requested, but her mind had been on Justin. The most ridiculous thoughts kept replaying in her head. What would it be like if Justin loved her? What would it be like to be held in his powerful arms every night?

She might not have been able to get that kiss out of her head, but Justin had clearly forgotten it. He'd been all business. She wouldn't be with him now except that she spoke some Spanish.

She knocked on the screen door. The chatter stopped. Someone called out, *"Si?"* from the kitchen.

"Es una amiga de Pequita." It's a friend of Pequita's. A fib but Kat didn't know what else to say. Her experience with Maria had told how wary of strangers the immigrants were.

IT TOOK KAT NEARLY HALF AN HOUR to pry the facts out of the women. She returned to the pickup with a plastic bag full of the dead woman's things. She handed the bag to Justin, saying, "Tony told you the truth. Pequita lived here. These are her things."

"Any chance there's a hairbrush in there?" Even in the darkness of the pickup, his gaze was blue and piercing.

"Yes." Redd nosed her from the backseat, and she gave him a quick pat. "You're going to compare the hair against the hair on the body."

"You bet." He turned on the headlights, started the engine, then pulled away from the house. "It's the only way we can positively ID her. She didn't have any dental work."

"I doubt her family could afford it. That's why she came here."

"True. What else did her roommates tell you?"

"Maria told me Pequita was very ambitious, and her roommates confirmed it. Pequita bragged about getting a lot of money. She went out late one night to collect this windfall and didn't return."

"They never reported her missing."

"No. They knew something must have happened to her, but they were too concerned about being deported to go to the authorities."

Kat hadn't been paying much attention to where Justin was driving. Now she realized he wasn't heading back to the *Trib*. "Where are you going?"

He turned to her and a slow smile curved his lips. "I'm taking you to dinner."

Kat was thankful it was dark inside the truck. She could feel the heat creeping up into her cheeks. She knew she should say no but she couldn't make the words come out. Truth to tell, she wanted to be with him—even if she knew better.

"ARE YOU AWARE that some aspect of your case must be still under investigation?" Justin asked.

"Really?" she replied in what she hoped was a surprised tone.

They'd eaten at the Ragin' Cajun Café, and Justin had driven her back to the *Trib* to pick up her car. He'd insisted on following her home and walking her to the door. The steps groaned as they went up, guided only by the light of the street lamp on the corner. Redd followed, his claws clicking on the wooden slats.

"They're investigating something," he told her with a brittle smile. "I thought you might know what it is."

"I don't know." This much was true. She was waiting to be contacted. No one had deigned to tell her what was really going on. She constantly checked her cell phone, but no one had called her.

He studied her a moment with a gaze that was way too penetrating. She thought he saw right through her and knew she was hiding something. She brazened it out, looking right at him and silently daring him to challenge her.

She took out her key and fumbled with the lock. It was difficult to see, and she wished she'd left the porch light on. But it would have burned all day and run up her electrical bill.

"You need a light that comes on automatically when something gets near it."

Her key finally slipped into the lock. "I need lots of things. When I get paid, I'm going to buy some of them."

She opened the door, reached in, and flicked on the porch light, then hit the switch to turn on the small lamp across the room. "Thanks for dinner."

He slid by her and went into the stuffy apartment. Redd trotted after him. "It's too easy to get in here. You need a dead bolt on the door." He inspected the two windows facing the alley. He opened one and a whoosh of air that was only slightly cooler than her apartment gusted into the room. "Do you keep these open at night?"

"When it's hot, I do."

He shook his head. "All anyone has to do to get in is come across the roof next door and walk along the ledge under your window."

"No one's going to bother me," she replied.

"What about your sister? I wouldn't be so trusting, if I were you."

"I'm not." She didn't like to think Tori would hurt her, but she was desperate to marry Clay. Anything was possible.

He closed his eyes for a second and took a deep breath as if he were thinking hard about something. He reached for her and pulled her flush against his powerful torso. His lips came down, and he kissed her slowly, taking his time. Her own eager response to the touch of his lips made her body warm and tingly.

Kat's thoughts spun. All last night and today when she least expected it, the memory of his kisses haunted her. She recalled the ecstasy of his lips on hers. Why had he stopped kissing her? She'd wondered if it had been her lack of experience.

She pulled away and gazed up into his eyes. "I'm not good at this. I haven't had much practice."

His look was so galvanizing it sent a chill through her. "I'm a great teacher." He swung her into the circle of his arms. "Just relax."

"We shouldn't be…involved," she protested but the words lacked conviction. "You're the law and I'm an ex-con."

"I'm reforming you," he told her, his voice low and husky. "You're going to take a lot of work."

He kissed the hollow of her neck, tasting her with his lips and tongue. She couldn't help sighing. She touched him now, her hands skimming across his powerful shoulders and inhaling the woodsy aroma of his aftershave. His tongue edged into her mouth, but she could feel the tautness in his body. He was trying to control himself, holding back for some reason.

She quivered at the sweet tenderness of his kiss, and allowed her tongue to greet his. Suddenly, a wave of moist heat unfurled between her thighs. She'd French kissed before, but nothing prepared her for Justin's technique. She returned his kiss without thinking of the future.

Her mind was on the past. She'd been the fat ugly duckling for so long that she couldn't conceive of anyone like Justin Radner giving her a second glance. She knew prison had changed her, but somehow the inner voice of the ugly duckling kept whispering to her.

You're repulsive.

Worthless.

Those days were over, she reminded herself. Now she realized how much of her personality she'd repressed over the years. *You've been given a second chance at life. Go for it!* She was a different person now.

She hugged him hard and pushed her body against his. Justin's hands slid down her back and cupped her bottom. He pressed her flush against him with a rock-hard erection. Oh, my God! She'd turned on Justin Radner! Could she handle this? You bet. She was a new woman.

Maybe Justin was one of those men who was duty bound to lay as many woman as possible in this lifetime. Tori always said a man's brain was behind his fly. Did it matter to her what Justin's reasons were? No. This undercover operation could get her killed or she could be sent back to prison. She was going to live in the moment.

She kept envisioning the same slow penetration of her body as the French kiss. He was huge, and sex might hurt, but she didn't care. Too much of her life had been wasted already.

She slipped her hands under his shirt and stroked his back. The corded muscles flexed beneath her fingertips. A low groaning sound came from his throat. She couldn't help being proud of herself. She was getting to him. Pretty amazing.

The creaking of the stairs and Redd's growl registered in her sex-starved brain, and she broke the kiss.

"Are you expecting anyone?" Justin asked.

"No."

"'Ellooo."

"It's Maria. I recognize her voice." Kat went to the door. "Is everything okay?"

Maria was now at the top of the steps, carrying a glass dish. "I brung you dis. Enchiladas."

"Oh, thank you." Kat didn't need the calories, but she couldn't bear to hurt the young woman's feelings. She made so little money washing hair that Kat didn't want her spending money making food for her.

Maria spotted Justin, and her eyes widened with fright. "Maria, come in. Justin is leaving."

"I am?"

"I'll see you tomorrow."

Justin walked stiffly out the door, Redd at his heels. Kat couldn't decide if she was sad or relieved. Things might be happening a little too fast with Justin anyway. In her rush to rejoin the living, she could be making a mistake she would regret. He was a cop who could ruin her if he chose. She needed someone to talk to—a friend. She would try to catch Lola Rae tomorrow morning.

"Maria, let's put the enchiladas in the refrigerator."

The woman's dark eyes gazed at Kat with fright. Kat motioned toward the fridge that dated back to the fifties. "Refrigerator," she repeated, knowing the woman wanted to learn English.

Kat opened the door and moved aside the nonfat yogurt to make room for enough enchiladas to feed her for a week. "Thank you."

Maria regarded her with solemn eyes. She couldn't be more than thirty, but Maria had a guarded way about her that indicated she'd seen a lot of the world and it had not been kind to her.

She pointed to the door. "He no tell Tony a me?"

"Tony doesn't know anything about you. The sheriff doesn't

care if you're here illegally." She repeated the message in her best Spanish to make sure Maria knew she was safe.

But, truth to tell, Kat didn't know if Maria was safe. Or if she was.

CHAPTER TWELVE

DAVID NOYES DID NOT have to look for a dog. One found him early the next morning as he walked out of the Shop 'N Go, a bag of groceries under his arm. He spotted two young children with a box of squirming puppies just outside the market.

"Wanna puppy, mister?" asked the little girl.

"They're mostly Blue Heeler," added the boy.

David had no idea what a Blue Heeler looked like, but these pups appeared to be the local version of Heinz 57—coon dogs and inbred hounds. Still, they were cute, and he was in the mood for a dog. Loneliness tugged at him more and more these days.

"How much?"

The little girl giggled, but her brother kept a straight face, saying, "Free to a good home, mister."

David put down his bag of groceries and inspected the litter. There were eight of them, but a tan one with a white spot on his rump caught David's eye. He picked it up and saw it was a male. The little guy licked his chin as he gazed at David with eyes like melted chocolate. Pick me, the pup silently implored him.

"He's the smartest one in the litter," the girl assured David. "He'll make a mighty fine hunting dog, he will."

David wasn't buying the intelligence bit. Clearly, the two had been sent by their parents to get rid of the pups. By the looks of it, they hadn't had any takers.

David cradled the pup in his arms and asked, "How big is he going to get?"

The brother and sister exchanged a glance. David bet the family had the mother, but they had no idea what dog fathered the litter.

"'Bout this big." The little boy raised his hand to his waist.

Not too large, David thought. The pup would grow up to be the size of a cocker spaniel. A good size, David decided. The dog would fit nicely in the seat of his T-Bird. He wouldn't be too big to have around the office.

"I'll take him, but you'll need to hold him for me while I go back in the store and get some puppy chow." He handed the pup back to the kids. "What kind of food does he eat?"

The two exchanged a troubled glance. Again, the brother answered. "We jist weaned him on cornmeal mush."

David nodded, thinking the bitch probably ate mush, too. His experience in Twin Falls had shown him that most folks let their dogs run and didn't give them the special treatment city dogs received. But David needed his dog to be clean and well behaved if he intended to have him at his side most of the time.

He put out his hand. "I'll take him now." He didn't add that he was going straight to the vet to have the pup checked and find out what the little guy should be eating.

BY THE TIME David got to the office it was nearly ten. He'd left the pup—hastily named Max at check-in—to be wormed.

Coming through the *Trib*'s door, he saw Kat typing away furiously at her desk. She looked up with a suggestion of a smile on her lips. She shot out of her seat and headed toward him.

"Guess what?" she said, her voice low. "We're close to identifying the dead woman."

We? Justin and Kat. Quite a team. "Good work. Come into my office and tell me all about it."

He sat at his desk and listened to the story of Justin tracking down Tony Mendoza, and Kat's visit to Pequita's roommates.

"At first, Justin wanted us to sit on the article until he receives the DNA results, but I convinced him to let us publish it, making clear it needs to be verified. Someone may come forward with helpful information."

David couldn't hold back a proud grin. "You're going to be a first-rate reporter."

Kat returned his smile. "You haven't seen my article yet. I'm almost finished with it. I need you to read it and give me your input."

She bounced out of his office. Kat needed him. He liked that. Max needed him, too. He wanted to be more…connected. Life had to be about something besides work. He wanted the warm pleasure of being close to someone. He hadn't known he missed the feeling until the car accident that had so severely injured his back. Months of rehab followed. He'd suffered through it all alone.

What about Kat? She'd been deserted by her family and faced prison all by herself. He couldn't fathom what her time there must have been like. If she were truly innocent as she claimed, this was a major travesty. He was going to help her reclaim her life.

Helping an ex-con and adopting a puppy—never mind that the dog had peed on the leather seat of his meticulously restored T-Bird—were giving him an immense sense of satisfaction. He thought about his past for a moment. He'd been a brilliant reporter—two Pulitzers proved it—but when had he ever made a difference in a person's life?

Mentoring Kat had been a wise choice. She was catching on more quickly than he could possibly have imagined.

He forced himself to pull up the "dummy" on his computer and check the copy editor's layout for tomorrow's edition. As usual, Connie had done a terrific job. The news holes were medium sized, so the article didn't have to be too long. David knew the statistics. People rarely finished long pieces. Medium spaces were perfect for local events like car washes to raise money for the football team. They didn't require much writing, and left room for a photograph.

Trouble was, the *Trib* couldn't afford to send a photographer to every podunk event. They were forced to accept photos from participants. The quality was often poor—the *Globe* would have been shocked—but David had discovered people loved seeing their pictures in print even if the photos weren't great. He always gave the locals a photo credit.

He checked the UPI and AP readout to see if there were any national stories he could rewrite to make them meaningful in ten inches or—hopefully—less. He anticipated that Kat's article on the identity of the murdered woman would run above the fold.

Half an hour later, Kat rushed in with a printout of her story. He quickly read it through. It was good but… "I have some suggestions."

Kat eagerly looked at him. He appreciated her willingness to accept criticism. She was determined to become a reporter. Already she seemed to have conquered what some reporters never mastered—the ability to get people to talk. Now, she needed to learn how to write articles with punch.

"I like what you've written. It's the angle that might need to be tweaked. One thing we learn to deal with is the 'who cares' factor. Some articles rivet a community. Any kind of child endangerment, from kids left in autos in the heat of the summer to abductions and molestation, is red-hot. Why? Readers fear it will happen to their children. They'll read every word in such an article."

"I suppose there's also a perverse sense of relief when you read about what you escaped."

Was she ever perceptive, he thought. "Exactly. If there's a fear that it could happen to you or yours, paper sales skyrocket."

Kat looked at him intently for a moment. "The brutal murder of an illegal alien won't interest them."

"Not much, I'm afraid. They'll breathe a sigh of relief that it wasn't a local and won't even bother to read the follow-up article when the DNA comes back."

"What happens to illegals isn't a threat to them."

He noted a dejected note in her voice. "I saw it too often when I was a reporter in Boston. Deaths in Roxbury were of little interest in the wealthy suburbs. It just reaffirmed why they had fled the inner city. In the ghetto, violence was a way of life."

Kat nodded, her expression grim. Prison hadn't hardened her as much as he'd expected.

"Do you have any suggestions?" she asked.

He thought a moment. "Spin it. Use the meth angle. Do you know how common consumption of the drug is?"

"Justin says it's the number one drug in rural America."

David harrumphed. "In America, period. Housewives take it to get through the day, to diet, to cope with the kids. It gives you a cheap high that lasts for days. Its use is rampant in this town."

"I get it. Show how meth is invading Twin Oaks and ruining our way of life. Pequita got caught up in a major drug operation."

"You might hint at a possible mob connection. We don't want to slip into yellow journalism, but refer to 'unsubstantiated sources' at that point."

"Justin says there were suspiciously few arrests for possession."

David nodded slowly. "I think Sheriff Parker let them off if their parents were wealthy or part of his good-ol'-boy group. A check of the records will probably show most arrests were in the north side."

"I'll look into it." She grabbed her draft off the desk and rushed out of his office.

He returned to the UPI and AP pickups he was rewriting.

Most of it was dumbing down stories that had little to do with life in Twin Falls. He put them in anyway. A few people would read them.

Travis called with the filler articles about the PTA meeting, the proposed addition to the library that was rarely used, and, of course, the weekend's sporting events. David hated rewrites. All reporters disliked writing articles phoned in from the field, but it had to be done.

Sports was the most read section of the paper, according to a survey the last editor had conducted. David didn't doubt it. Sports *ruled* in the South. Right now, Twin Oaks was holding a noodling tournament. Catching catfish with your bare hands was so big in the area that David had paid a local wedding photographer to go down to the river. He was looking forward to writing the copy on the noodling. Last year, his article had been picked up by UPI. It was a rare day that a small-town paper could make any money from a syndicated article, but he was sure it would get picked up again. Noodling was off-beat enough to attract attention.

He quickly rewrote the articles that had been phoned in, then sent them to the copy editor. Connie would come up with the heads and place the stories in the news holes. No doubt, she would come in to see if he approved of her work. Connie always found some excuse to talk to him. He suspected she was angling to have her title changed to managing editor.

By now, David was basically finished for the day. He could have run the numbers on the paper's finances, but he was too restless to bother. Instead, he called the vet to see how Max was doing. The pup would be released tomorrow morning. David studied the list of things he would need and decided to make a stop at Wal-Mart after work.

A soft knock on his doorjamb made him look up from his list. Kat stood there, papers in hand, an uncertain expression on her face. He motioned for her to come in.

"What's wrong?" he asked, taking the papers from her.

"I hope this article is better," she replied.

He quickly read what she'd rewritten, then gave her an encouraging smile. "Like I said, you're going to make a first-rate reporter."

AFTER THE MORNING BRIEFING at the station—expect more drunk and disorderly arrests at the noodling championship—Justin studied the articles David had given him about Kat's trial. He agreed with David. It sounded like a railroad job.

Are you sure? he asked himself. *Or is that what you want to think because you're hot for her?* He still couldn't believe she'd told him to leave after acting like a sex kitten.

He'd had to shift to relieve his erection and walked out of her place with a stick of dynamite in his pants. He was going to have blue balls for a week. The hell of it was he didn't know what to think about his physical reaction to Kat. Since his first sexual encounter at fourteen, he'd always controlled the situation.

But this was different. Why? He couldn't decide—and he couldn't stop thinking about her. Last night he'd dreamed he was making love to Kat on the banks of the Big Muddy, a ridiculous notion. Mosquitoes would have eaten them alive, but he woke up with a killer hard-on.

He needed to go over to the bank and get a feel for the others involved in Kat's case. Working hard should take his mind off sex. He left Redd shut in his office and was heading out the door when he decided to ask Nora what she remembered about the case.

"You did a great job downstairs," he told her. He'd already complimented her in front of the deputies at the briefing, but it never hurt to encourage a good employee.

She beamed at him. "Thank you. I just wish I'd found the missing file."

Justin nodded. "Do you remember much about the case?"

"Yes, indeedy!" Her voice rose several notches, registering her indignation.

"I thought you would," he said in a conciliatory tone. "Were you on dispatch that day?"

"Yes. Cloris Howard called and wanted to speak to Sheriff Parker. I asked what it was about. You know, the sheriff didn't like to be disturbed after lunch." She paused and measured him for a moment as if deciding whether to tell him more. "The sheriff needed a nip of bourbon, if you know what I mean."

"I do." He'd heard rumors about the late sheriff's drinking.

"Well, after lunch, he'd take a little snooze. I usually radioed a deputy in the field with any problem. Yes, indeedy, if you woke Sheriff Parker, he was like a rabid dog. But Cloris demanded I put him on. He bellowed at me, but when I said Cloris Howard wanted to speak to him, he immediately took the call."

"Have any idea what was said?"

Again, Nora studied him and hesitated before saying, "I listened in." She shook a bony finger at him. "Now mind you, I don't usually do that, but I had a hunch. That woman's been carrying on with Judge Kincaid for years. I thought she was doing his dirty work for him."

Justin hadn't heard a thing about this. "Really? How did you know?"

"It's a well-kept secret because of the judge's political ambitions, but my sister used to be the judge's secretary until she died of cancer."

"You never told anyone?"

"Sheriff, I'm an old maid with no relatives. This job is my only way of supporting myself. The sheriff was a good buddy of the judge. One word from him and I'da been fired."

"I'll keep the info to myself," Justin assured her, "but the judge couldn't persuade me to fire anyone, least of all you."

She arched one brow skeptically. "There's talk in town that you'll be gone before long. Buck Mason is after you. Yes, indeedy, that man can hold a grudge like nobody I've ever known."

"I'll watch my back," he replied, then realized he'd been sidetracked by news of the affair. "What did Cloris say when the sheriff came on the phone?"

"I don't rightly recall her words exactly, but I do know she didn't say there had been a robbery. She said something like they had a situation or a problem. But her voice didn't sound stressed the way you'd expect in a robbery."

Justin considered the information for a moment, then asked, "Did the sheriff go to the bank?"

"Flew out the door like Satan himself was on his tail. It was strange, I'm telling ya. I've been here a mighty long time. I never knew the sheriff to work a case himself. The deputies did everything."

David had also said that he'd found the sheriff's actions weird. "Did you happen to see the evidence the sheriff must have collected?"

"He had the girl's fingerprint from inside the bank vault. She wasn't authorized to enter the vault. Cloris and Elmer missed the money, knew it had to be an inside job, and they looked around and saw cash sticking out of Kat's purse in the employee's lunchroom."

"Sounds like an illegal search."

"The prosecutor didn't think so. Apparently, the money was clearly visible and that made it okay."

"What do you think?"

Nora's eyes narrowed. "Except for the print in the vault, I thought Kat could have been framed. It seemed just a little too…convenient. The judge huffed all around town that our funds wouldn't be safe if criminals weren't prosecuted to the full extent of the law."

Pompous ass. The judge took every opportunity to grab the spotlight and further his political career.

"There were quite a few of us who thought if Kat's family had stood behind her and hired a competent attorney, she could have beat the charges."

"Who do you think did it?"

Nora lifted her scrawny shoulders in an exaggerated shrug. "Who knows? Maybe one of the other tellers. Cloris or Elmer, more likely."

CHAPTER THIRTEEN

JUSTIN STRODE into the Mercury National Bank and asked to speak to Cloris Howard. The stunned teller—barely out of high school—took one look at him and scurried to the back of the building where the executive offices were. Obviously, word had gotten around and they knew he was the law in Twin Oaks. Just goes to show you what being an authority figure could accomplish.

He gazed around the bank, thinking little had changed since Kat had worked here. The tellers' stations were up front behind old-fashioned grills installed back in Bonnie and Clyde's heyday. A desk for the loan officer separated the tellers from the executive area where Cloris Howard, the president, and Elmer Bitner, the vice president, had offices hidden from view. The vault was there as well, its sturdy brass wheel partially visible from the tellers' area.

Why had it been left open that day?

Kat would have had to walk right by the tellers and the loan officer to enter the vault. Surely someone would have noticed. But according to the articles in the *Trib*, no one had seen Kat going into the vault.

The only damning evidence had been the discovery of the money in her possession. And the fingerprint. She could have been framed, he decided. It would be hard to prove. None of the tellers working at the time were still at the bank. One was now a dealer at the *Lucky Seven* and the others had moved out of state. They could be traced but it would take time and resources Justin didn't have.

He'd have to rely on gut instinct and his service on the force in New Orleans to help him. If something hinky had gone on, he trusted himself to sniff out any inconsistency.

Seconds later Cloris Howard appeared, her ring-decked hand extended. Justin remembered what Nora had told him about Cloris's affair with the judge. Old history—or current news?

Cloris was a slim, elegant older woman with a flawless peaches-and-cream complexion. Her hair was probably gray but she had it colored a glossy, natural-looking blond. She was still striking, but when she'd been younger, Cloris must have been a knockout.

Why hadn't she ever married? She came from one of "the" families, and she'd inherited her father's banking business after making her way through a fancy boarding school, then Vanderbilt. He supposed Turner Kincaid had married May Ellen before Cloris had returned to town.

"Justin!" she said as if greeting a close friend. "You're back in town."

He smiled to himself. He'd been a hero during his days at Harrington High School. Sure 'nuf. People around here didn't forget a football star.

"What can I do for you?"

"Kaitlin Wells has returned on a work furlough for good behavior."

"So I heard." Cloris shook her head in disgust. "Don't let her near the bank."

Justin manufactured a smile. "Isn't up to me, ma'am."

"I'm afraid of her."

Justin found that hard to believe. "Why?"

Cloris hesitated. "Kat's sneaky. She worked here for years without anyone suspecting what she was doing."

Justin waited for her to elaborate. Cloris motioned for him

to follow her into the president's office. Once inside, the heavy oak door shut on an office eerily like Turner Kincaid's, she continued, "We'd been missing small amounts of money—fifty to one hundred dollars—for some time."

"Couldn't you isolate it by the tellers' end-of-day reports?"

Cloris shrugged dismissively. "Yes, but this is a small bank in a very small town. At the end of the day, the tellers are in a rush to close out their drawers and leave. They balance, then stack their hundred-dollar bills in one pile, their fifties, their twenties and so on in the appropriate places. Later, we would discover we were short."

"You didn't try checking each teller?"

"Of course we did." Her tone was filled with righteous indignation. "There's no one but Elmer and me." She tried for a smile but failed. "When there was a shortage, we checked out the tellers for weeks. Nothing. We decided honest mistakes were happening. We can't pay a lot so our tellers aren't always the sharpest."

"Did you suspect Kat Wells?"

Cloris shook her head. "No. Kat was too honest—or so we thought. Unfortunately, she had everyone fooled."

Justin imagined the plump young woman from the *Trib* photograph. Nothing like the Kat Wells he knew.

"Why so many questions, Sheriff?" Cloris's eyes were shrewd. He sensed her suspicion of him, and he had the distinct impression she didn't like being questioned.

"I'm responsible for keeping track of the Wells woman," he said, telling a half truth. "I wasn't in town when the crime happened. I'm just filling in the blanks."

"You'll need to speak to Elmer Bitner," she replied evenly, as if there could be no question about what to do next. "He saw the money in Kat's purse the day of the robbery."

Justin thanked her, thinking she'd been a little too cool, a little too smooth. Something about her nicked at his brain. Or okay, could be that Nora had alerted him to something he'd never have suspected otherwise.

Cloris was very feminine in a Southern way, but there was a good reason such women were called steel magnolias. His mother had been one—all purpose and determination hidden behind a soft veneer. Even when he'd made enough money, she hadn't allowed him to support her. Despite Cloris's femininity, she probably had bigger balls than most men.

"We're going to see Elmer." In less than a minute, Cloris had whisked him down the hall into Elmer's smaller oak-paneled office. She introduced Justin, then left. Why such a rush to get rid of him?

Bitner was shorter and pudgier than he remembered, but he still had a full head of brown hair just beginning to go gray at the temples. Justin recalled his mother trying to purchase a run-down shack on the outskirts of the north side. Her income as a laundress/seamstress hadn't merited a second glance from the bankers. Never mind that his mother paid cash and didn't have a credit card to run up her debt. Bitner had been a loan officer back then, and he'd wanted no part of Justin's mother.

Elmer had just been doing his job. He was one of those men who always did his job. He didn't overreach and he didn't fall short. He merely did what was expected of him. Near as Justin could tell, Bitner had been born again and spent his free time at church.

Bitner's doughy handshake was slightly clammy. "Kat Wells is back." The words reflected the man's disappointment with the penal system. "What next?"

Justin lowered his broad frame into one of the two spindly French chairs Bitner had in front of his desk. "It shouldn't be any problem. She's working at the *Trib.*"

Bitner snorted. "We're thinking about hiring extra security."

Justin struggled to hold back a laugh. Kat a threat? Not on your life. "Why?"

"She turned this bank upside down. We're finally back on track and we're staying on track."

"You know, I wasn't around when the money disappeared. Do you have any idea how Kat got into the vault without anyone seeing her?"

"It wouldn't have been difficult. The vault isn't usually open, but we'd opened it to secure a very large deposit from Whitney's Feed and Seed." Bitner rolled his shoulders as if he had a kink in his neck. "The break room is down the hall beyond the vault. People wouldn't have thought it strange that she was going in that direction."

"Who opened the vault for the large deposit?"

Bitner cocked one shaggy brow. "I did. As God as my witness, I should have closed it. But the gall-darned wheel was sticking. I knew we had another deposit coming in, so I left it ajar."

Justin wondered if Bitner was being honest, but without proof, he couldn't call him on anything. On his way out, he checked the bank's floor plan. It seemed impossible for Kat to have slipped into the vault without someone noticing, but Bitner could be right. If people went by the vault to the break room all the time, it might not attract attention.

"THERE'S A PHONE CALL for you. A man," Connie said with a frown as Kat was rewriting a PTA story Travis had phoned in. Her heart lurched in her chest. Maybe it was Justin, calling with the DNA results.

She didn't know what she was going to say to him after last night. This morning she'd discussed the situation with Lola Rae, who advised taking it slowly. Men were notorious hound dogs who liked to hook up, have sex, then split. They didn't commit easily, and Lola Rae should know. She had been trying to get Gary Don Willingham to the altar for two years.

Kat had nodded, thinking about the man. She hadn't liked

him particularly and thought Lola Rae was lucky Gary Don refused to marry her.

What she *needed* to do was get her life in order before she became involved with a man. First she wanted to visit her mother. No matter what Tori said—and no doubt Tori was right—Kat had to see her mother.

She picked up the telephone. "Hello. This is Kaitlin Wells."

"Kat, remember me?"

Elmer. She would have known that voice anywhere. As vice president of the bank, Elmer supervised the tellers. He never lost an opportunity to tell the girls their souls would be saved if they attended services at Trinity Baptist Church.

"Yes, Elmer, what can I do for you?"

"Shh! Don't say my name."

She didn't trust the creep after he'd claimed to have found the money in her purse. "Why not? What's going on?"

"I need to talk to you—in private."

"I can't imagine what we could have to discuss."

"It's about the money you took."

Oh, my God! This must be the call she'd been told to expect. She had always wondered if Elmer had planted the money and lied to cover up his own crime. Or perhaps he'd been protecting Cloris. She'd never been able to decide what had happened. The only thing she knew for certain was that she'd never entered the vault, so her fingerprint couldn't have been found there.

"When do you want to meet?" she asked, justifiably proud of her calm voice.

"Tonight at nine. There's a picnic bench near the *Lucky Seven*'s dock. Meet me there. And don't tell anyone. I can't be seen with you."

Kat agreed and hung up. She considered calling Justin, but what would she tell him? No one was supposed to know she was undercover. She glanced around the city room. Connie was bent over her computer. David was out taking Max for a walk.

She pulled out her cell phone and called Special Agent Wilson, who answered on the first ring. She quietly explained what was happening.

"Meet him, but be sure to record the conversation."

"Right." He'd given her a miniature recorder that looked like a woman's powder compact.

"And take your cell phone. Do you have the undercover agent's number on speed dial?"

"Yes, and I keep the battery charged."

"Good. I'll alert the agent that you're meeting Bitner at nine. If there's trouble, call immediately. The agent will be close enough to help you should it become necessary."

KAT MANAGED to get through the day and return to her small studio. She hadn't heard from Justin, but she didn't call him, assuming the DNA hadn't come in yet. It was miserably hot in her apartment. She was too nervous to eat. She checked the recorder twice and made certain the speed dial on her cell phone had the correct number.

What did Elmer want with her?

She had two hours before the meeting. Enough time to drop in on her mother. She decided that if Tori's car was there, she'd visit another time. She didn't want to confront both of them together.

THE MODEST ROW of town homes where her mother lived was a lot nicer than the small bungalow where Tori and Kat had grown up. Loretta Wells had purchased the condo before Kat's father was cold in the grave. She'd been so proud of it. Kat had always suspected her mother bought it with the college fund her father had left, but Kat had been too dependent, too unsure of herself to question Loretta.

A tidal wave of memories washed over her as she pulled into the drive. She'd lived in the small condo until she was arrested for theft. They would watch television in the evening, but they didn't talk much. Every other night, Tori would call, and her mother's stone tablet of a face would light up. Kat always experienced a humiliating, deflated feeling, as if she were less than nothing to her mother.

It was almost dark, and Kat saw the lights were on in the living room. The television was visible from the path up to the house. A quivery feeling settled into the pit of her stomach as she knocked on the screen door.

"Come in," a feeble, barely audible voice called.

Kat stepped into the room. It took a second for her eyes to adjust to the dim light. *Oh, Lordy.* The once robust woman had been reduced to bare bones. Her skin, wrinkled as a ball of tissue paper, alarmed Kat with its chalky pallor. Her mother's silky hair must have fallen out during chemotherapy and was growing back in coarse gray sprouts.

"You," she rasped. She crossed her arms over her stomach as if holding herself together and coughed, a rattling sound like pennies in a soup can.

Kat had planned to lash out, to punish Loretta at last, but she was too shaken by her mother's appearance. It had been years— miserable, lonely years—since she'd last seen this woman. Her mother. Despite her betrayal and all the revenge scenes Kat had imagined in prison, she couldn't go there. Not now.

"I'm out for good behavior." Kat ventured closer, thinking the condo smelled strange. Death, she realized. Her mother was literally decaying. "I wanted to talk to you."

"I'm…not much…for talking…these days."

The aching pain in Kat's chest made breathing difficult, talking nearly impossible. Finally, she managed to say, "We may not have another chance."

Her mother rolled sideways, then pushed herself up from the sofa with great effort. "I'll get…us some…lemonade."

Her mother had a thing for lemonade. She made it from

concentrate and didn't add enough water. It was always too sweet. "Let me do it."

Her mother waved her aside with a spindly arm. "Nah. I need…to get up…once in awhile. 'Sides, I've had…rats. You don't…want to see…the kitchen. Sit down…and I'll fetch…the lemonade."

Kat reluctantly sat on the sofa. Her mother walked with a cane, moving as if she were knee-deep in wet sand. Kat lowered the volume on the television and waited.

She heard her mother trundling around in the kitchen. Kat tried to think of what to say to a dying woman. Her mother might not have loved her, but she'd taken care of her and never abused her.

Not all abuse is physical, she reminded herself.

It took an unusually long time because her mother now moved so slowly, but she finally shuffled back in, her terry slippers scuffling across the wood floor. She handed Kat a tumbler of lemonade, then slowly and very carefully lowered herself onto the sofa. Kat took a sip and found it was even sweeter than she remembered. She didn't want to insult her mother by putting it down, so she drank a little more.

"So…talk."

She had so many questions, but she could see her mother was in pain. Beneath Kat's anger was a bone-deep sense of sympathy. She'd seen too much in prison, witnessed too many degrading incidents not to recognize suffering when she saw it. And this was her mother, not some hardened con.

"Why didn't you help me when I was arrested?"

Her mother looked at her from across the top of her glass. Her once vibrant green eyes had a milky caul to them now. "Why waste…good money?…You…disgraced us."

"I didn't take the money." Kat drank a little more lemonade and waited for her mother to answer.

"They found…the cash…in…your purse."

"I was framed," Kat replied, but she could see her mother didn't believe her. Trouble was, her mother would be dead by the time she cleared her name.

"Could you just explain to me why you didn't love me—not even a little?"

Her mother leaned back, head bowed, shoulders slumped. Her eyes had a detached look, as if her soul had already left her body. "It…doesn't…matter."

Kat supposed she was right. What did it matter now? Nothing could be said or done to change the past. The gulf between them yawned wider than ever. Kat finished her lemonade and watched her mother fall asleep, the silence grating on her nerves.

This reunion was nothing like what she'd imagined in prison. She'd thought talking to her mother, telling her how hateful she'd been, would make her feel better and help her put her life back together. She'd been wrong.

Cancer had a timetable of its own. Loretta was going to slip away without Kat ever knowing exactly why her mother didn't love her. It was difficult to overcome the feeling of being alone in the world. She battled an unexpected urge to cry.

It's too late for tears, she decided. The past was behind her, and there was nothing she could do to alter it. She had to get on with her life. Be strong enough to accept what's happened—don't allow yourself to slip into victim mentality. She was going to make the most of her future.

Kat slipped out the door, forcing her mind away from her mother and thinking she had just enough time to make it to the *Lucky Seven.* The riverboat would be out trolling the Mississippi, but she was sure she could find the picnic table by the dock. She stood in the driveway and double checked her cell phone.

Something in the bushes caught her attention. Flesh crept on the back of her neck as if a spider had wriggled across it.

Heavy, hot air filled the darkness, silencing even the crickets that usually chirped. She thought she heard a noise but the dark, sweltering air muffled sounds.

Walking very, very slowly, she waited for the noise to repeat. Nothing. Probably a cat, she decided. She reached into the bottom of her purse and found the roll of quarters. Special Agent Wilson wouldn't allow her to have a gun—not that she knew how to use one—but he'd told her how to turn her hand into a deadly weapon.

"Wrap your fist around a roll of quarters. Land a solid punch and it's better than brass knuckles."

She was certain such a move would result in every finger being broken, but if need be, she would chance it. The impending meeting was making her jumpy. She climbed into the car. Despite the oppressive heat, she shut the windows, then locked the doors. She put the roll of quarters on the seat beside her purse.

She slowly drove through the unincorporated area toward the *Lucky Seven*, concentrating on the pavement ahead. She'd rarely traveled the snaky road, then only in daylight. Unable to stand the suffocating heat, she lowered her window. A breeze off the Big Muddy, rank with the scent of decaying moss, stirred the trees along the road, but with no moon, the landscape was a pitch-dark expanse. The only illumination was the swath of her headlights on the pavement. She rounded a bend and swerved to avoid a fat skunk waddling across the road.

A Mississippi Highway Patrol car blew by her, going in the same direction. A wave of hot air from the cruiser rocked her car. Where had he come from? she wondered. Why hadn't she noticed his lights? Perhaps he'd pulled out of a side road. The area was riddled with hundreds of old logging trails. This was the sheriff's jurisdiction, but apparently state troopers checked out the casino, too.

In her rearview mirror she saw high beams coming up behind her. Not surprising. Even though the riverboat had left for its evening cruise, many people from Twin Oaks worked there and would have to prepare for the *Lucky Seven*'s return.

A second later, the car was on her bumper, its lights blinding her. Sweat dampened her palms and made the steering wheel slip from her grip. She was afraid if she lost her concentration she would careen off the pavement into a tree. The idiot was driving as if he had a death wish, hanging on her license plate, not passing the way the highway patrolman had.

She struggled to maneuver the car through another turn. The glare on her mirror disappeared. She double-checked and found the car had vanished. Evidently, she was overreacting. Some local must have turned off on a side road she hadn't noticed.

"Don't be so jittery," she said out loud. "You need your wits about you to deal with—"

The blaring lights were back again. A second set appeared. Two cars? A third and fourth set of headlights. That many cars defied logic. Hunched over the steering wheel, she clutched it with all her might. What was going on?

"Stay calm."

The cars hurtled closer and closer. She had to squint hard to avoid the high beam lights trained on her mirror. She shoved the mirror upward, deflecting the glare. The first prickle of true panic skittered through her.

"Probably just kids," she assured herself in a whisper.

A spasm hit her colon and bile scorched the back of her throat. An odd sound like an avenging swarm of hornets buzzed in her head. The body dealing with raw fear, she decided. Why was she so terrified?

She'd been through much, much worse in prison. Nothing had happened yet. A gurgling sound purled up from her throat. She veered right, her teeth chattering, her body trembling.

Her front tire skidded on the soft shoulder beyond the

pavement, spitting gravel and sending a rooster tail of dirt into the air. She ventured a quick glance behind her while she struggled to control the vehicle.

More headlights. Dozens of them.

CHAPTER FOURTEEN

SON OF A BITCH! Things were whirling out of control. The *Trib*'s report had Twin Oaks buzzing. Radner had managed to identify Pequita Romero. Who the fuck had ratted? Could have been the beaner who worked with her making crystal meth. Could have been any of the beaners in town who knew Pequita and realized she'd vanished.

It didn't really matter, he thought with pride. None of them knew his identity except his partners, and they had too much at stake to squeal.

He'd taken great pains to make sure the drug operation couldn't be linked to him. What bothered him was that dickhead Radner—according to the paper—was going to push for more meth arrests. That would be a problem—big-time. Sheriff Parker had been paid to look the other way and not charge users, but that wasn't going to work now.

Radner'd had a tight-ass reputation when he'd been on the force in New Orleans. He swaggered around Twin Oaks like a fucking gunslinger. If Radner really started snooping into the meth problem, they would have to get rid of him. Translated it meant *he* would have to off Radner.

A lawman's murder might make the *Trib* suspicious. Never forget Noyes had won two Pulitzers for investigative reporting. And Kat Wells wasn't helping. Despite her being an ex-con, people around town were praising the article on the dead bitch.

He told himself his lucrative operation wasn't unraveling,

but if he didn't take steps, it could. Fortunately for all of them, he had a clever idea and had already put it in motion. Tomorrow, two of their enemies would be out of the way.

Thanks to him.

"Half past dead." That's what his grandpappy used to say about really old people who were too stubborn to die. They lived on and on, clinging to their money, forcing their kin to take care of them.

He liked the saying. It was ominous, mysterious—but he didn't think of it in terms of old people. No way. To him it described the people he'd marked for death. He allowed them to live until he chose to kill them. They walked around, not knowing they were going to die.

He could have said "as good as dead" but "half past dead" sounded more ominous. And mysterious. It fit his personality.

He wasn't sure how many people he'd have to eliminate, or how long it would require, but more than one person in Twin Oaks was half past dead.

JUSTIN STOOD on the bank of the Mississippi, where the noodling contest had been held. His deputies had things under control now, but when he'd arrived, it had been a near-riot. The guys from Arkansas who finished in second place were in a down-and-dirty brawl with the hometown team who'd caught a catfish that was one inch longer. The Arkansas boys claimed their catch had been mismeasured and they were the rightful winners. The judge, a stone-Okie who'd moved to Twin Oaks, refused to remeasure.

Justin had taken the first- and second-place catfish, measured them himself, then allowed one member of each team to measure. The Okie judge hadn't made a mistake, and the boys simmered down.

"Good work," Filpo Johnson told him, respect evident in his dark eyes. "You handled the situation like a pro."

"Let's hope," he replied. "I'm having my men stick around tonight to keep a lid on things."

Because noodling was a misdemeanor—cruelty to animals—a few contestants had been arrested in other counties where the sport was illegal. In Twin Oaks they had a heyday doing what most of them did along the riverbanks where they lived.

Most of the teams were from out of the area. They'd driven here in fifth wheels, campers, and motor homes to stay for the week-long event. They wouldn't be pulling out until tomorrow morning. More noodling. More fighting.

"I guess you're here with the north side team?" Justin asked.

"They're my boys," Filpo responded in a paternal tone. Justin knew Filpo had one son who was in law school at Tulane and the businessman was well known for helping out troubled teens in the north side. "We didn't place last year but this year we took third. Next year, I'm betting we'll win."

Justin managed a smile. Out of the corner of his eye, he noted the rebel flag flying over a nearby campfire. In the distance he heard some guy playing "Dixie" on a harmonica. It was tradition to cut loose with a rebel yell when you'd bagged a catfish.

Noodling was a redneck sport. The good ole boys wouldn't take kindly to a black team winning. Not that Justin cared. Anyone who groped around in the mud and caught a slippery catfish with his bare hands deserved to win, but next year Justin would need to have extra deputies out here to see there wasn't a riot.

"Come on over to my motor home," Filpo said. "We're grilling steaks for the team."

Justin's stomach rumbled at the word *steaks* and he accepted readily. It was late to be eating, but the contest had run over, then the fight broke out. He'd been planning on skipping dinner and finding Kat. He was going to use Maria as an excuse. Had she told Kat anything more that would help with the case? But he figured he'd better stick around here to make certain things remained calm.

"Just let me get my dog," he told Filpo. "It's too hot for him in my pickup."

"We're right over there." Filpo pointed to a brand-new, gleaming red motor home.

As Justin traipsed back to his pickup, he had an idea. Filpo owned a bank. Maybe he had some ideas about what had gone on at the Mercury Bank. He unlocked the door, and Redd hopped out. Tail between his legs, the dog looked uncertainly around at all the campfires and noisy guys. The nearest group was crunching beer cans on their foreheads. Justin doubted he'd need the shotgun on the rack behind the driver's seat or the Glock on his hip, but you never knew. Testosterone and alcohol were often a deadly combination.

"It's okay. Stick with me."

They walked back to Filpo's motor home, greeting the men at campfires he passed along the way. When the call had come into the station that the situation here was out-of-hand, Justin had quickly put on the khaki short-sleeved shirt from his uniform and pinned on his badge. He wanted the out-of-towners to know who he was and that he was monitoring the situation.

The scent of burning pine wood and catfish frying in cornmeal filled the night air. The smell brought back memories of his mother in the trailer's tiny kitchen, frying a catfish he'd caught. He'd never noodled, but he'd done his share of standing on the bank of the river in the cool shadows waiting for a nibble. He'd eaten too many catfish to ever want to eat another.

"Hey, you!" *You* came out *chew*.

Justin turned and saw Cooter skulking through the trees. In the flickering light from a nearby campfire, Justin could see liver spots like shrapnel on Cooter's hands as he clutched a fishing rod.

"Are you talking to me, Cooter?"

Cooter jerked his head, motioning for Justin to come into the trees where the old man was standing. Justin hadn't spotted the trailer park manager out here, but he wasn't surprised. Cooter claimed to have won the noodling contest forty-some years ago. When Justin had been in high school, Cooter's arthritis had gotten the better of him, and the old man had given up noodling for a rod and reel.

Justin walked toward Cooter, asking, "What do you want?"

"I sees things, I do." Cooter wielded the fishing pole like a scepter and pointed it skyward. "Thar's a bad moon rising."

"Cooter, it's the dark of the moon."

"Thass what I'ma tellin' ya. When the moon rises, someone is gonna die."

"Oh, for God's sake. That's an old wives' tale." He turned to leave, wondering if Cooter was still all there.

"This here's the truth. Lass time a still shut down, the beaner was killed."

Justin stopped, and Redd leaned against his calf. He dropped his hand to pet the dog. "What are you talking about?"

"The still out Shady Hook way. It jist shut 'bout when the woman died."

The still? Okay, an old-timer like Cooter might mistake the big vats in the meth shack for a moonshine operation. He wasn't surprised that Cooter had stumbled upon the shack. When he wasn't scavenging off the denizens of Shady Acres Trailer Park, he was tromping through the woods, shooting game for food. He had an old freezer in his carport where he kept enough squirrels, rabbit, and roadkill to see him through the winter.

Once when they'd been desperate, Justin's mother had asked Cooter to give her a squirrel. He'd handed over a squirrel that must have died of starvation. In exchange, Justin had to chop a cord of wood for the old geezer.

"Have other stills shut down?" Justin asked. His theory—and it was only a theory at this point—was the meth labs were deliberately moved with some frequency to avoid law enforcement.

"None a my bidness but a still out by Fox Holler is cattywumpus. Same as Fork Crik."

Fork Creek and Fox Hollow were deep in the woods. True, there were logging trails in the area, but it seemed a stretch to think of hauling supplies out so far. The protection it offered might be worth the effort, though.

"Did you see any people around the stills?" Justin asked.

"Nah, jist beaners."

Justin doubted there was anyone more prejudiced in Twin Oaks than Cooter. "Thanks for the tip, Cooter. I'll check out Fox Hollow and Fork Creek."

"Too late. Won't find nuthin'."

"Okay." Justin thought of a way to get some information. "If you see another still in operation, don't say anything to anyone. Just let me know."

Cooter shrugged noncommittally, but Justin could tell he was pleased to be asked for help. Funny, Justin had been a "worthless bastard" when he'd returned home and wandered through the trailer park.

He walked slowly toward Filpo's motor home, thinking about the types of people who didn't talk to authorities. In New Orleans, it had been criminals with something to hide or drug users fearful of losing their source. In Twin Oaks, it was people like the Latinos who were terrified of being deported and distrustful hollow folks like Cooter who lived off the land. Their "bidness" was private, no concern of the law. More than one of those men roamed the backwoods and might have seen something, but they weren't coming to him. He would have to seek them out, but it would be worth it to bust the meth ring operating in the backwoods.

Filpo was sitting in a lawn chair not too far from a huge grill where six or seven teenage boys were tending steaks, when Justin returned. "Steaks and barbecue beans. Pretty simple."

"Sounds good to me." Justin took the seat beside Filpo, and Redd curled up as close as he could get. Nearby a tree frog let out a deep-throated "ribbit."

"Do you ever have any dealings with Mercury National Bank?"

Filpo smiled, his white teeth flashing in his dark face. "Nah. My people are on the north side. Mercury's never wanted to lend to any of them, so I have a lock on their business."

"Mercury does pretty good, right? They're the only other bank in town."

One of the kids came over with an armful of sodas. They both took one. Filpo popped the lid, saying, "They've cornered the local white business—especially loans."

"What about checking accounts and credit cards?"

"Mercury is too small to make much from credit cards. I offer one, but it's allied with a bigger bank in Memphis. Unlike Mercury's customers, my people can't get a credit card anywhere else."

Justin took a swig of his diet soda, thinking Filpo probably charged astronomical interest rates. "Remember the robbery Mercury had a few years back?" When Filpo nodded, Justin continued, "Did anything seem strange about that case?"

"Possibly," he responded but didn't offer any explanation.

Justin waited a moment, hoping he wouldn't have to pry the information out of the cagey councilman. He finally asked, "What do you mean?"

"It was too damned convenient, finding the money sticking out of her purse. That woman had graduated at the top of her class. She couldn't be that stupid." Filpo silently appraised him for a moment. "Kat Wells is back and working for the paper. I guess you're supervising her."

"Yeah." Justin knew Filpo was one sharp cookie who had eyes all over town. No doubt he knew that he'd been seeing Kat. "I've had to acquaint myself with the case. Kat denies she took the money."

"Suppose she didn't," Filpo said carefully. "What do you think happened?"

Justin kicked back the rest of his soda. "Damned if I know. It focused a lot of negative attention on the bank."

"Damn straight." Filpo flashed him a full grin. "It delayed the FDIC inspection."

"Inspection?" Justin nearly shouted the word. "What inspection? No one mentioned it."

Filpo shrugged, still grinning. "Most folks in these parts wouldn't know what it meant."

"Some would," Justin said, his mind focusing on the growing list of suspects.

"Cloris Howard mighta needed to delay the FDIC visit." Filpo spread his hands wide and raised his shoulders in an exaggerated shrug. "Who knows? The thought occurred to me at the time, but…"

"Why didn't the prosecutor look at that angle?" Justin asked, then answered his own question. "The fingerprint convinced them a robbery had taken place."

"Prosecutors bask in the notoriety of a case. If they're not running for office, they're looking to be promoted up the food chain. Both types like a slam dunk."

"That's why Cloris called Sheriff Parker," Justin said, thinking out loud. "He lifted Kat's fingerprint from somewhere and claimed he'd found it in the vault."

"Could be." Filpo rocked back in his chair. "Could be."

"Not could be. It's the answer. I'm sure. It's been bothering me that Sheriff Parker discovered the print in the vault. The report said the print came from a half inch wide textured frame around the compartment where the bills were stacked.

Despite the bullshit you see on television, only the top crime scene techs can lift a print off anything but a smooth surface."

"Parker hadn't worked in the field in years," Filpo added, a cagey edge to his voice.

"Exactly. Yet he insisted on investigating the whole thing himself."

Justin's instinct told him this was the answer he'd been looking for. Kat had taken the fall because Cloris Howard had needed to delay a meeting with the bank examiners.

"Just what do bank examiners do?" He knew very little about the inner workings of banks, but Filpo had to be an expert.

"Check the books, see if money is reported and loans are recorded properly. Chickenshit stuff for the most part. Worst case—fraud."

"What type of fraud?" Justin was so excited he could hardly ask the question. He wanted to rush over and tell Kat. Hold her close and explain what he'd discovered.

"Most often illegit bankers borrow money from accounts to cover shortfalls. Sometimes they set up phony accounts to hide money or—"

"Launder it."

"You got it."

Could be money from drug sales, Justin decided. Or illegal funds that would be difficult to explain because they'd been skimmed from the casino. Delaying the bank inspectors would have given them time to cover their tracks.

The steaks were being served and Justin followed Filpo to the grill. He felt like roadkill flattened by an eighteen-wheeler. All he could think about was Kat having been framed. Sure, he'd had his suspicions about the crime, but he hadn't really had faith in her.

He'd been running on lust—or so he'd thought. Now he knew it went deeper than that. What he felt for her was different, more personal, more involving.

Okay, it was true he wanted her physically, but he needed to give her something as well. If he could just prove she had been framed, it would be a gift like none other. It wouldn't bring back the years she'd lost, but it would go a long way to restoring her pride.

The injustice of her situation made him break out in a sweat, suppressed rage a white-hot poker in his gut. Where did Cloris Howard get off sending an innocent woman to prison? Who in hell else had been in on it? His fingers itched to ram his fist down someone's throat, but anger would do more harm than good. He needed proof.

"Rare, please," Justin said to the kid serving the steaks. His cell phone vibrated, and he balanced the plate with one hand and pulled his phone out of his pocket with the other. "Radner," he said, walking away from the noise around the grill.

"It's Buster. Can you talk?"

It was the night duty officer/dispatcher. "Yes. Go ahead."

"There's trouble at the *Lucky Seven*."

Oh, great, Justin thought. The riverboat was south of the city. He was at least half an hour north where the noodlers had set up camp.

"There's a body—"

"I'm on my way."

CHAPTER FIFTEEN

DAVID GLANCED at his watch. Nearly eleven. Was it too early to take Max out for his final potty run of the night? Could the pup make it until morning? He hadn't last night. Max had begun squirming in the cozy dog bed that David had bought for him. He'd been forced to get up and let Max out at three. The pup had done his business, come in, curled up in his bed, and fallen back to sleep in a minute. David had been awake until dawn.

"Okay, Max. Let's go," he said to the snoozing pup.

Max lifted his head from the Oriental rug beneath David's chair. At least he responded to his name, David thought. Why had he told the vet's receptionist the pup's name was Maximillian—Max for short? What happened to doggie names like Fido and Spot?

Pets had become members of the family, he decided, not merely pets. You could hardly call a person "Spot." There might be an article in this trend. He was always looking for human interest stories. The pet revolution would be a great one.

"Come on, boy. Come on."

He coaxed Max to his feet, the puppy gazing up at him sleepy-eyed. David headed toward the door, and Max stumbled over his paws to follow him. Cute, David thought, really adorable. He opened the back door and Max trundled out to the half-dozen steps leading down to the backyard. It was a little difficult for the puppy, but David resisted the urge to carry him to the bottom.

He went down the steps, squatted on his heels, and called, "Come on, Max. Come on."

Max shambled down the steps and crashed to his tummy on the bottom one. He picked himself up without a whimper and scooted over to David. He jumped up, wanting to be held, to be petted. David gave him a quick pat on the head, then rose. "Come on, now. Do your business."

Max didn't seem to have any idea what "his business" was. He flitted around the well-lighted yard, interested in everything from the watering can to a low-hanging gardenia, giving off a fragrant smell. Suddenly, Max stopped in his tracks and coughed, a deep gut-wrenching sound.

"What's the matter, boy?"

Max kept gagging and coughing until he threw up his dinner. In the center of the brown goop was a still-bright gold button. "No wonder you horked up your dinner. You were chewing on my blazer."

Max gazed up apologetically, then trotted off toward the back of the yard.

The ring of his telephone startled him. Who would be calling so late? The paper had been put to bed hours ago. He looked around for Max and smiled when he spotted the pup squatting like a girl-dog on the lawn, relieving himself. He called to Max and rushed inside to catch the telephone.

He was too late. The call had clicked over to his answering machine. A disembodied voice David didn't recognize filled the room. "You're gonna wanna git to the *Lucky Seven*. Big trouble out thar. Murdur."

Another murder?

David checked his watch, but the secret source he had in place at the casino wouldn't be working at this late hour. Too bad. It had taken a lot of effort—not to mention money—to find a contact there. It would have been fantastic if his source had funneled him this information—if there really *had* been a murder. This might be a prank.

David arrived at the riverboat a half hour later. He saw several squad cars, the county crime scene van, and a few onlookers from the crew awaiting the midnight return of the *Lucky Seven.*

"What's going on?" David asked the first deputy he met. He didn't recall the man's name, but he'd seen him writing parking tickets on Main Street.

"Somebody got himself shot."

"Will he survive?" David asked, his voice full of hope. Maybe the mysterious caller had been wrong. Justin didn't need any more crimes to solve.

"Nope. Shot dead."

Oh, God. No homicides in years, then two in six months? What were the odds? David pulled out his cell phone to call Kat. He could use another reporter to interview as many people as possible. "Know who the victim is?"

"Oh, yeah. It's Mr. Bitner from the bank."

Bitner? It took David a moment to reorient himself. He remembered the first time he'd met Elmer Bitner, when David had opened an account at the bank. Elmer had insisted David use the bank for a home loan. Bitner had pestered him to attend his church every Sunday. He'd gone on and on about "staying the Lord's course."

Kat's cell phone rang and rang. No voice mail picked up. David imagined she was in bed. Since she didn't have a regular telephone yet, he had no way of reaching her. He would just have to do all the interviewing himself.

A shame.

He liked working with Kat. She was sharp and she had something about her that made people open up. Not to mention that she had the sheriff's ear. Justin was taller than the other men and easy to spot in the distance, hovering around what appeared to be a picnic area adjacent to the wharf where the *Lucky Seven* docked. A bulging black body bag lay off to the side.

What had Bitner been doing out here at night? With luck, David's source would shed some light on the situation. At least David could find out if Bitner had frequented the casino.

JUSTIN HAD RARELY MADE this type of call when he'd been working in New Orleans. A beat cop usually delivered the bad news to the next of kin, but tonight he had to tell Ida Lou Bitner that her husband was dead. He wanted to give her the message in person, not just because he felt it was his duty as sheriff but he needed a few questions answered. What on earth had Bitner been doing in the picnic area adjacent to where the riverboat docked?

There were no lights on except a yellow bug light on the porch when Justin pulled up to Elmer Bitner's modest home. If Bitner had been in cahoots with Cloris, he hadn't plowed the money into his home or his car, Justin decided, thinking of the seven-year-old Ford parked near the crime scene. He left Redd in the pickup with the windows down and walked up to the front door. After ringing the bell, he waited. A light came on in the back of the house. A chunky woman in rollers and an inside-out bathrobe opened the door a crack.

"Miz Bitner? I'm Sheriff Radner."

She swung the door open. "Elmer. Where's my Elmer?"

Justin stepped in beside her. She looked up at him and he could see she…knew. Suddenly her eyes were glassy with un-shed tears. "Sweet Jesus. What happened? A car wreck? Is he gonna be okay?"

He led her to a brown sofa with faded yellow flowers the size of hubcaps. As gently as possible, he lowered her down.

"Tell me," she whispered, her eyelashes glistening with tears. "Tell me."

"I'm afraid…Elmer's been killed," he said in a harsh, raw voice.

She trembled, rocking back and forth. Justin had no idea what to say. He had many questions to ask, but now wasn't the right time. He spotted a Bible on the coffee table. He picked it up and handed it to Bitner's widow. She clutched it to her chest, silent tears coursing down her cheeks. Just holding the well-worn Bible seemed to comfort her.

"Is there someone I should call?" he asked after a few minutes of silence broken only by Ida Lou's sniffles.

"Reverend Applegate," she replied in a tear-choked voice.

Justin found a wall phone in the kitchen, called information, then contacted the head of the Trinity Baptist Church. Evidently, the man was accustomed to being awakened at all hours. He told Justin that he would be there in fifteen minutes.

"How?" Ida Lou asked when Justin returned to the living room, a box of tissues in his hand. "How did my Elmer die?"

Justin didn't want to hurt this poor woman, but he owed her the truth. "Someone shot him." He could have added *point-blank in the back of the head.*

A glazed expression of utter disbelief clouded her face. "Elmer? You sure?"

Justin pulled Elmer Bitner's wallet out of his pants pocket and handed it to Ida Lou. "Yes, ma'am."

She put the wallet between the Bible and her body. Her breasts rose and fell under her labored breathing. Finally she managed to ask, "Was it an accident?"

"No, ma'am. He was sitting at a picnic bench out by the *Lucky Seven*—"

"No! I don't believe it! Elmer would never go near Satan's den. He didn't hold with gambling."

Justin waited a few seconds for Ida Lou to calm down. "The riverboat was out. I think he must have been meeting someone. Did he tell you where he was going or who he was meeting?"

She stuck out her chin defiantly. "He wasn't going to the river-boat. He was meeting Buck Mason at the Rebel Roost. They were talking business. Buck's going to expand his drugstore."

Great, Justin thought. Just what he needed. Buck Mason in the middle of a murder investigation.

JUSTIN WASN'T EVEN TEMPTED to put off visiting Buck Mason. He could have left it to a deputy who would get to it in the morning, but cases that weren't cracked within the first forty-eight hours often went unsolved. He needed to track down as many leads as he could as quickly as possible.

He drove his pickup to Buck's house on Allendale Lane, a few blocks from Judge Kincaid's home. Hidden by a stand of trees and a high hedge, the mansion wasn't visible from the street.

Unbidden, a memory resurfaced. Justin was coming to pick up Verity for their first date. It had been fall and black-eyed Susans and orange butterfly weed grew wild along the road in front of the entrance to the Masons' house. Weeds, he'd thought. His mother pulled out every weed around their trailer. Didn't the Masons have a gardener?

He'd driven his mother's rattletrap car into the yard and caught his first glimpse of Verity's three-story brick home with its sweeping white balcony and towering columns. A lawn lush as a golf course, trimmed with well-tended flowers, surrounded the mansion. Obviously the weeds along the road were the city's problem.

Tonight the house seemed less impressive. Time and maturity, Justin thought. He'd traveled. Seen bigger mansions, attended parties at them, investigated homicides in more splendid homes.

Low voltage lighting illuminated the curved driveway up to the front door. A single lamp was on in the living room. It had been on a timer when Verity had been alive. Probably still was. Buck Mason refused to change. Refused to stop living in the past.

Justin lowered the windows, got out of the pickup, and left Redd behind. Two flickering gas lanterns cast a warm glow across the brick walkway. Justin walked up, dreading the inevitable confrontation. He rang the bell twice, two short bursts, and waited. He knew Buck's bedroom was on the second floor down the hall from where Verity's room had been. No doubt her room hadn't been touched.

A few minutes later, Justin heard the heavy, plodding thump of Buck's feet on the wooden staircase. A light came on in the foyer.

"Who is it?" Buck called, his voice thick with sleep.

"The sheriff."

The door flew open, and Buck glowered at him. "What in hell?" Buck clenched his fist, poised to strike Justin. "You've got your goddamned nerve showing up here! Get off my property, you son of a bitch!" Buck lunged toward him, but Justin moved aside. "You're worthless white trash!"

"Elmer Bitner's been shot," he said evenly. "He's dead."

Buck staggered backward, slack-jawed. Justin stepped into the foyer and gestured toward the library off to the side. Gathering his thick velour robe around him like a shield, Buck led the way into the library and flicked on the lights without a word. The mahogany wood paneling gleamed as it had all those years ago when he'd arrived to pick up Verity for their first date. The hand-tooled leather books with gold embossed spines still sparkled. But the men's voices were like echoes in an empty tomb.

The house hadn't changed, Justin decided. He had. In more ways than he'd realized. Most important now—he was the law. Regardless of their past history, Justin had a job to do.

Buck sank into the leather wingback chair where he'd sat

the night he'd grilled Justin before his first date with Verity. "What happened?"

Justin sat in the same chair he'd used all those years ago. "He was shot," he said again.

"Really? Shot dead?" Despite his well-toned body, Buck sounded like an old man now.

"You saw him this evening?"

Buck nodded, his grizzled fringe of hair catching the lamp's light. Two shards of pure white hair shot upward from his head. "Yeah. We met for drinks at the Rebel Roost."

The Roost was known as a haven for the good ole boys around town. It served nothing but beer and liquor made in America. Most nights a poker game went on in the back room. The stakes weren't as high as out at the riverboat, but guys went there to get away from their wives for the evening.

"I didn't think Elmer drank," Justin said.

"He doesn't," Buck said, his voice low. "He had a root beer."

"Why were you meeting?"

Buck hesitated, then said, "I wanted to break the news to Elmer easy-like. I'm expanding the drugstore. Elmer expected me to get the loan from Mercury, but Jackson Mutual offered me a better rate."

For a moment Justin thought about what Filpo had said about Mercury having the lock on loans to whites. Apparently, their grip had weakened. "What did Elmer say?"

"He was upset. Real upset. Said he thought he could count on my business." Biting his lower lip, Buck looked away. "Now he's dead. I can't believe it."

Justin let the silence hang there for a few minutes, broken only by the cicadas chanting outside the library window. Finally, he asked, "What time did Elmer leave the bar?"

"'Bout eight-fifteen or so."

"Did he say where he was going?" Justin hadn't mentioned the riverboat. Since it was an unlikely destination for Bitner,

Justin wanted to know if he'd told anyone where he was going or why.

Buck vaulted out of his chair. "You worthless shit! Why make you sheriff? You haven't even found out he was going to the riverboat to meet Kat Wells."

Like a knock-out punch, Justin almost doubled over at the revelation. Kat? Why? It didn't make any sense at all. Justin kept his voice level, determined not to reveal his inner emotions. "Did Elmer say why they were meeting there, of all places?"

"She called him and insisted they meet at the riverboat." Buck spat out the words contemptuously. "She didn't want to be seen with him."

It made sense, Justin decided. Once the riverboat pulled out, the area was usually deserted until just before the Lucky Seven returned. That's why there had been no witnesses to the crime.

"I told him to stay away from the scheming bitch. Damn Elmer wouldn't listen. He said he was afraid of her, but he went anyway."

A bitter ache of disappointment arced through Justin. He'd been so sure she'd been framed for the bank robbery. Now he didn't know what to think. It could still have been another setup designed to frame Kat for murder.

He was far more emotionally involved in this case than he should be. His feelings for Kat impaired his judgment. Don't jump to any conclusions—one way or the other. Analyze every detail. Stick with the facts, he cautioned himself.

But the fact was, this didn't look good for Kat.

CHAPTER SIXTEEN

IN FRONT OF All Washed Up, Justin parked his pickup behind David's immaculately restored Thunderbird. He'd spotted the *Trib*'s editor out at the riverboat but they hadn't spoken. What was he doing at Kat's?

Justin glanced up and down the street lit only by the gas lamp at the corner. Kat's blue Toyota wasn't anywhere in sight, but there was a light on up in her apartment. From the dim glow, he decided it was the small lamp on the end table.

He rounded the corner of the building to take the steps up to Kat's place and saw a man coming down. Justin tensed, then the light caught the man's silver hair. "David?"

"Justin?"

"Yes. What are you doing here?"

David had reached the bottom step now, and they were standing eye-to-eye. "I'm looking for Kat, but she's not home."

"It's nearly midnight. Where could she be?" Justin didn't want to believe she'd gone to the riverboat to meet Elmer, but Buck had been more convincing than Justin cared to admit. Investigate this as if you don't know the woman, he thought.

"I don't know," David replied in a troubled voice. "Her car was spotted on the road to the *Lucky Seven*."

Justin's body stiffened in shock. "Where did you hear that?"

"I called Highway Patrol. They make a run by the riverboat a couple of times a night. At eight-twenty-seven a patrolman logged in a blue Toyota with Kat's license number driving toward the casino."

Christ! Justin cursed his own stupidity. Buck could be right about Justin. He was next to worthless—a real amateur hour sheriff. Why hadn't he thought to check with Highway Patrol? "Why did HP run her plate?"

David shrugged, his shoulders hunched over. He stepped down from the last stair onto the sidewalk. "No real reason except she was going slower than normal. You know how folks speed out in the unincorporated area."

Justin fell into step beside David. "Did you find anyone who actually saw her at the riverboat dock?"

No one Justin had talked with had reported any woman out by the dock, but David might have picked up on something he'd missed.

"No one I interviewed saw anyone until the grounds crew in charge of docking the *Lucky Seven* arrived and found Elmer Bitner slumped over at a picnic table. They thought he was a drunk sleeping it off until they were close enough to see half his head had been blown away," David replied, verifying what Justin had learned when he'd spoken to the men.

"My source doesn't work the late shift, but in the morning I'll check to see if Elmer frequents the place."

The knowledge that Kat had been out there twisted inside Justin. Until now, Justin hadn't quite admitted to himself how much he wanted her to be innocent. Needed her to be innocent. *Evaluate the facts; don't jump to any conclusions. Keep your personal feelings out of this.*

"Did Kat mention meeting Bitner to you?"

"Not a word." David stopped beside his T-Bird. "Bitner was shot. Kat doesn't have a gun. Her furlough specifies no weapons."

Justin wanted to believe someone else had killed Bitner, but common sense told him Kat was somehow involved. He didn't quite trust Buck—not after the way he'd hounded him for Verity's death. But the bartender at the Rebel Roost verified Buck's story. He had been there with Elmer early that evening. Why had she wanted to meet with Bitner?

"A gun's easy enough to get," Justin responded, unable to keep the bitterness out of his voice.

"I think Kat will come home soon and settle this," David said. "I'm going to wait in my car until she returns."

"No. Go home and get some sleep. I'll have one of my deputies stake out her apartment."

David hesitated a moment. "Will you call me the minute she shows up?"

"Yeah." Justin stood on the sidewalk and watched David drive away. He didn't call a deputy to watch for Kat's return. He sat in his pickup, Redd at his side, and waited for her himself.

NORMALLY TORI DIDN'T "do" breakfast. She usually gulped a Chocolate Royale Slim-Fast and relied on the pot of coffee at the office to get her through to lunch. At noon she would have a salad—no dressing. That way in the evening she could enjoy a meal with Clay and not worry about gaining weight.

This morning was different. Tori was meeting Doris Purtle at the Bits N Grits Café for breakfast. The elderly widow had a mansion not far from the Kincaids. Doris had been toying with selling it and moving to Atlanta to be near her only child. Tori had drawn up the papers twice and each time, Doris backed out at the last second.

It would be a real coup if Tori could list the place. The way the house was situated on the vast grounds, it could be sold and the rest of the property subdivided into at least two, maybe three lots. She'd already contacted a developer in Jackson who was anxious to take on the project. Of course, Doris didn't have to know anything about this. The estate had been in her family for generations. Subdividing was an ugly word to old-timers.

"Doris, you're early." She greeted the widow with her brightest smile when she walked into the café. She signaled the waitress for coffee and inhaled the aroma of their home-made cinnamon rolls. Fattening but heavenly. "I hope you haven't been waiting long."

"I just got here," the widow replied. Doris had beautiful sil-ver hair that glistened in the morning light. It made Tori think of her mother. Her hair had had the same sheen before the chemotherapy. "I wanted to tell you in person."

Tori asked, "Tell me what?"

The waitress delivered Tori's coffee and a piping-hot cinna-mon roll to Doris. The short hairs along the back of Tori's neck bristled. Something was wrong. Doris had that imperious look that May Ellen got when she was about to criticize someone.

"I want you to know I truly like you," Doris began. "You're smart and you've made something of yourself despite…"

Despite my sister, Tori silently finished the sentence.

"When I got the news…well, I just couldn't…"

"What news?" Tori asked as calmly as possible.

"You don't know?" Doris plunged her fork into the cinna-mon roll and broke off a ladylike bite. "Elmer Bitner was shot and killed last evening. Fayrene Weston called me just after midnight and told me."

"Elmer? He's harmless. A sweet guy. Who would shoot him?"

Doris thoughtfully chewed the roll and swallowed before answering, "Fayrene's cousin's son-in-law is a deputy. She says Elmer went out to the *Lucky Seven* to meet your sister."

"Kat? That's ridiculous! After what happened, Kat wouldn't go near—"

"As I understand it, the Highway Patrol saw her car on the road to the casino."

"I'm sure there's a reasonable explanation." But Tori couldn't think of one. If what Doris said was correct, Tori was finished in Twin Oaks.

Doris helped herself to another forkful of cinnamon roll. "Look, I've decided to sell. My daughter has found me a condo in Buckhead near where she lives. But I can't give you the listing. With all this scandal…well, I'm sure you understand."

Tori managed to gracefully leave Doris to the cinnamon roll. Outside Bits N Grits, she tried to reach Clay at his office. She'd forgotten that he was going into Jackson today. If he had his cell phone on, he wasn't answering.

DAVID HOVERED outside the sheriff's station for almost an hour before Justin Radner appeared.

"Justin," David called as the sheriff emerged from his pickup.

Justin halted, the red-colored dog at his heels. "Yeah?"

"Kat didn't come home, did she?"

Radner shook his head. "No. I've put out an APB on her Toyota."

"No results?" David asked, walking closer.

"I did it less than an hour ago. What can we expect?"

David detected the bitterness in Justin's voice and knew he had counted on more from Kat. Who could blame him? David had had faith in her as well. Even now, Kat's denial of her role in the bank robbery echoed in his ears with haunting truthfulness. It didn't seem possible she would have lied. To him. To Justin.

"I'm worried about Kat," David said.

Justin shook his head. "Forget it. She fooled us both. We're nothing but suckers. I'm the law. It's up to me to find her now."

David shuffled back to his T-Bird. Max was in the passenger seat watching him with baleful eyes. *Something's wrong*, David silently told the dog. *I feel it. Kat couldn't have shot a man. It's not like her.* The pup licked his chin.

"Did you contact your source?"

"Yes. Elmer wasn't a regular visitor to the casino. I did get a list of license plate numbers. I'll run them through Lexis-Nexis and see what comes up."

Justin gave him a curt nod and walked away. He obviously knew better than to ask for confidential information provided by a source.

David stared at the dark clouds hanging low in the sky. Rain was on the way. He needed to work on tomorrow's edition of the newspaper. What could he say? One of the *Trib*'s own was the prime suspect in a murder case?

BY LATE AFTERNOON, Justin was more than a little disturbed. All day his deputies and the Highway Patrol had been searching for Kat's Toyota. Nothing. How could such a distinctive car disappear without a trace?

"Special Agent Wilson is on the line," Nora told him.

Justin had been trying to reach the agent in charge of Kat's furlough all day. He was finally returning the call. "Wilson? Sheriff Radner here."

"Is there a problem?" Wilson asked in a lazy drawl typical of Bureau types stationed in the South.

"Kaitlin Wells has disappeared. She's wanted for questioning in connection with a murder that took place by a riverboat casino."

"Murder? Who was killed?" asked Wilson.

Justin gave him the details including the link to Kat's robbery conviction.

"What about her mother? Her sister? Have they seen Kat?" Wilson sounded interested but not particularly disturbed.

"Tori Wells hasn't seen Kat lately. Her mother has but she's so out of it with cancer drugs that she can't remember when she saw her daughter last."

"Lemme contact a few agents in the field. They may be able to help," Wilson said. "I'll call you if I find out anything."

Justin hung up and stared down at his knees. Redd was curled up beneath the desk the way he'd been all night in the pickup while Justin had waited for Kat. By now she had enough time to be across the border in four different directions. He should have put out the APB last night, right after Buck had told him Bitner was meeting Kat.

Why? Why would Kat shoot Bitner? It didn't make any sense except for revenge.

Something Wilson had said kicked in. *Agents in the field.* What did Wilson mean? Did the Bureau have other agents in the area? Or did Wilson mean Jackson, where he was located? The guys in the Bureau were a tight-ass bunch. You never knew what they were doing. Sure as hell they weren't paying much attention to a con on a work furlough.

IT WAS ALMOST SIX O'CLOCK when Tori walked into her mother's condo.

"A deputy sheriff was here earlier," the nurse informed Tori. "Asking if your sister had been around."

"She wouldn't dare," Tori said, her tone clipped. She'd heard all she ever wanted to hear about Kat today. Her sister had cost her a valuable property listing. Everyone was whispering behind Tori's back. Worse, she hadn't been able to reach Clay. He'd know what to do at a time like this.

The nurse stopped. "Your mother says Kat came to see her. She just doesn't remember when exactly. It's probably the drugs."

Kat wouldn't have come here, would she? Tori had warned Kat about visiting their mother, but Kat wasn't the same easy-to-manipulate girl she once had been. Obviously not, now that she was being sought in a murder investigation.

"Mother," Tori called. "How are you doing?"

"The...same." She was staring at the television. A weatherman seemed to be forecasting rain.

"Did Kat come by to see you?" Tori asked as casually as possible.

After a long silence, her mother replied, "She…mighta'. I…don't rightly…recall. I think…it was…a long time ago…before prison."

CHAPTER SEVENTEEN

DEAD MEN TELL NO TALES.

A comforting thought. With Bitner on ice, they had one less problem. Not that Bitner was a threat exactly, but since the dickhead had been born again, he'd become less reliable. Bitner had insisted on being cashed out—claimed he was starting a mission in Guyana. The candy-ass probably planned a Jim Jones-type commune where he could be king.

Shit on a stick! Had Bitner seriously believed he could just walk away? Maybe. Times changed and so did people. He needed to remember this. He'd been operating the same way for years but things evolved. People developed different agendas. He easily manipulated everyone it was necessary to control, but he didn't like becoming too involved and risk exposing his position. Things should be okay now. Smooth.

His business had been running like a well-oiled machine until lately. When Kat Wells and Justin Radner had returned to Twin Oaks, things started to go south. He couldn't blame them directly, but their return marked a change.

You had to know when to hold 'em, know when to fold 'em, he reminded himself. This time he'd done neither. He'd pulled a card out of his sleeve.

An ace. He'd trumped the sons of bitches. They'd be in a tailspin now, sniffing around—sniffing around Kat Wells.

THE RAIN BLASTED downward in hot, steamy torrents. Justin stared out his office window at the cascading water. It was almost time to go home, but he didn't intend to leave the office. Why bother? There was nothing for him at the place he'd leased except stacks of unpacked boxes.

"I'm leaving," Nora called from outside his office.

"See you tomorrow."

One of the deputies would be working dispatch/front desk, but Justin didn't bother to ask who was on duty. It didn't matter. Kat was long gone. Her handler at the Bureau hadn't been able to locate her and neither had the Highway Patrol.

Revenge. That's all Justin could figure. What else would make Kat kill a man? Bitner had done something—possibly framed her—and Kat wanted revenge for the time she'd spent in prison.

There was a knock on his doorjamb. As usual the door was open. His deputy Phil Lancaster stood there. "David Noyes is here to see you."

"Send him in," Justin said even though he didn't feel much like talking. Noyes had been as close to Kat as Justin. Maybe closer. What did a few kisses count for?

David walked in, looking exhausted. His new puppy, Max, was on a leash beside him. "Any news?"

"None," Justin responded as Redd sidled out from under his desk to get a peek at the puppy. "Did you find out anything?"

"I spoke with Lola Rae. She hasn't seen Kat since yesterday about closing time."

Justin nodded. He'd interviewed the owner of All Washed Up this morning when she'd arrived at the beauty shop. She'd told him the same thing. "Was Maria in?"

David shook his head. "No, but I doubt she knows much. Her English is limited. I can't imagine Kat telling her anything that she wouldn't have shared with Lola Rae."

"You're probably right, but Lola Rae was surprised Maria hadn't shown up for work. I drove over to her place, but she wasn't there."

David dropped into the chair opposite Justin's desk, and the pup obediently sat down beside him. "Do you think they're together or something?"

"Nothing would surprise me," Justin said with a weary smile. "But I don't think so. I spoke with the state trooper who spotted Kat's car. He said only one person was in it."

"Did he ID Kat?"

"He didn't get a good look. He just saw it was one person—female—driving more slowly than usual. That's when he ran a check on her license."

"I'm worried about Kat. I think she'd call me—"

"How long have you known her?" Like Justin, David had been gullible for a pretty face and a sob story.

"I haven't known Kat long," David admitted, "but I—"

"Exactly. I've asked a judge in Jackson to issue a search warrant for Kat's studio. I also want to see the phone records for the *Trib* and her cell. If she called Elmer, we'll find out."

Their eyes held each other's for a moment, and Justin could see how badly wounded Noyes was by Kat's behavior.

"Cloris Howard keeps dodging me," David finally said, breaking the silence. "Were you able to interview her?"

"Yes. I spoke with her just after the bank opened. Bitner never mentioned Kat's call. Cloris seemed stunned that he would go out to the riverboat to see anyone. His church was death on gambling, liquor—the whole riverboat scene. Cloris is determined to help catch Bitner's killer. The bank is offering a five-thousand dollar reward for info leading to the killer's arrest."

Deputy Lancaster burst through the door. "The mayor's here, sir."

Mayor Peebles pushed by the deputy into the room. "I need to talk to you," Peebles said in a coolly impersonal tone as if he were speaking to some clerk in his office.

David stood up. "I was just going." He hustled his puppy out of the office. The deputy nodded to Justin and followed David out.

Justin's temper had flared at Peebles' tone, but he refused to allow his emotions to show. Peebles was a politician, bound for the state capital or even Washington. Unsolved murders in his town couldn't be tolerated.

Peebles took David's seat. "I just had Judge Kincaid, Buck Mason, and Reverend Applegate in my office, howling for your blood. Is it true that you've refused to arrest Kat Wells?"

"We can't find her," Justin countered, seething but struggling not to show it. "But if we could locate her, we haven't sufficient grounds for an arrest. There's no evidence she was at the crime scene."

The primal glint in Peebles' dark eyes indicated what a fearsome competitor he'd been—and still was. He didn't easily take no for an answer. "HP reported her car on the road to the casino."

"But not *at* the casino." As calmly as he could manage, he added, "Being on the road is not a crime. We want to question her, of course. She's a person of interest in the case."

"I'd say she's a prime suspect," Peebles shot back, the cold edge of irony in his voice. "Who else would want to kill Elmer Bitner? He never harmed a fly, but he did testify against that woman."

"True," Justin conceded. "Her disappearance makes me very suspicious. We have an APB out on her and the Toyota. So far—nothing."

"Buck says he had to tell you that Elmer was meeting the Wells woman at the riverboat. You didn't know."

Justin reached under the desk with one hand and petted Redd. He waited a beat before explaining. "How was I supposed to find out? When I interviewed Elmer's wife, she didn't mention it."

Peebles shifted his bulky frame in the chair. "Bitner met Buck at Rebel Roost and told him about the meeting."

Justin understood what Peebles was doing. A politician to the core, he was trying to please everyone. No doubt, Kincaid and Mason had ratcheted up the pressure on Peebles, hoping to get rid of Justin.

"I went to see Ida Lou Bitner just after the body was found. Gossip flies around this town. I didn't want her hearing about Elmer's death from some old biddy over the phone," Justin explained, keeping his tone even with an effort. "As soon as she told me Elmer had gone to meet Buck, I went to interview him."

"You did the right thing." Peebles sighed. "Buck just has a hard-on for you. And the judge—"

"Doesn't want Kat around. It could hurt his political plans."

"You're right," Peebles admitted. "He keeps squawking about leaving cons in prison where they belong. He's tuning up for the election. He wants her back in jail."

Justin didn't tell him that being out of touch with her handler, not reporting to work, and a number of other things—not to mention murder—would get Kat's furlough revoked. Apparently, the men weren't familiar with work furlough rules. "Crime is a hot button. Two murders in six months defies the odds. We went years without a homicide. Could be coincidence, but I don't buy it. The crimes are linked somehow."

"I guess you would have called me if you'd found the murder weapon."

Yeah, right. Keeping the mayor posted wasn't a top priority. "We dragged the river. Nothing. But with the current, the gun could have been washed downstream. My men searched the woods around the *Lucky Seven*. Nothing there, either."

"What about clues at the scene? Footprints or something."

"There were lots of footprints. They all appeared to be men's shoes. The guys who discovered the body tramped around pretty good. I doubt we'll get a usable shoe print."

With a shake of his head, Justin added, "The crime techs didn't find much either."

"The murderer had to have driven out there. Walking to the casino is out of the question." The mayor rose. "I guess the perp could have come by boat."

"No way. The kudzu vines have choked off the shore. It costs the casino a bundle to keep their pier open."

It all came back to Kat, Justin thought. Motive and opportunity.

IT WAS ALMOST MIDNIGHT before Justin's deputy returned from Jackson with a search warrant signed by a judge. Justin could have saved time by going to Kincaid, but he didn't want the prick horning in on his case and telling him what to do—or worse—using information against him.

The phone records would have to wait until morning when the telephone company in Jackson opened for business. Justin took two deputies with him to Kat's studio. The place was so small that he could have searched it on his own easily, but he wanted witnesses.

He was determined to find Kat and get to the bottom of this. She'd used a lot of good people, gotten them to trust her. Justin burned with frustration. She could be miles away by now, and he wouldn't be the one to collar her. Still, there might be a clue in her place to tell him where she'd gone. He'd take off after her even if it meant leaving his jurisdiction.

David Noyes was sitting in his T-Bird with his puppy when Justin drove up. Justin cursed under his breath. Noyes did not know when to give up. He'd become way too attached to Kaitlin Wells.

David stepped out of his car. "You've obtained a search warrant."

"Yes, and tomorrow we'll be looking at the phone records."

The older man's brow knit into a tight frown. "You might

want to get a warrant for Elmer's phone records—at the bank and at home."

"Why's that?"

"I spoke with Connie, my copy editor, after I left you. She says Kat received a call from a man yesterday afternoon."

"Okay, so? Could have been the guy monitoring her furlough or something."

"Connie thought it was Bitner. She knows him."

For a moment, doubts swirled through Justin's brain. *Don't go there,* the reasonable part of his conscience thought. *Rely on the facts.* On the force in New Orleans, he'd learned to cleave his emotions from cold reality. *Don't become any more involved than you already are,* an inner voice warned him.

"If Bitner's number doesn't turn up on Kat's phone or the *Trib*'s, I'll check Bitner's phone records. But why would he call Kat? I spoke with him earlier in the day. He didn't want to have anything to do with her."

Noyes shrugged. "We're missing something important. I can feel it."

"Why don't you go home? This will take us some time."

Noyes leaned against his car. "I'll wait and walk Max. I'm betting you don't find anything."

DAVID WAS STIFF from sitting in the car so long. These days he had more than just a touch of arthritis. He sluggishly strolled down the street, letting Max sniff at will. The pup was curious about everything and not particularly interested in doing his business. The muggy air was still heavy from the earlier rain. The scent of azaleas mixed with the fragrance of jasmine, but David was too stricken with anxiety about Kat to really notice. Unanswered questions twisted through his mind.

What would make Kat simply vanish? She seemed so interested in being a reporter, so eager to have a second chance at life. He remembered the way her green eyes narrowed when she was concentrating on writing copy. It didn't seem reasonable that she would blow her opportunity by killing Elmer Bitner.

He believed Connie was correct. The woman rarely made any mistakes. Elmer had called Kat. Why? What could he want with her? Why meet in the dark out by the riverboat when no one would be around?

He turned and gazed up at Kat's studio. Justin had forced the lock and entered the apartment. The lights were blazing. With a pang of sympathy, he imagined them rifling through Kat's things. After years in prison and a meager furlough allowance, she couldn't have much.

"Come home, Kat," he muttered. His breath hitched. "I'll help you."

From a nearby tree, an owl hooted once, twice. David waited in the darkness, still perplexed by what had happened. He slowly turned and headed Max back toward All Washed Up.

The lights went off in Kat's studio above the shop. That was a fast search, David thought. He waited beside Justin's pickup. Redd stuck his head out the window, inviting David to pet him for the first time. He usually cowered under Justin's desk or hid behind his legs.

"Good boy." He stroked the dog's head. Max jumped up against his knees and pawed him, begging to be petted, too. He stroked the puppy with his other hand.

He spotted Justin striding across the street. The gas lamp at the corner was a quaint touch but provided little light on a moonless evening. Justin had something in his hand, but David couldn't see what it was.

"Find anything?"

Justin stopped a few feet away from David. "Off the record?"

David's heart rapped against his ribs like an unanswered knock, and he managed a nod.

"We found a thirty-eight hidden in the trunk she uses for a coffee table." He held up a plastic bag with a gun in it.

A wild flash of grief and disappointment ripped through David. Elmer Bitner had been shot with a thirty-eight. It was a moment before he could muster the strength to ask, "Why would she hide a gun, then disappear? Why wouldn't she throw it away?"

"Don't you think the answer is obvious?"

Justin asked the question with a grin, but David could see Justin was just as disturbed and disappointed as he was. He was romantically involved with Kat. This couldn't be a cakewalk for him.

"She didn't think anyone knew she was meeting Elmer," continued Justin. "How would we have known, if he hadn't told Buck Mason?"

David nodded, not trusting his voice. He felt his throat constricting as if he'd swallowed a bale of cotton. Right now he felt like an old fool with one foot in the grave and the other close behind.

Justin said emphatically, "Something or someone tipped her. She hightailed it without returning for the gun. But I believe Kat hid the gun because she thought she might need it again."

CHAPTER EIGHTEEN

IT WAS ONE O'CLOCK in the morning when Tori heard her doorbell ring. She was online, checking the requirements for a Georgia real estate license. She dreaded the hassle of studying for the exam, finding a broker to work for, and developing clientele all over again. What choice did she have? She was through here, thanks to her sister.

She rose from the workstation in the small home office on the first floor of her condo. A quick peek out the window revealed Clay's silver Porsche Boxster at the curb. She'd tried to reach him all day, but he hadn't returned her calls. She knew she would have to get over him. That, besides burying her mother, would be the most difficult part of leaving. She would be giving up on a dream she'd had since high school. She would never be Mrs. Clay Kincaid.

Everything in her body went slack at the thought. She considered not answering the door. What would be the point in prolonging her agony? The bell rang again, a long, sustained buzzzzzzzzz that told her Clay was leaning on the bell.

She walked out of her office and down the hall to the front door. She would have to sell her condo, she realized. Her mother's, too. It would be months at least, before she could leave. She certainly couldn't move until her mother passed away.

A thought hit her. Did her mother have a will? She'd assumed so, but she should have found out before now. If she didn't have a will, the estate—small as it was—would have to go through probate and Kat would receive half. She would squander it on attorney's fees.

Tori threw open the door and found Clay grinning at her.

"Hey, babe," he said, his breath thick with Johnnie Walker. He moseyed into the living room, dropped onto the sofa, and waited for her to turn on the lamp.

She flicked on the light without a word. Clay was shitfaced. He'd been drinking and hadn't bothered to respond to her frantic calls. She'd never seen herself as a weak woman. She'd sacrificed so much for this man. But where he'd been concerned, she now realized that she'd been a simpering Southern belle, waiting at his pleasure.

With a stab of anger, she mentally kicked herself. Once. Twice. It hit her that Kat's years in prison had transformed her into a stronger woman, while Tori had become weaker by trying to please Clay and the self-important Kincaids. What *had* she been thinking?

"Where have you been?" she demanded. "I've been trying to reach you for hours."

He patted the seat beside him, saying, "I wanted to have something positive to tell you."

"What could be positive about this situation?" Tori sat next to Clay. "My sister is a prime suspect in a murder."

"I just left Dad's place."

The only time Clay called his father "Dad" was when he'd been drinking and the judge wasn't around. Otherwise, he called him "Father." In front of people he wanted to impress, he referred to him as "the judge." Had he ever called his father Daddy? She dismissed the ridiculous thought.

"Dad got a call. A search of your sister's apartment turned up a gun. They'll have to run tests, but everyone knows it's the murder weapon."

Tori didn't bother to say anything. She would only have to live with this nightmare until she could move to Atlanta. But her mother was another story. She was already weak, near collapse. The endless humiliation Kat rained down on them would kill her.

Clay grabbed Tori and crushed her to him, his lips claiming hers. The expensive whiskey on his tongue swirled through her mouth. A pleasant taste, well-remembered over the years. Her body warmed in response but she told herself to forget it. They were history. She shoved out of his arms.

"Babe, things are going to be all right." Clay gave her a smile that was borderline evil. She'd seen it before and knew he was up to something. "This is going to be a win-win for all of us."

The Kincaids always came out on the winning side. Her family had been nothing but losers. She'd tried her best, but nothing had changed her luck.

"Dad gave me this." Clay reached into his pocket and pulled out a ring. He picked up her left hand and slipped it on Tori's ring finger.

"What?" She stared down at an old-fashioned ring that was several sizes too big. The center stone was a diamond so small that a magnifying glass wouldn't help make it much larger. Clustered around the stone were diamond chips the size of pinheads. At least they glittered a little.

"Great-grandmother Swain's engagement ring," Clay said with unmistakable pride. "Dad got it out of the safe just a little while ago."

Tears welled up in Tori's eyes. Wait until her mother saw the ring. Never mind that it wasn't the impressive diamond Tori coveted. She had a Kincaid heirloom on her finger. Her mother could die in peace, knowing Tori would become a Kincaid.

"Now it's official." Clay pressed a sweet kiss into the palm of her ring hand. "We're engaged."

Engaged. She could finally say the word and flaunt her

ring, the way dozens of her friends had over the years. She'd waited so long for this moment.

Hold it, she thought, staring at the ring on her finger. Why had the judge agreed to this engagement? Her name was now synonymous with scandal.

She swallowed with difficulty and found her voice. "I'm surprised your father agreed to let us marry, considering the mess my sister's caused."

His eyes darkened as he held her gaze. "Your sister has given Dad a tremendous opportunity."

Warning bells clanged in her brain. A heavy silence hung in the air. Nobody's fool, Tori knew there was a downside to this.

"You see, Dad's hired a high-priced political consultant. Rob Everett is the best. He helped the President carry the South. Rob says people are interested in law and order and moral values. Dad can get a lot of free publicity by coming out against work furloughs. Cons should do their time."

Great. Just great. She was being used by the judge to further his career. She smiled smoothly, betraying none of her annoyance. Did it really matter? She was going to be Clay's wife.

"He's planning a news conference. We'll be at his side. Dad's going to say how devastating it is to a family when one of their own commits a crime."

"We're only half sisters," Tori reminded him.

Clay nodded but he had a faraway look in his eyes. "This will give Dad a running start on his opponents. With the reward the bank is offering to find Elmer's killer, people will be riveted to their televisions."

Tori tried to look on the bright side. Maybe she would get some free publicity, too. The judge's speech might even turn Doris Purtle around, and Tori could sell her estate. She would need that commission to throw the kind of wedding the Kincaids would expect. At the very least, becoming a Kincaid would save her career in Twin Oaks.

Tori hated being involved in politics, so she tried for a smile and kept her thoughts focused on the wedding. If they had it soon enough, her mother might be able to attend. *Please, God. Keep her alive until the wedding.*

"Don't worry, sweetheart," Clay said with a smile. "This ring is only temporary. I'm going to buy you the big diamond we saw in Jackson."

"YES INDEED, you're not going to believe this," Nora told Justin when he walked into the station on the morning following the discovery of the thirty-eight.

"Tell me the state crime lab has run the ballistics test on the gun." He'd sent it over to Jackson with one of his deputies within half an hour of finding the weapon. It was a top priority test, since there had been only one murder in the state in two weeks.

"No. Of course not." Her taut features scowled. "They're slower than a dyin' June bug. I'm talking about the tip line. Yes, indeedy. We've received over fifty tips on the Toyota. Kat Wells has been spotted more often than Elvis."

"The reward has brought them out of the woodwork." Redd trotted by Justin's side as he walked into his office with Nora. "Any of the tips seem promising?"

"Hard to say. Some are outrageous. I doubt Kat's dancing in a strip joint in New Orleans."

He struggled not to think about Kat. He'd predicted this from the get-go. The rate of recidivism among ex-cons was astronomical. He had thought he could help change her and like a fool, he'd tricked himself into believing it was working.

"A trucker claims to have sighted her south of Memphis at about six this morning."

Justin considered the information as he watched Redd curl up under his desk. Memphis was a big town. It would be easy to get lost there. If he were on the run, he would head in that direction.

"Get the police chief in Memphis on the line. I'll talk to him myself."

Justin looked through the tips while Nora contacted the Memphis police chief. None of the tips looked terribly promising, but you never knew.

"An old guy by the name of Cooter phoned and wants you to call him," Nora told him while she waited for the police chief to speak with Justin.

He thought about Cooter and the meth labs hidden in the forest. It could wait. Busting the operation wasn't a priority right now. The chief came on the line, and Justin explained the situation. He promised to alert his officers in the field to be on the lookout for the Toyota and Kat.

"Lola Rae called," Nora told him. "She said to tell you Maria is at work today. Her car broke down in Jackson. That's why she didn't make it in yesterday."

Justin decided he would question Maria when he had time. He remembered the way she'd unexpectedly appeared at Kat's studio. Perhaps she'd seen something that could be helpful.

DAVID WATCHED the trucks roll away from the loading dock with the special edition of the *Tribune*. He'd come back last night after the gun had been found and worked until dawn to produce a two-page Extra! He rehashed the murder, the sighting of Kat's car by the Highway Patrol, but his major focus was on the gun found during the search.

It had killed him to write the special edition. Somehow he felt as if he were betraying Kat, when the reality was she had let him down. What Justin had said made sense. Kat had thought no one knew she was meeting Elmer. That's why she'd kept the gun.

"Come on, Max," he said to the puppy on the leash beside him. "Let's go for a walk."

The puppy scampered in a circle, twisting the leash around

David's knees. Usually David would have smiled at Max's antics, but today he felt lower than he ever had since his accident. Christ! Where did he go wrong? He shouldn't have allowed himself to become emotionally involved. He'd liked Kat and had wanted to help her. He should have known better.

He walked down the street and saw a paper vending machine. Through the glass, he saw the Extra! headline: WEAPON FOUND? His stomach took a dive south as he thought about what he'd written. He'd told the truth, stuck to the facts. Still, he'd condemned Kat, and something inside made him hate himself for it.

He found himself standing, Max at his side, in front of All Washed Up. He looked through the window and saw the shop was empty except for Lola Rae. David opened the door and walked in.

"Hello, I'm David Noyes. I spoke with you on the telephone yesterday about Kat Wells."

The brunette looked up from the reception desk where she appeared to be totaling receipts on a small calculator. David recalled Kat telling him how friendly and helpful Lola Rae had been. The woman eyed him with unconcealed suspicion.

"I'm her friend. I want to help her."

Lola Rae nodded. "Me, too. I just never expected…this."

"What did Kat say the last time you saw her?" he asked although he had already asked her this when he'd phoned.

"Like I told you, I wanted her to join us for dinner."

"Us?"

"Maria and Gary Don and me. Maria works here and makes awesome Mexican food. Know what I mean? Maria should open a restaurant. And Gary Don is my boyfriend." She rose up on tiptoe and called, "Maria, *aqui por favor.*"

From the rear room came a diminutive brunette with creamy cocoa-colored skin and intelligent brown eyes. "You need Maria?" she asked in a Spanish accent.

"This is Kat's boss," Lola Rae explained. "I was telling him about the last time we saw Kat. You'd made tamales, but she couldn't join us."

"Why not?"

Lola Rae shrugged, but Maria said, "She go see *madre*. Mother."

"Someone called for an appointment," Lola Rae said. "I didn't hear Kat say she was on her way to her mother's." Lola Rae thought a moment. "I'm not surprised though. Her mother treats Kat like dirt, but she's near death. Know what I'm sayin'? What daughter wouldn't want to say goodbye?"

A husky man with sandy hair and a pack of cigarettes in the rolled-up sleeve of his T-shirt shouldered his way through the door. "Hey, cutie," he said to Lola Rae. "What's the haps?"

"Just talking with Mr. Noyes. He's with the *Trib*."

"The paper?" The guy turned to David and stuck out his hand. "Gary Don Willingham. I tend bar out at Moonin' N Coonin'. This here's my gal."

David had never been to the seedy tavern on the outskirts of town. He'd heard the walls were festooned with raccoon skins nailed up by guys who'd shot them. Using flashlights to "tree" raccoons and kill them was a local sport that David preferred not to think about. Moonin' N Coonin' attracted a young crowd and was known as a place where you could score any type of drug and gamble in the back room.

"Babe," Gary Don said. "Let's talk. I can't see you tonight. Jimmy called in sick. I have to work his shift."

Lola Rae's lips thinned. She moved out from behind the counter and walked into the back room, Gary Don at her heels.

David turned to Maria and spoke slowly to make sure she understood his question. "Did Kat say anything else about where she was going?"

Maria gazed down at her small hands and flexed her fingers. "No. She leave. No see again."

CHAPTER NINETEEN

IT WAS ALMOST DARK and Nora had just left for the day. Justin looked up and saw David coming through the door of his office, his puppy at his side. *Uh-oh.* Justin had the mother of all headaches from chasing his tail all day and coming up with nothing on Kat. He needed to go home and crash.

"Any luck finding Kat?" David asked.

"None. Lots of tips generated by the reward, but nothing panned out. She vanished into thin air." He massaged the knot in the back of his neck with one hand and stroked Redd under the desk with the other.

David sat in the chair opposite Justin's desk. "I spoke with Maria Sanchez."

"Really? Did she have anything to say?" Justin had been meaning to interview the woman, but he'd been too busy.

"Kat told Maria that she was going to visit her mother."

"What? Lola Rae didn't mention it to me."

"I went to Loretta Wells' condo. She's pretty strung out on morphine. She doesn't know if she saw Kat, didn't see her, or Kat came to her in a dream."

This case is really screwed-up. So what else was new? "Does the woman have any idea *when* she might have or might not have seen her daughter?"

David shook his head. "No, but she's clear on one thing. Before she 'goes to glory' Tori is going to marry Clay Kincaid."

"Is she sure? They've been dating for years."

"When I dropped into the No Latte Café for a sandwich, everyone was talking about the heirloom ring Tori is wearing."

"I'll be a son-of-a-bitch! I never thought Tori and Clay would actually get hitched. I figured the judge had other plans for Clay."

"According to Loretta, it's going to be a big wedding, and the reception will be at the judge's home."

"There you go. A marriage made in heaven." An inexplicable feeling of urgency came over Justin. "She told you all this yet couldn't remember if Kat came to see her?"

"It took me more than an hour to pry this gem from her. She kept fading in and out." David leaned forward and rested his arms against the desk. "Know what I think?"

"I'm afraid to ask."

"Lola Rae hit it on the head. Despite the way Loretta treated Kat, the woman is her mother and she's close to death. Loretta might be confused, but I believe Kat dropped by." David let his words hang there for a few seconds. "This would definitely be the case if Kat was planning to leave forever."

If she'd been planning to leave, Justin thought, why hadn't she taken the gun with her? Redd nudged his way out from under the desk and went over to see Max. The puppy licked him and Redd jumped back. David chuckled, but Justin couldn't see humor in anything right now.

"Did you come up with anything from that list of license plate numbers your source gave you?"

"Not really. A lot of Louisiana plates. Several are registered to a car service that's a front for Drexel Sartiano."

"Figures. The casino is connected to the most powerful crime family in the area."

"Do you know Gary Don Willingham? He tends bar out at Moonin' N Coonin'."

Justin shook his head. "I don't know him, but I know that joint. Not a weekend goes by that we don't get a complaint that some guys are mooning passing motorists. Why?"

"He's Lola Rae's boyfriend. There was something about him…"

"Let's run him through the computer and see if he has a record." Justin opened the National Correctional Facilities database and typed in the man's name, then looked up at David. "Willingham did time in Arkansas for armed robbery. That was twelve years ago. Nothing since then. No local problems."

"I could be wrong," David admitted. "It was just a hunch."

JUSTIN HAD DINNER at the counter of the Gator Grill. He'd ordered his usual, chicken fried steak, but he barely ate two bites before asking for a to-go box. Redd would have a feast tonight.

He was in his pickup and nearly to the home he'd leased when the cell phone in his pocket pulsed. He pulled it out and saw the sheriff station's number on the caller ID screen. "Radner here."

"Sir," the night duty/dispatcher said. "A Mr. Hobbs called."

Cooter. The ornery cuss had called earlier in the day, too. "What does he want?"

"Wouldn't say. He has to talk to you in person. He doesn't trust the telephone."

Honest to God, some things never changed. The old geezer had always been secretive, paranoid. "Did it sound like it could wait 'til morning?"

The deputy hesitated a moment. "No, sir. It might have to do with that Wells woman. Mr. Hobbs asked if anyone else had claimed the reward."

"Okay, I'll swing by his place," he replied even though he seriously doubted Cooter had any relevant information.

Justin turned the pickup around and drove toward Shady Acres. The trip took him past Moonin' N Coonin'. He decided to stop. David Noyes was a perceptive, intelligent man. If he picked up strange vibes from Willingham, the guy might be worth investigating.

He drove into the parking lot. Two gray clapboard out-houses slouched in the beam of his headlights, one marked Bulls while the other said Heifers. Perfect. The clientele here would be rednecks right down to the mud on their cowboy boots. He left Redd locked up in a lot full of vehicles.

It was busy for a weeknight. The riverboat had put most roadside taverns out of business, but not this place. Justin figured they sold enough drugs on the side to keep the bar open as a front. When he had time, he was going to see what really went on at this place. He had no doubt this would be a point on the meth trail.

He walked in and saw a couple of guys playing pool on the far side of the room. They didn't notice him, but a hush fell over the rest of the group. A bluish haze hung in the air from the cigarette smoke. The joint reeked of tobacco, beer, and cheap hooch. He went straight to the bar even though the man behind it didn't look a bit like the mug shot of Willingham.

"I'm looking for Gary Don Willingham," he told the bald-ing man who was drying a glass with the dirtiest rag Justin had ever seen.

"He's off tonight."

"Where does he live?"

The bartender hitched his head to one side. "Trailer out yonder."

"Thanks." Justin turned to leave.

"He ain't there. He's with his girlfriend."

Justin left, deciding he'd check on the man later. Tracking down Lola Rae might take some time. He needed to see if Cooter had any valuable information first.

The drive to Shady Acres Trailer Village took longer than it should have. Justin had swung by Kat's place to see if she—by some miracle—had come home. Yeah, right. The studio was dark and there was no sign of her car. S'okay. What did he expect?

When he drove into the trailer park, he noticed most of the

lights were on in the rows of single-wides. The one where he'd
lived was dark. In the dim light coming from the neighbors,
the place appeared more forlorn than it had during the day.
He tried not to remember how cheery his mother had managed to make it look.

He parked in the back where Cooter lived in a trailer
pocked by thirty years of rust and corrosion. The television
was blaring and sounds of some reality show filled the night
air. From his pickup, Justin could see a TV screen that
dwarfed the small space. Cooter always had the biggest television he could fit into his trailer. He didn't spend a nickel on
anything else, but he had to have a big new TV set every eigh-
teen months.

"Hang in, boy." He petted Redd's nose. "I'll be right back."

The thunk of the pickup's door slamming brought Cooter
to his door. "Thass you, Justin? Took your dadgummed time."

Justin stopped a foot from where two planks on cinder
blocks led up to Cooter's trailer. "You have some information
about the Bitner case?"

Cooter put his index finger to his lips and shushed Justin.
He motioned for him to come inside. The fine hairs across the
back of Justin's neck prickled to attention. Never once—not
ever—were the tenants invited into Cooter's trailer. Justin
bounded up the planks, anticipating catching a case of terminal herpes just by crossing the threshold.

Well, I'll be a dawg. He'd expected the inside to be trashed,
but it wasn't. It was small and clean with a brand-new plasma
television. A well-worn Naugahyde recliner was positioned
in front of the set. The only other furniture visible from where
he stood was a tiny kitchen table with one chair.

"I don't want no one to hear what I'm sayin'. Next, they
be claimin' the reward."

Could Cooter actually know something? The man was so
agitated that Justin might have thought he was on something,

but past experience told him Cooter was actually excited. The only other time he acted like this was when he was expecting the delivery of his newest television.

"Okay, what do you know?"

"Not so fast. My reward—"

"Cooter, the bank is offering a reward for the person who provides information that leads to the arrest and conviction of Elmer Bitner's killer. You know how long trials take…."

The old man grunted. "A year at least."

"It's late. Did you drag me out here for nothing?"

"Quitcher sassin', boy. I seed that blue Toyota yer lookin' fer."

Any hope Justin had been harboring evaporated. Everybody and his mother had spotted the car. That many blue Toyotas in Twin Oaks. Who knew?

"This mornin' the car was parked near Dwayne Hill's pickup."

"What?"

The Hill family owned a big chunk of the unincorporated area not far from the casino. They were hollow people who didn't come into town much. They lived on the land that had been in their family since before the Civil War. The Hills claimed to be related to the Southern general, A.P. Hill. It might be a lie or just wishful thinking, but no one dared dispute the tough bastards.

Justin had been in classes with Dwayne Hill after the courts forced the folks in the hollows to send their children to school. They'd played football together, but they hadn't been friendly. Dwayne rarely talked to anyone. When he did, it was just before a fight. The kids had taken to calling him "Dwayniac."

Justin suspected Dwayne was much smarter than he looked or acted. His father, Throck Hill, had outsmarted everyone when farmers had given up on growing sugarcane and rice. Throck plunged ahead and planted soybeans, and it had paid off—big time. They'd made so much money that Dwayne refused to accept a football scholarship to LSU. Instead, he worked with his father.

Kat couldn't possibly know the Hills, could she? Maybe their paths had crossed in high school. They both had been loners with few friends. But how had they reconnected—and why?

"Early this morn, ya know, afore dawn, I followed a deer. Jeez-a-ree! I didn't know I was on Hill land. Leastways I didn't see any signs."

Justin wasn't buying this. The Hills were notorious for having their land posted every twenty feet. Not that they were opposed to hunting. They just didn't want anyone taking their game. If Cooter went after a deer, he must have been positive he could bag it and haul the carcass away before the Hills spotted him.

"The dogs started barkin' 'n spooked the deer. Whoo-ee! It took off like a shot. I hightailed it."

Justin bet Cooter had run as fast as his bandy legs would take him. No telling what the Hills would do if they caught anyone hunting on their land.

"Thass it. Thass when I seed the Toyoter."

Running for all he was worth, Cooter couldn't be relied upon as a credible witness. Still, Justin couldn't help thinking about two loners who just might have reconnected—somehow. The bank could have been their connection. Justin instantly dismissed the idea. The hollow folks—especially the Hills—never trusted banks. What money they had, they kept God-only-knew-where.

"I'll pay Throck a visit and check it out," he told Cooter.

"No can do. Throck's gone yonder."

Gone to glory meant you were heaven bound. *Gone yonder* meant gone to hell. Aw, shit. He would have to deal with Dwayniac. The sullen boy with a dirty look permanently imprinted on his face was now in charge of his own kingdom.

Common sense said to round up a few deputies before

marching onto Hill property. But no one had ever accused Justin Radner of having a lick of sense.

He had no doubt that the Hills would be armed to the teeth, but other than that he had no idea what to expect. He hustled out of Cooter's trailer, wondering if he had a death wish.

"Don't cha be forgettin' my reward."

"Can it. We're a long way from a reward."

CHAPTER TWENTY

JUSTIN CHOSE the direct approach to the largest house at the compound of wood frame homes on cinder blocks. He'd considered going around to the back to check on the Toyota, but he wasn't within a hundred yards of the complex when the dogs started baying and motion sensors flooded the yard with blinding light. Seconds later, a hulking shadow with a shotgun flung open the front door.

A gruff voice yelled, "Whoze out there?"

"Sheriff Radner."

There was no response. Justin opened the chain link fence's gate even though seven blue-tick hounds, fangs bared, were gathered, snarling on the other side.

"Stand down," the man called to the dogs as Justin strode through the gate. The hounds sat on either side of the flagstone path, still slavering, bodies twitching for his hide.

"Dwayne?" he asked, still unable to see the man because of the floodlights.

The figure stepped forward. "You're on private property."

Justin immediately recognized Dwayne Hill, although the guy had gained weight, his body now bulked-up but still muscular. Dwayne's face had filled out, too. Deep creases at the corners of his eyes and skin toasted brown and crispy like a campfire marshmallow said he spent his days in the fields.

"Want me to come back with a warrant and a dozen highway patrolmen?" Justin was bluffing. No judge would issue a warrant on Cooter's suspicious sighting.

"Better come in," he replied with a smile that seemed to darken his brown, almost black eyes. Just then, Justin remembered something about Dwayne—he'd always smiled at things that weren't funny. This and his combative personality made most kids in school avoid him.

Justin walked inside and was surprised by the pale yellow interior, tastefully furnished with a moss-green sofa and matching chairs. The wood floor had been buffed to a high shine and matched the handrail on the staircase leading to the second floor. The parlor opened up to a family room where a huge television was tuned into *West Coast Choppers*. A very pregnant woman waddled toward them from the family room. He recognized her but couldn't come up with a name.

"This here's Betty Jo," Dwayne said as he shelved the shotgun on the wall rack with a dozen other weapons. "'Spect you remember her."

Justin remembered Dwayne's cousin now. He'd had a couple of classes with her. "Hey, how are you?"

"Mighty fine." Betty Jo said, revealing tiny, even white teeth. She looked at Dwayne.

"G'wan. I'll be down here a spell."

Betty Jo mumbled good-night and went up the stairs, hiking her skirt as if she were wading through a stream. Dwayne motioned for Justin to have a seat on the sofa while he took a matching easy chair opposite him.

"Now what the hell are you lookin' for? You have no call to tear this place apart." Dwayne flashed another ill-timed smile. He picked up a tin from the glass coffee table between them, took a pinch of Copenhagen, and wedged the tobacco between his jawbone and cheek. "I've got three young'uns upstairs. You can see my wife's about to pop out another. I don't want her riled up."

Justin exhaled slowly, his eyes on the seascape that dominated the wall. He wondered if Dwayne had ever seen the ocean. Somehow he doubted it. Hollow people seldom ventured far from the backwoods.

"I don't have to search your home. I can rely on your word just the way I relied on you when we played ball."

This time Dwayne didn't smile. With his tongue, he switched the chaw to the other side of his mouth. And kept staring.

"An informant tells me there's a blue Toyota out behind your house."

"Yeah, so?"

Justin had expected shock or surprise or even a lame excuse but not Dwayne's casual reaction. He went rigid, every muscle tensed and his breath rattled against his ribs. "So? Haven't you heard about Elmer Bitner's murder two nights ago?"

Dwayne treated him to another off-beat grin and sucked on the wad of tobacco. "No. Don't get into town much. My brother Billy Dean gasses up the trucks and takes the gals shopping. Don't watch the news much. Just a bunch foreigners tryin' to kill our boys."

"The Toyota was spotted on the road to the riverboat where Bitner was shot." When Dwayne didn't comment, Justin asked, "How did you get the car?"

"I don't 'xactly have the car," he replied.

"Come on, Dwayne. Don't fuck with me. Is there a blue Toyota behind this house?"

Eyes gleaming savagely, Dwayne stared him down. After a moment's silence, he grinned and cocked his head to one side like a bird. "Car's behind Ma's house."

For a gut-cramping second, the room froze. Holy shit! Cooter had been right. The car was here. Kat must be around, too, or Dwayne knew where she was. His mind again scrambled to make the connection between them but came up empty except for the school connection. "There's a seven-state APB out on that car. Explain what you're doing with it, and where's the driver, Kat Wells?"

Dwayne threw his head back and laughed. An image came to Justin of Dwayne laughing after they'd lost a close game. He hadn't made any noise when he'd laughed. Still didn't.

Justin wondered if Dwayne was "a little skippy" as his mother used to say. He figured it came from too many cousins marrying each other. It had earned him the nickname Dwayniac, but Justin had the feeling it might be his way of keeping people at a distance. Whatever. It worked.

"Betty Jo and I were driving back from Jackson," Dwayne said, his voice slurred slightly from the wad of tobacco. "She gets these…cravings. Gotta have Cherry Garcia. The nearest place they sell the friggin' ice cream is the capital."

Get on with it. Justin couldn't believe the guy who rarely said two sentences was making a long story out of this. Justin tuned out the bit about the long line to get the ice cream, his mind on Kat.

He'd been missing Kat so much that it amazed him. Missing her tentative smile. Missing the way the breeze flirted with her hair. Missing the way her eyes held him. Missing her and hating himself for it.

He was going to find her. And then he'd have to haul her off to jail. He could do it, he assured himself. It was his job. His personal feelings didn't matter one damn bit.

"We ran into Billy Dean and Ma coming back from the Gator Grill. She fancies their chicken pot pies. They followed us back here. We hauled ass to get home before the ice cream melted. Know how much that stuff costs?"

Justin nodded as if he cared. "Ben & Jerry's is damn expensive."

"That's Yankees for you." Dwayne shrugged. "We come upon this car piddling along. A blue Jap car goin' real weirdlike."

"What time was that?"

"A little before eight-thirty. I know 'cause Betty Jo wanted to make sure the kids were in bed so'z she could watch some TV show."

"What happened?"

"The car fishtailed off the road into the bar ditch."

Justin mentally kicked himself. His deputy had checked area hospitals and doctors and ruled out an accident. He hadn't considered Kat could be in a private home. He'd been too quick to condemn. Too willing to believe she was a con who would never reform.

"I jumped out to help. So did Billy Dean."

"How bad was it?" Justin forced himself to keep his voice level even though a speedball of rage was shooting through him. What had he been thinking? Why hadn't he given her the benefit of a doubt?

"Not bad. She wasn't goin' that fast. She was wacky, though. Thought there was a bunch of us. She was yellin' 'n kickin' 'n shiverin' like it was the dead of winter."

This sounded like a concussion to him. "Had Kat hit her head?"

"Nope. Not a mark on her. The car had a bent fender where it plowed into the bank, was all. It still runs. Didn't take Billy Dean but two shakes to pull the whole shebang outta the bar ditch with the winch on his pickup. Ma drove it home. The woman rode with us, rantin' all the way."

You stupid shit, he silently cursed himself. His judgment had been so clouded by Kat's status as an ex-con that he'd assumed she'd run. He'd never considered the possibility something had happened to her.

"Where is Kat now?"

Dwayne studied him a moment, and Justin wondered if he sounded more personally involved than someone would expect the sheriff to be.

"Ma checked her. Said the gal was sick. That's why she was acting so…goofy."

"Where is she?"

"Ma's takin' care of her. She's better. 'Spect she can go home tomorry."

Justin nodded slowly. Most people would have taken Kat to old Doc Walther's twenty-four-hour clinic. A nurse was on duty every night. If someone was seriously injured, Doc lived in a cottage behind the clinic.

Hollow folks were different. They treated their own when they could. Dwayne's mother, Mavis, was well-known in these parts as a healer. Of course she would have taken care of Kat.

"I need to see Kat." Justin stood up.

"I'll ask Ma if it's okay."

Justin followed Dwayne out the back door. Light from a new moon shafted through the clouds. A whorl of June bugs danced around the light posts along the path. They walked over a swale toward a smaller home where a single lamp burned in the front window, the pack of dogs at their heels. Dwayne knocked softly and waited.

The door opened and a stout dumpling of a woman with silver hair hanging to her shoulders answered the door with a frown. She spotted Justin and her scowl deepened. "Who's he?"

"It's the sheriff, Ma. Remember Justin Radner? I played football with him."

"'Course I remember."

"He needs to see that gal we found."

She turned to Justin and trained her dark brown eyes on him. "What fer? She's sleepin'."

"She's wanted for questioning in a murder case," Justin responded, although he now thought Kat had an ironclad alibi.

Mavis stared at him in a way that sent a cold, liquid tingle down the back of his spine. After a long moment, she asked, "Whose murder?"

Justin explained but omitted that the crime had occurred after the Hills had come upon Kat.

Mavis gazed at him from between drawn brows. "When was this exactly?"

Smart woman. Not much got by her. No doubt she was the Ma Barker of this clan. Planting soybeans had probably been her idea.

Justin explained when Bitner's body had been found. Dwayne cut loose with one of his soundless laughs. Mavis stopped him with a look that would have felled a charging rhino.

"Couldna' been Kat. We picked her up at eight-thirty. She was fixin' to feel puny. Weak. Upchuckin'. We brought her back here." Mavis offered him a proud smile. "I cured her with one of my potions."

"Food poisoning," Dwayne told him. "Betty Jo heard the symptoms on TV."

Mavis harrumphed. "What does Betty Jo know? She's a Buford." Mavis turned to Justin. "Someone tried to poison the po' thing."

The softly spoken words rang in his head like a furious shout. Pequita Romero had been poisoned, too. He barged his way by Mavis into the small parlor where a marmalade cat was curled into a ball on the sofa. "I need to see her—now!"

Mavis stared pitchforks at him. "Your mother wouldn't cotton to you bein' uppity."

How did she know his mother? They must have talked years ago while in the stands watching their sons play football.

"Look, this is official business," he said with all the patience he could muster. "Two people have died already. Someone might have tried to kill Kat."

She stepped aside without uttering another word and gestured to a room nearby. Justin rushed into a small bedroom where a single lamp not much brighter than a night-light cast a mellow glow. A four-poster brass bed was centered in front of a fireplace that must be the room's only heat in the winter.

Justin paused in the doorway to allow his eyes to adjust. Ahead of him he saw a small figure dwarfed by the bed. Dark hair spread across a stark white pillow. A petite form, sleeping, encased in a quilted comforter.

Kat.

Thank you, God.

He heaved a sigh of relief and stepped forward. The scent of pine mixed with lavender greeted him. The light flickered, and he realized it was a pillar candle lighting the room, not a lamp.

In the dim light Kat seemed unusually pale. The vision shouldn't have shaken him so much, yet it did. He knew she'd been in a crash—but a minor one. Could Mavis be right about the poison?

"Is she okay?" he whispered to Mavis.

"She's just weak and needs her rest. Don't you be long." Mavis turned and left the room.

Walking softly across the wooden floor, Justin ventured closer. He stood over Kat for a moment, then lowered himself to his knees on the rag rug beside the bed. "I'm sorry, babe," he whispered. "I was thinking…bad things. You've done nothing wrong since I met you."

He gently brushed a wisp of hair off her forehead with his fingertips. "I'm crazy about you. That's why I was so upset and—" he stopped himself, not realizing the truth until this moment "—hurt. I'll make it up to you." He lightly kissed her cheek. "I promise."

CHAPTER TWENTY-ONE

TORI THANKED HEAVEN for the trees protecting the dais from the tyrannical sun scalding the town square. It was barely ten o'clock, but spring seemed to have passed over Twin Oaks in favor of summer. The navy linen suit she was wearing felt hot and itchy. Rob Everett's idea. Judge Kincaid's "Call me Dad" media advisor insisted black, navy, and gray were the only appropriate colors for the campaign circuit.

"Don't worry," the judge had assured Tori and the equally mortified May Ellen. "I'll treat you to new wardrobes in Atlanta."

Tori had gamely agreed, but May Ellen had balked, insisting her "Southern" clothes were just fine for a Mississippi campaign. Rob had patiently explained the crime angle would give the judge national exposure, priming him for who-knew-what in the future.

Tori hated dark colors, preferring peach, lavender, and yellow, but Rob insisted her blond hair and delicate features were better highlighted by darker, more fashionable shades. Conservative, Rob had told her, was the operative word. Her wardrobe was too eye-catching. She took that to mean people would be looking at her—not the judge.

Despite his flattering words, Tori knew manipulation when exposed to it. Rob Everett needed to control the situation at all times. This morning the judge was to give his first statewide press conference. Last evening she'd joined the family at Oakhurst. Rob had rehearsed and rehearsed and rehearsed them. The judge was to speak out on violence in America and the necessity to keep convicts in jail for as long as possible. Tori was supposed to give a short, teary speech about how crime can touch every family, ruin lives.

The speech irritated her. It sounded canned. She knew the message they wanted to impart. She could do much better on her own. When her moment to shine came, she was giving the speech she'd spent the wee hours of the night practicing in front of the mirror.

Tori looked out over the crowd of reporters. Thanks to Rob, television crews from Jackson, New Orleans, Memphis, and Atlanta were covering the press conference. He thought with luck some of the footage might be shown on national television. Scores of print media people were huddled in the dappled shade beyond the dais. Clay gave her a reassuring smile, and Tori returned it, but she couldn't help feeling annoyed. Truth to tell, she was here because the judge wanted to use her.

And Clay allowed it.

To Tori's way of thinking, Clay should have insisted that he loved Tori and married her long ago. Where would she be if the judge hadn't seen Elmer Bitner's death as an opportunity?

EMPOWERMENT. A great concept. Fucking A! Power was everything. You either had it or you didn't.

He was edgy, jazzed up. Things were changing. The stakes were higher now, much, much higher.

He'd been awake for over forty-eight hours. He should be exhausted, but the opposite was true. He was fully awake, energized. Most days he lived his life in shades of gray. Nothing interesting happened. But now that things were changing, his world was alive with vibrant color.

Power was intoxicating. He would be the first to admit it.

He'd been a young boy when this fact first presented itself, and he'd capitalized on the knowledge ever since. He was becoming more powerful with each passing day.

Just one loose end gave him a ping of uncertainty. Where was Kat Wells? They hadn't counted on her disappearance. They'd mulled the problem over many times already. Luck—as always—was with him. Having her run played into his hand. She looked guilty as hell.

Still, she was out there somewhere. A wild card. He hated wild cards unless he had one up his sleeve.

DAVID STOOD IN THE TOWN SQUARE with Max at his side in the shadow of a pecan tree. He had the small notebook he always carried in the pocket of his suit. Judge Kincaid was to announce his candidacy for senator. It was a bit premature, as Senator Foster hadn't yet said he was retiring, but everyone knew this was his last term.

David figured the judge wanted to get a head start. After all, the man was well-known in the county and a familiar person in the Delta area, but the rest of the state had never heard of Turner Kincaid. The judge had been wise to hire Rob Everett. The scumball was as wily as they came but he'd successfully steered numerous campaigns. David expected the judge to sling enough political bullshit to bury Twin Oaks.

A catspaw of wind brought the sweet scent of honeysuckle through the hot, moist air. Somehow it reminded David of Kat. He bent down to give Max a pat and thought about her. This was the third day since she'd disappeared. He kept imagining her breezing through the *Trib*'s door the way she had in the short time he'd known her. He'd been convinced she was innocent—even though it defied logic.

"There's no fool like an old fool," he muttered under his breath. Kat was long gone. Whatever she'd done…well, was done.

He forced himself to concentrate on the crowd gathered in the square. The whole town had turned out. It wasn't often a favorite son announced he was running for such an important office. Even Gary Don Willingham was here, a woman at his side. It wasn't Lola Rae. He scanned the square but didn't see either Lola Rae or Maria.

His gaze came back to Gary Don. The woman next to him leaned close and whispered in his ear. As she did, she slipped something into his pocket. They turned and slithered through the crowd until David lost sight of them.

The intangible vibes David had picked up on when he'd first met the man must be correct. Willingham was up to something. The man was taking or dealing drugs. Probably crystal meth. He reminded himself to mention what he'd seen to Justin.

David checked the gathering again and spotted Justin standing alone across the small square. He considered joining him, but it was too crowded to move. Justin had called late last night after David had gone to bed and switched off his answering machine. He saw Justin pull his cell phone out of his pocket and answer it.

Mayor Peebles mounted the platform. Behind him trooped Reverend Applegate, Filpo Johnson, and two other men David didn't know. Interesting, but not unexpected. To carry this state Judge Kincaid would need the Christian right and the African-American vote. Who better to have at his side than a former NFL star and a minister?

Rob Everett tapped on the mike, testing the audio system, then he nodded to Mayor Peebles. Apparently the mayor would introduce the judge. Off to David's left a man fanning himself with a magazine caught his attention. Buck Mason. Mason did nothing to hide his disgust. Obviously, Buck wasn't enthusiastic about his friend's campaign, or he resented the mayor introducing the judge. David couldn't tell which, but the pharmacist was an odd man.

He'd given a fortune to Waycross Christian University. Several buildings there were dedicated to his daughter, Verity Anne Mason. Despite his generosity to the school, Buck Mason never gave a nickel to any local charities. He wore his isolation like a shield and refused to join Kiwanis or the other civic organizations, calling them a waste of time.

Buck had a body like a tombstone. The guy was less than ten years younger than David, but he was still in superior shape. Of course, Buck didn't have to contend with four crushed—now fused—vertebrae.

Why hadn't he remarried? David considered Buck to be the type of man who would attract women. He wasn't movie star handsome, but he was tall and well-built-and he had money to go with a family name.

David leaned over and stroked Max's silky ears, encouraging the pup to keep behaving. He half listened to the mayor's introduction of Judge Kincaid. The PA system amplified his words with a slight ring. Rob Everett walked forward and adjusted the speaker.

The mayor resumed his introduction. Same old, same old. The judge stepped up to the mike with a smile worthy of a televangelist. After thanking everyone for coming and fawning over the men on the dais, the judge launched into what was obviously a very well-rehearsed speech delivered in his authoritative courtroom voice. No doubt he would go far in politics.

"Many of you have called upon me to run for office for some time." A concerned, reflective smile followed this announcement. "I've considered it, but I've been reluctant to leave Twin Oaks."

That was a crock. David knew the judge spent half his time in Jackson. The capital was far more interesting than a small town like this.

"A family tragedy, a community loss has forced me to reconsider." He gazed fondly at Tori for a moment and she smiled shyly at him. David immediately saw Rob's orchestration of this touching scene. "My son's fiancée, Tori Wells, is the daughter I never had. She's had the misfortune to have a sister—half sister, actually—who was convicted of a crime."

Bastard! David saw the scheme clearly now. Kincaid was going to spin it so he seemed personally involved.

"Kaitlin Wells was released...prematurely on a work furlough. I don't condone this practice. Convicts should receive the maximum sentence and be forced to serve every day."

A low buzz rippled through the crowd. David couldn't detect any words, but an excited hum filled the air. David realized crime was a hot button. With two recent murders in the normally peaceful town, people were on edge.

"After Kaitlin Wells arrived here, our good friend and neighbor Elmer Bitner was murdered. The Highway Patrol reported Kaitlin's car near the scene shortly before Elmer's body was discovered."

So much for innocent until proven guilty, David thought as the judge droned on about criminals being kept in prison and how a crime like this hurt innocent family members like Tori. The judge cast a sympathetic glance at Tori. Kat's sister deserved an Emmy. She appeared to be on the verge of tears like a soap queen.

"This murdering woman has yet to be apprehended. We're all concerned that someone else may die before she's sent back to jail where she belongs."

Tori nodded, her expression profoundly troubled. His instinct told him that Tori Wells didn't give a hoot about Kat. He thought about how this would play on the news. Like carrion-eaters, the media would devour Kat. She didn't stand a chance.

"Situations like this devastate families. They unnecessarily put God-fearing communities at risk. That's why I've—"

"Ask the sheriff why he hasn't found Kat Wells," shouted Buck Mason.

For a second the judge looked like a poleaxed grizzly, but he quickly recovered. "That's a good question. A state trooper reported—"

"We know that," Buck yelled. "Why hasn't she been arrested?"

Judge Kincaid sent Rob Everett a furtive look. Clearly, this wasn't part of the script. "I see Sheriff Radner over there," the judge said, sarcasm in every syllable. "Maybe he would like to explain to the good folks of Twin Oaks why there hasn't been an arrest in this case."

The television cameras swung toward Justin. David clicked his pen, ready to write. He pitied Justin. This was going to be like dogpaddling in a riptide. Not bringing in the prime suspect by now could cost him the job as sheriff.

Justin strode up to the podium with an easy, confident gait. He might have been walking up to the checkout at the mini-mart. The men on the dais scuttled aside to make room for him. David noted that none of them looked the sheriff in the eye except Filpo, who nodded a greeting.

"Sheriff," the judge demanded the second Justin was on the dais, "why haven't you arrested Kaitlin Wells?"

Justin stared at the judge as if explaining this to Kincaid would be as futile as pitching tax exempt bonds to the homeless. "This is America. You're innocent until proven guilty—"

"She's guilty," shouted Buck Mason. "Just bring her in and make her confess."

A rumble of agreement passed through the crowd. An edgy pause, then total silence. David could hear Max panting but no one was saying a word. Then Justin glared at Buck in a way that made the crowd collectively gasp.

"Can't do that, Buck," Justin replied smoothly. "Kat Wells has an ironclad alibi. She was in a minor accident just after the trooper saw her. Dwayne and Billy Dean Hill pulled her car out of a ditch and took her home. Mavis Hill's been taking care of her."

"I knew she was innocent," David heard himself shout.

The mayor had a startled expression as if he'd just been caught in bed with his best friend's wife. Filpo Johnson was beaming.

"I don't believe it," snarled the judge.

"Suh." *Sir.* The deep-fried Southern voice boomed from the back of the crowd. "You doubtin' my word?"

Dwayne Hill stepped forward, his hands on his hips. A hulking man well over six feet, Dwayne had close-cropped brown hair. An odd smile creased his bronzed face. Beside him stood a smaller version of the big man. Billy Dean, guessed David.

"O-of course not," the judge said with all the enthusiasm of a man receiving the last rites.

CHAPTER TWENTY-TWO

TORI SAT in the living room at Oakhurst, listening to Rob Everett discuss what had gone wrong at the news conference. "Never give up the spotlight. Never. You should have—"

Tori tuned out. For once May Ellen had the best idea. She'd pleaded a migraine from all the beastly heat and had gone upstairs. No doubt she planned to pop a few pills and have a swig of gin.

Of all the damned luck! Kat was still around. Was there no getting rid of her? Bad enough that her presence was making Mother's condition worse. Now she'd stolen the spotlight from Tori. She could have been on television. Imagine what that would have done for her real estate career.

But no. Kat was here to stay. Something had to be done about it, but Tori didn't have a plan unless one of Clay's contacts at the casino could help to scare her off.

She glanced over at the judge, who was still listening to Rob. Every time the man mentioned Justin, the judge turned the color of an eggplant, the way he had when Justin had announced Kat's alibi. Tori thought Rob was exaggerating the scope of the catastrophe so he could make money. But who knew? Maybe the consultant was right. This fiasco could ruin the judge's election hopes.

That would be okay with Tori. This had been her first real taste of politics, and it had been much worse than she'd anticipated. All that rehearsing for what? To be upstaged by backwoods hicks?

The Hills were hollow folk, worse than white trash, but they'd made a lot of money on stupid soybeans. And they could trace their ancestors back to some long-forgotten Civil War general. If that wasn't enough, Mavis Hill was a respected healer. Her horehound soup was famous for curing colds. God only knew what she used but she had a reputation in the Delta for helping infertile couples. Kat couldn't have come up with a better alibi had she tried.

"I WANT THE WHOLE STORY," David demanded. "I know you left a message last night, but you should have called this thing in this morning."

He was with Justin at his office in the *Trib* building, where they'd come after Justin astonished everyone at the press conference and made a fool of the judge. Max was snuggled up under the desk, seemingly bored by the monumental turn of events. Justin appeared calm, almost relaxed, but David knew better. There was a tension to his shoulders, a lethal glint in his eyes as he lounged in the chair across from David.

"I was real busy this morning. Do you know what it takes to cancel a seven-state APB and persuade the authorities not to revoke Kat's furlough?"

David nodded, silently conceding that contacting him couldn't have been a top priority.

"Want to know details—off the record?"

Under his breath, David muttered a curse. Off the record did not sell papers, but in this case, sales didn't matter. Kat hadn't killed Elmer Bitner. He'd known all along that she was innocent. He wanted to help her any way possible. "Okay. Off the record."

"Mavis Hill believes Kat was poisoned. That's why she had an accident. She became disoriented and drove into a bar ditch. Apparently Kat was hallucinating. She thought a group of men were after her, but Mavis swears it was only Dwayne and Billy Dean."

Poisoned? The word ricocheted through David's brain. When he'd heard Justin tell the crowd Kat had been in an accident, he'd assumed it had been a simple car crash. He'd been concerned, but nothing like this. He felt as if a hand had closed around his throat, choking the life out of him, and he was powerless to do anything about it.

He finally managed to croak out two words. "Who? How?"

"Good question. Kat doesn't remember anything."

"Pequita Romero was also poisoned. Could it be—"

"It's not fluoroacetate. That works too quickly," Justin replied. "Mavis suspects nightshade."

David rifled his brain for a moment to come up with the type of plant Justin was talking about. "Belladonna? Does it grow around here?"

"Could you get on the computer and check?" Justin shifted in his seat. "Mavis thinks it comes from Asia but can be grown here. According to her, a little bit can cause hallucinations and amnesia."

David tapped the keys on his computer to log onto Info-National, the special search engine newspapers paid to use. He typed in the word *belladonna*. In seconds the screen filled with lines and lines of information.

"It can be grown here, and it causes selective amnesia. She may remember bits and pieces of her experiences, but not everything. Hallucinations are common, apparently."

"Does it say anything about how long after ingesting it the substance kicks in?"

David scrolled through the rest of the text. "Interesting. Belladonna was taken by women in the Renaissance to dilate their pupils and give them a wide-eyed and beautiful appearance."

"How long after taking it does belladonna affect the person?" Justin repeated impatiently.

David quickly skimmed the material. "An hour to several days, depending on the part of the plant ingested. The berries and the roots are more potent than the leaves or stalks."

"Great. So we have no idea of where or when Kat was given belladonna." Justin gazed out the window for a moment. "Maybe where or when doesn't matter. What we need to know is why."

"And why was Bitner murdered?"

"This comes down to motive." Justin gave him a slow nod with an expression that was wise beyond his years. "I think I have a motive for the bank robbery. Totally off the record."

Waiting for his explanation was like holding a live grenade. "Off the record."

"Bank examiners were coming to inspect Mercury's records. A robbery was staged so the inspection would be put off for weeks. It would give them time to cook the books."

Sometimes David felt like a brittle old man past his prime. Why hadn't he seen this? He hadn't known about the inspection—it hadn't been reported in the *Trib*—but he should have guessed.

"I understand," David said slowly. "Kat was a foil for money laundering, bank fraud…who knows? But why try to frame Kat for Bitner's death?"

"She would be a natural suspect, diverting suspicion from the real killer." Justin's lips edged into a bitter smile. "I think someone else slipped her poison and fouled up the plan."

"That would mean she has more than one enemy."

"Bull's-eye."

"Seems far-fetched."

"Bitner knew something and was about to spill the beans."

"The answer is at the bank."

KAT GAZED OUT the window of Justin's pickup. They were well down the road from the Hills' compound. Trees skimmed past in a blur of green. A cold numbness permeated her and settled in her bones. She seemed detached from her body, as if she were observing all this from a distance.

It must be some type of psychic shock, a reaction to knowing someone had deliberately tried to kill her. She'd counted on being relatively safe, she'd counted on seeing her enemy charging at her. She'd been wrong and now she couldn't handle it.

After being told someone had tried to poison her, Kat felt a column of light rise up from somewhere inside her, and she left her physical being behind. Now she watched from afar. The weight of the knowledge of her situation was too crushing to deal with right now. It was easier, more comforting to be absent from herself.

She saw Justin's lips moving. He was talking but the words weren't coming through. She didn't want to hear them. He touched her arm, his fingers brushing over her skin, then gently clamping down. All she felt was a slight warmth.

"Kat? Kat, are you okay?"

His words echoed through the tunnel in her mind and vanished into blackness. Her brain stubbornly refused to process the facts and allow her to deal with reality. He frowned, pulled the pickup to the side of the road, and stopped.

"Kat? Should I take you to the hospital in Jackson?"

The word *hospital* detonated on impact and forced her to respond. "No," she whispered in a strange voice that didn't sound a bit like hers. "Mavis says I'll be fine in a day or two."

His commanding blue eyes met hers and she experienced a familiar lighthearted squeeze in her chest. *You're attracted to him,* some distant part of her brain told her. Then she drifted off to Neverland again.

Justin pulled the pickup back onto the road. "I'm taking you to my house. You'll be safer there."

Safe? It took several seconds for the word to register. Would she ever feel safe again? Spasms hit her stomach, then tightened into a cold knot of fear. She squeezed her eyes shut, battling the onslaught of terrifying memories. Her arrest. Jail. The trial. Prison.

She hadn't been *safe* in years. Nothing, it seemed, could keep her out of harm's way. Safety was merely an illusion.

When she'd first come home from prison, there had been so little left of her old self that she felt like a stranger. But a stronger person. Now she was back to square one. A victim again.

He drove up to a beige ranch house with dark brown trim. The neglected yard was overgrown, and the grass hadn't seen a lawn mower in months. She spotted Redd in the fenced yard under a big leafy tree that shaded half the lawn.

"David's going to bring your things here." He turned off the ignition in front of a large detached garage that apparently had a shop in the back. The pickup coughed twice and shuddered while the engine shut down.

"Don't move," he told her. "I'll help you get out." He opened the pickup door and extended his strong arms.

It seemed as if someone else—not her—slid out of the pickup into his arms. He pulled her against his powerful chest. She held onto him, concentrating on drawing each unsteady breath.

"It's going to be all right." He held her close, and one hand gently massaged the back of her neck, fingers moving up and down in a slow, caressing path.

It was a highly charged embrace, she realized, but it wasn't sexual. It was a life-affirming bear hug, something a couple would share after escaping a plane crash. She buried her nose in the crook of his shoulder and let his masculine scent fill her lungs. Burrowing against him, she permitted herself to enjoy the solid security of his body pressed against hers. Tears pricked at the backs of her eyelids.

He kissed her temple and whispered, "I was damn worried about you. I don't know what I would have done if you'd died."

His words seemed to be coming from far, far away. Lost in thought, it took a moment to comprehend what he'd told her. She realized she'd heard how much he cared for her in his voice. Cautiously she lifted her face from his shoulder and looked at him. He had amazing eyes. So insightful, seeing right through to her soul. Then he smiled and she was truly lost.

Someone cared about her, and knowing it made her feel a little less forlorn. When was the last time she'd mattered to someone? Years ago before her father had died. The memory unleashed a pent-up sob, and she began to shake.

"It's okay to be upset," he said in a husky tone that made her hold him more tightly. "You've been through a lot."

At last her sobs wrenched her completely out of Neverland and into the present. Someone had tried to kill her. Panic mushroomed inside her, cutting off her breath and becoming pure terror. What was she going to do?

She couldn't quite come to terms with her own weakness. She despised herself for allowing fear to immobilize her. She recognized her reaction for what it was—a throwback to those terror-filled days in prison. Hadn't that trip through hell made her stronger than this?

It had. Of course it had. So why was she cowering in a man's arms? She jerked away from Justin, disgusted with herself. Her surge of anger gave her the stamina she needed, a source of inner strength that replaced her lethargy. Fear evaporated in a dizzy rush, morphing into a fury beyond anything she'd ever experienced.

"I'm okay now." Her voice had an edge to it.

"Good," Justin replied, but he looked skeptical. He kept his arm around her while he slowly walked her toward the house. She was so exhausted she could hardly stand. It was like heading into a gale force wind, yet with every step she became a little stronger mentally. He unlocked the front door and ushered her into a living room furnished with a maroon paisley sofa and two mismatched easy chairs. Moving boxes lined the walls.

"It came furnished except for a television," he explained. "I haven't had time to buy one."

"It's okay. I'd rather read than watch TV."

"Want something to eat?"

Kat shook her head. Her stomach still felt queasy. She was afraid she'd embarrass herself by throwing up again. She'd been sick at least a dozen times while Mavis had been caring for her. The older woman had been a total sweetheart, telling Kat that throwing up was good. It was her body's way of healing itself. She'd kept down the broth Mavis had given her last night and this morning, but the ride had upset her stomach.

"I'd feel better if you let Redd in," she said with an attempt at a smile.

"You got it!"

While he went to get the dog, Kat quickly inspected the house. On wobbly legs she discovered there were three bedrooms and one bathroom. A good-sized kitchen was off the living room. Unpacked boxes were everywhere.

In the back of her mind, she wondered who was after her and what she could do to save herself. The work furlough. She'd been sent here for a reason. She had never been told exactly why she was here, but the authorities knew. She had to contact Special Agent Wilson.

She settled herself in one of the easy chairs. A second later the door opened and Redd bounded into the room.

"Hey, boy." She held out her hand. "How are you?"

Redd hesitated, glanced over his shoulder at Justin, then

approached her. He sniffed her fingers before moving close enough to allow her to pet him.

"Good boy, good boy," she crooned, running her hand over his head. She looked up at Justin. "His hair is beginning to grow back."

"Yes. He'll be downright handsome when his coat comes in."

Petting the dog gave her a way to avoid more physical contact with Justin. Kat longed to touch him, to be secure in his arms. Oh, Lordy, was she a mess. She knew she had to depend on herself. "Which bedroom should I use?"

"The second one down the hall." He gestured toward the short corridor off the living room. "Sorry about the atrocious green spread in there."

"It doesn't matter," she assured him.

He moved closer, his expression concerned. "I've got to run into the station. There's food in the fridge. Yogurt, eggs, soup. Stuff Mavis said you can eat."

He'd gotten special food for her. He'd arranged his schedule so that he could bring her home. He cared. Tears filled her eyes as she realized this, but she managed to blink them away. Prison had taught her the futility of tears. "How can I thank you?"

He bent over and kissed her forehead. "No thanks are necessary. Just stay alive."

Kat listened while he gave her instructions on locking the door, and he told her there was a gun in the nightstand in her room. He assumed she knew how to use a gun. Most people in the area had several guns, but Kat's father had never owned a gun. Unlike most men in Twin Oaks, her father hadn't believed in hunting. Kat decided to tell Justin when he returned.

"You won't be alone long. David's on his way with your things. Don't open the door for anyone but him."

The minute Justin left, Kat rummaged through her purse and found the cell phone. It had been too long without a charge and was dead. She decided to use Justin's phone. He might check the numbers called, but she supposed he would understand she had to contact her handler.

Special Agent Wilson answered on the first ring. Kat had him call her back to avoid running up Justin's bill.

"Where are you?" he asked when he called several seconds later.

Kat hesitated. She didn't want to admit she was with Justin, but she didn't have a choice. He was bound to find out.

"I'm staying with Justin Radner."

He was silent for a moment before asking, "Do you think that's a good idea?"

"Yes. Someone tried to poison me."

"I know all about it. Remember, I have an undercover agent working there. The last time you called you told me Elmer Bitner had asked you to meet him out by the casino."

"I did?"

How could she have forgotten something so important? Bitner had been her nemesis. His testimony had sent her to jail. Justin had told her Elmer had been murdered and how her car had been sighted by the Highway Patrol. The accident had saved her from being framed for murder.

Her mind had tried to process the situation. She wasn't glad Elmer was dead—exactly—but she couldn't help feeling he might have gotten what he deserved. He liked everyone to think he was a Christian of the first order, but he hadn't hesitated to frame her. Who knew what else he might have done?

"You told me you were meeting Bitner, and I said I would have my undercover operative in the area in case you needed help."

"I did? I don't...recall—"

"Small wonder. I contacted our experts at FBI headquarters. Belladonna triggers amnesia and hallucinations. From what I understand, it isn't like other drugs when you realize you're hallucinating. Belladonna has people believing they actually experienced the event. They don't realize it's an illusion."

She remembered cars—lots of them—chasing her, but Mavis insisted it was just two cars. They hadn't been after her. They'd merely been going home. Her mind kept telling her otherwise.

"Even more interesting," he said, "the drug can erase memories from several hours before it was ingested."

"You mean, it might have been slipped to me at lunch, and I wouldn't recall incidents from that morning?"

"Exactly."

How strange, she thought. Had someone been trying to erase her memory or had it been a murder attempt? It was hard to believe an ugly duckling with no friends could attract such determined enemies. Something else had to be going on.

"Did someone try to kill me because of your investigation?" she asked, unable to keep the bitterness out of her voice.

"No. Your problem doesn't appear to be related to our investigation."

"But you're not positive."

"Ninety-nine percent sure."

Kat released an exasperated sigh. "Any ideas who might want me dead?"

"No. With luck Radner will be able to track it down."

Kat wasn't trusting luck. She needed to save herself.

CHAPTER TWENTY-THREE

KAT GAZED at David Noyes across Justin's kitchen table and tried without much luck to swallow a little of the soup he'd brought her from the No Latte Café. Max and Redd were tussling over a doggie toy nearby.

"Delicious," she told him, although her taste buds seemed to be dead. All she could feel was the soup's heat.

"What's the last thing you remember before the accident?" he asked.

She'd already told him about feeling funny, then imagining a pack of cars following her. How many times could she go over this?

"I was at my desk doing rewrites."

His brows drew into a deeply concerned frown. "That was the day before your accident."

"I know." She put down her spoon. "I went over this with Justin and Mavis. Except for the accident, I can't recall anything else about that day—no matter how hard I try."

He offered her a sympathetic smile. "I've been able to trace some of your activities before the accident. Elmer Bitner called the *Trib,* and Connie said he asked to speak to you."

Again a rising tide of disbelief flooded her. She would have sworn that she couldn't possibly have forgotten a call from Elmer Bitner, but obviously she had. She knew the poison caused the memory lapse, but it still seemed inconceivable. While she'd been in prison, she'd mentally told off Elmer thousands of times for being a lying skank. On his knees he'd begged her forgiveness. Of course, it had only been a day-dream, but still, the man was so firmly embedded in her mind that she couldn't imagine forgetting his call.

"Any idea why Bitner would want to meet with you?"

Kat shook her head. She had the lurking suspicion it might have something to do with the undercover operation, but she couldn't tell David about it. He studied her intently for a moment, and she wondered if he suspected she was withholding information.

"You stopped in to see Lola Rae around dinner time. You told Maria that you were going to visit your mother."

Her throat seemed to close up. It was a moment before she could reply, "I did?"

David hesitated before adding, "Well, that's what Maria claims, but Lola Rae didn't hear that part of the conversation. Apparently she was on the telephone at the time."

"It's difficult to believe I could have seen my mother and not remember. But Maria wouldn't lie. Why would she?"

"Maria knew Pequita. It's possible she's mixed up in the meth deal."

"Maria?" Kat responded, her voice charged with anguish. She sighed wearily. "I don't believe it. She's too innocent to be involved in illegal activity."

"Can you be sure? You don't speak enough Spanish to re-ally know the woman, do you?"

She slowly admitted, "I guess not."

He regarded her with a searching look. "I spoke with your mother. Her mind is fuzzy from the morphine. She didn't seem to remember a recent visit, yet she wasn't positive."

Kat thought about her mother and tried to recall her face, but nothing came up on the screen in her mind. Instead, a dark, ominous impression of a stern woman who disliked Kat took over her brain. Why couldn't she see her mother's face?

Your mother is close to death.

How did she know? Of course, Tori had said their mother was terminal, but an inner voice was saying death was closer than Tori had indicated. She examined her feelings, wondering if she *had* seen her mother. The memory might have been erased by the drug, but in some remote part of her brain *something* had registered.

"I have a feeling—not a memory—just a feeling I was with my mother," Kat confessed to David.

"What makes you think so?"

She explained that she knew more about her mother's condition than Tori had told her. She thought he might find her strange for relying on a vague feeling but if he did, David's face didn't reveal it.

"If you visited your mother, would you have eaten anything?"

"I doubt it. My mother rarely baked. Now that she's so ill, I guess her nurses are preparing meals." She considered his question before adding, "She used to make very sweet lemonade."

"Did she garden?"

Several beats of silence passed before his words sank in; Kat could see where David was going with this. "Yes, she grew roses. She made extra money by selling them to the local florist. I'm sure she hasn't been out in the small garden behind her condo in a year—or longer." An ache lodged deep inside her chest, making it painful to draw a breath. In a low voice, taut with emotion, she told him, "I didn't get along that well with my mother, but she would never try to kill me."

David nodded, but it was impossible to tell what he was thinking. He gestured for her to eat more soup. She forced down a little more, her mind on the imminent death of her mother.

David surprised her by asking, "Have you met Gary Don Willingham?"

She still couldn't bring up her mother's image, but she instantly recalled the redneck bartender Lola Rae was crazy about. "Just once. Why?"

"What was your impression?"

"He's not good enough for Lola Rae. I have no idea what she sees in him. Why?"

He told her about his suspicions. He relied on his instincts, too. No wonder he didn't find her intuitive feelings outrageous. She gazed at him for a moment, realizing he reminded her of her father. David didn't look like her father, but he had a way of listening, a way of concentrating on a person that had characterized her father.

"You think Gary Don might be dealing meth?" she asked.

"It's possible. Moonin' N Coonin' is notorious for being a place to buy drugs. As a bartender, he has to know what's going on out there. I'm betting he's involved."

She couldn't help recalling how eagerly Lola Rae had welcomed Kat. She'd been expecting a much cooler response. Now she wondered about the hair stylist's motives. Had it been an act?

It crushed something inside her to be suspicious of so many people. But what choice did she have? Someone had slipped her poison. She didn't suspect her mother, but there were many people who'd had the opportunity. Lola Rae was one of them. Come to think of it, so was Maria. She was always appearing uninvited with tamales or enchiladas. They could have been laced with belladonna. It was even possible she'd eaten something poisonous at the *Trib.* The break room was loaded with homemade goodies, and David brought in food when they worked late.

DARKNESS HAD FALLEN and Kat was sitting in one of the easy chairs in Justin's living room, Redd at her feet. David had insisted she take a nap after lunch. He'd stayed until Justin returned. She'd awakened to find Justin banging around the kitchen. He'd given her raspberry Jell-O and a tiny piece of chicken. Her stomach warned her not to eat but after all he'd done, she forced herself. She was weak and the best way to regain her strength was food.

Justin had refused to let her help him clean up, and she'd gone into the living room to read. Her mind kept drifting to her predicament. Who would want to frame her? Who wanted her dead? Maybe she was supposed to meet Elmer, then keel over. That scenario didn't really play. Timing her reaction with belladonna would have been impossible.

After Justin had finished in the kitchen, he'd announced he needed a shower. He'd disappeared into the bathroom just visible down the short hallway. She tried to concentrate on her book, but hearing the running water brought up images of Justin naked, the shower spray sluicing down his powerful body. You have more pressing things on your mind, she told herself. Her brain refused to listen. Lordy, wasn't he a hunk? She could only imagine what he looked like nude.

Get over it!

Her sole experience with a naked man had been years ago when she'd first gone to work at the bank. Every week a man from Jackson delivered boxes of deposit slips and other paper supplies to the bank. They'd gone out for several months when she'd agreed to go back to Corbin Gutcheon's motel. They'd had sex that still made her cheeks hot when she recalled the awkward situation. Immediately, she'd known she'd made a mistake. Corbin had asked her out many times after that, but she never went.

Kat heard the water shut off. She tugged down the hem of the board shorts she was wearing and adjusted the wrinkled blouse she'd pulled out of her things, when David had brought them over. She was a little self-conscious about not wearing a bra, but she'd been too exhausted to rummage though her clothes to find one.

With a sidelong look, she caught a glimpse of Justin as he emerged from the bathroom. His wet hair stood up in glossy black spikes. She quickly averted her eyes, but she couldn't help noticing his great shoulders, broad and muscular. Tufts of dark hair arrowed downward and disappeared under the towel knotted around his waist. That didn't stop her from appreciating his powerful thighs and long, lean legs.

Don't go there, she warned herself, realizing her body was flushed with warmth. She had no business being around Justin. She should have asked David to take her home with him. Surely, she would have been just as safe there.

A few minutes later, Justin emerged barefoot from the bedroom, wearing cargo shorts and a black Miami Heat T-shirt that couldn't possibly survive one more washing. She'd only gotten a quick peek at his chest before, but the well-worn cotton emphasized every masculine line and contour. Her gaze traveled up the lean, solid length of him until his eyes met hers and held. She struggled to bend half a smile while the pleasing scent of soap floated through the room.

Why did Justin have to be so heart-stoppingly gorgeous?

He went over to the window air conditioner in two long-legged strides that reminded her of what an exceptional athlete he'd been. "This swamp cooler isn't worth a damn."

She mustered a reply in what she hoped was a level voice. "The air is sort of cool."

He didn't respond while he tinkered with the dials. The swamp cooler wheezed and belched out a gust of colder air. He looked over his shoulder, and she admitted to herself that he had the most amazing blue eyes she'd ever seen.

He rose to his full height, saying, "Want some ice cream?"

"No, thanks. Today I've had more than I've eaten since…before."

"It's strawberry." A playful smile tilted the corners of his mouth upward, giving him a boyish, yet sexy expression. Obviously, David had told him that strawberry was her favorite.

"Okay, just a little." She used her thumb and forefinger to indicate a tiny bit.

"Feel up to helping me?"

"Sure." She put down the book and pushed to her bare feet, wobbling slightly on the cool wood floor.

He reached out and grabbed her arm to steady her. "Maybe you shouldn't—"

"I'm fine."

He slipped his strong arm around her waist, and pleasure radiated outward from every place his body touched hers. "It's a good idea for you to move around a little. In a hospital they always make you get up and walk as soon as possible."

She managed a nod, totally aware of his rock-hard body pressed against hers. The warmth of his powerful torso was reassuring. She told herself she could walk on her own, but she couldn't quite manage to pull away. They crossed the small distance to the kitchen, Redd at their heels. Justin let go of her to open the freezer.

Gingerly, she took a step backward so she was no longer so close to his appealing body. Rummaging through the frozen food, he seemed oblivious to the devastating effect he had on her. He said, "The bowls are over the sink beside the plates. I'll get the spoons."

Still a little woozy, she retrieved the bowls and set them on the counter. He dished out a generous dollop of strawberry ice cream. She shook her head. "Half that."

He cut down the portion with the spoon and dropped it into his dish. He added a huge scoop with a cocky grin. "My stomach's fine."

It was more than "fine," she thought. His stomach was so flat and taut that you could bounce a penny off it. She doubted he ate ice cream often. As they took seats at the kitchen table, she thought about the chubby girl she'd been, then told herself this small amount of ice cream couldn't hurt after days without food. They ate in silence, but she couldn't help noticing how relaxed he seemed, while she couldn't help being on edge.

Justin rinsed off their dishes and left them on the drain rack. "Come on." He held out his hand to her. "Let's get you walking. It's the only way to get strength back in your legs."

His arm encircled her waist in a no-nonsense manner. He exuded sexual magnetism, but he was all business now, and she forced herself to concentrate. With baby steps she walked barefoot across the living room toward the bedrooms. Redd followed beside them, peering up at Kat and seeming to be concerned.

"I guess you found the bathroom," he told her. "Just open the cabinet on the wall for fresh towels."

They approached the bedroom she was using, and Kat realized she was walking a little faster now. Inside the room her things were piled in one corner. She didn't know where to put them. Maybe she wouldn't need to move them; she could be leaving anytime. He reached for her hand and turned her around.

"Let's go another lap."

"Lap? How far did we go? Forty feet?"

"Less than that."

He didn't drop her hand. His fingers twined between hers, warm, reassuring. She wasn't in this alone, she told herself. It was profoundly disturbing not to know who her enemies were, to suspect most people around her, but at least she knew she could rely on Justin and David for help.

Pulse racing, she did her best not to lean against him as she walked. Having his arm around her was more comforting and, admit it, more pleasurable than holding hands, but Justin was all business. He might have been a little attracted to her at one point, but now he had two murders to solve—and she was the key to one of them. Who knew? Maybe she was linked to both.

"Pick up the pace." His voice had a husky edge.

She walked faster, focusing on putting one foot in front of the other. She'd never be able to solve the mystery unless she regained her strength. Still, having Justin at her side was distracting. Tempting.

Kat had been in prison too long, away from any men except the disgusting guards. She might have been an ugly duckling who could boast of just one brief relationship, but that hadn't kept her from looking at men. And daydreaming about them. For as long as she could remember, Justin Radner had lurked in her romantic thoughts.

"How do you feel?" he asked when they reached the kitchen.

"I'm fine. Ready to do it again." She made herself say this even though she longed to collapse into the easy chair again. *No pain, no gain,* she reminded herself.

She twisted her fingers out of his grasp and marched toward the back bedroom. Her calves burned but she kept going. If prison had taught her one thing, it was to never show weakness. She walked briskly until she was in the bedroom she was using, her toes up against a black duffel with *Boston Globe* in white script. David had stuffed her things into one of his duffels when he'd discovered she had more clothes than would fit into the satchel she'd brought to the apartment. She pivoted, ready to do it again, or fall flat on her face trying.

Justin was right behind her. He held up his hand. "Whoa! That's enough for now."

She set her chin high and sailed by him just the way she would have a prison guard. *Show no fear.* In this case, she wasn't afraid of Justin; she was afraid of being too weak physically to defend herself. Who knew what would come next? She had to be prepared, to rely on herself.

Justin grabbed her and pulled her so close that her breasts flattened against the solid wall of his torso. The rapid rise and fall of his chest sent her pulse skittering. "Don't overdo it. You'll have a relapse and it'll take longer to recover."

His breath feathered the wisps of hair at her temples. Her throat went dry, but heat throbbed in her veins, then shafted downward, warming her lower tummy and thighs. Face facts, Kat told herself, she'd always been a sucker for Justin Radner. His gaze met hers and another rush of heat surged to the area between her thighs. The air between them was suddenly charged with sexual attraction.

Before she could utter a word, his mouth slanted over hers. His lips were moist and firm, the way they'd been when he'd kissed her before, but this time there seemed to be…an urgency to the kiss as well as a tenderness that she hadn't felt with previous kisses. The faint prickling of his emerging beard heightened the sensation. Her already weakened legs turned to rubber and she sagged against him. His arms supported her like bands of steel while his tongue nudged between her lips.

Oh, my.

His tongue filled her mouth, mating with hers, the way she'd imagined over and over and over in her dreams. Desire, dark and urgent, swept through her, eradicating rational thought. She wrapped her arms around his neck and kissed him back for all she was worth.

She craved each touch, each movement of his mouth, his powerful body. The reality was even more exciting than anything she'd ever dreamed. Kissing Justin was so much…more thrilling than she ever could have anticipated. Why stop here? her body asked. Why?

She'd never felt like this in her whole life. True, she hardly had any experience with men, but this seemed to be so much *more* than she expected. This was the *bomb!* She was almost dizzy with the heat suffusing her body. One of his hands crept downward to cup her bottom, and she couldn't resist the urge to rub her chest sensuously against his torso. Her nipples were tight nubs while her breasts felt heavy and aching with pleasure as she moved. His hard, swollen penis pressed against her belly from behind his fly.

His hand caressed her buttocks, then inched upward under her blouse. She pulled back, still kissing him, still clinging to him, to allow space for his hand to touch her. He cradled one breast in his palm while he slowly traced his thumb across her erect nipple. A purring sound rose from deep in her throat.

Don't stop, she silently prayed. If someone was going to kill her, Kat wanted to go to the afterlife knowing what it was to really make love to someone. Instinct told her Justin wouldn't be a wham-bammer like Corbin. As if reading her thoughts, Justin swooped her up in his arms and carried her over to the bed. Gently he lowered her to the sheets and in the dim light coming from the luminous dial of the alarm clock she saw the blaze of heat in his eyes as he gazed down at her. His breathing uneven, he traced the high arches of her cheekbones, then eased his fingertips into her hair.

Kat's whole body quivered with amazement that he could want her as much as she wanted him. Sensing his desire, her pulse kicked up another notch. Maybe his burgeoning erection had taken over his brain. This was a man who could have any woman he wanted. This might just be about sex and nothing more.

Who cares? Right now, she needed him to make love to her. If it meant more to her than it did to him, Kat was willing to take the risk. Who knew what tomorrow might bring? She could indulge in soul-searching later.

He angled his body across hers. "Am I too heavy?" he whispered.

"No." Actually, she found his size, his weight reassuring. She slid her arms around his neck and surveyed the shad-

owed contours of his face while he unbuttoned her blouse. He
brushed the panels aside, revealing the soft mounds. Cool air
whisked across her heated flesh, and goose bumps like pin-
pricks sprang up.

"Damn," he muttered. "You're beautiful."

She'd never thought of herself as beautiful. Her "assets,"
as her mother called them, were small compared to Tori's, but
there was no mistaking the reverence in Justin's tone. Now,
in this moment, she did feel beautiful.

CHAPTER TWENTY-FOUR

KAT GAZED UP at Justin through her long eyelashes. His hands pulled out of her hair and slowly trailed downward, caressing her cheeks and neck, finally coming to rest on her taut nipples.

"I've wanted you since the moment I set eyes on you," he told her.

"Really? When I was a fat kid?" She was justifiably proud of her irreverent tone.

He paused and smiled at her, his thumbs still on her nipples. "I wish I did remember you back then, but I didn't pay much attention to younger kids."

Unless they looked like Tori, she silently amended.

"But when I spotted you outside Jo Mama's, I was a goner."

This was something, she supposed. A belated victory. Once again she thought about the way prison had changed her. Hell on earth had made her tougher—and more attractive. *What doesn't kill you makes you stronger.* Her father used to tell her that. Now she knew what he meant.

"I wanted you, too," she admitted. She'd always had a thing for Justin, but the night when Hank Bullock had attacked her in Jo Mama's parking lot marked a milestone. She'd never been so physically close to him before that evening. The impression he'd made had been powerful. She hadn't been able to get him out of her mind since.

"Make love to me," she heard herself whisper.

"What in bejesus do you think I'm doing?"

"Who knows? You're takin' your sweet time."

His pupils had dilated until they were black with a narrow rim of Arctic blue around them. He whispered in a raw, thick voice, "Are you a virgin?"

"No!" she snapped back. Undoubtedly, he believed the ugly duckling had never had sex and it bothered him.

"Thank God for small favors."

He sounded so relieved it was all she could do not to punch him. Then she stopped herself. A virgin was a huge responsibility, and Justin realized this. Corbin Gutcheon had not. Her first and only sexual experience had been a disaster because the man knew she had no experience but never thought about anyone except himself. At least Justin cared enough to ask.

With a sigh, she surrendered. She wanted him inside her with such intensity that she was dizzy with anticipation. Get a grip, her mind kept telling her, but Kat's body had other ideas.

CHILL, JUSTIN TOLD HIMSELF, but it was impossible. Beneath him was the sexiest, most erotic creature he'd ever envisioned. How had this happened? A parade of women had tromped through his life, but not until now—until Kat—had a woman made such an impression on him. He wanted her, sure, but even more he was desperate to protect her. Who wanted her dead? He hadn't a clue, and it frustrated him more than he could say.

"Kiss me again," she whispered, her voice low, seductive.

"I want you to understand," he said, then forgot what he wanted her to know. She pivoted in his arms, turning just a degree but the friction of the movement sent scores of nerves in his body tingling. Aw hell, what was she doing to him?

He didn't blame Kat. She wasn't a virgin, but she wasn't experienced enough to play him like a fish on the hook. Her moves were uncalculated. She wasn't like other women who took seduction to the highest level.

Kat was different, special. She had a guileless, emotional honesty that he found refreshing. And intriguing.

For a moment, he regretted she'd been with another man. He couldn't be jealous, could he? Okay, he conceded, maybe he was a tad jealous. Justin longed to know who her lover had been. Had he left her to face prison by herself? Then, suddenly, unexpectedly he didn't care. She was his now. His alone.

Kat's tousled hair was fanned against the pillow. The glimmer of light from the hall kindled her red highlights. He'd dreamed about having her on her back like this, but the reality was so much more pleasurable. He needed to make this good for her, to bond her to him in a special way that only true intimacy could accomplish.

Her arms encircled his neck and held tight. His lips touched hers, and he stopped thinking while he kissed her. His erection had become painful now, begging for release, but he couldn't rush it. He wanted her to remember this night forever. She'd had sex, but there couldn't have been that many men in her life. He needed to be exceptional.

Justin unzipped her shorts, then hooked his thumbs in the waistband and yanked them downward. She wasn't wearing any panties. He sucked in a gulp of air to keep from losing it. Her shorts slid down her trim thighs, and she wiggled her legs to free herself.

Justin reared back on his knees, inhaling sharply, his breathing harsh, unsteady. She tugged at his shoulders as he unzipped his cargo shorts, shimmied out of them, freeing his erection. With one knee, he nudged her thighs apart, then rested between them. His heart thundered against his ribs as if this were a marathon. He forced himself to try to breathe normally. This wasn't a race. They had all night.

With heavy-lidded eyes, he gazed down at her for a moment, not saying anything. Damn, Kat was beautiful. He'd told her that a few minutes ago, and she'd seemed startled.

Hadn't anyone ever told her how pretty she was? What about the creep who'd taken her virginity? Hadn't he appreciated the way she looked, the interesting person she was?

Where had she been his whole life? It seemed as if he'd been journeying toward this moment for years.

"Are you sure about this?" he asked, a warning note in his voice.

She pressed her hand flat against his nosily beating heart. "You bet I'm sure."

There was a quaver in her voice, but he barely noticed. With one fluid movement, he shucked the T-shirt and threw it to the side. It landed on Redd's rump. The dog was watching them intently.

Kat's lips were parted and she gazed up at him with adoring eyes. He lowered his mouth to her round, soft breast and flicked his tongue across the beaded nipple. Her body shuddering, Kat arched upward, tilting her pelvis against him. Her nails dug into his shoulders, and he smiled inwardly. She wanted him just as fiercely as he wanted her.

He gave her other breast its due and sucked on the nipple greedily. He eased one hand between her thighs. There he discovered the slick, wet proof of her desire. She was ready for him, but he wanted her at the brink. She gasped as he stroked between the folds of soft, moist skin and found the tiny bud.

"Hurry!" She squeezed her thighs against his hand.

Justin had no intention of speeding up the pace, even though his erection felt ready to explode. Rolling the nubbin with his thumb, he slipped one finger inside her. The moist sheathing heat sent his pulse skyrocketing. She moaned with pleasure and rocked her hips, arching off the mattress. He slowly withdrew his finger, then burrowed two fingers into the wet channel.

"Oh, wow! Wow!" she cried.

The relentless heat scorched Justin's skin, and he pulsed

with the burning need to take her this second. His breath erupted in short bursts that caused pain to lance through his side. He trembled with the need to possess her. He managed to hold himself in check even though his jutting penis throbbed to be deep in her sweet body. He was vaguely aware of a distant, chiming noise.

"Your phone," Kat muttered.

"Oh, crap!" He recognized the distinctive sound now. "It's the station. Something must be wrong."

He rolled to his side, his erection ramrod straight, hot and throbbing. It took a moment of fumbling in the dark to locate his cargo shorts and pull his cell phone out of the pocket.

Gazing up at the ceiling, Kat groaned out loud. From what Justin was saying, he was going to leave her to go out on a call. Just her luck!

"It's the Randolphs next door," he told her, his voice raw. "The prick's beating up his wife again." With a grimace, he pulled on his shorts and managed to get his penis inside, although a quick glance would tell anyone he had an erection. "I won't be long. The gun's in the nightstand."

"I know," she managed to say. "I saw it this afternoon."

"You're not going to need it." He bent over and kissed her forehead. "I'll be back in no time. I'll leave Redd with you for company." He pointed to the old-fashioned rotary telephone on the nightstand. "Call if you need me."

GROGGY WITH SLEEP, Kat opened her eyes. Where was she? It was too dark, too quiet to be prison. Of course not. She had been released on a furlough. If she let her mind stay there long enough, she would *feel* the prison walls closing in around her. She forced herself to think, and by degrees, reality tiptoed into her muzzy brain. She was in bed, at Justin's home, where she'd been when he'd received the phone call.

What had awakened her? She glanced at the luminous dial

of the clock on the nightstand. Justin had been gone for almost an hour. What was keeping him? Her heart thumped noisily as cold-blooded fear took over her body.

Someone's out there.

It's probably Justin, she decided, but she strained to listen for another sound. She waited…and waited. All she could hear was the low, rhythmic wheeze of the swamp cooler in the living room. Redd was curled up asleep on the throw rug beside her bed. Dogs had more acute hearing than people, didn't they? If she'd actually been awakened by a noise, it hadn't bothered the dog.

Listen, a voice in her head insisted. Trying not to freak, she scooted to a sitting position, pulled up her legs, and rested her chin on her knees while she strained to hear something besides the air conditioner. Nothing. It must have been her imagination working overtime.

Where was Justin? He'd said he would be right back. Being alone in the house, so far from everything was creeping her out—big time.

Get over it. You're okay. No one's out there.

Rationally, she knew no one was around, but she'd feel a lot better if Justin were in bed with her. She groped for the lamp on the nightstand. To soothe her nerves, she could read until Justin came home.

Her hand on the lamp's switch, she froze. A noise. This time Redd heard it, too. A low growl rumbled from his throat as he lurched to his feet. She detected a dull click that seemed to have come from the kitchen. Maybe it was the back door that opened to the yard.

There was probably a logical explanation for the sound, she reassured herself. The refrigerator might have cycled on. The darkness and the still house magnified any noise. Redd growled again, and the fine hairs on the back of her neck shot upward.

She slid open the drawer in the nightstand and grabbed the gun. How would anyone know she was here? *Duh!* How many places could she be? A determined person could find her easily.

Guns had safety catches, didn't they? By the light of the alarm clock, she examined the weapon. It was cold in her hand and had a deadly gleam. She didn't see any catch to disengage.

Redd growled again, and the fur on his back bristled upward like a hedgehog's. She wished he would bark. That might frighten off an intruder, but she knew the dog wouldn't be much protection. Not only did Redd jump at his own shadow, golden retrievers didn't rank up there in the guard dog category.

Holding the gun, she tiptoed across the small room to her pile of clothes and slipped into a pair of shoes she'd pulled from her things earlier that afternoon. Thankfully, she'd been sleeping in her shorts and T-shirt.

Another faint click.

Redd snarled and bared his teeth. Now the house was deadly silent; only the low wheeze of the swamp cooler filled the darkness. If someone was there, he was as silent as a cat.

She reached for the telephone. The old-fashioned rotary dial must be a legacy of the previous owner. It was going to make noise, but she had no alternative. She hadn't recharged her cell. Even if this turned out to be a false alarm, it was better to be safe than sorry.

The line was dead.

She gripped the gun to her breast and silently prayed the phone had malfunctioned. After all, it was older than Egyptian dirt. Justin used his cell all the time. He might not have known the land line was out.

And pigs might fly.

It was just too much of a coincidence to hear a noise, have a growling dog, and find the phone dead. Someone was here. Were they in the house yet or lurking outside?

She slipped out of bed, tiptoed to the door, and kept her body out of sight as she peered around the doorjamb. The porch light was yellow and cast a golden sheen across the small living room. No one was there—unless they were behind the couch, out of her view.

A floorboard creaked and she nearly screamed. Someone was in the kitchen. *Go out the bedroom window,* an inner voice urged. She ventured across the room to the only window. The lever lock released with a low ping that sounded like a shot in the dark house. She paused, expecting to hear footsteps.

Nothing.

She pushed on the window. It wouldn't budge. She put the gun on the sill and used both hands to shove harder, but it didn't do any good. The window must have been painted shut or something.

"Going somewhere?" The deep, guttural voice filled the room.

A huge ape of a man stood in the doorway, blocking her only escape route. The air left her lungs in a low moan. Fangs bared, Redd trotted over to her side.

"What do you want?" She tried to sound tough, the way she had been in prison. Taking advantage of the darkness, she reached behind her back for the gun on the sill.

"Whoo-ee! I could use me some pussy."

Numb with terror, she realized he had a gun in his hand, and it was aimed at her. Somehow she managed to get the revolver off the sill. She kept it behind her back, saying, "Justin will be back any minute. He—"

"Will find a dumb cunt tied spread-eagle to his bed."

CHAPTER TWENTY-FIVE

KAT DIDN'T RECOGNIZE this demented stranger. She didn't recall seeing him around town. But with complete certainty, she knew he was going to rape her. Chances were he would kill her before Justin returned.

She whipped out the gun from behind her back and pulled the trigger as she jumped to the side, hoping he couldn't react quickly enough to shoot her. Nothing! The gun didn't fire.

The hulking creep belted out a derisive laugh. "Forgot the safety, bitch."

Acting on instinct alone, she charged forward and hurled the gun at his face while kicking toward his groin. Redd lunged with her, taking Kat by surprise. Kat's foot missed the target, but the dog chomped down on the brute's leg just as the gun hit him square in the nose.

"Shee-it!" he howled, staggering backward into the hall, blood spurting from his nose. He dropped his weapon. It clattered onto the wood floor with a deafening bang.

Run!

In a split second, she exploded out of the bedroom and bolted down the hall. Out of the corner of her eye, she saw Redd hanging onto the man's calf like he was a pit bull instead of a scaredy-cat retriever. Heart pounding in her ears, already weak and short of breath, she dashed toward the front door.

Fumbling with the chain on the safety lock, she heard a pain-stricken yelp. He'd clobbered poor Redd. Suddenly, there was movement behind her. She managed to open the door and sprinted out onto the porch. *Keep moving,* she told herself even though her weakened body trembled with the effort.

With a shriek she was positive could be heard all the way back in town, she stormed down the steps into the yard. Bathed in a bone-chilling sweat and disoriented by the darkness, she struggled to recall the layout of Justin's place. A wisp of a breeze fluttered around her, causing silhouettes to twist and lunge, every shadow a threat.

She'd been so out of it when they'd driven up that all she remembered was an unkempt fenced yard and a detached two-car garage with a workroom or shop built onto the back of it. A dense layer of clouds blanketed the new moon, blocking out the stars as well. It was nearly impossible to see where she was going, but she rushed forward.

In the distance, she detected a glimmer of light through the trees. That must be where Justin had gone. She screamed again for all she was worth. A tromping sound startled her. *Oh, no. Oh, no.* The creep was chasing her, running her to ground. He would pounce on her before she could reach the house beyond the trees.

The garage. He wouldn't be able to see where she went, if she could manage to make it to the back of the garage. He would expect her to head toward the lights. She might be able to fool him by running in the opposite direction, toward the thicket that she vaguely remembered seeing behind the garage. The whole unincorporated area was riddled with dense stands of old-growth trees—perfect for hiding.

Her stomach heaved and her legs threatened to buckle beneath her, but she forced herself to race across the unmowed grass. Behind her, Kat heard footfalls like a charging buffalo. The guy might be clumsy, but he was shockingly fast, and he was rapidly closing the distance between them. She screamed again—just in case someone was out there and could hear her.

"You're dead, bitch!" he yelled as if he'd gone berserk.

He was just seconds behind her now. Kat knew she wouldn't make it to the rear of the garage and into the woods without him seeing where she went. She veered right and crashed through the partially open door into the workroom attached to the garage. She slammed the door shut a split second before he reached it. The only lock she could feel in the darkness was a small button in the knob itself.

Not much protection.

He rammed the door with his shoulder and dust filled the air. Coughing and struggling to gain control of her senses, she fumbled in the dark for something to use as a weapon. Undoubtedly, he would bust through in less than a minute. Her hands discovered a long handle. A rake or a hoe? she wondered hopefully. No. A broom.

Oh, great! How could she defend herself with a broom? Her sixth sense told her to stand beside the door. The way he was pummeling it with his whole body, when he broke through, his momentum would carry him into the small narrow room. With luck, she could escape out the door behind him while he was struggling to get his bearings.

He battered the door again and again, apparently charging the barricade from a running start a short distance away. A moment later, he punched a hole with his fist in the door near the handle. In the dim light coming from God-only-knew-where she spotted his white hand, flapping around, searching for the knob. She grabbed two of his fingers and snapped them backward with all her might.

"Muth-fucker!" he shrieked from the other side of the door. He yanked his hand out of range. "Yer dead meat, bitch!"

An eerie calmness had overtaken Kat. She wrapped her arms around her waist, attempting to hold herself together. She'd been in terrible situations before, but then death hadn't been riding on her shoulder like an avenging angel. She waited, no longer trembling, knowing she would have just one chance to get away from this monster. He smacked the door again with his beefy shoulder.

Off to the side, Kat waited, biding her time while striving to organize her thoughts and keep panic at bay. The way he was thwacking the door, the madman would fly into the room any second.

"Fuckin' A!" he ranted, then rammed into the door so hard the wall against her back shook.

Something in his tone alerted Kat, and she pressed her body as close to the wall as possible. He would sail by her in a heartbeat. With luck, it would be enough time for her to flee across the yard to the trees where she could hide. The next instant, the door splintered on its hinges and the creep hurled into the room.

Kat leaped out the door and stormed toward the thicket of trees and underbrush.

"Stop, bitch! Or I'm gonna kill him as soon as he comes home!"

Him?

Kat stumbled to a halt, not trusting what she'd heard. Her breath left her lungs in labored pants. Did this monster mean Justin? Duh! Of course he did. What could she do to help him?

He pounced on Kat and grabbed her by the hair, yanking her backward so hard her teeth rattled. With an open fist, he slapped her with such force her vision blurred and her ears rang. He pulled her against him. The sour odor of sweat rank with rum filled her lungs. She slumped, making herself dead weight, but it didn't faze him. One arm around her waist, he dragged her toward the house.

Please, save me, Justin, she silently prayed.

He hauled her up the two steps to the front door. It was wide open, but the house was still dark inside. He heaved her onto the sofa, then came down on top of her like a sack of wet cement. The force of his weight knocked the air out of her lungs with a whoosh. She felt the gun, shoved into the waistband of his pants, dig into the tender flesh of her belly. If only she could distract him long enough to grab the gun.

Terror mounting, she gasped for breath. There was just enough light glowing from the digital clock on the oven in the nearby kitchen for her to see his white teeth as he grinned down at her and the fireworks detonating in his eyes. Blood dribbled from his nose and was smeared across his cheek.

He slammed one meaty hand down on her breast and squeezed—hard. It hurt, but she refused to cry out. He dug in his fingers more, determined to cause as much pain as he could. His dirty, smelly body ground against her like a rutting boar.

"You're gonna pay for breakin' my nose, bitch!"

Kat's pulse spiked; her breath came in choppy, terrified pants. Oh, Lordy, her life couldn't end like this. Raped and murdered. A wave of horror unlike anything she'd ever experienced—even in prison—engulfed her.

Desperate and savage as a cornered wildcat, she reminded herself of the lessons she'd learned in the school of hard knocks. His huge body, smoldering with heat and reeking of rum and BO had her overpowered. She had to use her wits if she intended to survive.

"Why are you after Justin?" she asked, hoping that getting him to talk would stall him.

"He killed my brother." He released her breast and shoved his rough hand under her shorts and across her stomach to her crotch. "Shee-it! Nice pussy Radner gots hisself."

Kat's stomach heaved, and for a second she thought what little she'd eaten would come up. Droplets of sweat popped out on her forehead. She thought she heard the click of Redd's nails on the wooden floor, but couldn't be sure. If the dog would just bite him again, she might be able to grab the gun.

Headlights cracked the dark yard like twin bolts of lightning. Justin was back. Voices. Someone was with him.

His hand locked around her throat. "One sound and you're dead."

He was crushing her Adam's apple, cutting off her air entirely. A hard rim of pitch-black limited her field of vision. Any second she would pass out from lack of oxygen. She bucked upward as best she could, but he didn't loosen his grip. He was going for the gun. She attempted to knee him in the groin, but he shifted to the side.

As his weight shifted, he took his hand off her neck. The bile welled up in her throat and the lack of air had sent her queasy tummy into a backflip. She gasped for air and told herself to hurl. *Come on. Just let it go.*

Her stomach clenched then heaved upward in a sickening rush. She aimed right at his face. The putrid-smelling vomit hit him in the eyes. He punched at her viciously, but she managed to duck to the side.

The lights flashed on, blinding her. She kicked upward, counting on the element of surprise and knowing the sudden brightness had to have affected him, too. Before she realized it, she had her hand on the gun. They grappled for control of the weapon. She was aware of voices yelling, but she was too intent on disarming him. If he had his finger on the trigger, she was certain the man would shoot Justin.

A shot split the vile-smelling air.

The beast looked at her blankly for a moment, grabbed his crotch, then toppled over. Redd hovered nearby, growling. Justin and a deputy stood not far away, guns drawn.

Kat stood up, covered in puke and blood. He was still alive, writhing on the floor, clutching his penis.

"Are you all right, honey?" Justin asked.

"Y-yes, I...think so."

Justin came over and helped her to her feet. He slipped his arm around her and gave her a hug.

"Yow-zer!" cried the deputy. "Gal, you shot him in the balls."

Unexpectedly, both men began to laugh. Justin squeezed her tighter.

"I didn't shoot him," she told Justin. "The gun just went off."

While the deputy cuffed the man, Justin said, "It doesn't matter, honey. You're safe. That's what counts."

"He was after you."

Justin pushed on the man's foot with the toe of his boot. "Gunning for me, Lucas? If you hadn't taken a bullet, I'd ream you a new one for being such a chickenshit to pick on a helpless woman."

"Helpless?" The man grunted, both hands locked on the crotch of his blood-soaked jeans. "She's a ballbuster. This here's bleedin' like a muther!"

"Call an ambulance," Justin told his deputy. "Go with him to the hospital ward at the jail in Jackson." Justin turned to Kat. "Are you sure you're all right?"

"Yes. You arrived in the nick of time."

"Sorry I wasn't here sooner. Randolph's wife will never learn. He busted her nose, but she fought us. When we calmed her down, we spent almost an hour trying to convince her to press charges."

"She flat refused," added the deputy. "We can't charge him unless she agrees."

"Get him out of here before I do something I'll regret," Justin told his deputy.

"You got it." The deputy hauled Lucas, still moaning, to his feet.

Justin guided forward. "Let's get you into the shower."

The adrenaline rush and the bout of pure terror caught up with her. Trembling as if she were freezing and knees buck-

ling with every movement, Kat did as she was told. In the
bathroom she peeled off the shorts and shucked the T-shirt.
She could have washed the clothes, but decided to pitch them.
She could never look at either garment again without thinking of the brute's hands all over her.

She caught a glimpse of herself in the full-length mirror
on the back of the closed door. Ohmigod! Smudges of blood
crisscrossed her cheek and neck. Somewhere along the way,
she'd skinned her elbows—probably when he'd hauled her up
the steps. Bruises were beginning to form on her throat where
he'd choked her. An angry purple and blue splotch covered
most of one hip. Dirt and leaves clung to her skin, along with
disgusting patches of vomit.

Kat managed to shower and rinse out her hair. She dried
herself and toweled the water from her hair. She was so rattled and exhausted she couldn't concentrate much less blow
her hair dry. She noticed Justin had removed the stinky clothes
and left one of his well-worn T-shirts.

Justin knocked softly, calling, "How are you feeling?"

She opened the door. "I'm a little light-headed."

He gazed down at her, his expression concerned.

"Is Redd okay?"

"He's fine," Justin replied. "Why?"

"He bit the guy's leg. The man must have hit or kicked
Redd to get him off."

"You're kidding."

"Seriously."

"I'll be damned." He grinned. "Now, let's get you into bed
before you collapse."

"What about the mess in the living room?"

"I cleaned it up."

"I'm sorry. When I thought he was going to shoot, I forced
myself to throw up. It wasn't that hard. My stomach's been
really upset."

"Good thinking." He guided her out of the steamy room toward her bedroom. "It's worked for other women when men have tried to rape them."

Redd was waiting in the hall for them. He spotted Kat and his tail began to whip through the air.

"Good boy. You're an attack dog now." She turned to Justin. "Who was that man?"

"Lucas Albright. When I was on the force in New Orleans, I killed his brother during a drug bust." The steely edge to his voice told her there was a lot more to the story. "Lucas swore he'd kill me as soon as he got out of prison."

"You didn't know he'd been released?"

"Nope. That's the system for you."

She shuddered, thinking how close they'd both come to being killed. "You came back at just the right moment. I—"

"We heard you yelling down the road. That's why we high-tailed it back here." He stopped her and cradled her breasts in his hands. "That's some set of lungs you've got."

She managed a wry smile. "I'm exhausted. I—"

"Don't worry. I'm not going to jump your bones, after all you've been through. I'll stay with you while you sleep."

Kat didn't say anything, but she knew he meant he would guard her. This convict had been after Justin. Whoever had poisoned Kat was still out there. Waiting.

CHAPTER TWENTY-SIX

KAT AWOKE in the darkness. The luminous dial on the alarm told her it was a little after three in the morning. Redd was sleeping next to the bed, and nearby in the armchair he'd brought in from the living room was Justin.

With heart-pounding clarity, terrifying memories filled her brain. Gasping for breath, she recalled being chased. The pressure on her chest felt so great that the brute seemed to be on top of her again. She levered herself up with her elbows and stared at the featureless shadow across the room to make sure it really was Justin.

"You okay?" he whispered.

"I'm fine." She knew her voice sounded strained.

He stood up, walked over to the bed, and sat on the edge. He put his arm around her waist. She shivered, though the room was undoubtedly warm. She rested her cheek against his shoulder and placed one hand on his chest. His heartbeat against her palm was steady, reassuring. Calming.

He held her close, his grip tightening as if he sensed her anxiety. "Everything is going to be all right. I spoke with my deputy. They've got Lucas Albright in jail in Jackson. He can't hurt you."

"Did the shot take off his…penis or anything?"

Justin chuckled softly. "No. The bullet grazed one of his balls but lodged in his thigh. He has a pretty bad dog bite on his calf. Don't worry about him. He'll be back in the pen soon."

"That's good. I didn't want him to kill you."

Justin didn't mention the poison, and neither did she. But Kat was positive that the knowledge someone was out there, determined to kill her, weighed on both their minds.

"Don't worry about it." He eased her down onto the pillow. "Go back to sleep."

She refused to release him. It might be weak or silly but there was a certain measure of comfort just being in his arms. She heard herself saying, "Make love to me."

"I don't think now's a good time. You've been through a lot tonight."

"That's why this is the best time. Anything can happen." She slipped her hand up under his T-shirt and caressed the springy mat of hair on his solid chest. Her heart revved, and warm blood purred through her veins. "If you hadn't gotten that call…"

"I know. We were well on our way." He stood up and pulled off his shirt. His chest was tanned and broad with rippling muscles. The wedge of hair on his chest narrowed to his waist where his cargo shorts hung low on his hips. A bod to die for. He unzipped his shorts, and in the dim light, she saw he wasn't wearing underwear. Her gaze traveled along his lean, strong body and saw his penis was already erect.

She sat up and took off the T-shirt while he lifted the sheet and moved in beside her. Electricity arced between them as she scooted into his arms, parting her lips for his kiss. His tongue brushed hers, and she drew it into her mouth with astonishing eagerness.

She strained forward, eager to have her throbbing nipples against his chest. Crisp hair greeted her breasts; she instinctively moved to heighten the erotic sensation. Arching her back, she moaned her delight in having the hard contours of his bare body against hers. A craving like nothing she'd ever experienced overcame her—a total meltdown. She wanted him inside her—now.

"Hurry, hurry," she muttered against his lips.

He broke off the kiss, raised up on one sturdy elbow, and leaned over her. "I'm not rushing this."

He allowed the words to sink in before his mouth sought hers again, and this time he kissed her fiercely, his need matching her own. Yet something was different about the kiss now. It seemed to bond them in a way she'd never anticipated. This just wasn't about sex. Something…more was happening.

The ache in her loins intensified. All she'd gone through—even prison—had brought her to this moment, this man. She wouldn't change any of it. Without going through hell, she would never have been here. Nothing mattered except being with Justin.

Justin pulled her tighter to him and explored the curve of her back and sexy bottom. Oh, my, she was soft. She was vulnerable, too, and he knew it. This wasn't going to be a one-night fling. They belonged together, but he had to keep her safe at any cost—even if it meant sending her away while he remained here until he solved this case.

He pressed her bottom against his jutting hardness and rolled her onto her back. Parting her long, slim legs with his knee, he settled himself full length between them. He lifted his head and stared down at her. Even in the shadowy darkness, he could see her green eyes were dilated yet ablaze with passion.

"Justin." His name slipped from between her lips on a breath that wasn't quite a whisper. It was the most erotic pronunciation of his name he'd ever heard.

She moved against him again—just a little shimmy of her hips. The desire building by the second inside him nearly exploded. He forced himself to hold on, make it good for her. She might want him to hurry, but he had enough experience to know not to rush. He concentrated on drawing even, calming breaths.

He trailed moist kisses down her neck, then nuzzled one breast before turning his attention to the other. He flicked his tongue over one taut nipple, then blew across it. As the moist skin cooled, she shuddered with pleasure. He sucked on her puckered nipples and circled each tight bud with his tongue. She uttered a low moan and dug her nails into his shoulders.

She gyrated her hips sensuously against his. His penis was so hot and hard that it ached when the downy hair between her legs rasped his sensitized skin. The heat in his veins had become a fever, a gnawing hunger that only this woman could satisfy.

Her hands skimmed down his back and caressed his buttocks. Another surge of erotic pleasure stormed through him. His kiss turned savage, hot and mindless. *Be tender, be gentle,* argued some part of his brain but testosterone had taken over his body.

Kat moved her head to break the kiss. She announced, "I'm ready. Really ready."

It was the absolute truth. Even though her experience with lovemaking was extremely limited, she realized she was totally aroused. Entranced. Earlier that evening she'd had a glimmer of what it would be like to have him inside her, but now her senses were heightened. Some distant part of her brain told her this happened when someone had a brush with death, but right now, she didn't care about the reason.

"I need you—now, Justin!"

"All right! All right!" His voice was hoarse with desire.

She gazed at his heavy-lidded eyes and clenched jaw. *Why, he's struggling to maintain control.* She should have found this enormously pleasing, but her frustration was mounting with every heartbeat.

He slipped his hand between her legs, and his thumb found the tiny, throbbing nubbin between the moist folds of flesh.

He rolled the delicate bud for a moment, then rubbed the velvet smooth head of his penis against it. A low moan broke from her lips, and she scored his back with her fingernails.

He whispered against her ear. "You're a little hellcat, aren't you?"

"Sorry…I got—" The sensations were so exquisite she could hardly eke out the words "—carried away."

He eased the tip of his penis inside her. "That makes two of us."

She arched upward, needing him deeper. Fiery-hot and hard, the thick head of his penis probed at her but didn't nudge forward. "Come on!"

"You're a little tight," he replied in a low, raw voice. "I don't want to hurt you."

He gradually edged forward, stretching her until she was certain she would split in half and die on the spot, loving every second of it. Finally, he was deep inside and her body had adjusted to accommodate him.

He took her hard and fast, his thick shaft thrusting back and forth like a supercharged piston. She came quickly with a series of shattering tremors from a place inside her she'd never known existed.

"Justin!" she screamed.

He kept pounding into her for a few seconds, then she heard him groan as release came with a final deep, deep thrust. His powerful body shuddered and went slack. He fell forward, taking the brunt of his weight with his arms so he wouldn't crush her. Breathing like a racehorse, he buried his face in the curve of her neck.

She lay there, stunned by the magnitude of her orgasm. Her body was limp as if every bone had been sucked out of it, but somehow she felt complete in a way she could never have expressed in mere words.

Arms linked around her, Justin rolled onto his back, taking her with him. Unable to muster the strength to move, she lay sprawled on top of his body, sated and happy.

ANTSY, UNABLE TO SLEEP, the man stared out into the darkness. Kaitlin Wells was a cat for sure. She had nine lives. Who would have guessed the Hills had taken her to their place? No one would think of contradicting those crazy fuckers.

The best-laid plans of mice and men.

If something can go wrong, it will, he reminded himself. This scheme to take out Bitner and blame it on Kat Wells had been a little too…risky. He'd said so—more than once—but in the end he had gone along with their plan.

Now what?

They had to get rid of the bitch. She was a liability they couldn't afford to have around. It was just a matter of time before the authorities reopened the case. A competent fingerprint expert would know Kat had never been inside the bank vault.

Sheriff Parker was six feet under. He couldn't help them with another cover-up. Radner was straighter than Cochise's arrow.

Or so it appeared.

Personally, he believed *every* man had his price. Problem was no one had been able to get close enough to Radner to determine what it would take to lure him into their camp. Worse, Radner had the hots for Kat. Long as she was spreading her legs for him, he would do his damnedest to help her.

A disturbing thought resurfaced, like an itch in a spot you couldn't reach. Someone else wanted Kat dead, too. Poisoning Kat had been a diabolical move. Who would be that desperate? That ballsy? You had to respect—and fear—a person like that.

Too much was at risk. He might even end up dead. He

shoved that prospect to the back of his mind. He was a big-time player and had been for years. They wouldn't *dare* kill him.

Leave nothing to chance, he reminded himself. It had long been one of his favorite mottos.

A low beep indicated a message coming through on his police scanner. It hadn't been much help. Radner never used the radio. He took calls on his cell. It was possible to monitor cell calls, but it took special equipment that he didn't have.

He unlocked his desk drawer and pulled out the scanner. It was nearly four in the morning, late for activity at the sheriff's station. A staticky squawk belched from the black box, then a man's voice came over the air waves.

"Leavin' Jackson." The disembodied voice of the deputy then told the dispatcher his location.

That old bat, Nora, worked the day shift. At night the deputies rotated turns being the dispatcher and front desk officer. The other deputy on duty was assigned to field operations. It wasn't much of a task force, but it had been all Twin Oaks needed—until now.

Why would anyone on the force be in Jackson? The man stared at the black scanner, more than a little troubled. The sealed records of the Kaitlin Wells trial were in Jackson, but the prosecutor's office wasn't open at this hour. Even if the office had been open, they'd left nothing to chance. No one would ever find the file they'd destroyed.

"What's happening?" the dispatcher asked.

The man listened through bursts of static while the deputy explained. He'd known all about Radner's problems with Lucas Albright. It paid to have the goods on everyone.

From the sound of the conversation, Albright had attacked Kat Wells while looking for Radner. Interesting. More than interesting. He'd been right about Radner and the bitch with a talent for getting into trouble. Now he knew exactly where to find her.

The news brought him out of the funk he'd been in earlier. What he needed was a plan of action. This time she wouldn't escape alive. She'd used up her nine lives.

Didn't she know she was already half past dead?

CHAPTER TWENTY-SEVEN

TORI SAT ALONE in a booth at the back of Bits N Grits Café and ordered one of their homemade cinnamon rolls for breakfast. After what she'd been through with the Kincaids, she deserved a treat. Since the fiasco in the town square, the men had spent endless, agonizing hours rehashing events and strategizing. Tori had the sickening feeling she'd seen a glimpse into the future. And she hated every second of it.

Sure, she was willing to become the perfect daughter-in-law to further the judge's political ambitions. She'd brownnose and smile at dinner parties with celebrities, but she'd imagined a certain amount of private time. She saw herself walking the quaint streets of Georgetown on Clay's arm. Shopping in elegant boutiques. Dinners—just the two of them—in famous restaurants.

The reality might be quite different, she realized with a pang of disappointment. Would it be endless days in the stifling heat of backwater towns like Twin Oaks, campaigning—groveling—for votes? Her intuition warned her that more time than she'd ever bargained for would be spent on the campaign trail.

She could use her career as an excuse and duck out of some events, but the judge was a shrewd man. He would notice if she were magically free for parties in Washington, but not available for his speeches to hillbillies. She studied her long, immaculate nails and tried to decide how to handle this.

Maybe the Kincaids should have dumped her when Kat had gotten into trouble again. Atlanta was sounding better and better. Not Washington, but a fresh start in a lively city.

What about Clay?

Good question. She gazed at the heirloom ring gracing her left hand. If she married him, Tori knew she would be committing to a life of utterly boring political campaigns. From what she'd learned, the judge saw this senate seat as a stepping stone to the presidency.

Granted, the White House had its allure, but at what price? Rob Everett was always ordering them around. Where to go. What to say. What to wear. If the judge ultimately became president, Tori would lose her freedom. The Secret Service would be all over them like ants at a picnic.

And what about Clay?

She couldn't imagine breaking the engagement—even if their marriage had been the judge's idea. She'd loved Clay *forever.* She'd always envisioned herself as Mrs. Clayton Kincaid. Her mother would be devastated beyond belief if Tori broke the engagement.

But what about Clay?

How did he really feel? He'd contributed little during the strategy sessions, but then, even the judge had found it difficult to get Everett to shut up long enough to express his own opinions. Clay had spent last night with her. He'd rolled over, his back to her, and had fallen asleep immediately. He'd left early this morning for a deposition.

Gabby Anne trundled toward Tori, a pot of coffee in one hand and a plate with a decadent cinnamon bun in the other. There but for the grace of God, Tori thought. Gabby Anne had been in Tori's class, but she'd had to get married a week after graduation. The first of five—or was it six?—kids appeared that fall. Her no-good husband bounced from job to job. That meant Gabby Anne had to support the family by waiting tables. She lived off tips and Tori always left her double what a waitress would expect.

Gabby Anne looked closer to forty than thirty, yet she always had a smile for every customer. Tori detected a well-spring of regret beneath Gabby Anne's relentless smile, but frowns didn't earn tips. Just seeing the woman made Tori realize how lucky she was. Other than Cloris Howard at the bank, Tori earned more money than any woman in town.

No doubt, Gabby Anne would love to trade places, to wear fab clothes, to have a handsome, rich fiancé—and go on the campaign trail. So why was Tori giving in to self-pity and belly-aching?

Another unpleasant thought assailed Tori. The judge expected her to produce a grandson—immediately. She needed several years of marriage before embracing motherhood. Children were okay…but she couldn't imagine being pregnant. One look at Gabby Anne made Tori shudder. Having children ruined your figure. Imagine the stretch marks under the woman's rumpled uniform!

Gabby Anne grinned and placed the cinnamon roll in front of Tori. The sweet scent of melted sugar and cinnamon wafted through the air. Tori's stomach rumbled in anticipation, and she rallied a bit, already savoring the long-denied treat.

"Your poor, poor sister," Gabby said in hushed tones.

Tori almost snapped that Kat was only her half sister, then the words Rob Everett had drummed into all of them surfaced. *Take the high ground. Show sympathy, but distance yourself.*

"I know." Tori tested the softness of the warm roll with her fork and sectioned off a piece. "Terrible, isn't it?"

Gabby Anne tsked and replied, "Who says lightning doesn't strike twice?"

Tori halted, fork just an inch from her mouth. "Twice?"

"You didn't hear about what went on out at Justin Radner's place in the middle of the night?"

Tori silently listened while the talkative waitress launched into an amazing tale of how Kat had narrowly missed being killed by a paroled convict who was gunning for Justin. Her sister was like a noose around her neck, choking her more and more as each day passed. It was as if some malevolent power was using Kat to torture Tori.

Gabby Anne lumbered off to wait on a customer, and Tori stared down at the roll. She tried to eat it, but the treat now tasted like a lead biscuit. She took out her cell phone and called Clay to see what he would make of this latest event. His secretary told Tori that Clay hadn't come in yet.

Tori clicked off, puzzled and upset. How could that be? He told her he had a deposition. The light dawned. The deposition must be elsewhere—possibly even Jackson. She tried his cell, got his voice mail, and left a message.

KAT STUDIED the dummy of the *Trib*'s next edition on her computer screen. There was a news hole on the front page above the fold for the story of Lucas Albright's attack. Connie Proctor had informed her the second she'd arrived that David was still at home interviewing someone over the telephone. When he returned, David would write the article, insisted the copy editor. No, Kat couldn't do it. She was personally involved, which meant a conflict of interest.

Connie had been almost sweet—nicer than she'd ever been—but firm. The *Trib* must feature David's article. Still, Kat hadn't been able to resist typing in a few of her more vivid memories of the incident in the background section for David to review before he wrote the story.

When Kat had finished, she pulled up the issue about her car accident and her rescue by the Hill family. She skimmed it quickly, puzzled.

"Here's some herbal tea to soothe your nerves." Connie placed a steaming crockery mug on her desk.

"Thanks," Kat replied and made an effort to return the woman's sympathetic smile. She wished Connie would go back to copy editing. Lord knew the woman had plenty of headlines to create. There was no way Kat was going to drink or eat anything she hadn't personally prepared. Well, if David or Justin gave her something, she wouldn't refuse.

She thought Connie was looking at her oddly. She didn't suspect the older woman but Kat intended to be vigilant every moment. She didn't want to hurt Connie's feelings, so she tried to divert her attention from the herbal tea.

"I notice there's no mention of belladonna in David's article about my accident."

Connie frowned, deepening the lines between her eyes and on her forehead. Her eyebrows were a dark contrast to her overbleached blond hair. Kat couldn't help thinking that Lola Rae could do wonders with the copy editor's hair, but didn't say a word. Kat couldn't help feeling that Connie disapproved of her and resented the time it took for David to train Kat.

"You know how David is," Connie said with a smile that made Kat wonder if the woman had a thing for her boss. Probably not, she decided. David was the type of man who earned his employees' respect. Small-town papers very rarely had editors from publications as prestigious as the *Globe*. He could teach them things they would never have learned at a small paper. "Mavis Hill was only speculating. The *Trib* deals in facts."

"Of course." Kat reached for the mug and warmed her hands on it, hoping Connie would assume she was going to drink the tea. Connie muttered something about getting to the heads and walked over to her cubicle. Kat put down the mug.

She struggled to keep her focus on the rewrites about the upcoming fair, the Boy Scouts' Jamboree, and other local events. David was right, she realized, and not for the first time. Rewriting reports phoned in from the field was a total bore. There was nothing like original material.

She glanced up and almost jumped out of her chair. She hadn't heard a footstep, but Dwayne Hill was standing in front of her space in the cube farm. He grinned, the off-beat smile that chilled her somehow.

"Dwayne. It's good to see you." She stood up slowly, every muscle still aching from the ordeal with Lucas Albright. "I didn't get a chance to tell you how grateful I am to you and—"

"No need. You thanked Ma. Thass good enough."

"I need to thank all of you." She switched the weight of her sore body from one foot to the other, a little uneasy. "Is there something I could get your mother? What do you think she'd like?"

He stared at her and chawed on a wad of tobacco, as if the concept of a gift was alien to him. "Don't you be gettin' her nuthin'. I'll buy whatever she needs."

Something in his tone curtailed any further discussion. He flipped the keys to her Toyota over the Lucite divider. She lunged and managed to catch them with both hands.

"Car's all fixed. Billy Dean and me straightened out the bumper. Yer good to go."

"Thank you so much! It's hard to be without wheels."

Dwayne looked at her with eerie intensity and chuckled, a silent laugh that spooked Kat. She forced a smile and a little wave as he turned and left. She was too nervous to ask if there was anything she could do for him.

"What was that all about?" Connie asked in a voice loud enough to carry across the cubicles from where she was working to Kat's station.

"He was just returning my car. That's all."

Connie rolled her eyes and sat down again to work on the heads. Kat knew what she was thinking. The Hills were a bit strange, was the consensus of the locals. But Kat knew from experience that you could count on the Hills for help, unlike most of the other people in this town.

Half an hour later, David sailed through the door, Max at his side. He beamed when he spotted Kat at her desk. Connie popped up from her cube and waved to him. "Check these heads."

"Later," he called and motioned Kat to come with him.

She jumped up, relieved to get away from the rewrites and wondering if he'd discovered anything that would shed light on her predicament. He bear-hugged her. "You're looking so much better today."

Kat hoped she wasn't blushing. A night in Justin's arms and several rounds of sex had energized her. She felt a special sense of truly belonging to a person, of finally experiencing both physically and emotionally, the meaning of love. Not that Justin had uttered the *L* word, but that's how she felt—in love.

His arm still around her shoulder, they walked into David's office. Max trotted on ahead of them and scooted under the desk. "I spoke to a source in the FDIC," he told her in a low voice. "I wanted to know about the inspection set for the bank just before you were arrested. The FDIC randomly audits banks. Their visit is announced less than a week before they appear. They don't want to give the bank time to cook the books."

"The best way to rob a bank is to own a bank." Kat didn't recall where or when she'd heard this but the saying came out. Just before she'd been accused of robbery, Kat hadn't paid much attention to the auditors. Cloris and Elmer had been sprucing up the place for days, anticipating the visit. Their activities hadn't seemed unusual considering it had been nearly twenty years since the last FDIC inspection.

"The robbery caused a postponement of the FDIC audit," David added, his tone unusually solemn.

Kat had read every scrap of information about her case. All of it was related to her arrest and subsequent trial. Nothing about the audit had appeared in those reports. They wouldn't have, she realized. It would have been documented in federal records. Could this have something to do with the reason her record was sealed and the federal authorities were involved in sending her here to work undercover for them?

She realized her thoughts had caused a lull in the conversation, and David was regarding her with solemn speculation. "Did they ever complete the audit?"

"Not until six weeks after you were sentenced. When the bank became a crime scene, it was closed for a week while the investigation was conducted. The auditors were forced to reshuffle their schedule."

Now Kat got the picture. "They didn't want the auditors in the bank. That's why I was framed. They needed the time to hide something."

David collapsed into his chair, suddenly looking much older and world-weary. "Very possibly, but it'll be hard to prove, especially now with Elmer Bitner dead."

"They think I'm a threat," she said, unexpectedly relieved to finally put together the motive behind the scheme that had sent her to prison. "But why would they want to kill me now?"

"This is more complicated than it appears." He ran his hand through his silver hair. "Before the final report could be submitted by the team of examiners, one of them was killed in an automobile crash."

Kat picked up on an odd tone in his voice and looked at him more sharply. "Was there something suspicious about the accident?"

David shrugged, but she detected a glint of doubt in his expressive eyes. "Not really. I spoke with the husband. He's remarried and wants to put the past behind him. He claims he didn't know what his wife was working on at the time of her death."

"You suspect he's not telling the truth?"

"When he was talking, I kept thinking he knew more than

he was willing to tell me." He loosened his tie with a shrug. "Call it reporter's intuition. They have a grown daughter who's attending Duke. I'm going to drive up there and talk to her."

"What could she possibly tell you that the father wouldn't reveal?"

"Who knows? She would have been in her teens. She must have been close to her mother. Maybe they discussed the case."

Kat was about to mention that not all mother-daughter relationships were close. David surprised her by telling her to write the front page article about Lucas Albright to save him time.

"Just be sure to use my name on the byline," he concluded. "I don't want anyone—even Connie—to know. It's really not kosher to have you involved since you're part of the story, but I believe you can do a superior job."

CHAPTER TWENTY-EIGHT

KAT CONCENTRATED on the words on her computer screen, doing the final rewrite on Lucas Albright's attack on her and his botched attempt at killing Justin. It sounded like David, she concluded after rereading the piece. It was a tersely worded, professional article. Nobody would think the person who wrote the story had almost been killed by that madman.

"Someone's here to see you," Connie announced in a tone that made it clear this was a personal visit, another unnecessary interruption during working hours.

Kat quickly closed her screen so Connie wouldn't see what she'd been writing. David was supposed to have written this article, but Kat knew he had been busy downloading as much information as he could on FDIC investigations and the death of the inspector. She turned her attention to the *Trib*'s reception lounge where Lola Rae was huddled in one of the hard-back chairs. Why wasn't she at the shop?

"Hey, how are you?" Lola Rae asked in a soft voice that didn't carry beyond the reception area.

It was apparent that the hair stylist had been crying. Kat wasn't certain what to say. Lola Ray had coffee and pastries available in her shop each morning. Could Kat have consumed the nearly lethal dose of belladonna there? Or had Lola Rae hidden it in the Mexican food Maria had prepared for Kat?

She smothered the ache of discomfort that came with each

step and forced herself to focus on Lola Rae—not idle suspicions. Anyone could have slipped her the poison.

"What's wrong?" Kat sank into the chair beside Lola Rae, careful to keep her voice low and not disturb Connie and the others. There were only a handful of people working in the cube farm, but they were all rushing to meet the two-o'clock deadline to put the *Trib* to bed for the day.

"It's Gary Don," confessed Lola Rae and a fresh stream of tears dribbled down her cheeks. "He has another woman on the side. Know what I mean?"

It wouldn't surprise Kat, but she didn't voice her opinion. She really didn't know the man at all, but in her opinion he seemed cocky and reckless. There was something else about him that bothered Kat, but she couldn't quite put her finger on it.

"Why do you think there's another woman in the picture?"

Lola Rae pulled a scrap of tissue out of her pocket and dabbed at the corners of her eyes. "The other night, Gary Don claimed he was working, but I drove out to Moonin 'N Coonin. He wasn't there. I went around behind the building to where he keeps his trailer. He didn't see me, but I spotted him getting into this old Chevy with Teresa Evans." Lola Rae paused for a moment, sucking in air to keep from crying out loud. "Everyone knows she's nothin' more than a ho."

Whore. The word reverberated through Kat's brain. She wondered what people had called her. Kat knew Teresa from school. She'd served a short sentence in Jackson for possession of marijuana. As far as Kat knew, she'd never been accused of prostitution. But folks around here were quick to judge. Once you'd been in jail…you never lived it down.

"Last night I followed him," Lola Rae continued, oblivious to Kat's silence. "I was smart. I didn't use my car. I borrowed one of my brother's motorcycles. I put on a helmet and a leather jacket. No way could Gary Don see it was me dogging him."

Sensing something was coming, Kat's pulse kicked up a beat. "You followed him out to the bar or when he was leaving it?"

"As he left. He sleeps most afternoons and gets up in time to work or party, depending on his schedule. Last night, he took off from the bar and drove out to one of the levee roads. It's just a dirt path leading through the cane breaks in fields that haven't been planted for years. I hung back and turned off my lights to keep him from spotting me. In the middle of nowhere, he stopped. I was too far away to tell what he was doing exactly, but I saw a huge old tree had fallen down and blocked the ruts that pass for a road. I thought he'd taken something out of the old hollowed-out part of the tree."

As casually as she could manage, Kat asked, "Did you see what he took?"

Lola Rae hunched forward in her chair and studied the rhinestone-studded jeans she was wearing. "I was wrong. He didn't take a blasted thing. He left a bag of money for that two-bit tramp."

Kat nearly gasped at her friend's convoluted logic. Why leave the woman money out in the middle of nowhere? He could easily have handed it to her in private somewhere. The money couldn't be for this woman. It had to have been left in secret for someone else.

Kat needed to end the awkward break in the conversation. "Was it a lot of money?"

"I didn't count it but it had to be thousands of dollars. In small bills. There wasn't anything larger than a twenty that I saw."

Drug money, Kat silently concluded. She vividly recalled what Justin had told her about "double blind" drops.

"Where would Gary Don get that much money?" she asked, testing Lola Rae's logic. Love was blind, deaf, and dumb—too often.

"Gamblin'," Lola Rae replied without hesitation. "There's

always a game going on in the back room at the bar. He takes a cut for running the table. A lot of times he bets." Lola Rae's lips drew into a grim smile as tight as a corpse's. "He gave me a wad of cash to start All Washed Up. Now he's handing that ho money for something."

Kat could hardly wait to tell Justin about this development. It could be related to the case somehow. Twin Oaks was simply too small to have the drug running and murders not be linked. There must be a lot of cash floating around and an extreme need for secrecy to force the group to stash it in a log. It had to be retrieved and brought to a central point...like a bank. The casino was another possibility, she reluctantly admitted to herself. This wasn't going to be simple. She would need Justin's help to unravel this mess.

"Did you take the money or leave it in the old log?" she asked, attempting to sound nonchalant. Don't make Lola Rae suspicious. Go along with her assumptions.

"I left it." Lola Rae barked out a sound that might have been an attempt at a laugh. "I thought I'd catch Teresa picking it up. Know what I mean? I waited until the sun came up but she never showed."

It was almost two in the afternoon—plenty of time for the next link in the drug network to have picked up the money. Maybe they'd left more drugs to be sold. She wasn't sure what any of this meant, but she firmly believed this was a piece of the puzzle.

Justin needed to be informed of this development as soon as possible, but she didn't dare alert Lola Rae. Let her assume this was about another woman until they knew the truth.

"Is there a good place to hide and watch the tree?" Kat asked.

"Yeah. I rolled my brother's old Triumph behind a stand of bramble bushes and scrub oak. Even in a full moon, no one could spot me in that thicket." Lola Rae's dark eyes narrowed. "Why?"

"I'll go out there with you. Teresa might have been work-

ing. Let's see if she picks up the money today. Who knows?
It might be someone else."

"Like who?" There was a serrated edge to Lola Rae's
voice now.

Game's up, thought Kat. Lola Rae knows where I'm going
with this. Be straight with her. "Didn't it seem odd that Gary
Don would leave the money out in the boonies rather than
hand it to Teresa directly?"

Lola Rae brushed a limp hank of hair off her shoulder. "Not
really. Gary Don's a tease. He told me I'd find what I needed
in an old coffee can behind the post office." She smiled wist-
fully as if remembering those days with youthful happiness.
"Sure enough. There it was."

"Small bills?"

"Uh-huh. Gary Don told me to keep it hidden and feed it
into my cash drawer a little at a time." Lola Rae's lips trembled for a second, then tears welled up in her eyes again. "Every
night, I'd check the coffee can. You have no idea the security
it gave me to know I had enough money to run my shop."

Lola Rae was one of eight children, and her parents had
struggled constantly to keep up with the bills. Lola Rae had
no one to count on but herself. A familiar feeling, Kat decided.
From the moment her father had died, Kat had known she
must support herself. Oh, her mother allowed her to live with
her—but she was expected to pay rent. If she hadn't come up
with the money, she would have been out on the street.

Too bad Lola Rae's security had come at such a price.

JUSTIN GRINNED across the wide mahogany desk at Cloris
Howard. "I'm not asking to see any personal information
from the bank's files." He blasted the bank president with a
good ole boy smile even though he was pissed big-time that
she'd kept him waiting for over a half hour. "But I'll get a
court order if I need to."

Cloris inhaled, her delicate nostrils flaring just slightly, but she didn't respond. Beneath her cool demeanor he detected a cunning ruthlessness that he'd encountered in powerful men who saw themselves as above the law.

"I'm here to do a little more background on Elmer. I'm sure you want to see his murder solved."

"Of course," she replied smoothly. "I was convinced that Wells woman had shot poor Elmer but…"

"She has an airtight alibi."

"So it seems." Her observant eyes were a flawless blue, but with no depth of emotion. "How may I help?"

"What was Elmer working on when he was killed?"

"I would have to check." A note of defiance underscored her words as well as a subtle challenge. "The usual, I'm sure. He handled all our loans."

"Any problem transactions?" Justin was fishing here, slowly leading up to the questions he really needed to ask.

"I'm not aware of any, and I'm sure if there had been something, Elmer would have conferred with me."

Justin didn't doubt it. Any jerk could see Cloris Howard called the shots around the bank. Elmer wouldn't be able to take a crap without her okay.

Justin decided now was the time to drop the bomb. "Did Elmer mention that Buck Mason was getting his new loan from Jackson Mutual?"

"That's a lie," Cloris blurted out before she could stop herself, and Justin smiled inwardly, knowing he'd struck a sore spot. Cloris glanced down at her calendar for a moment, then responded in her usual detached voice. "Buck has always done his banking here. Why would he go all the way into Jackson?"

"A better rate?"

"Impossible. Ask anyone. We offer the best rates and services around."

Her haughty tone was like a burr under his saddle. How could the woman be so sure? Unless… "Buck and Elmer had met just hours before Elmer was killed. Buck himself told me that he'd broken the news about the Jackson bank to Elmer then."

"That's absurd! Buck would never do that."

He opened his mouth to ask the million-dollar question: Why not? A loan was a loan. A good businessman could get one anywhere. What was so special about Mercury? The service? Yeah, right.

The cell phone in his pocket vibrated—three quick bursts. The code he'd given Kat. "Gotta take this." He stood up and pulled the cell out of his pocket as he walked over to the window, his back to Cloris. "Radner here."

"It's Kat," she whispered.

"The reception's lousy," he told her, not wanting Cloris to guess who was on the line.

"I don't want anyone to hear me. I'm with Lola Rae. We're heading out to a spot along the levee. I think it's a drug money drop-off point."

Holy shit! She could get herself killed. "I'll meet you. I—"

"That'll blow everything. I'm leaving my cell phone on. It'll act like a microphone, if you don't turn yours off."

Justin started to protest, then stared at his cell phone for a second. What choice did he have? He flipped it shut, put it in his pocket, but didn't disconnect. He'd planted a miniature GPS tracking device in the heel of Kat's shoe. With the hand-held monitor he kept in his truck, he could follow her anywhere within in a sixty-mile radius. But this way, he could track her and hear the conversation.

"Is there a problem?" Cloris asked, her voice just a touch too interested.

He gazed at her a moment, thinking of Kat out in the woods with Lola Rae. Anything could happen. He'd planned to string Cloris along with a little game of cat-and-mouse to see what he could discover, but he didn't have the time now.

"No problem," he assured the oh-so-cool Ms. Howard. "I spent time with Ida Lou Bitner. Did she tell you Elmer planned to retire in two months and move to Guyana where he'd start a mission?"

Cloris started to giggle. "Elmer? A mission in the middle of nowhere?"

"Who said it was in the middle of nowhere?"

Cloris didn't miss a beat. "Elmer did. He mentioned his plan to move to Guyana and start a religious school. It was just talk, that's all. Elmer wouldn't venture off on his own to some small outpost north of Brazil that most people can't find on a map."

"Ida Lou tells me the funding was in place. Elmer had even made a deal with a realtor in Guyana to purchase a school and orphanage once run by a Jesuit order."

"Really?" Her tone expressed surprise, but Justin had a gut-deep feeling that she knew all about Bitner's plans to leave the country. "Reverend Applegate never mentioned—"

"I don't think he knew. This wasn't going to be a Baptist mission affiliated with Applegate's church. Elmer alone would be in charge."

It sounded a lot like a cult thing to Justin, but he wanted to get Cloris's reaction. After all, she'd worked with Bitner for almost twenty years. Hadn't they talked?

"Interesting." She appeared to be weighing her answer, debating whether to say more. But she kept her response to the single word. Justin had no idea what was really going on in her head.

Could she have pulled the trigger and shot the man who'd worked for her for over twenty years? Justin wouldn't bet against it.

CHAPTER TWENTY-NINE

TORI NOTICED the feathery trail of white powder on the garage floor when she went to check her mother's car battery. She should sell the old clunker, but that would only emphasize to her mother how near death loomed. The powder had spilled from a small green box shoved behind the old refrigerator her mother insisted on keeping in the two-car garage. Tori pried out the small box.

Rat poison.

Had rats invaded the pantry again? None of the nurses had mentioned it. She walked back into the house, calling softly, "Emilie, Emilie."

Emilie Yates was the night nurse. Almost sixty, with thinning white hair pulled back in a knot at the nape of her neck, Emilie had a lumberjack's body and a sunny disposition. No matter how ill Tori's mother felt, Emilie could make her smile. She was a rock and Tori had counted on her for most of this year.

Emilie poked her head around the corner, a finger to her lips. "Shh! Your mother's asleep."

Tori didn't point out that her mother was so heavily sedated these days that she usually slept twenty-three hours a day. She held out the small box of rat poison. "Are we having problems with rats again?"

Emile shook her head, adding, "I found it on the kitchen counter the other evening. I wanted to throw it out, but your mother insisted on taking care of it herself."

"Oh." Tori let out the word slowly. Why on earth had her mother shoved it behind the old fridge where they kept extra sodas?

"Your mother's going fast," Emilie said, her grizzled brows knitting into a tight frown. "It won't be long now."

Tori swallowed hard. Emilie had years of experience with these situations. No doubt what she'd said was true. Why not allow her mother to die in peace, believing Tori was going to become a Kincaid? Why tell her that Tori was seriously considering giving back the ring and moving to Atlanta?

"I'm not sure your sister should visit again," Emilie said carefully. "Your mother was really upset after the last visit."

"What visit?" Tori struggled to keep her voice down. She'd asked the day nurse and her mother if Kat had come here, but she hadn't seen Kat.

"The other evening when I arrived your mother was sitting in front of the television all agitated. She claimed Kaitlin had been bugging her."

"Bugging her?"

"About the past. Why she didn't love her." Emilie's gaze sharpened. "I guess your sister had popped in real unexpected like between nursing shifts and asked questions that disturbed your ma."

"Mother told me Kat hadn't visited."

Emilie tapped her head. "It's all the medication. Addles the brain. I've seen patients forget their own names and babble like loonie-tunes. Next day after the medicine cleared out of their systems, they became themselves again. It's best to talk to them just before they receive pain medication."

"Okay, when Mother wakes up, don't give her anything. I need to talk to her."

Emilie nodded thoughtfully. "Tie up any loose ends before it's too late."

Tori busied herself sorting through things in the garage,

making piles for charity and throwing useless items into the
trash, while she waited for her mother to wake up. Had her
mother poisoned Kat? Tori knew she wanted to get rid of
Kat—they both did—but would she have gone that far? No.
Her mother would never have resorted to poisoning her own
daughter.

She finished what she could do in the garage and returned
to the small condo, but her mother was still sleeping. She
could go through things in the second bedroom. It would cut
down on the sorting she would have to do later, but Tori was
afraid her mother might notice.

Tori tried Clay's cell phone again. Still no answer. Either
he'd left it in his car or he had it off. She didn't bother to call
his office again.

Where *was* he?

Clearly, he'd lied. He wasn't at a deposition or his secretary would have known. Could he have gone home to
Oakhurst for some reason? She couldn't imagine why he
would have. The judge and Rob Everett had driven into Jackson to confer with political honchos. Only his mother would
have been at home—assuming she didn't have a club meeting or a luncheon to attend.

"Your mother's awake," Emilie informed her in a whisper.

"I'll go talk to her."

The older woman studied her for a moment before saying,
"Some medications have half lives and remain in the system
for days if not longer. It could be some time until she's herself again. That'll mean she may suffer a lot."

Tori's throat closed up and she drew in a harsh breath. "I
need to talk to her. I'll make it quick."

Emilie nodded her approval, and Tori went into the bedroom. Her mother was sitting propped up against a bank of pillows, her skin a parched gray against the stark-white fabric.
She seemed to have shrunk since Tori had visited yesterday,

and she realized with heart-knocking alarm that Emilie was absolutely right. The end could be days or even hours away.

"Mom," she said. "How are you feeling?"

Her mother managed an indifferent shrug. Tori sat beside her on the bed, attempting to gauge how lucid her mother was. She took her mother's frail hand in hers and stroked her palm with her thumb. She noticed her mother's eyes drift to the engagement ring. Let her mother go to glory believing Tori would become a Kincaid. Tori could put off any decision about Clay until her mother was gone.

"Ma, listen to me. I need to ask you a few questions."

Her mother's gaze rose to Tori's face. She appeared to be more clear-headed than she had when Tori had arrived. "'Bout what?"

Tori swallowed hard, then asked, "Do you have a will somewhere?"

"Will? I don't...need a will."

"Ma," she said gently as she touched her mother's cheek. "You're not getting any better—"

"I know," she responded with a suggestion of the smile Tori remembered so well. "I'm...how do they say it? Terminal."

The word tore at something inside Tori's chest. It was the first time her mother had used it. She ventured a slight nod, silently acknowledging they'd crossed a line and were facing death head-on. "If something should happen, you wouldn't want Kat to get half of everything you have. Would you?"

"Don't worry about it," her mother said in a voice that seemed stronger than it had been in weeks. "Every-thing...goes to you."

Tori wondered if the combination of so many medications had confused her normally rational mother. If she had no will, the state would equally divide her property between her heirs. Kat would get half.

"You think I've lost it," her mother said.

"Well, you may not be thinking clearly because of the drugs."

"I'm a little fuzzy after an injection," she admitted, "but I haven't had one for hours. It hurts to breathe, let alone move, but my mind is crystal-clear at the moment."

Tori wondered how lucid her mother actually was, but didn't dispute her. She ran out of energy very quickly. Tori needed to settle this now before her mother was exhausted.

"There's something important I need to tell you." She patted the sheet for Tori to move closer.

Tori scooted over, more than a little uneasy. Why would her mother wait so long to tell her something important?

"All I have to leave you is this place." She waved one frail hand to indicate the small condo she'd purchased after Kat's father had unexpectedly died.

It was in good shape thanks to Tori's contributions for upkeep and decorating. It would bring top dollar—not as much as a home like Oakhurst—but enough that with the sale of her own condo Tori could reestablish herself in Atlanta. Of course there would be outstanding medical bills and a funeral to consider, but Tori calculated that she would have enough to begin again without scrounging for pennies—if she decided not to become Mrs. Clayton Kincaid.

"I signed and recorded a quit claim deed to this place. It's yours now."

Tori stared at her mother, unable to believe she'd taken this step without consulting her. A dozen thoughts whirled through her brain. As a real estate agent, she'd dealt with enough quit claims to know they were binding. The owner assigned all his property rights to another party. The loan and the liabilities transferred to that person as soon as the document was recorded. This condo and its small loan were now Tori's responsibility.

"What do you need to tell me?" Tori asked and her mother grinned, a strange, secret smile that frightened Tori.

"The truth." Her mother laboriously scooted into a more upright position.

The word *truth* rang a warning bell of dread deep inside Tori. Her mother hadn't been harboring a secret, had she? Tori always believed they were close in a way that other mothers and daughters weren't. They seemed more like sisters or best friends. They didn't keep secrets from each other.

As soon as that thought rushed through her brain, Tori admitted that she didn't tell her mother everything. Even now with death so close, her mother didn't know her doubts about Clay. But Tori had always believed she knew everything about her mother.

"Truth?" Tori asked. "What are you talking about?"

"My deepest shame." Tears filled her mother's stricken eyes and trickled down her cheeks.

What on earth was she talking about? Tori grabbed a tissue from the nightstand and dabbed at the tears. Her mother brushed her hand away.

"I never wanted to taint you and ruin your chances of being part of society."

Tori didn't doubt it. Her mother had been obsessed with what passed for society in Twin Oaks for as long as Tori could remember.

"You did your best," Tori assured her. She silently added that she'd done her part as well. She'd worked hard and made something of herself. Until the fiasco at the town square, Tori had discounted her achievements. Seeing how easily the judge had been taken down made Tori realize she didn't have to rely on family position. She had a track record. She could start all over again in Atlanta and be just as successful.

Judge Kincaid and his family relied too much on name and reputation. Even though May Ellen had a family name and a degree in botany from Ole Miss, she wasn't in any position to support herself. Clay and the judge had law degrees but she wondered how they would fare with the legal sharks in Atlanta or Memphis. Their success here was based too much on who their families had been.

The judge might come out a winner again, she decided. He had a predator's cunning that his wife and son didn't. She tried to imagine Clay going head-to-head with the cutthroat lawyers she'd encountered in Jackson—but couldn't. She loved him, yet sometimes she wondered if his heart was really in the law. What would he have become if he'd been raised in a single-wide trailer like Justin Radner?

Would she have wanted to marry that Clay Kincaid? He'd still be handsome and charming, but her mother wouldn't have relentlessly pushed him at her. Would Tori have been so determined to marry him?

"I didn't want the truth to ruin your life." Her mother's words came out in an agonized rush. Her mother's flat, unspeaking eyes prolonged the silence between them. Finally, she went on, "Your father didn't die in a car accident in Florida. After you were born, Vince just up and walked out. He didn't want the responsibility of a baby."

It took a moment for the words to register. Her father had loved her dearly. He'd been tragically killed while on a business trip to Miami. Even though she'd never known him, never heard him speak her name, she'd felt his love.

Love.

The word floated through her brain. It took several seconds to realize what she'd felt wasn't her father's love. It had been her mother's love. Always. What little she'd known about her father had been filtered through her mother.

His love had been nothing more than an illusion. She closed her eyes for a moment in an attempt to come to grips with reality. The ghost of a father she'd always adored and had believed loved her—hadn't existed. He'd deserted her mother because he didn't want...Tori.

It had happened a long time ago, she reasoned. It shouldn't

ache like a raw wound, but it did. It wasn't easy to let go of a lie you'd lived with for over thirty years. It became part of you, who you were, how you saw yourself. How others saw you.

"What was I supposed to do?" Tears strangled each word from her mother's lips. "I had a baby and rent to pay but no job. What do you think people would have said if they knew Vince had up and left me?"

Still numb with shock, Tori silently acknowledged that people sympathized with widows in a way they didn't with women who'd been divorced or deserted. It wasn't fair but it was true.

Torn by conflicting emotions, Tori asked, "What about Daddy's family in Memphis?" She'd never seen her aunt and cousins. Her mother had always made excuses not to visit them. Now Tori knew why.

"Vince's mother died just after we were married. His only sister married a no-good bum. Vince's pa had up and disappeared just after Vince was born. Like father, like son." Her mother shook her head. "There was no getting help from our families. I was on my own."

Tori tried to imagine how frightening that must have been. True, she'd worked to make something of herself, but she'd always known she had her mother as a fallback. What would it be like to have no one?

Unbidden, Kat's image appeared in her mind. Kat had known love—her father's love—just as Tori had been assured of her mother's love. But after her father had died, when Kat had needed her mother the most, Loretta had turned her back on her. Having been deserted herself, their mother must have known how devastating it could be, but she hadn't cared. *And neither had I,* Tori reluctantly conceded. Oh, she'd been tempted to help Kat, but it had been easier to walk away without getting involved.

At the time she'd assured herself that she'd chosen the

best course. She'd been convinced she didn't have the knowledge or the money to help Kat. But had she been honest? Not really. If she'd put up a fight, at the very least, Kat might have been assigned a more competent public defender. *Don't go there,* Tori warned herself. There had been hard evidence against Kat. Getting mixed up in her problems wouldn't have helped.

"I went to work in Dr. Cassidy's office, keeping patient records and filing," her mother continued, "but I was barely earning enough to get by. I had no choice but to look around for another husband while I was still young and pretty."

"Without getting a divorce? What if Daddy returned?"

Her mother let out a derisive snicker. "I'm not dumb. I scraped together enough money to hire a private investigator in Jackson. Seems your daddy only made it as far as Panama City Beach before hopping in the sack with another woman. They claimed to be married."

Dazed, Tori attempted to compare the various images of her father that she'd culled from the few pictures her mother had of a handsome young man with a wide smile and twinkling eyes. She'd always thought of him as loving and supportive, a man who would be with her every moment he had to spare.

A father like…like Parker Wells.

She'd never envied Kat. Actually, she'd felt superior to her sister because she had a mother and a father who doted on her. True, her father was dead, but she'd basked in his love just the same. Tori had always assumed her father would have been exactly like Parker.

If only he'd lived.

The opposite had been true, she realized with a wild flash of grief.

As if reading her thoughts, her mother said softly, "You had me. I loved you more than I should have to make up for the loss of your father."

"I'd like to—" Tori stopped herself before she asked how to contact her father. It could wait, she decided, until her mother was gone. What would be the point in hurting her by letting her know how much Tori had dreamed about her father? How much it now hurt to know he had been living a few hours away and had made no attempt to see her in all these years.

Again seeing through to her soul, her mother said, "Your father died 'bout eight years ago. Lung cancer. He'd been a chain smoker. No one—not even his new woman—could convince him to give it up."

Tori stared out the window, her heart unable to accept what she'd just heard. Her world was shutting down like a curtain falling after the final act. The play was over. Life as she knew it was over.

For a fleeting second she wondered if this was how Kat had felt when she'd been alone in jail. She let the thought go as quickly as it had come. This was different; Tori's life was special. She'd made something of herself. Nothing could take that away from her.

She'd been a winner from the day she was born. Kat was—and always would be—a loser. Kat had suffered—she'd grant her that much—but if she'd had character she would have been more like Tori.

"I wanted to protect you," her mother added. "I didn't consult a lawyer—least of all the Kincaids—and have to explain why I didn't want to write a will."

Tori didn't get it. "Why not?"

"I was afraid someone might find out that I had inherited Parker Wells' money illegally. Your father and I never divorced. As his next of kin, Kat should have inherited everything her father had."

"Why didn't you divorce him when you found out the skank was living with another woman?"

Her mother shrugged as if it didn't really matter. "Parker

came along before I had time to scrounge up enough money to go to Florida and get a divorce."

Now Tori understood. "You'd said Daddy wasn't alive. You couldn't file for divorce here without everyone knowing you'd lied."

Her mother's mouth quirked as if a bolt of pain had lanced through her. A moment later, she said, "I didn't want to ruin your chances with folks like the Kincaids." She slumped back against the pillows. "Right away Parker was smitten with me…"

And you saw a meal ticket, Tori silently added.

"I never wanted another child. Kat just happened. I didn't love her." She managed a low snicker. "I didn't have to. Her daddy loved her enough for both of us."

The way you loved me.

"Now you can marry Clay and take your rightful place in society like I've always known you would."

CHAPTER THIRTY

KAT LEANED against Justin's sturdy shoulder and gazed out at the gathering dusk casting an amber glow across the yard. Lola Rae had dropped Kat off after a long, hot afternoon on an amateur stakeout of the fallen tree. Justin had been home waiting for her, Redd and Max at his side. The relief on his face told her just how worried he'd been.

When was the last time anyone had been concerned about her?

Images of her father sprang into her mind. The look on his face as she rode her bike up the drive for the first time without training wheels. His puckered brow as she'd competed in a spelling bee, which she'd ultimately won. His attempts to control a grimace as Tori had swanned out the door with Clay on prom night, when they both knew Kat wouldn't have a date when her own prom rolled around.

It had been years ago, yet the memories triggered a bittersweet ache. What would her father say if he could see her now? She wasn't a shy, ugly duckling any longer. She knew he would be proud of her—despite the years she'd spent in prison.

"Okay," Justin said, his warm breath fanning her cheek. "Give me the details. What I heard over our cell phones was garbled. I could tell you weren't in trouble but the signal kept cutting out."

She'd already explained she'd seen the money being picked up, but she went over the story again, taking care to give him every fact she could recall. "After we arrived on the motor-cycle Lola Rae's brother loaned us, we hid it in the underbrush and walked over to the old log."

"Good thinking." He gazed down at the area rug where Max and Redd were snoozing.

"Several other packets had been placed on top of the one Lola Rae had seen Gary Don leave."

"Lola Rae must have realized this wasn't about another woman."

"Of course. We talked it over. She believes Gary Don must be dealing drugs. She doesn't want anything to do with him. She's terrified she'll end up in jail."

"Did she know he'd already served time?"

"Yes." Kat looked up at him and tried for a mischievous smile. "I gave her the whole spiel about the rate of recidivism that you dished out at me. She promised not to tell anyone about this. She doesn't want to be involved."

He chuckled and kissed the top of her head. "Finish telling me about the pickup."

"The sun was dropping behind the trees, but it was still hotter than Hades. Swarms of mosquitoes were eating us alive. We were about to leave." Her body was still hot and sticky despite the swamp cooler blowing right on her. "We'd been so sure the money would be picked up during the day that we hadn't bothered to bring flashlights. We knew it would be useless to stay after dark.

"That's when Lola Rae heard a motor. She thought it was a dirt chopper like the motorcycle her brother had loaned us. I noticed a chugging sound, and I knew it must be a motorboat."

"The levee meets the river not far from there, but the inlet is choked with kudzu," Justin interjected.

"Did you know exactly where we were?"

Justin's smile seemed a tad guilty. "I planted a mini-GPS transmitter the size of a button in your shoe—just in case."

"Without telling me?" Sometimes she didn't understand him. It would have been comforting to know the device was there.

"People act differently if they don't realize they have a fallback."

"I see," she replied slowly. He came from a different world, where drug busts were an everyday occurrence. In some ways she'd been through hell, but this was her first brush with the dark underworld of drug dealing.

"Go on," he prompted.

"A guy neither of us recognized tromped up the trail. He made no attempt to conceal himself or to stay quiet."

"Young? Old? How tall? What did he weigh?"

"It was a little too shadowy to say for sure, but I thought he was in his late twenties. Average height. About one-eighty. He was dressed in beige slacks and a navy polo shirt. A little dressed-up for the backwoods. He must have come from work somewhere."

"A navy blue polo. Did it have the casino's logo above the pocket?"

Kat shrugged. "Possibly, but neither of us got a close enough look. He knew exactly where to go. He marched up to the old log, loaded the packets into a backpack, and was out of there in less than a minute."

"He's done this before. Lots of times."

"Probably. I listened carefully when he started the motor. The engine wasn't more than fifty horses. I know because my father fished. Bigger engines have a deeper rumble." She didn't add how much her father had wanted a larger motor for his small skiff, but insisted on banking the money for "his girls' education."

"Figures," Justin replied with a thoughtful nod. "Meth generates lots of cash in small bills. New York, Chicago, L.A.— every major city you can name and authorities have found money stashed away, waiting to be picked up. Sometimes it's left so long the bills are mildewed. Boxes have been found in storage units when people fail to pay the rent. There's so much cash floating around that people forget or lose track of it."

"Amazing." She thought of how little money she had. It was difficult to imagine allowing a dollar to get away from her.

"Someone working a double-blind operation doesn't want anyone to know who he is. So how is the cash counted without a lot of workers?"

Kat considered his question for just a second. "They must have machines at the casino to automatically count money and slot machine change, right?"

"Hey," he said with a teasing smile, "you're smarter than the average blonde."

"Ya think?"

"Absolutely." His expression turned serious. "There's nothing average about you."

She kissed him lightly on the cheek. "You think there really is mob money behind the riverboat? Are they pushing drugs, too?"

"Gambling has always been tainted by the mob. The Sartiano family operates out of New Orleans. They control the riverboats there but not with a heavy hand. Gambling is regulated by the state. Getting around their accounting procedures is tough but not impossible."

"You're saying the mob wouldn't funnel a lot more cash into the casino and make the state auditors suspicious."

"Exactly. The take from every table, every slot machine is recorded, then checked in and placed in steel cases with a special lock."

Kat thought a moment. "Couldn't the supply boat that delivers goods take the drug money back to New Orleans to avoid state inspectors? Remember, we thought the supply boats might be delivering the supplies needed to make meth."

"It's possible, but I have the feeling the ringleader wouldn't want to involve that many people. Crews on small service boats change overnight. Having those boats transport cash would mean letting more and more people in on the secret. Our guy doesn't operate that way."

"Guy? Why not a woman?"

"A woman could be involved," he conceded, "but this is still the South. Guys rule."

"Get out!"

He smiled, then compressed his lips. "Sad but true. A woman may be involved, but she wouldn't deal directly with the Sartianos. They're Italians from Chicago who intermarried with a Cajun family living outside of New Orleans. It's a male-dominated society. I suspect the drug money is processed through the counting machines at the riverboat to quickly and accurately tally the cash. I'll bet the Sartianos take a cut, then turn over the rest of the money to someone locally."

"What happens to the money then?"

He gazed off across the room for a moment, then said, "Good question."

Kat couldn't imagine how the drug operation might be connected to her—except through the bank. She verbalized her hunch. "It goes through the bank somehow."

"That's my guess, but it's just speculation. Question is: Why did Bitner ask to meet you? I can't see him telling you about the operation."

Kat had no idea either—unless it was somehow tied to the undercover operation the Feds had going. She was tempted to tell Justin, but decided to wait until David returned. With luck, he would know more about what had gone on with the bank examiners. It might explain what had happened without her having to go back on her word and tell anyone why she was here.

His thumb gently kneaded the back of her neck. "Let's go to Jo' Mama's for ribs. I think we've done all we can for one day."

She tried to resist the urge to melt into his arms. "What about having a deputy stake out the log?"

"I don't have the manpower. Even if I did, I don't know who to trust. This is a small town. I don't want word getting back to the ringleader that I'm onto this. Besides, I seriously doubt if they leave money more than once a week. We have time."

How much time did she have? *Don't think about it. Live in the moment.* She shifted positions, pulled his head toward her, and crushed his lips with a kiss.

He returned the kiss, one hand creeping up her leg and caressing the tender flesh of her thigh. She fumbled with the buttons on his shirt as his mouth opened and their tongues met. She finally managed to wedge her hand under his shirt and stroke his bare chest. A low growl rumbled from his throat.

"Hey, if you're not careful, we won't get to Jo'Mama's."

"Ask me if I care."

He chuckled, then began to kiss her neck and the sensitive spot behind her ear. She threw back her head and allowed him access to her breasts. He palmed her through the fabric of her blouse, the normally soft material abrading her sensitive nipples. Her legs weakened and parted as a low moan became a sensuous purr.

Before she knew what was happening, he swept her into his arms and with long, purposeful strides crossed the living room. This time he took her down the hall into his room and kicked the door shut with his foot before the dogs could follow them.

He gently laid her on top of the covers as if she might break. Stretching out beside her, he kissed her slowly, his fingers tunneling though her tousled hair. She arched her back and snuggled closer. Before she knew it, he had her blouse undone and her bra unhooked.

They kissed. And touched. And caressed. By silent agreement they took time to explore each other's bodies.

This was how a man and a woman made love. It wasn't just about sex, she told herself. This was so much more...fulfilling.

She'd fallen hopelessly in love with him. She'd realized this yesterday, but now knew with absolute certainty this man was the love of her life. How could she love him and not tell him the truth about why she'd been sent here? Hiding this secret seemed almost like cheating, like being with another man behind Justin's back.

"THERE'S A MESSAGE for you," Connie informed Kat when she walked into the office the following morning with Max in tow. She thought it might be from David. He hadn't called last night, and she wondered if he'd found out anything from the bank examiner's daughter at Duke.

"Thanks," Kat replied as she tried to ignore the flush rising up her neck to her cheeks. She was positive the copy editor had seen Justin drop her off and knew just how they'd spent last night.

Connie hovered nearby. "Your sister left a message on the machine just before the paper opened. I guess she didn't know how to get a hold of you."

Kat stared down at the slip of paper Connie had given her. What did Tori want? She guided Max into David's office and let him settle under his desk before she used David's telephone to return the call. Whatever Tori wanted, Kat didn't need Connie to overhear her conversation.

Kat waited while Tori's cell phone rang several times. She was getting ready to hang up when Tori answered. "Tori? It's me. Kat."

A muffled noise followed as if Tori had put her hand over the phone. A moment later, she said, "It's Ma." Tori's voice cracked and the rest came out with a sob. "She went to glory last night. I'm at Gaylord's Funeral Home. You need to come right away."

Without another word, the line went dead. Kat collapsed into David's chair. How could her mother have died so suddenly? Not that it hadn't been expected, Tori had warned her, but Kat hadn't had the opportunity to see her mother and set things straight. Had she?

Some dark corner of her brain wondered. She'd been so convinced her mother's death was imminent—was it possible she had visited her mother but didn't remember?

A wellspring of guilt rushed through her. Instead of spending last night in bed with Justin, she should have gone to see her mother. Her father used to say "you never have a second chance to make a first impression." Now she could add "you never have a second chance to say goodbye."

CHAPTER THIRTY-ONE

CURSING UNDER HIS BREATH, the man walked across the town square and mentally reviewed what had happened yesterday. Being Jekyll and Hyde was no longer as much fun as it had been. Until Radner and the Wells woman had returned to Twin Oaks, he'd seldom had to revert to Hyde. Usually, he played Dr. Jekyll, the man no one suspected of running the most lucrative drug operation in the Delta.

He had the world by the short hairs. When necessary, he ruthlessly and cleverly killed anyone who got in his way. He'd eliminated the Mexican broad who'd tried to blackmail him. Only dumb luck had led to the discovery of her body. He'd needed a little help tricking Elmer, but he would have pinned Bitner's death on the Wells bitch if fate hadn't intervened.

He controlled the world around him, but fate—usually his closest ally—could be the downfall of even the smartest man. He'd planned to get rid of Kat yesterday. Then her lowlife friend from the beauty parlor showed up at the paper. From there he'd tailed them to a decrepit shack just outside of town where they'd left the car and had ridden off on an old motorcycle they'd taken out of the garage. In the middle of the day. Why?

Then it came to him. PnP. "Party and play"—the Internet lingo for meth parties. When he was bored, he tracked meth parties advertised online. In cities they were usually held in abandoned buildings. In rural areas like this, "players" gathered in the woods. There the druggies met, got high, had sex, then split.

Kaitlin Wells was on furlough from prison. She couldn't be too careful. She needed to be completely out of sight before she used drugs. It bothered him—a little—that they'd driven off into the woods a few miles from one of two drop-off points his operatives used. There was no way he could follow them without being spotted.

He chalked up his suspicions to being overly cautious. There hadn't been a single sign his operation had been compromised. True, Willingham had gotten his rocks off with the broad from the beauty parlor, but their sources told them that Willingham was humping someone else now.

Willingham didn't know who masterminded the operation, but the laser would never divulge what little he did know. The last thing Willingham wanted was to find his ass behind bars again.

He returned to his office and had tried to work, but he kept his eye on the clock. The cryptic call had come in from the casino just as it always did. He'd written down their count of the weekly take and subtracted the Sartianos' cut.

Business as usual, he'd reassured himself—except for one small hitch but not an unexpected one. The team of Mississippi state inspectors had arrived at the casino to verify the tallies and calibrate the slot machines, the way they always did.

Not a problem, he assured himself. The state sent its team around once every month. The machines that generated the checks had to remain hidden along with the packets of drug money while the inspectors were onboard the riverboat. His money wouldn't be brought back to Twin Oaks until tonight, when the inspectors left for another riverboat and the cover of darkness made it easy to transport his money.

Last evening he'd concealed his car behind some scrub oak and wrangled his way through the woods until he found a hiding place in the thicket behind the sheriff's house. Radner and his scruffy dog had driven up a short time later. Not long after, the floozy of a hairdresser dropped off Kat.

Un-fucking-believable! The broad did have nine lives. They didn't even open a door except to let the dogs out to piss around midnight. He had no opportunity to isolate her for the kill.

He could have whacked them both as easy as shooting a treed 'coon. But murdering a law officer brought out all his brethren. The place would be crawling with cops. If the FBI were called in, his operation could be exposed to unnecessary scrutiny.

The others would go ballistic. They had a game plan and went nuts whenever it wasn't followed to the letter.

Only a dumbfuck would snuff Radner and the bitch while they were together. But he had a plan—one he had no intention of sharing with the others. Let them sit on their asses in the woods being chawed on by mosquitoes and no-see-ums. He'd had an entire night to devise a foolproof scheme.

Gone missing.

Did he love that term! Once upon a time—a more rational time—people vanished or disappeared. Now they'd "gone missing." How could anyone *go* missing? The phrase wasn't even grammatically correct. It didn't really make any sense, if you analyzed it, but what the fuck did he care?

Kaitlin Wells was going to vanish into thin air. This time he'd make certain people believed she'd fled by planting drugs in her things. They'd all assume she was avoiding a return to prison. The trick was to kill her and dispose of the body where no one would ever find it.

No Pequita Romero situations this time. No dumb luck. No

more half past dead. As far as he was concerned, Kat Wells was all the way dead.

JUSTIN TOOK the precautions that David had insisted upon when he called. Evidently the reporter had discovered something that he didn't want anyone else to know about. Without telling anyone where he was going, Justin had driven out to the pier at Cully's Landing. The resort on the spring-fed lake hadn't opened for summer yet and no one was around. David pulled up a few minutes later with Max.

"Where's Kat?" Justin called.

David walked toward him without answering, and a frisson of alarm rippled through Justin.

"She's at the mortuary," David replied. "Kat's mother died just before dawn. She's helping Tori make plans for the funeral. When I returned from Duke, Connie told me."

The news lanced through him like a shaft of ice. Aw, hell! Just what Kat didn't need. She had enough stress in her life for ten women. Why did her mother have to die now, before they'd had a chance to talk?

Sure, the woman had been cruel to Kat, but Loretta Wells had still been her mother. The emotional shield Kat had worn like a straitjacket had slipped away as he'd gotten to know her. She was softer than he'd first thought, more sensitive. Faced with death, she would forgive her mother anything.

Justin suspected that Loretta had tried to poison Kat. Now they might never know the truth. Hell, for all the evidence he'd discovered, the killer might still be out there. He hated loose ends that left him wondering. The pit of his stomach burned with anxiety.

"Maybe I should head over to the funeral home," Justin told David. "I don't want Kat alone with Tori. She might have been the one who tried to poison Kat."

David leaned his back against the wooden pier rail. "She's

not alone. Connie told me the mortician was meeting with them and so is Reverend Applegate. It'll take awhile to plan the funeral."

Justin nodded without speaking. Too clearly he remembered how long it had taken to arrange a small private service for his mother. Every second had been agonizing.

The type of coffin. Wood or faux wood? Should the casket be lined with satin or polyester? Would the dearly departed want her Bible in the coffin? Where would the dearly departed wish to spend eternity? On a hill? Near the pond?

David turned to him, his expression solemn. "I asked you to meet me out here so I could tell you what I discovered."

Already alarmed, Justin's pulse kicked up a notch. "Why? Do you think your office is bugged or something?"

"No," David replied after a moment's hesitation, "but experience has taught me to be extremely careful."

"So what did you want to talk to me about?"

"Pamela Nolan, the bank examiner's daughter, had a lot to say about her mother's death. Before she was killed in an auto accident, Ethel Nolan had been engaged in a disagreement with her partner, a man who'd been recently hired by the FDIC."

"About the inspection of Mercury National?"

"Exactly. Ethel told her daughter she suspected certain loans taken out for real estate and automobiles were actually set up under false names to hide funds. Her partner disputed her assessment."

This confirmed what Justin already suspected but couldn't prove—yet. "Laundering money by creating phony real estate and auto loans to conceal drug money."

"You're probably right."

Justin considered what David had said for a moment. "The daughter just told you all this? Why didn't she go to the police when her mother died?"

"She wanted to, but her father wouldn't let her."

"Someone paid him off."

"Possibly. A check of his bank records would tell us if he deposited money he can't account for." David let Max off the leash. The puppy scampered to the end of the pier and hung his head over the dock to check out the wind-whipped waves lapping the pilings. "His daughter's still pretty upset that her father remarried so soon after her mother's death. I think that's the reason she told me all this."

"She's getting back at her father."

"That was my impression. She doesn't like the woman he married, but I also think she feels guilty about not doing something sooner."

"What about the partner, the other bank examiner?"

"He filed the report after Ethel Nolan's death, and it went through. He's been promoted. The man is FDIC regional supervisor now."

"And Mercury hasn't been inspected again."

"Not surprising," David assured him. "I checked. With all the federal funding cutbacks, banks are being inspected only once every ten years or so—unless there's reason to suspect fraud."

"We were right. The answer is at the bank. Question is, how do we prove it?" Justin spent the next few minutes telling David about the drug drop-off in the woods, and his theory that the automatic counting machines at the casino were being used to tally the take before the cash was returned to town.

"A slick deal. Simple, efficient, yet hard to trace," David said.

"Drexel Sartiano isn't about to let someone run a drug scam under his nose without getting his cut."

David nodded, then said, "I had time to think about this on the drive back from Duke. Cloris Howard is the key, right? She has to be in on this, if the money is going through the bank."

"Right. Bitner, too." Justin had already calculated how this had gone down. "Bitner wanted out so he could start his mis-

sion in South America. That's what got him killed." Justin
paused for a moment, then continued. "Pequita Romero's
roommates claimed she was going out to pick up money. This
may be a stretch, but I'm thinking both of them asked for
money. Pequita was probably blackmailing someone, while
Bitner wanted his cut so he could move on."

"Interesting theory."

"Hell. It's the only thing that makes sense."

"I say we get Cloris to roll over on the others and cop to a
lesser charge."

"Never happen." Justin leaned over the rail and studied the
clear blue water below the pier. "Cloris is tougher than nails."

"People bend if they think they can avoid spending the rest
of their lives behind bars."

Justin thought David's smile was a little smug. Obviously,
the man had an idea. "Okay, I'll bite. How do we get her to
cooperate?"

"Remember my source out at the *Lucky Seven?*"

"Yeah." Justin didn't say that so far his source hadn't come
up with jackshit.

"He's working as a parking valet and he's made some interesting observations in addition to the license plate numbers
he provided me. He's taken photographs of visitors using his
camera phone. Clay Kincaid appears in several of them. And
in two, I spotted Maria."

"The woman who works at the beauty parlor?"

"Exactly. I wasn't surprised to see Clay there—I hear he's
quite a gambler—but what would Maria be doing at the *Lucky
Seven?*"

Justin recalled the first time he'd met the woman when
she'd been delivering food to Kat. *Food.* Shit! Double shit!
That could have been the source of the belladonna.

"She could be visiting other illegals who work there,"
David suggested.

"Possibly, but remember that Maria was the one who gave Kat info about Pequita when no one else would. I think she's involved in this somehow."

REVEREND APPLEGATE AND the mortician, Willis Benton, finally left Kat alone with Tori. They'd been at the funeral home since noon. Each minute had seemed like an eternity, but Kat hadn't complained. She could tell this was more difficult for Tori than it was for her. Kat hadn't seen—or didn't remember seeing—her mother for several years. Tori had been with her every day. She'd suffered with Loretta until the end had finally arrived.

Kat had concurred with each of her sister's decisions. Tomorrow would be an open-casket viewing. Reverend Applegate had assured them the ladies in the church auxiliary would supply cookies and punch in the mourning parlor after the viewing. The funeral service was set for the same afternoon.

Tori had stoically agreed and murmured her thanks. Her eyes were puffy, and although she wasn't crying now, it was clear she had been. The only time Kat could remember her sister crying was when she hadn't been elected homecoming queen. *Get over it,* Kat told herself. *That was then. This is now.*

Kat said, "I'll get you my half of the money to pay for the funeral as soon as I have it."

Tori leveled her red-rimmed green eyes on her. "It's not necessary. I earn plenty of money, and Mother quit-claimed the house to me. I can afford it."

"I want to contribute my share. I—"

"Don't you understand? You're not inheriting a dime from Mother."

Kat wasn't surprised in the least. Considering how her mother had treated Kat when she'd been put in prison, Kat knew better than to think her mother would leave her anything. "I didn't expect to inherit a cent, but I still need—"

A lone tear crawled down the high arch of Tori's cheek. "She got pregnant with you by accident."

An accident.

The word hit her with the force of a physical blow, and she had to suck in a stabilizing breath. Well, that explained a lot. An ache too deep for tears filled Kat, but she forced herself to focus on the positive aspects of her life. At least she'd had her father's love. No one could take that away from her.

Tori swiped at her tears with the back of one hand. "Let's go. We need to talk."

DAVID RETURNED to the *Trib* and Connie greeted him in the foyer. "You put the paper to bed?" he asked, bone-weary and wishing he could go to sleep. He was too old for an all-night drive followed by a full day of work.

"Yes. Kat wasn't here to help. I guess she's still planning the service for her mother."

David walked toward his office, Max beside him. "She'll need a few days off for the funeral and to settle things."

"I was going to run a death notice about Loretta Wells."

David sat in his chair and did his best not to let his shoulders slump. "Check with Kat for a photograph, blow it up, and run it. Don't charge Kat a dime."

Connie nodded but the scowl she tried to conceal told him that she didn't approve. Obituaries were just a few lines, giving the deceased's name, date of death, funeral arrangements, and a bit of other data. Funeral notices with photographs and information submitted by the family were a source of revenue for every paper. Connie had turned them into a cash cow for the *Trib*, but David refused to take money he knew Kat didn't have.

"We've received lots of e-mails and calls about your article on Lucas Albright," Connie said with a smile he found a little flirtatious.

"Good," he replied, ignoring her attempt to be overly friendly. "Have we had an update on Albright's condition?"

"Kat was supposed to call this morning, but she ran out after I gave her the message from her sister. I phoned the police in Jackson. Lucas has been transferred to a regular cell until he can be returned to the penitentiary."

"Thanks. I knew I could count on you. Did you run an article about it?"

"You bet." Connie beamed at him. "Check it on the dummy sheet. I told about the transfer and reused some of the article you wrote."

David kept his concern to himself. Today, he'd revealed more information about a source than he should have. He prided himself on being a professional. He didn't want anyone—even Connie—to know Kat had written the article and used his byline.

CHAPTER THIRTY-TWO

"You visited Mother just a few nights ago," Tori told her.

Oh my God, Kat thought. Her temples throbbed and she was suddenly light-headed. It took a second to reorient herself. "I did?"

She stared wordlessly at her sister. How could she have possibly forgotten something so important? But some distant part of her brain had remembered. She'd had a *feeling* her mother was going to die.

"Yes. She served you lemonade."

They were standing in the living room of her mother's small condo, having stopped to pick out a dress for their mother to be buried in.

"I can't imagine forgetting, but I don't remember seeing Mother."

Tori looked away for a moment, then gazed at Kat with bloodshot green eyes. Tori motioned for Kat to sit on the sofa. She dropped onto cushions that had been recovered since she'd lived here, and Tori sat beside her.

Her sister had behaved differently today, she thought—less self-absorbed, less intense. Death takes something out of you, changes you. Kat was sorry her mother was gone, sorry they hadn't had the opportunity to make their peace, yet she wasn't as distraught as Tori seemed to be.

That's because I lost my mother by degrees, Kat reasoned, then corrected herself. No. She'd never had a place in her mother's heart. She'd learned at a very young age not to expect affection from anyone but her father. Even if she foolishly kept hoping to earn her mother's love, she'd never counted on it.

Kat realized she'd let go of her mother almost completely while she'd been in prison. Loretta Wells had been alive, but in Kat's mind she'd died when she refused to return Kat's calls after her arrest.

Now she knew why.

Kat couldn't imagine not loving a child, but her mother had always been a little bit like Tori. Her world revolved around herself. There had never been much room in it for anyone—except Tori.

Her sister interrupted Kat's thoughts. "You don't remember visiting Mother?"

"No. Didn't you hear about it? Someone must have slipped poison into my food. I don't recall much before I woke up in Mavis Hill's bed."

"It's strange that you would go blank like that."

"Mavis believes someone gave me a rare drug called belladonna. It causes amnesia, and it's usually fatal."

"It wasn't belladonna," Tori said in a low voice charged with emotion. "It was arsenic."

"Arsenic? I don't think so. It doesn't cause—" The expression on her sister's face stopped Kat cold.

"It could," Tori said, a whipcord-thin muscle in her neck pulsing. "Drugs and vitamins and even herbal supplements interact with each other and cause all sorts of problems. I saw it with Mother, and read about it in a magazine. Hundreds of thousands of deaths are caused each year when people mix drugs and harmless things like vitamins and herbal supplements."

Kat nodded her agreement but her brain was riveted on a single word. *Arsenic.* "What made you say it was arsenic?"

Tori's face clouded with an uneasy expression. "I found a box of rat poison here, at Mother's condo."

"That doesn't mean—"

"Yes, it does," Tori emphatically insisted. "Mother talked about getting rid of you."

Jagged, painful memories like shards of glass pierced Kat's emotional shield and triggered a raw ache. She'd known her mother hadn't loved her, but at least Tori had always tolerated her. At times, her sister had actually been nice to her. "Did she hate me that much?"

She inclined her blond head and studied the carpet for a moment, then raised her eyes. "Mother was deceiving herself. I'm just a pawn that Judge Kincaid can play when it suits him."

Kat didn't know how to respond to the self-ridicule she detected in her sister's voice. At least Tori realized the judge was using her. A small step, Kat decided.

"You know how obsessed Mother always was about my marrying Clay." Tori rushed on without waiting for a response. "She thought your troubles would ruin my chances."

"I know she never loved me. That isn't a surprise, but trying to kill me … Well, I just can't believe Mother—"

"Believe it," Tori countered in a voice like acid. "Mother was capable of things that neither of us could have imagined."

Kat had heard enough. She couldn't bring herself to ask what else Tori knew. Part of her didn't want to know. *You've been through enough,* the rational side of her brain reasoned. *Let the past go.*

"She was crazy about my father," Tori told her after an awkward silence.

That wasn't news to Kat. How many times had her father been forced to endure stories of how wonderful, how handsome, how exceptional Vincent Conway had been? Nothing Parker Wells did could measure up to the myth of

Tori's father. Loretta had never let Kat's father forget he'd been second best. If Vince had lived, Loretta wouldn't have looked twice at Parker. How devastating that must have been for her father.

Tori stood, gracefully unfolding like a long-stemmed rose, Kat thought. Her sister walked over to the window and opened the set of shutters facing the street.

"Neither of us really knew Mother." Tori pivoted slowly and faced Kat, a steely resolve firing her green eyes. "She lived a lie her entire life."

Kat's thoughts spun in disbelief as she listened to how Tori's father had walked out on his wife and infant daughter. Tori was right; in her wildest dreams, Kat couldn't imagine her mother doing this. "Mother never divorced him?"

Tori shook her head and a wealth of glistening blond hair skimmed the shoulders of her expensive dress. "No. She married your father to get a meal ticket."

Kat's pulse began beating erratically. Her father had loved this woman and received nothing in return. Nothing. He'd been a kind, gentle man who'd deserved better.

"Funny, I always felt superior to you. I arrogantly believed I had it all. Both my parents adored me. In truth, we each had the same thing. One of our parents loved us. The other didn't."

Unexpectedly, Kat's temper flared. "My father would have loved you like his own daughter, but Mother wouldn't let him. She didn't want to share you, so he was stuck with me."

Tori dropped onto the sofa again and spread her hands wide. "It doesn't matter now, does it? They're both gone."

Kat wanted to say: All we have is each other. The words refused to leave her lips. She waited for Tori to say something—anything—that would bridge the differences between them. All her sister said was, "I have a black suit you can wear tomorrow for the funeral."

KAT DIALED Justin's cell phone and he picked up immediately. "It's me," she said, attempting in vain to keep the distress out of her voice.

"Where are you?"

"At the *Trib*. Everyone's gone home." She opened the car door to let the heat escape. Even though dusk was falling, the air was still warm and laden with moisture and the faint scent of wild honeysuckle.

"Where've you been?"

"With Tori. We had to plan the funeral. We talked…a lot." She didn't want to discuss their conversation over the telephone. "I think we're all set for tomorrow."

"I'm glad you called. I was getting worried. You were at the funeral parlor a long time."

"After we made all the arrangements, we had coffee, then picked out a dress for Mother to wear."

There was a long pause. "Are you two getting along better?"

Kat wondered how she could put into words what had happened with her sister. "A little, I guess. She told me some stuff." She heard the quaver in her voice.

"Are you okay?"

She braced herself and said, "Tori told me that Mother poisoned me."

For a moment there was complete silence. "Oh, babe, I'm sorry. I wondered about your mother, but it just didn't seem possible a mother could—"

She cut him off. "Let's discuss this when I see you."

"I'm onto something. I can't leave," Justin told her. "I want you to go by the station and pick up Redd. Spend the night at David's. I don't know how late I'll be."

"Okay," she reluctantly agreed. She'd been anticipating spending the night in his arms again.

"Call me when you get there. I want to know you're safe."

Safe? Now there's a concept, she thought as she slid into

her car. How could she ever feel safe again, knowing her own mother had tried to kill her?

Tori was standing in the living room of her condo when she heard Clay drive up. She didn't bother going to the door with a welcoming smile the way she normally would have. Instead, she kept opening the mail she'd brought in after Kat left. Already, dozens of friends—business acquaintances really—had sent or dropped off condolence cards and bouquets of flowers.

A few seconds later, Clay opened the door with the key she'd had made for him and breezed in. "Tori, sweetheart, I heard about your mother."

He gazed down at her with loving eyes. For an instant, it was the way it always had been—just the two of them. Without their parents hovering in the background, his disapproving, her mother insisting she'd been born to be Mrs. Clayton Ambrose Kincaid.

Things had changed, Tori thought while he murmured his sorrow for her loss. Loretta Wells had departed from the world of the living. Tori was finally free. Her mother's dying confession had somehow released her.

Clay guided Tori over to the couch. "Babe, I can't tell you how sorry I am that I wasn't there for you."

Clay sat, pulling her down with him. She didn't ask where he'd been or why he hadn't taken the time to call. He knew she'd been trying to reach him. She'd left enough messages for him.

"When are the services?" he asked.

"The viewing's tomorrow at nine," Tori replied in a wooden voice. "Kat and I—"

"Your sister is going to—"

"She's Mother's child as well."

"I just thought that under the circumstances…"

She glared at him. "We'll receive people in the mourning room right after the viewing. The funeral will be at two."

"My family sent a special arrangement from Mother's florist in Jackson. It's all white orchids."

Orchids, of course. His mother's favorite. Loretta Wells had loved yellow roses. Over the years, Clay had stopped numerous times with Tori when she'd bought her mother yellow roses for various occasions. Obviously, he hadn't remembered, or maybe it was easier to do what his parents wanted than to think for himself.

Tori forced herself to say, "That's very kind of your family."

Clay rose and went over to the armoire that served as a bar. "Want something?" he asked, reaching for the bottle of Johnnie Walker Blue Label that she always kept on hand for him.

She watched him splash a lot more than his usual two fingers of scotch into the cut crystal glass. He kicked back first one swig, then another. He exhaled with a satisfied grin.

"What's the matter, babe? You're awfully quiet."

Aren't you going to explain where you've been? Why couldn't I reach you when I needed you the most? "My mother's gone."

He tossed back the remainder of his drink. He walked toward her, saying, "I know how you feel, babe."

"How can you?" she blurted out. "You still have both your parents."

"True," he conceded, sitting down beside her. "I didn't expect you to be so upset. You've known for a long time your mother was going to die."

"That doesn't make it any easier."

He slid his arm around her shoulders and gave her a smile that could almost pass for genuine. His father's smile. Until now, Tori had never realized that Clay by subtle degrees was morphing into his father. He'd never possess the judge's cunning instincts or razor-sharp intelligence, but it was clear to Tori that Clay had begun to pick up his mannerisms.

"About the funeral," Clay said in a tone that some might have mistaken for regret. "Tomorrow isn't a good day for me. I have to be in Memphis with Dad and Mac, but I'll send Mother."

Tori stared into the blue eyes she'd adored for much too long. For once, she didn't say anything.

CHAPTER THIRTY-THREE

JUSTIN WAITED, concealed by a stand of snowball bushes growing wild along the frontage road by the casino. Laden with white blossoms the size of oranges, the bushes were taller than the squad car that Sheriff Parker once used. Justin was driving the cruiser instead of his pickup to appear as official as possible. David's source claimed that on the nights following the state inspection, a lone car, one of the fleet of black Lincoln Town Cars the *Lucky Seven* used to shuttle gamblers to and from the casino, left without any passengers. It returned less than an hour later. Just enough time to drop the money counted and sorted by the casino's electronic machines.

His cell phone rang, and he reached across the high-powered field glasses to grab it. The caller ID told him it was Kat.

"It's me. I picked up Redd and we're at David's. He's fixing lamb chops for dinner."

Relieved, Justin replied, "Good. Stay there. Lock all the doors."

"We already have, but we'll need to go out with Redd and Max before bed."

"Okay, just be extra careful."

He hung up, recalling what Kat had told him earlier about the poisoning.

Kat's own mother.

He fondly remembered the loving woman who'd raised

him. His mother would have killed herself rather than let anything happen to him. Life had cursed Kat with another kind of mother.

Motive and opportunity, he reminded himself. Loretta had been determined to make Tori a Kincaid for over thirty years. It was demented, but Loretta had a definite motive for wanting Kat out of the way.

One loose end tied up. With luck, the other loose end would be taken care of tonight. This "end" was more like taking a tiger by the tail. It depended on a string of "ifs" almost too long to count. *If* his source was reliable. *If* the Town Car was carrying the cash. Most important—*if* he could get Cloris Howard to crack.

He'd prepared as best he could, considering the short notice. He had his badge on and his gun in a regulation holster at his hip. He'd asked Nora, the only person he could trust at the station, to handle the night shift.

A black car sped by him, and Justin leaned forward, ready to trigger the siren and activate the flasher on the roof, but stopped himself. It was a Taurus, not a Town Car.

He settled back, engine idling, and watched several cars zoom by. It was a little after eight. He imagined Kat helping David clean up after the lamb chops. Was he ready for a domestic scene like that? You bet. Time to settle down with the woman he loved.

Love? Where had that come from? He'd never uttered the word out loud. He'd never considered committing himself to anyone. He'd labeled his feelings for Kat as a challenge, attraction, desire, and lust. He'd even admitted he was crazy about her.

Don't lie to yourself! You do love her. It was true, and if he were totally honest, he'd have to admit he'd loved her for some time. When it had happened he couldn't say exactly, but after she'd been missing, he'd been so worried that he hadn't been able to sleep. When he'd finally found her, every pore in his body had been filled with pure joy. He needed to sit down with Kat and tell her how he felt so they could begin to plan a life together.

First things first. He had to clear Kat's name before they could start over. And "starting over" might mean getting out of town, because he was about to break the law. Okay, maybe not break it but sure as hell, he was going to bend it. When this was all over, he might be out on his ass looking for another job.

Shortly before eight-thirty a black Lincoln Town Car drove past. It was traveling at least five miles under the posted speed limit, a disgrace for any red-blooded man in the county, but exactly what Justin would expect for a courier who'd been instructed not to risk being stopped by the authorities. Justin hit the siren button and the accelerator at the same time. The squad car shot onto the highway, blue-and-white lights flashing, siren wailing. He was on the Town Car's bumper in two seconds.

The car slowed, and Justin saw a pale face with dark hair checking in the side mirror. The car pulled over to the dirt shoulder. Justin drove up behind him, threw the cruiser into park, switched off the siren, but left the police lights flashing. He took his time getting out and sauntered up to the car, his flashlight in one hand, his other hand resting on the butt of his holstered pistol, a citation pad dangling from his fingers.

"Is there a problem, Officer?" The flip question came with an irreverent smile from a clean-cut kid in his mid-twenties, just the type the casino would use. One of Sartiano's usual goons would have attracted unnecessary suspicion.

Justin blasted him square in the face with the high-beam flashlight. "Let's see some ID."

The guy shied back from the intense light and reached in the back pocket of his khaki trousers, smile still in place. The punk was a cool number. Made sense. They trusted him to transport the money. This wasn't his first job for the Sartianos, but he wasn't very far up the food chain either.

"Slow and easy," Justin told him as if he expected the kid to draw a gun.

The kid's unflinching smile now held wariness as he pulled his license out of his wallet and handed it to Justin. He trained his flashlight on the ID but didn't bother to read it. He took the opportunity to covertly check what was in the backseat. Just as David's source claimed, a gray plastic container like those used by the postal service rested on the backseat. Justin didn't spot any bundles of money, but the bin was full with what appeared to be envelopes on the top.

Aw hell! Not regular mail or something innocuous, he prayed. The ball was rolling. It was too late to back out now.

"Step out of the vehicle," Justin told the kid.

"Now wait a minute, I—"

"You heard me. Out of the car!"

The guy leaped from the vehicle. "What's the problem? I wasn't speeding."

Of course not, and he would have an unblemished driving record, and the Town Car's plates in the state computer would be as clean as the day it had been driven off the showroom floor.

"I clocked you at seventy-nine," Justin fibbed. "I'm gonna need to run your license and plates."

"No way! Your speed gun must be broken."

Justin walked around to the back of the sedan, aimed the flashlight on the rear plate, while unclipping his cell phone from his belt and hitting speed dial.

Nora answered before the first ring was over. "Run this plate number," he said in a voice loud enough for the kid to hear, then he began to rattle off the letters and numbers in a lower tone. Could he help it if he accidentally transposed a digit so that this car matched one reported stolen?

Mistakes happen.

"Ten-four." He snapped shut his cell phone and stalked over to the punk kid. "Turn around. Hands on the car. I'm gonna have to frisk you."

The kid belligerently held his ground. "Why? I wasn't speeding."

"I say you were, dickhead. Speeding *and* driving a stolen vehicle."

"No fucking way!" The kid stared at him with the wild eyes of someone who couldn't quite believe he was in big-time trouble.

"The state computer is never wrong. You've got one second to turn around, spread your legs, and put your hands on the car, or I'll throw in resisting arrest."

The kid turned, muttering under his breath, and Justin frisked him. He wasn't carrying much other than some loose change and a cell phone. "Okay, you may face me now."

The kid turned, his eyes narrow slits.

"What's in the backseat?"

"You've got no right—"

Justin smiled at him. "A stolen car means I have the right to search for weapons or stolen goods. Want to tell me what's in the back seat before I look? The record will show you co-operated with authorities."

The punk shrugged, maintaining admirable composure. "Nuthin' much. Just a delivery to the bank from the riverboat."

"Really?" Justin feigned surprise. "Without an armed guard?"

"I think it's just checks."

Checks? Christ! Justin hoped not. He was betting on cash being laundered, not checks. Then he considered a different angle.

"Wait a minute! Doesn't the casino do all its banking in New Orleans?" Justin asked even though he knew damn well a Brinks truck made a daily pickup at the casino before heading back to New Orleans.

The punk lifted one shoulder in a subtle show of defiance. "All I was told was some checks missed the pick up."

"Where were you taking them?" he asked as if he didn't know.

"Mercury National's night deposit."

Justin managed to conceal his smile. He and David had suspected all along that the money gathered by the drug operation was going to Mercury National. Now was his chance to prove it.

A lot was at risk. His career was over if anyone could prove he hadn't made an honest mistake. No one—not even David or Nora—knew he'd spent time at an Internet café in Jackson to prevent anyone from tracing his online activities. He'd searched the Patrol's database until he'd come up with a stolen Town Car matching the description of this one. Now if only his luck held, he'd be able to link Mercury to money laundering for the drug ring.

He'd been ignoring another, more troubling problem. This bust would piss off Mayor Peebles big-time. He'd been specifically warned not to go near the casino, let their security handle their own problems.

No doubt this kid's arrest would infuriate the Sartiano crime family as well. He'd dealt with them in New Orleans and knew how ruthless they could be, but he figured he didn't have any other choice. How else could he help Kat?

BACK AT THE STATION, Justin threw the kid into one of their two cells. In his office, he inspected the bin full of envelopes. About two dozen computer-printed checks and deposit slips were on top of money pouches with the Mercury National logo embossed on the front. Justin didn't recognize a single name on the slips, but each one bore a similar notice in the

"memo" section: *approved auto loan. Approved home loan.*
A check of Twin Oaks' telephone directory confirmed his
suspicions. The casino was printing phony checks and making deposits to hide the drug money, laundering it through
supposedly legitimate loans.

Beneath the envelopes Justin found pouches of cash con-
taining deposit slips from local business addresses that didn't
actually exist.

Jackpot!

A classic case of money laundering. No wonder Ethel
Nolan had been suspicious. By cross-checking records, the
FDIC would easily uncover a scam like this. The bank had
needed time to cover their tracks, so Kat had been framed for
a robbery that never occurred.

Cloris had to be in on this. But who masterminded the
scheme?

CHAPTER THIRTY-FOUR

A LITTLE AFTER NINE-THIRTY, Justin waited in the squad car outside of Cloris Howard's home. The brick mansion with its fluted columns proclaimed a romantic time in the past when gentlemen bowed as ladies in hoopskirts mounted the marble steps. He'd already tried the bell, but no one had answered and it was dark inside. He wondered where she could be. Twin Oaks had a lot of places where guys could hang out, and there were spots like Moonin' N Coonin' where a certain type of woman could go. Cloris was not that type.

Nora had said Cloris was having an affair with Judge Kincaid—risky business now that Kincaid was running for the senate. Could she be with him? Maybe they were still hot and heavy. No, a lot of guys thought with their dicks, but Justin didn't see Kincaid in that group. Not now. Not with so much at stake.

But he could be wrong, Justin mused. Look at him, putting his career on the line for a woman he hardly knew. Granted, Kat had proven herself in many ways, but the things she'd been through had to leave scars—and his experience with Verity Mason had proven he was no judge of women.

Headlights swept around the corner and Cloris's silver Lexus pulled up the driveway into the six-car garage. Justin waited until he saw the lights come on inside the house before walking up and ringing the bell. A few moments later, the front door swung open. Obviously, two murders and a poisoning didn't have Cloris frightened enough to ask who was at her door before answering it.

Cloris had a welcoming smile on her face as if she were expecting someone else. When her eyes met his, her jaw dropped slightly. She immediately recovered and asked, "Sheriff, is something wrong?"

Justin had already removed his hat like a true Southern gentleman and now he played the good ole boy to the max. "Yes, ma'am. I need you to come down to the station. I believe we've recovered some of Mercury National's stolen property."

She stared wordlessly at him for a second. "Stolen?"

"Yes, ma'am. We need you to identify it."

"What is it?" she asked, clearly suspicious.

"You'd better come and have a look."

She appeared to be on the verge of refusing, but changed her mind. "I'll get my purse and meet you there."

"I'll drive you. A deputy will bring you back." The last thing he wanted was to give her the opportunity to call the guy behind the money laundering.

She hesitated, again seeming to consider whether or not to insist on using her own car. "All right," she said with a sideways glance. "I'll get my purse."

Justin followed her inside to make certain she didn't use the telephone. "Nice place."

She glared at him as if he were some lower life form incapable of appreciating the grandeur of the home that had been in her family for generations. She finally mumbled a grudging "Thank you."

Once they were in the car and on their way to the station, she commented, "I'm surprised you're working the night shift, Sheriff."

"We're short-handed. I can't expect my guys to pull all the late shifts."

They traveled the remainder of the short distance in silence, but the air in the car seemed electrified. Once they arrived at the station, Justin took Cloris inside and greeted Kyle Martin with a nod. He'd called in the deputy who'd been hired shortly before Justin arrived. Justin didn't trust any of his men at this point, but he figured Martin hadn't been around long enough to be taking bribes yet. Martin had been assigned the task of dusting the car for prints and gathering evidence from the vehicle.

"We stopped a car for speeding," he told Cloris as they approached his office. "Turned out to be a stolen vehicle. In the backseat was a box of deposits for Mercury National."

The color leached from her patrician cheeks and her blue eyes widened. He gestured toward the gray plastic box sitting on his desk. She stepped toward it, disbelief etched on her features like a death mask.

"Wait!" Justin grabbed a box of latex gloves. "We don't want to destroy any prints."

She stared at the box of gloves as if he'd offered a can of worms. After a slight hesitation, she snatched a pair out of the box. It took her a minute to pull on the tight-fitting gloves. He could almost hear the mental gears in her brain whirling at breakneck speed, trying to figure out what was happening and how to play this.

"Where did you say these came from?" she asked a shade too casually as she began to inspect the contents of the box.

"A stolen car. They don't appear to have been processed. Could someone have broken into the night deposit box?" Justin delivered the information as if this were the holy writ, not pure bullshit.

She shot back a tight, "No!" Then added in a softer voice, "The second the alarm goes off, your station is notified, then I'm called."

"That's what I thought," Justin told her, still playing the

dumb good ole boy. "I went by the bank on the way to get you, but the night deposit box didn't appear to have been disturbed. You never know. Electronics being what they are these days, the contents could have been removed without anyone knowing."

"True," Cloris reluctantly conceded as she peeled off the gloves. "I've heard of such cases in larger cities, but the night deposit vault at my bank doesn't receive large sums of money worth going to all that trouble." Cloris was no fool. She smelled a rat, but didn't know where it was exactly.

"I noticed the security camera over the night deposit box isn't working."

"Really? It must have just gone out or the security service would have taken care of it."

"It's possible the thief disabled it." Justin knew this wasn't true, but his check earlier in the evening had revealed the camera was out of order.

"These do appear to be our deposits." Her brows drew into a tight frown. "What did the driver tell you?"

"Very little," he hedged. "He's cooling his heels in a cell."

"Has he called a lawyer?"

"No. He hasn't been charged with anything…yet."

Right on cue, Nora, who was stationed just outside his door, interrupted them. "Sheriff, I have the Federal Prosecutor in Jackson on line two."

Cloris couldn't disguise the glazed look of fright that came over her face. Justin pretended not to notice.

"Tell him I know it's getting late but I'll call him back," he told Nora. She nodded and left.

"Federal prosecutor?" Cloris asked in a low, troubled voice.

"That's why the kid hasn't been charged. A stolen vehicle is the least of his problems." Justin dropped into his chair and motioned for Cloris to have a seat. "As you know, stealing bank deposits makes it a federal crime. He'll have to be charged in Jackson by federal authorities. I guess he'll call a lawyer from there."

David Noyes poked his head in the door. "Hey, Sheriff, I heard—"

Nora was right behind him. "I told Mr. Noyes you were busy, but I couldn't stop him."

Justin jumped to his feet and did his best to appear angry. He'd called David and told him what to say. Justin was counting on the presence of the press and the threat of bad publicity to convince Cloris to cooperate. "I don't have anything to say right now."

David ignored him. "Cloris, is it true? Were bank deposits found in a stolen car?"

Justin took David by the arm. "This is an ongoing investigation. I'll have a statement in the morning."

He escorted David into the hall and Nora followed them. He whispered, "Is someone with Kat?" Even though he knew that Kat's poisoner was dead, the kingpin of the drug operation was still out there. Kat still needed to be very careful.

"I called Connie Proctor. She should be at the house by now."

"Good. Stick around. I may need you again."

David tapped the pad of paper he had under his arm. "I'll work on the story while I wait. I may want to put out an Extra! in the morning."

Justin walked back into his office, shaking his head as if in disgust. "Police scanners should be outlawed. Every jerk in the county listens to our calls. The *Trib*'s already here. In no time the media from Jackson will be camped out like pagans at the gates of Rome."

Cloris gazed at him, her mouth set in annoyance—or apprehension. Justin sat down again, hoping this was a sign she was beginning to crack. His case was as flimsy as a house of cards. If Cloris didn't cooperate, he didn't have squat.

"Know what I find strange?"

"What?" she countered in a strained tone.

He held up a clipboard with a list written on it. "I wrote down the names and addresses of the depositors listed on the deposit slips. All of the addresses were in Twin Oaks. I've never heard of any of the businesses, and the people aren't in the telephone directory."

He waited for some excuse, some denial, but Cloris was one smart cookie. She knew when to keep her mouth shut.

He rocked back in his chair and gazed at her for a moment. "Know what I think? Money's being laundered through the bank. That's why I don't recognize any of the names on the deposit slips. Those people, those businesses don't exist."

She swallowed hard, but didn't say a single word.

He rose to his feet, walked around to the front of his desk, and stood right before her with his arms folded. "Let me be straight. As soon as I call the prosecutor in Jackson, the feds will swarm all over Mercury National. The investigation will be out of my hands."

She inclined her head slightly as if to indicate she understood.

"I'm between a rock and a hard spot here."

"What do you mean?" A thick chill hung on each word.

"In a few months, I'll have to run for office. I won't get any credit for this bust if I have to turn it over to the feds. But if you cooperate and I crack the case here before giving it to the feds, it's a win-win."

"I don't know what you're talking about."

"Here's what I'm prepared to do if you cooperate." He shot her a penetrating look. "I'll investigate this under the assumption that you knew nothing about the money laundering. This bin of phony deposits is the first you knew of the situation. The money that passed through the bank over the last few years was handled by Elmer Bitner. He was the crook—not you."

Cloris replied cagily, "What do you mean by cooperate?"

"I want to know who's doing the laundering."

"The casino, I assume. This *really* is the first I've heard of this."

Justin walked over and closed the door to his office. She was a tough nut to crack, but he felt a slight give in the way she was denying her involvement. "It's not the casino. They may be counting the money, but I've had a drop-off staked out. Couriers leave drug money from local sales." He took his position in front of her again and leaned, half standing, half sitting against the desk. "I don't think you want the media raking your good name through the dirt and linking it with a meth lab, do you?"

She colored fiercely, the blood rising to her cheeks. "Of course not."

"We've already learned this is a double-blind drug operation. The team making the meth in the backwoods and those distributing it don't know each other, and they don't know who the linchpin is. But you do."

"I don't know—"

"Cut the crap. Cooperate. I'll see to what I can to see the crime is blamed on Elmer. What's the harm? He's already dead."

She flinched, then said, "They'll kill me. All Elmer wanted was to be cashed out. He really was going to Guyana to start a mission. He was killed anyway."

They? Proof this was a wider ring than he'd thought. There might be one guy heading up the local operation, but others were involved. The Sartianos, no doubt.

Her voice faltered. "I need time to get away."

Justin figured she was smart enough to have money in offshore or Swiss accounts. Apparently they'd been doing this for years. Who knew how much she'd stashed? She could disappear and live like a queen without even bothering to liquidate her assets here.

"I'll tell you who killed the Mexican woman and Elmer. Proving it will be your problem. Elmer did set up all the phony accounts. Before I made him vice president, he'd been a loan officer. There's nothing on paper that says I handled any loan—ever."

"The idiot defense. Several major CEOs have tried it." He didn't add that they'd been found guilty anyway.

"I'll need a little time or I'm dead."

Wouldn't that be a tragedy? "Not a problem. I'll tell the federal prosecutor that I'll get back to him, and I'll just charge the kid with driving a stolen vehicle."

Justin made it sound as if he were doing her a favor. In truth, he was already pressing his luck by holding the kid under false pretenses. "I have no reason to hold you, but I'll find one if you don't give me the name I want."

A knock on the door interrupted them. Justin stalked over to the door. He'd told Nora that if he closed the door he didn't want to be interrupted. He swung it open, and asked Nora, "What is it?"

"There's someone here. You need to see her immediately."

"I'll be right back," he told Cloris. "Don't touch anything. We don't want your prints on the evidence, do we?"

He didn't wait for a response. He followed Nora into the reception area. A wide-eyed young girl with red hair was standing in the reception area.

"She says her name is Abby Lester," Nora said in a low voice. "She was in prison with Kat. She won't talk to anyone but you. She claims it's a matter of life and death."

He walked up to the girl and Nora went back to the dispatch desk. "I'm Sheriff Radner. What's the problem?"

"I'm Abby Lester. I'm out of Danville Correctional Facility while I'm awaiting a new trial." She gazed at him with troubled eyes. "I need to find Kat Wells. She's on furlough from Danville. I think she had to check in with you."

This girl seemed too young, too innocent to have been in prison. "That's right. She did register with me when she arrived."

"She's my friend. Kat helped me when I needed her." Abby's lower lip trembled. "I tried to find her. She doesn't have a telephone number. I don't know where to start."

"What's this about? I can't just release information to anyone who happens along."

She looked around to make sure no one was close enough to hear them, then whispered, hand on her breast. "I have to warn her. They'll kill her."

The word *kill* triggered a depth charge of fear in him. "Who's they?"

"I don't know, but when I was being discharged, I found out one of the inmates who works in the warden's office had snooped through confidential files. She sold information about Kat's record. The furlough is just a front. Kat's helping federal authorities. As soon as word gets out, she'll be killed."

Fear and anger knotted inside him. Sonofabitch! Here he was putting his career on the line for Kat, and she hadn't bothered to tell him this. Why not? Didn't she trust him?

He'd had a funny feeling about her from the get-go. He'd imagined a lot of scenarios—but never this. If she'd been undercover for the feds, why hadn't she confided in him? There had been plenty of opportunities.

Why are you surprised? he asked himself. He had a long history of misjudging women that went back to Verity Mason. He'd all but convinced himself that Kat loved him. What a crock! For all he knew, the whole thing had been an act. She'd made a deal with the feds; it was as simple as that.

He didn't know where he fit into her life—or if he fit in at all. An abject hollowness, a deep-seated sense of betrayal left him dazed. He'd been planning a life, a future with a home and children. What had Kat been planning?

Who knew? He tried to tell himself he didn't care, but he was hurt.

"Don't worry," he assured the girl. "I'll make certain she finds out."

"You're sure? My mother's waiting outside in the car, but I don't want to leave if Kat needs me."

He was so pissed he could hardly choke out a response. "Don't worry about Kat. I'll warn her."

CHAPTER THIRTY-FIVE

HE LIFTED HIS HEAD off the pillow, not certain what had awakened him. His bedroom was dark. Too dark. A shadow had slipped over the moon, stealing the pale light that usually filtered through the drapes and across the buffed wood floor. An ominous, bone-chilling thrill of apprehension snaked up his spine.

Something was wrong.

He sat up, unsure of just how he knew this, yet he did. All his senses were on heightened alert, a preternatural response he'd come to expect in tense situations. But there was nothing unusual in his bedroom. Everything was in its place and in perfect order.

Had he been dreaming? He didn't remember. He rarely dreamed, and if he did, he didn't recall them often. His lips thinned in irritation.

A face appeared on the screen in his mind. Kaitlin Wells. He should have whacked the bitch today, but she'd been with people until midafternoon, when he'd been forced to stop shadowing her and go to an appointment. If Loretta Wells hadn't died at such an inconvenient time, Kat would have simply "gone missing," and his problem would have evaporated.

The Sartianos would go apeshit if he attracted attention to the money he was funneling through the casino. The best way to divert everyone's interest was to get rid of the troublemaker. But he kept hitting road blocks. How long could he follow her before someone noticed?

He had to act fast. That was what was troubling him. The reason he'd awakened was simple. Self-preservation. When Kat Wells "went missing," he could sleep peacefully again.

His scalp prickled a warning and he inhaled a deep breath to calm himself. Kat Wells had eluded him twice, but that didn't mean he'd lost the magic touch. Mr. Hyde would get rid of her tomorrow, he assured himself. Still, he couldn't shake the uneasy feeling building inside him with the fury of a hurricane.

His sixth sense, and an attention to detail that bordered on compulsiveness, had always served him well. He rested his head against his pillow and stared up at the coffered ceiling. Outside his closed window, an owl hooted from a nearby tree.

He wasn't superstitious but his mother had always said, "If the owl calls your name, the angel of death is coming for you."

He listened more closely, but the owl didn't hoot again or call anyone's name. All he heard was the creak of the house, already ancient when he'd been born. It made noises at night— friendly sounds. He could be Jekyll or Hyde and the house didn't care. It always welcomed him home like a long-lost son.

Thunk.

The muffled noise alerted him, and he rose up on his elbows. That wasn't a sound the house made. It might have been a car door, but he wasn't sure.

Like a dry twig, something brittle inside him snapped, and he swung his feet to the floor, then grabbed the bathrobe he always kept folded into a precise square at the foot of his bed. Over his shoulder he checked the clock glowing on his nightstand.

2:00 a.m.

He tiptoed to the window and peered down to the sweeping drive below.

What the fuck?

There were at least a dozen cars—police cars—on his driveway. Twin Oaks didn't even have that many squad cars!

Through the glass, he detected low, muffled male voices and caught the *clack* of a gun bolt on a high-powered rifle. A steel fist grabbed his gut in a death grip. He couldn't think straight, but he did notice none of the cars were using their lights. Why not? Only the moon and the tubular beams of flashlights illuminated the darkness.

Get a grip!

He drew back, telling himself there had to be some logical explanation. But he couldn't think of a damn one. Could his years of anonymity have been compromised without him knowing it?

What the fuck could have happened?

The Sartianos wouldn't roll over on him. Never. They were tough, prepared for anything. The only other option was… Cloris. He'd thought killing Elmer had eliminated their weak link, but something must have forced Cloris to talk.

What?

Could she have been convinced to reveal his identity? She had as much at stake as he did. In a heartbeat, he realized she must have cut a deal. Made sense. She had balls of steel; ratting on him wouldn't bother her for a second.

Run!

He sprinted across the room, then halted. He wasn't a quitter. He knew when to hold 'em and knew when to fold 'em. This game wasn't over until he ended it—on his terms.

JUSTIN STOOD in front of the pitch-dark mansion. A few minutes ago, he thought he'd detected a movement at the window on the second floor. He'd squinted hard, then decided it had merely been a shifting shadow on the glass. Next to him, Special Agent Wilson gave orders to his men in a terse, low whisper.

Justin had had no choice but to contact the federal authorities in Jackson. As soon as he'd learned the identity of the drug linchpin here, he'd decided not to call in his own deputies until he had the feds backing him up. He couldn't afford to let the prick slip away.

Cloris had pointed them to the right man, but it was up to the authorities to make a case. Proving the bank was laundering money was going to be easy, but getting convictions for two murders would be more difficult. A good lawyer might convince a jury that the mastermind had been framed by the cops, had been abused as a child…pick your favorite "victim" defense.

The feds seemed to know more, but they hadn't clued him in yet. When he'd called with the money laundering info and the identity of the kingpin, they weren't surprised. If Kat was working with the feds—and he had no reason to doubt Abby Lester's story—the government had been trying to build a case against the Sartianos for a long time.

How Kat tied in, he wasn't sure. He was still all kinds of pissed at her. He hadn't bothered to call and let her know Cloris had squealed. He wasn't sure he could control his temper.

What kind of woman slept with you, let you protect her, let you put your career at risk for her—then didn't tell you she was working with the feds? Hadn't he proved she could trust him not to tell a soul? She'd used him.

He was positive the danger to her would be over once the feds made this arrest. Special Agent Wilson hadn't been concerned about her safety. If it appeared she might still be in danger, he would insist the feds move Kat into Witness Protection tomorrow.

If that happened, she would be gone months, maybe a year. That would be plenty of time for him to sort out his feelings for her. Get over her. Get on with his life.

"We're ready," Special Agent Wilson whispered to him. "You want to ring the bell, then read him his rights?"

"Yeah, thanks." Justin was pretty sure the darkness concealed his smile. Wilson was a good guy. Most career feds would have busted the ringleader themselves, but Wilson was allowing a small-town sheriff to take the credit.

Justin didn't have to glance over his shoulder to know David was back there somewhere. As soon as Abby Lester had left and Cloris had given Justin some details, David had raced out the door to the *Trib* for a camera. Justin knew he'd be ready to document the biggest story to hit Twin Oaks since General Lee's surrender.

Justin's stomach churned in anticipation as he led the phalanx of officers up the steps to the front door of the mansion. They all took care to walk silently but their footfalls echoed in the humid air. He ran the bell and waited, every muscle tense.

The light in the foyer went on, its soft glow gleaming through the majestic fanlight over the entry. The door swung open and Buck Mason stood there, fully dressed in a suit and tie as if he planned to drive to the office. Had he been tipped? Justin wondered. It didn't seem possible. He'd confiscated the cell phone Cloris had in her purse and warned her if she called Buck, she wouldn't be given any credit for helping the authorities.

"You're under arrest for the murders of Pequita Romero and Elmer Bitner." Justin barked out the words in an attempt to conceal the immense satisfaction this arrest was giving him. "You have the right to remain silent. If—"

"I'm aware of my rights," Buck said—not to Justin but to the men behind him with a hostile, unyielding stare. "You're making a big mistake. I—"

"Can it!" Justin waved the piece of paper he held in his hand. "We have a search warrant for your home and another for your pharmacy. Federal agents are already searching the bank and the riverboat."

The news didn't seem to faze Buck in the least. He'd always been cold as ice, Justin thought. No wonder Verity had taken her own life. How depressing must it have been to have a father like Buck?

A flashbulb went off behind Justin—David, recording the event for an *Extra!* that would hit the streets just after Twin Oaks woke up. What a shock! The leading citizen who'd donated thousands to Waycross Christian University was actually a drug pusher.

"I'm not talking to any of you. I want to call my lawyer," Buck said.

Justin wondered if he would call Clay Kincaid, then decided Buck was smart enough to have an attorney in Jackson. Clay was a lightweight with an addiction to gambling, just one of the secrets he'd learned when Cloris talked. She had been involved with Judge Kincaid, but the affair had ended last year when Kincaid became serious about his political career. A woman scorned, she'd been happy to talk about the Kincaids, but nothing she said would lead to their arrests. Justin had decided she'd hoped word would get back to David Noyes, and the salacious details of the judge's family life would appear in print. But Justin knew the Pulitzer Prize winner wouldn't trade in gossip.

"You can call your lawyer after we book you." He held out a pair of handcuffs. "Hands behind your back."

The flash went off again and again. Buck snarled into the blinding light.

"You've got an army with you. Is cuffing me necessary?" he asked, his face a study in self-control. If he'd been a card shark, it would have been impossible to tell if he held a winning or losing hand.

"Standard procedure," Special Agent Wilson said before Justin could.

Buck took his time turning and stuck one arm behind his back. Justin handed the search warrant to an agent near him, then reached forward to cuff Buck. Quick as a snake, Buck whipped around, grabbed Justin by the arm, and rammed a pistol into his ribs.

"Step back! Anybody moves and Radner's dead."

The men around him froze. Justin cursed himself. The minute he'd seen that Buck was dressed, he should have searched him.

"Okay, boys. Step back," the special agent told his men. "What do you want, Mason? You can't get away."

Buck jabbed Justin with the gun—hard enough to crack a rib. Justin stifled a gasp. "Don't bet on it. The good sheriff here is going to take me for a ride. If I even see so much as a headlight behind us, he's a dead man."

"Sonofabitch!" muttered Special Agent Wilson.

"Let's go!" Buck again jammed Justin in the ribs with the pistol.

Justin walked ahead of Buck, who held onto Justin's arm and kept the gun crammed against his side. The men parted like the Red Sea. Out of the corner of his eye, Justin spotted David clutching the camera to his chest.

How in hell was he going to get out of this alive? He had the fleeting thought that he'd gloated waaaay too early. Buck had outsmarted people for years. Justin should have anticipated this He wasn't ready to die, but Buck Mason was a desperate man. He wouldn't hesitate to kill.

He thought about Kat. How would she take his death? Would she care? Had she ever cared about him or had she merely been using him to help the feds? Unless he thought fast—and got lucky—he would never find out.

"Get in your car," Buck told him when they reached the fleet of vehicles parked at the far end of the sweeping driveway.

Justin had no choice but to lead him over to the cruiser he'd been using all night. "You won't get away with this."

"If you don't shut up, you won't live to find out if I do or not."

Justin opened the door to the squad car and climbed into the vehicle. Buck walked around the front, the gun trained on Justin the entire time. He opened the passenger door, plopped down on the seat, and thwacked Justin on the side of the head with the pistol. A stab of pain arced through his head and radiated downward to his jaw.

"Drive. Head south on the river road."

He wants to go out to the riverboat? Could there be someone at the casino who will help him? Justin turned on the ignition, then drove out of the driveway. In the rearview mirror, he saw the feds scrambling for their cars.

"You're just making things worse for yourself," Justin said.

"You think I'd put myself through some damn trial that would last months and months? Why make some wise-ass attorney rich?"

In that instant Justin realized Buck Mason wasn't trying to escape the way he'd originally thought. The maniac wouldn't allow himself to be taken alive. He'd die first, but so would Justin. Somewhere from the back of his mind came the negotiation techniques he'd learned at the New Orleans Police Academy.

Keep them talking.

"I can't understand why you would stoop to selling drugs," Justin said.

Buck snorted and poked Justin in the ribs with the pistol. "What do you know about me? I learned a few tricks at pharmacy school and found out I could make more money selling stuff to my friends at Ole Miss than my father or grandfather ever saw in their lives."

He got that right. Justin knew a lot of the "old money" in Twin Oaks had actually been played out several generations earlier. The Masons, Kincaids and their friends coasted on the coattails of the family name.

"You were running the meth operation around here," Justin said, trying to put a note of awe in his voice and make Buck think he was really clever.

It worked. "I had it all to myself, except I had to give

Cloris a small cut to launder the money when my take got too damn big to hide from the IRS." Buck sounded very pleased with himself. "My operation was running like a well-oiled engine until the riverboat arrived and the Sartianos insisted on getting a percentage."

Justin took a guess. "They made you kill Bitner when he wanted out."

Buck was silent for a long moment, and Justin didn't think the man was going to answer. "They demanded a lot of things. That's what happens when you become too successful."

"It doesn't seem like you spent the money," Justin commented, trying to keep the conversation going.

"I spent a fortune in Verity's name."

"Oh, yeah. I forgot," he retorted in a low, sullen voice. "The buildings at Waycross Christian."

Buck snorted. "Just the tip of the iceberg. What people can see. I set up a slew of perpetual scholarships in her name. I don't want my baby to ever be forgotten."

Verity had been Buck's whole life. His wife had died young and he'd devoted himself to his only child. When Verity killed herself, something in Buck had died as well. Her death had been tragic, but it didn't justify building a drug empire just to keep her name alive.

"Buck, I just want to say I'm sorry about Verity's death. If I'd known how depressed she was, I—"

"Depressed over you?"

Buck battered Justin's head with the gun again. Justin saw stars and swerved, barely able to control the cruiser. He swallowed hard to steady himself but his mouth was like dry clay.

"Verity wasn't depressed over you. She was happy at Ole Miss, and she could have been Clay's girlfriend again. But you'd ruined her. Completely ruined her."

Justin waited a moment for his head to clear and to concentrate on the road ahead before asking, "How did I ruin her?"

"She and Clay were together, just the way I wanted—then you stole her away."

Justin didn't want to set the record straight and piss him off more, but Verity had been the one to come on to Justin. She'd followed him around and flirted with him until he'd asked her for a date.

"You were scum. A nothing who lived in a trailer. God only knew what she saw in you except a number on a football jersey," Buck said, generations of inbred superiority in his voice. "When she went to Ole Miss, she fell in with even worse scum."

"I thought you said she'd dated Clay." Keep him talking, Justin told himself.

"She did but she kept slipping out with...niggers on the football team." As dangerous as a wounded bear, Buck ground out, "She thought I wouldn't find out, but I did."

Poor Verity. Justin could just imagine Buck going ballistic on her.

"If it hadn't been for you, Verity would never have stooped so low. She would have realized Clay was the man for her."

Justin didn't know the guys Verity had dated, but he'd known a lot of black guys who were a vast improvement on Clay.

"What did you say to upset Verity so much that she killed herself?" Justin took a guess. "You had the black guy thrown out of school."

"You never were half as bright as you thought you were," Buck rasped. "I didn't go near the bastard. I stopped my baby before she disgraced herself."

He couldn't believe this convoluted, mind-boggling revelation. This man lived for Verity, named buildings after her, funded scholarships. "What do you mean 'stopped her'?"

"Sent her off to glory before it was too late. She never saw it coming—I didn't tell her what I knew. Why fight? She loved me up until the end. One drop of poison in her Coke and she went to sleep."

"You killed her. Just like Pequita Romero."

"Exactly. I didn't study chemistry all those years in pharmacy school for nothing."

The man was a seriously demented lunatic, but a very clever one. He'd eluded detection for years. Fear crystallized in Justin. He was dead if he didn't think of something—fast.

"You're overdue," Buck told him in a disturbingly calm, quiet voice. "You've been half past dead since you came back to Twin Oaks."

"You won't get away with it. They'll catch you."

"Don't you wish! We're going to die together. I've got enough bullets for both of us."

"You sick bastard. You're too chicken to face a trial."

"No. My work's done here. I'm ready to go to glory." He waved the gun as if to hit Justin again but didn't. "Pedal to the metal. Let's get to the Moss Bend levee road."

Justin accelerated and inhaled a deep, steadying breath, then slowly released it as he came up with a plan. It might not work, but it was his only hope.

He knew the seldom-used dirt road. It was in an overgrown, deserted area concealed by old cane fields where the authorities wouldn't find them easily without a helicopter or dog teams. It was a sharp ninety-degree turn off the highway about a mile from where they were.

When they were close, Buck asked, "Know where to turn?"

"Yes, it's up around the bend to the right." He did his best to keep his voice solemn as if he were contemplating his last moments on this earth.

Buck ordered, "Cut the lights just as you turn. I want them to have to search long and hard for the damn car."

They approached the turnoff for the old levee road. "This is it, I think," Justin said as if he wasn't quite sure.

"That's it. Slow down."

Justin stomped on the brakes, throwing Buck forward.

Justin already had his left hand on the door. He flung it open and launched himself into the air just as the car slammed to a halt.

"Cocksucker!" Buck screeched.

Justin catapulted upward, then hit the ground with a bone-crunching thud. Hot, salty blood gushed into his mouth. Roll! Roll! Roll! He spun side over side until the gnarled root from the base of a tree snared him.

Shots split the night air like cracks of lightning. He looked up at the moon. It cartwheeled, then vanished into a burning blackness.

CHAPTER THIRTY-SIX

DAVID WAS AT LEAST six cars behind the lead cruiser following Justin and Buck Mason. They were traveling as fast as
possible, considering none of them had their headlights on.
Ahead, he saw a patch of white veer off the road at a right
angle. It was the car Justin had been driving.

They'd been ordered to maintain radio silence so Mason
wouldn't know what was happening, but now Special Agent
Wilson's voice blared out, "Shots fired! Shots fired!"

"Officer down!" shouted another voice. "Officer down!"

Please, God. Don't let it be Justin, David silently prayed.
All the cars' headlights came on almost simultaneously. The
patrol car Justin had been driving was wedged in a ditch. A
man in a suit leaped out of the passenger side, his gun aimed
at the cars closing in on him.

"Get down," the deputy driving the car ordered David.

Pop! Pop! Pop! David hit the floor, hearing the sharp re-
tort of gunfire. Where was Justin?

He huddled on the floor until the shots stopped. The front
door of the car opened and he heard the deputy yelling to someone. David rose to his knees and peered over the front seat.

"Send two ambulances," squawked a voice over the radio.

David bolted out of the car. He'd covered enough crime
scenes to know the police sent for an ambulance even when
it was clear the person was no longer among the ranks of the
living. Suddenly, men were swarming toward the patrol car

from all sides. Some were special agents in suits while others were deputies and reserve officers in uniforms.

Was Justin alive?

David charged forward, elbowing and shoving his way through the group. Ahead, awash in light from the headlights on high beam, David spotted Buck Mason's body. He'd collapsed backward, blood forming an ever-widening stain across the front of his expensive gray suit.

David spun around and spotted a small group of men huddled near a body. Justin! He raced over and saw his friend sprawled facedown at the base of a cypress tree.

"Is he alive?" David yelled as he ran up to them.

Special Agent Wilson nodded. "He's lucky."

David dropped to his knees beside Justin. In the distance, he heard the wail of an approaching ambulance. Oh, God, he prayed. Don't let him be too badly injured. He gazed down at Justin. Seeing him like this evoked feelings David didn't have time to analyze right now. Kat and Justin had come to mean more to him than he'd admitted even to himself.

"Hang in there," he told Justin. "Help's on the way!"

Justin moaned and valiantly tried to lift his head.

"Don't move," David said. "You'll just hurt yourself more."

Justin rolled onto his side, blood trickling from his mouth. "Wh—a-a-a...B-b...uck?"

"Don't worry. He's dead," David assured him.

Justin grunted a reply, but David couldn't be sure what he meant. His chest was moving a bit, his breath coming in quick, shallow bursts. David noticed Justin's clothes were smeared with dirt and blood, but he didn't see any bullet holes.

Justin levered himself up on one arm and swiped with the other hand at the blood oozing from his lips. "I—I'm," he said feebly. He gulped in some air, surged onto all fours.

"Hey! Don't move!" David cried.

"I—I'm…okay. Just…knocked myself…friggin' bat shit."

"Are you okay?" Special Agent Wilson asked.

Justin touched his side and winced. "Mighta' broken a few ribs."

"What about the blood?" David asked.

"I bit my cheek, is all."

"Let's have the medics check you over." Wilson turned around and waved at his men to make a path for the paramedics.

David let them take charge of Justin. As they were working on Justin, David pulled out his cell phone and dialed his house. It rang and rang, but there wasn't any answer. He hadn't called earlier because he didn't want to wake up the women, but he knew Kat and Connie would want to know about this. He needed both of them at the *Trib*, if he hoped to get out an Extra! in the morning.

He snapped his phone shut. Let them sleep; he would call them again when he was closer to town. He hung around, taking notes as the men worked the crime scene around Buck Mason's body. Half an hour later, Justin had managed to convince the paramedics and Special Agent Wilson that there was no way he would be taken back to Twin Oaks in an ambulance.

"I'll be sore as hell for a week, but I'm good to go," Justin told David with a self-deprecating smile. "Gotta practice those hard landings a little more."

David chuckled at Justin's gallows humor. The sheriff might very well have died tonight. Both of them knew it, felt it.

"Are you going to just stand there gawking at me or do you want an exclusive?" Justin asked.

Special Agent Wilson overheard them. "Hold it! I need to take your statement before the press gets it." Wilson pointed to the car he'd been driving. "Let's talk over there, Radner."

"Hey, what about me?" David asked.

"No reporters."

Justin halted. "You can trust him. If it weren't for David,

I wouldn't have cracked this case. Anything you say is off the record. Right, David?"

"Abso—fucking—lutely!"

Wilson glared at them both. "No leaks. We've been working for two years on this case. We've had an agent in deep cover here the entire time. Warrants are being issued right now. I don't want any of the Sartianos hightailing it before we can arrest them."

"I understand," David assured him.

David climbed into Wilson's car with Justin, where he listened to an amazing tale of drugs and greed. He couldn't help smiling inwardly. This story was much bigger than he could possibly have imagined. It was earmarked Pulitzer, if anything ever had been.

Share the byline with Kat, whispered an inner voice. She'd put her life on the line to get these bloodsuckers, and she would help him write the story. He brought himself up short. No! She would report it. She'd earned it.

David continued to listen as the special agent wrapped up the details about the case. He took notes for what promised to be a series of columns that would appear after the crime family was in jail. Reuters. AP. UPI. They would swarm all over this.

"Wow!" Justin said to David as they emerged from the car. "This is some case. Bigger than anything I worked on in New Orleans."

"With this to your credit, you won't have any trouble getting elected sheriff." He touched Justin's arm, taking care not to hurt him. "Give Kat a break. She didn't tell anyone that she was working for the feds. She didn't know who to trust and she must have been afraid."

Justin's eyes narrowed speculatively. "You're right. Given what she'd been through, I probably would have reacted the same way." He gazed off into the darkness for a moment.

"Know what I regretted the most when I thought Buck might kill me? I never told Kat that I love her." He bit back a wince and reached in his pocket for his cell phone. "I'm going to tell her about Buck right now. The personal stuff can wait. What's your number?"

"I already tried to call Connie and Kat, but we're out of cell range."

"No, we're not. The riverboat's not far from here. They put up a special receiver to keep gamblers happy."

David heard his own quick intake of breath. He was almost certain he hadn't misdialed. He told Justin his number and watched him punch it into the small cell phone. Justin held it up to his ear. A few seconds later, he frowned.

"No answer."

"Maybe they went over to Connie's," David said, doubt echoing in his voice, "but I can't imagine why they would."

Justin shook his head and spun around. "Deputy!" he yelled to one of his men. "Give me the keys to your car."

"YOU WON'T GET AWAY with this," Kat said with more certainty than she felt.

The gun pointed at her never wavered. "Get in the trunk."

Kat had no choice but to climb into the small trunk of her own Toyota. Her wrists and ankles were quickly bound with duct tape. A second later, the top shut over her like the lid of a tomb.

It was dark inside and suffocatingly hot. She told herself to stay calm and breathe as normally as possible to avoid using what little oxygen there was in the cramped space. *Don't panic!*

The car lurched into drive and slowly pulled out of the place where Kat had parked it in David's driveway. It picked up speed when it reached the street. Where was she being taken? Kat wondered. And why? That didn't matter. What counted was saving her life—somehow.

It was almost three in the morning. No one was around to help her. David had gone off to the sheriff's station to help Justin and wouldn't miss her for hours. The special chip that Justin had planted in her shoe must still be there, but no one would activate it until it was too late. Justin believed she was safe at David's with Connie. She would have to save herself.

But how?

She should never have opened David's door. If she'd even suspected—which she hadn't in a million years—she would have remained locked in his home with the dogs.

She'd been asleep in her clothes on the sofa when David had gently touched her shoulder.

"What?" She'd sat up, her mind still gauzy from sleep. "Justin needs me at the station," David explained. "I don't know how long I'll be gone. I've called Connie to come stay with you."

"Don't bother her." Kat gazed down at Redd and Max who were curled up on the floor near the sofa. "I'll be fine by myself. I won't open the door to anyone."

David shook his head. "Justin and I talked it over. We don't know who to trust. Drug money buys a lot of people. That's why I have to help him now. He can't rely on his deputies." He grabbed his reporter's pad from the desk next to the sofa. "We both want someone guarding you until it's safe."

"All right," she agreed as he rushed out.

She lay on the sofa, still a little groggy. When would this be over? She thought of Justin and couldn't help smiling. Soon, she promised herself. After this case was solved, her life could move forward.

She must have fallen asleep. The next thing she heard was a sharp knock on the front door. Max wagged his tail, but in the dim light of the lamp, Kat saw Redd's fangs were bared.

The rattletrap Toyota, its suspension shot from years of use, hit a bone-jarring bump. Her head slammed into the roof of the trunk. She cried out, a sound lost to the clanking of the car's tires as it sped over the railroad tracks.

Railroad tracks. We're going north, Kat realized. They hadn't been traveling long so they must be somewhere near the river. Where was she being taken?

Where didn't matter, she reasoned. What was her best chance for getting away?

She should never have climbed into the trunk, but she'd been too numb with shock to think clearly. She should have run, screaming, from David's house. His yard was big and surrounded by trees and bushes that would have muffled her cries, but at least a neighbor might have heard her. She hadn't yelled because the gun trained on her was equipped with a silencer. There was no chance anyone would have been disturbed by shots.

Now she remembered an article she'd read when she'd had time to burn in prison. Even an expert marksman had only a fifty-fifty chance of hitting someone running in a zig-zag pattern. It had been one of several tips in a story about what to do if accosted.

She should have made a dash for it when she'd had the chance. Another opportunity might present itself if—and it was a big if—she was allowed to get out of the trunk. For all Kat knew, she might be shot right here.

Running with bound ankles would be a joke. She'd have to hop. Could you hop in a zig-zag pattern? Probably, but first, she would need to get as far out of shooting range as possible.

The car gradually began to slow down. From the feel of the tires, they were still on pavement. Her judgment wasn't the best right now, but she thought they must be just beyond town. There the back road cut over toward the river and ran along the Mississippi until it reached Vicksburg.

The car stopped and Kat heard the front door slam shut a

moment later. This was her last—and only—chance to save herself now. Be prepared!

A second later the trunk lid popped open. Dank river air rushed at her, and Kat gulped it in. Fresh oxygen would give her much-needed strength.

"Get out!"

She thrashed her legs, not even trying to get out. They were cramped from being curled up to fit into the trunk.

Bzz-tt Bzz-tt. The cell phone clipped to Connie Proctor's belt rang. She slammed the trunk lid shut again, but Kat could hear her talking.

"I have no idea," the woman was saying in the businesslike tone they'd all come to trust. "I went by your house but no one answered the bell."

David must be on the line, Kat decided. He'd been just as taken in by this conniving woman as she had. He'd even called her to "guard" Kat.

"I know. I kept ringing the bell." Another long pause followed this lie. "Her car was gone so I thought she must have driven over to the *Trib.* I went there but didn't find her."

Come on, David, she silently pleaded. *You're smart. Pick up on something in this lunatic's voice.*

"I'm checking at her mother's right now." Another pause. "I remembered the address from the obituary I wrote."

Kat heard Connie say goodbye. It's now or never, she thought. The trunk popped open again and more of the Big Muddy's steamy, heated air gushed in. Along with it came swarms of no-see-ums and bloodthirsty mosquitoes.

"Hurry up and get out!" Connie grabbed her by the arm and hauled her from the trunk.

Kat swung her weight downward so she fell to the ground at Connie's feet.

"Get up!" the older woman screeched. "I don't have much time."

"Just tell me why," Kat said as she pretended to be trying to push off the ground with the palms of her bound hands.

Connie watched her, as alert as a wolf on the hunt. "David loves *me*. I'm the partner he never had at work or at home. He was just realizing it—then you had to come along."

Connie's admission caught Kat totally by surprise. True, she'd noticed how protective Connie had been, but she'd never suspected Connie had fallen in love with her boss. She was completely certain David had never encouraged the woman, but Connie was too delusional to realize this was a one-way attraction.

"I almost got rid of you the easy way—"

The light dawned. "*You* poisoned me!"

Connie smirked. "I slipped a little belladonna into that yogurt you like so much, but it wasn't enough."

"Thank you, God," she said to the earth below her nose. "I can die knowing my own mother didn't try to kill me."

"Get up!" Connie yelled, kicking Kat in the side. "Get behind the wheel."

"Why?" Kat levered herself up, ignoring the stabbing pain in her side.

Connie's menacing smile seemed even more frightening in the moonlight. "I'm meeting David at the sheriff's station. They want me to help hunt for you. Of course, you will have had a little accident. What you were doing out here will be a mystery but you'll end up in the river in your car."

"Wait a minute! How are you planning to get back?" she asked, still stalling and mentally calculating her chances.

"My car's not far from here." Again, Connie smiled her diabolical smile. "Get moving! I don't have time to waste. I'll have to run all the way to my car."

Kat stood her ground. "A forensic team will discover that my wrists had been taped. Justin will start investigating. He'll track you down."

Connie belted out a laugh. "Have you ever seen what a body looks like after a few days in water?"

The woman was right. It didn't take water long to destroy evidence on a body.

"Know what working for a paper has taught me?" Connie asked, but didn't wait for a response. "Investigation techniques. I found out how deadly belladonna is and that they grow it at the arboretum in Memphis."

"You're smart, all right," Kat said, buying time.

"You bet. I've studied the charts of the currents. Ol' Miss is deep here and the current is faster than most other places along the river. In this tin can of a car, your body will be halfway to New Orleans before they find it. If they ever find it." Connie prodded Kat with the gun. "Now move."

Kat held onto a sliver of hope. "Aren't you going to cut off the tape?"

Connie swiped at her with the gun. "Don't underestimate me, you little bitch. I'm not giving you a chance to get away. I'll cut the tape off—after you're in the car."

Go for it!

Kat swung her bound arms directly at Connie's face. The woman managed to hang on to the gun, but the blow knocked her sideways. Kat vaulted into the shadows beyond the car. She jumped one way, then leaped in the opposite direction. She gasped for breath, but kept springing from side to side like a frog on meth.

Hell-bent for leather, Kat bounded first one way, then another. She kept furiously hopping into the wooded area. Jumbled thoughts raced through her mind: her mother in the coffin, Justin smiling at her, Redd cautiously licking her hand. David reading an article she'd written. Tori's beautiful face framed by long blond hair. Standing on top of the toilet and looking out the window.

She was in dense brush now. The river rumbled along, not

far away. She might fall into it, if she weren't careful. Bound like this, she would drown in no time.

Knees rubbery now, she kept hopping. Behind her, Kat heard scrambling noises. What was Connie doing? She didn't have time to wonder. She had to put as much distance as possible between herself and that madwoman.

"Stop! Stop!" called a familiar female voice.

Kat kept bouncing one way, then the other, frantically ducking hanging branches and slipping on mossy rocks. Blood thundered in her ears, she gasped for breath, but kept springing along.

A shot blasted through the night air like a round from a cannon followed by another. They weren't near her, but the next shots undoubtedly would be. She hurled herself through the underbrush where it would be harder to see her in the darkness.

An odd fact registered. Connie Proctor's gun had been muzzled by a silencer. It would never make such a loud noise. Oh, my God! She jumped up and down wildly, struggling to keep a coherent thought. Someone was helping Connie. She had two people after her.

You don't stand a chance.

Despite the futility of her effort, Kat kept up her hopping spree. Justin's face floated before her eyes. Thank heavens she'd taken a chance and let herself become involved with him. At least now she knew what it meant to truly love a man.

She heard crunching sounds behind her and knew the end was near. What chance did she stand with her ankles and wrists bound?

Her foot caught on an exposed rock and she pitched forward. Both knees hit the ground at once and she toppled over, her head hitting the trunk of a tree. Clusters of stars blinded her. She could hear sounds but it seemed as if they were coming from underwater. She didn't have the strength to utter a word.

A blast of light from a flashlight hit her face. "It's me, darling," a low voice told her. "Are you okay?"

She squinted up into the blinding light. Was she dreaming? Or was she dead? "J-Justin?"

He gathered her into his arms. "Are you hurt?"

She managed to shake her head. "C-Connie?"

He slit through the tape with his pocketknife and rubbed her wrists. "Don't worry about Connie. She can't hurt you." He worked on the tape wrapped around her ankles. "I shot her, but she'll live to stand trial."

Her mind filled with a million questions, as she stared up at a swag of Spanish moss hanging from the tree that had taken her down. Only then did she notice the woman standing nearby.

"Maria?"

The other woman smiled. "That's my cover name. I'm Special Agent Teresa Hildago. I've been following you. Justin didn't know it. We both started shooting at Connie to keep her from killing you." The woman smiled. "Justin's the better shot. He took her down."

CHAPTER THIRTY-SEVEN

A SINGLE MEADOW LARK TRILLED from the branch of a nearby magnolia tree on the hillock where Kat's mother was being laid to rest. That morning when Kat arrived at the funeral home, the sky had been marbled with charcoal and white, but now shafts of sunlight punched through the clouds. Hours had gone by and the viewing followed by the service in the chapel was over. A rain-scented breeze had scuttled the clouds into an ominous mass with leaden underbellies. In the distance short pulses of lightning flickered, accompanied by the muted rumble of thunder.

"How are you doing?" Justin asked her in a low voice.

"I'm fine," she replied even though she was still shaky from the narrow escape last night and the emotional stress of the funeral. She leaned into the curve of his arm and permitted herself to be comforted by the bone-deep strength of his body.

The brief service had been delivered by Reverend Applegate. They had come out to the graveside to say their final goodbyes. Loretta Wells had attended his church for over thirty years, but it was apparent that the minister had never gotten to know Kat's mother. Nor had any of the other parishioners who'd been kind enough to attend the funeral.

In the short time since my return, I've made more friends than my mother made in a lifetime, Kat reflected.

Those who had taken the time to attend the funeral had drifted off after the service. Only a handful of people still stood at the graveside. Kat was grateful for the supportive presence of David and Lola Rae. They'd been accompanied by Maria—Teresa. None of them had suspected the shy illegal immigrant was actually an undercover FBI agent who'd been investigating the Sartiano crime family and the casino for over a year.

Tori stood opposite Kat on the other side of the grave, not far from the freshly dug mound of earth that would soon cover their mother. With her sister was a portly, balding man in his early forties. He shifted from one foot to the other while he waited for the minister to deliver his final words. The man owned the realty where Tori worked. Kat couldn't immediately recall his name but realized he seemed to be Tori's only friend.

Where was Clay? Kat had wondered this earlier when none of the Kincaids had attended the viewing or the service in the chapel. She'd considered asking Tori, then decided against it. The Kincaids had sent a spray of orchids in an exquisite rhapsody of whites that dwarfed the other arrangements.

"The Lord is my shepherd," the minister began. Kat and Tori had agreed to limit the graveside service to one final prayer before their mother was interred.

Justin gently squeezed her as the minister continued. Kat barely heard the prayer. Out of the corner of her eye, she caught sight of the headstone marking her father's grave. For a moment a sheen of tears obscured her vision. She forced herself to glance upward and concentrate on a dark wedge of migrating birds flying overhead.

Neither of her parents had ever known true love. They'd loved their children, but hadn't shared the love of a spouse. An ache lodged deep inside her, a feeling made even more powerful for its emotional honesty. She wasn't living her life that way.

I loved you, Mother. Even though you didn't love me, I loved you. I always wanted to please you the way I pleased Daddy.

Now it was too late, Kat silently admitted the truth to herself. Nothing could change the past. It was behind her now, but its lessons were not.

"...the kingdom, the power, and the glory, forever," continued the minister. "Amen."

Kat gazed down at the casket as it was being lowered into the ground. She'd insisted that Tori take money for the garland of yellow roses draped over the polished mahogany. Some of the blossoms were fully open while others were buds the size of a thimble. It was an exceptional display, far more beautiful than any floral arrangement her mother had received while she'd been alive.

"I don't think you need to see this," Justin said, his voice pitched low.

The casket was now at the bottom of the grave. Carrying shovels, two workers from the funeral home began to fill in the pit with the dark, loamy earth piled up on the other side of the grave. Kat stepped back, Justin's arm still around her, and from across the open pit, her eyes met Tori's.

"I need to talk to my sister for a moment," Kat said.

"All right. I'll be at my mother's grave," Justin replied as he reluctantly released her. They'd hardly been apart since he'd arrived at the river to save her from Connie. "Tell Tori we're going back to David's. She's more than welcome to join us."

Kat walked to the foot of the grave and waited for Tori. Her sister spoke for a few moments with her boss, then joined Kat. They silently took a few steps, keeping their backs to the workers who were quickly filling the grave before the storm hit.

"A few of us are going back to David's. I'd like it if you came over."

"I can't," Tori said. "I'm in a hurry. I need to start for Atlanta before it's raining too hard."

"Atlanta?"

Tori's mouth pulled into a tight line that might have been

an attempt at a smile. "I've decided to move there. You see…"
She took Kat's hand and turned her around to face their
mother's grave. "I want to start over—on my own. I loved
Mother, but I'm not going to be bound by her ideas."

Kat wasn't certain what to say. She'd never seen her sister
so emotional, yet so determined.

"See this?" She held up her left hand. "It represents all the
years I waited for Clay."

"I thought you loved him."

"I convinced myself that I loved him," she sourly retorted.
"It was easy with Mother constantly telling me what 'quality folk' the Kincaids were and how wonderful my life would
become once my last name was Kincaid. Clay was handsome and charming. It was easy to buy into Mother's
dream."

A tight knot formed in Kat's throat. "You've changed
your mind?"

"Yes. Clay gave me this ring because his father told him
to—not because it was his idea."

"I'm sure he loves you. He's always—"

"Done what his father wanted. That's why he isn't here
today. Daddy needs him." Tori tried for a laugh but it was more
of a croaking sound. "I followed Clay to Ole Miss and worked
two jobs just to be near him. Know what? His father told him
to start dating Verity again, and he did even though he *swore*
he loved me."

Kat couldn't imagine confident, beautiful Tori taking this,
but then, she'd never really known her sister.

"He would have married Verity the way his father
wanted except she dumped him for some black football
player."

Kat wanted to say she was sorry, but it was such a hollow
word. She thought of her parents. They'd both been like Tori.
They'd continued to love someone even though they'd known

it was futile. At least Tori had come to her senses before it was too late.

"What will you do in Atlanta?"

Now, Tori managed a genuine smile. "Sell real estate. I like doing it and I'm good at it."

Kat knew this was true. It had been hard to say no to Tori when they'd been younger. She could only imagine how easily this sophisticated, beautiful woman could close a deal.

Tori gazed at Kat for a moment, then slipped the heirloom ring off her finger. She tossed it into the loamy earth. The men filling the grave must have noticed, but they kept shoveling dirt. In a few seconds, the ring was no longer visible.

Ohmigod! Did her sister know what she was doing?

"That part of my life is over," Tori announced. "The ring is with Mother where it belongs."

Kat wished she knew how to respond to the angry defiance she heard in her sister's tone. *Leave it,* cautioned an inner voice. *This is between Tori and the Kincaids.*

Tori opened the designer handbag hanging from her arm and handed Kat an envelope. "This is for you."

"What is it?"

"A quit claim deed to Mother's condo. It's all yours."

"W-why?" she stammered in bewilderment. "Mother didn't want me to have—"

"Mother didn't leave it to you, but I insist you take it from me," Tori said in a firm, final voice. "I need you to take it. When you were arrested, I should have…"

"It's okay. In a strange way, the experience has made me stronger…a new person really." She attempted to return the envelope to Tori, but her sister shoved it away.

"It's the least I can do…considering everything. I want you to know how much I regret the way I behaved. I—"

"I know you're sorry. I don't want to take something Mother didn't want me to have."

Tori looked sideways at the grave. "It doesn't matter what she wants now, does it? We're on our own." Her sister's eyes were awash with unshed tears, pleading for forgiveness.

"I don't know what to say. I—"

"Don't say anything. Just be happy." Tori hurried away.

Kat wanted to call after her, but the words wouldn't come. She turned, clutching the envelope, and walked to her father's grave. The spray of red roses in a heart shape that she'd ordered early this morning stood beside the grave.

"Guess what?" she told the marble headstone that had taken her months to save for. "Tori and I made up...at least, I think that's what happened."

Let her go. Some lessons you must learn on your own. You did, and look at you now.

Had her father spoken to her or was it merely her imagination? Both, Kat decided. Love was so strong that time and place didn't matter. Her father was always with her—an angel on her shoulder—guiding her in the way she lived, the way she loved.

A roll of thunder shook the earth. Spring storms descended with a burst of speed and heavy rain—Kat had so much to tell her father and so little time right now. She would have to return on a sunny day and share with him the way she felt about Justin.

"Daddy," she said. "I am what I am because you loved me. Your love gave me the will to survive in prison. Without it, I don't know what might have happened to me."

She let out a low, tortured sob, then permitted herself to give in to the unrivaled solace of tears. Drops of rain pelted her head and shoulders, but she hardly felt it. She wept out loud, her body shaking.

Strong arms encompassed her and held her tight. "Sweetheart, don't cry," Justin said tenderly. "Let's get out of here before lightning hits one of us."

She took a few deep breaths until she was strong enough to raise her head. She looked up into Justin's eyes and saw what her mother and father had never known.

Love.

"I love you," she whispered.

"I love you more," he replied. "I've been waiting my whole life for you."

Turn the page for a look at the next exciting romantic suspense tale from Meryl Sawyer!

Coming from HQN Books, January 2007

PROLOGUE

Adam Hunter, you're dead.

THE MOMENT ADAM KNEW he was at death's door flashed back into his brain so vividly real his gut cramped. A split second before the incident, he'd realized his life was over. The other guys hadn't spotted the danger, didn't know death was an instant away. Adam had watched—stunned—unable to utter a word.

His body hadn't seemed to belong to him. It was almost as if he were seeing a film, as if this were happening to someone else—not him. He wasn't meant to die—not like this.

Then blood had coursed through his veins and reality had arced through him like a jolt of electricity. This was real. Move! Run! But there hadn't been time to run—nowhere to run—no place to hide.

In a heartbeat his world had exploded in an all-consuming pain and the bleak darkness of hell.

SHREDS OF MEMORIES DISSOLVED into the present. By some strange miracle, Adam had survived. He'd cheated death.

The others had not been so lucky.

Adam hadn't had a good night's sleep since escaping death. He thought if he could go home, he would be able to finally get some rest. He would put his head down on his soft pillow and stretch out on his own bed—home at last.

Home.

What a concept. He didn't have a home. All his so-called worldly possessions were in a storage unit, gathering dust.

He was still alive and traipsing around in paradise. He was a long way from the hellhole where he'd come within inches of dying. By some twist of fate, Adam Hunter had now arrived at his uncle's home in the Greek Isles.

Calvin Hunter greeted him with a smile some might have mistaken for the real deal. "Adam, how was the flight?"

Adam shrugged dismissively. He realized it was a rhetorical question. Hell, his uncle knew the flight to Siros Island on Calvin's private jet had been spectacular. His uncle would expect Adam to be impressed, but once you've looked death in the eye, it's hard to be impressed. Damn near impossible.

"Nice place," he said because he felt it was expected. Nice was an understatement, like saying Versailles was "nice."

His uncle gazed at him for a moment with shrewd eyes. Adam tried to gauge what the older man was thinking, but didn't really give a rat's ass.

"Let me show you—" Calvin gestured with a strong hand that sported a pinkie ring with a large canary-yellow diamond "—your room."

Adam looked down a hallway that he could have driven a Hummer through with room to spare. The villa on Siros was over the top just like the Citation jet. Well, hell, what did he expect? His uncle had always been larger than life and an enigma.

He trudged behind his uncle, still wondering why Calvin had sent for him now. He'd always distanced himself from their small family. Calvin Hunter hadn't bothered to come to San Diego when his half brother had died. Adam had handled his father's funeral arrangements alone. Of course his father's friends had offered to help, but there had been no other relatives at his side. He was still pissed with his uncle. Calvin had sent an arrangement and a condolence telegram, but hadn't bothered to telephone after the services to see how Adam was doing.

He supposed that cheating death had somehow gotten his uncle's attention. That must be why he'd stepped into Adam's life and sent the jet to pick him up.

Calvin Hunter was in his late sixties, but he retained a military stride from over thirty years in the navy as an arms specialist. The hell of it was—Calvin Hunter was a dead ringer for Adam's father. Adam hadn't been able to feel much since "the incident" but now memories of his father resurfaced. And he hated Calvin for resurrecting the past with all its sadness.

"This is it," his uncle said as he gestured toward the open door of a suite with a sweeping view of the harbor.

Without a hint of enthusiasm, Adam muttered, "Nice view."

Calvin studied him with cool blue eyes as if he were an egg about to crack. "Why don't you change into fresh clothes and join me on the terrace for a drink?" Without waiting for a response, Calvin pivoted in place, then walked away.

Adam sauntered through the room and tossed his well-worn duffel on the brocade bedspread. Fresh clothes? Yeah, right.

He crossed the marble-tiled room and went out onto the balcony. The timelessness of Greece and its long history awed Adam. He was the center of his own universe but the world was bigger than one man.

Others had died violent deaths. Others had cheated violent deaths. He wasn't unique. In the long history of this earth, he was merely another man who had been granted a second chance.

Adam stood silently and gazed at the boats bobbing at anchor and the crescent-shaped stretch of cafés lining the quay until he lost track of time. The sharp, frantic barks of a dog sent him back into the suite, which consisted of a sitting area that opened through a vaulted archway into the huge bedroom where Adam had carelessly tossed his duffel.

He rummaged through his things and found a pair of jeans

and a Coldplay Rules T-shirt. Neither were what his mother—God rest her soul—would have called clean, but he didn't possess anything better.

He scrounged around and came up with his dop kit. If his clothes weren't pristine, at least he could shave. He wandered into the bathroom and spotted the claw-footed bathtub with a handheld shower.

"When was the last time you showered?" he said out loud.

The words echoed in the high-ceilinged room. He shucked his jeans and shirt, then peeled off his shorts. They puddled on the floor beside the tub.

He turned on the taps but didn't wait for warm water before stepping into the tub. It had been over two years since his last hot shower. A fine spray of water misted over his still bruised body. Unexpectedly needles of scalding water pummeled his skin. He stared at the showerhead for a moment before the thought—hot water—registered. He adjusted the taps.

Using the bar of soap from the wall-mounted wire rack and a washcloth, he scrubbed his entire body twice. The shampoo on the rack smelled like peaches, but he used it anyway. His fingers told him how long his hair had gotten without him quite realizing it.

He dried himself, then found his comb in the dop kit and slicked back his hair behind his ears. It hung down to the nape of his neck. He found a throwaway razor in his kit, but there wasn't any shaving cream. He used the bar of soap to lather up.

Adam caught his reflection in the gold-rimmed mirror. Beneath intense brown brows a shade darker than his hair, Calvin Hunter's emotionless blue eyes stared back at Adam. Well, shit, what did he expect? He and his father as well as Calvin had all inherited Grandpa Hunter's eyes. But his father and grandfather's blue eyes sparkled with life and good humor. He'd had those eyes once, too.

Dressed in the black T-shirt and jeans, he wandered down the hall in search of the terrace. The villa was obviously old but immaculately maintained. Potted palms with ivy cascading from their bases were dramatically placed among what had to be authentic antiques.

"Thees way, meester," called a small man who must be one of the servants. He pointed to a double set of French doors that were opened onto a terrace that overlooked the magnificent harbor. The setting sun washed the sea with an amber glow.

His uncle, attired in white slacks and a navy sports jacket, rose from a round garden table. In his arms was a small dog that had no fur on his body except for tufts of hair on his paws and tail. His head had hair, too, with long hanks of fur sprouting from his ears. The poor mutt had to be a genetic mistake.

"Feeling better?" his uncle asked in a deep baritone that matched his military bearing.

"Ask me after I've had a drink."

Uncle Calvin gestured to a chair facing the view. "Have a seat. What would you like to drink?"

His automatic response would have been "beer," but he stopped himself. "Got a good pinot noir?"

"Of course." His uncle turned to the servant and said something in Greek. The little man scuttled away.

His uncle introduced him to the dog and proudly explained the goofy-looking canine was an international show champion. Not only had the dog taken Westminster "by storm," the pampered mutt had won Frankfurt International.

Adam decided his father would have hooted at how taken Calvin was with a dog. When Calvin had retired from the navy, Adam's father had expected him to spend time in San Diego, golfing and hanging out at the officers' club. Instead, Calvin had gone into dog breeding with baffling enthusiasm. An arms dealer turned dog breeder? Who'da thunk? After a few short years of breeding—what kind of dog Adam couldn't remember—Calvin had taken to the show circuit. He'd become a judge and had flown around the country to dog shows. Soon he'd gained quite a reputation and had become an international judge.

The little guy arrived with a glass of pinot noir. Adam took a sip. He couldn't remember the last time he'd relaxed with a glass of pinot noir.

"You're probably wondering why I brought you here."

"Didn't give it much thought."

Two beats of silence. "Adam, what was it like to be in the crosshairs of death?"

"I don't want to talk about it."

His uncle gazed into the distance for a moment. "I need to know—"

"What in hell for?"

"I think someone is going to try to kill me. I—"

"Who? Why?"

"You don't need to know. It would only put your life in danger." He fed the dog sitting in his lap a bit of cheese from the platter of appetizers on the table. "As my only living relative, if anything happens to me…"

HQN™

We *are* romance™

Chocolate can make a girl do the craziest things…

By *USA TODAY* bestselling author

JENNIFER GREENE

Lucy Fitzhenry has just discovered the best chocolate in the world…and it makes her do the craziest things. How else can she explain sleeping with her boss? Nick is so far out of her league that she's determined to forget that night and act the professional that she's supposed to be. Yet every time they taste test her brilliant recipe, they wind up in each other's arms and there can only be one explanation…

Blame It on Chocolate

Available in stores in January

www.HQNBooks.com

PHJG145

HQN™

We *are* romance™

She changed his life, but could she change his heart?

CAROLYN DAVIDSON

Civil War veteran and widower Jake McPherson lives as a
recluse. But it's clear that his young son needs a mother's
touch and new schoolteacher Alicia Merriwether seems
the ideal solution. Their marriage is only to be one of
convenience, but with each passing day it grows to be
something much more. Yet all is not as idyllic as it seems
and soon Alicia must decide if she can love her
new husband...in spite of himself.

Redemption

Available in bookstores in January.

www.HQNBooks.com

PHCD149

HQN™

We *are* romance™

The high-speed thrill of NASCAR meets the high-stakes game of love in this whirlwind romance by

PAMELA BRITTON

When the going gets rough, the tough get going…

The only job ex-kindergarten teacher Sarah Tingle can find is driving the motor coach for racing star Lance Cooper. She doesn't know a thing about NASCAR—and she's off to a rocky start when she doesn't recognize her ultrafamous and supersexy new boss! But as things heat up on and off the race track, Sarah's presence helps Lance shake off the slump that has been plaguing him all year. But is she only a good-luck charm…or the only woman for him?

In the Groove

The race begins! In bookstores this February.

www.HQNBooks.com

PHPB098

From #1 *New York Times* bestselling author

NORA ROBERTS

come the first two stories in the classic
MacGregor family saga that has touched
readers' hearts the world over.

THE MACGREGORS:

SERENA
CAINE

Serena MacGregor met Justin Blade during a Caribbean
cruise and the arrogant man wouldn't take no for an
answer in *Playing the Odds*.

The attraction was immediate between Caine MacGregor
and Diana Blade despite a strict professional relationship,
or were they merely *Tempting Fate?*

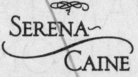

Silhouette®
Where love comes alive™

Available in trade paperback in January.

Visit Silhouette Books at www.eHarlequin.com   PSNR513

If you enjoyed what you just read,
then we've got an offer you can't resist!

Take 2 bestselling
love stories FREE!

Plus get a FREE surprise gift!

Clip this page and mail it to Harlequin Reader Service®

IN U.S.A.	**IN CANADA**
3010 Walden Ave.	P.O. Box 609
P.O. Box 1867	Fort Erie, Ontario
Buffalo, N.Y. 14240-1867	L2A 5X3

YES! Please send me 2 free Harlequin Intrigue® novels and my free surprise gift. After receiving them, if I don't wish to receive anymore, I can return the shipping statement marked cancel. If I don't cancel, I will receive 4 brand-new novels each month, before they're available in stores! In the U.S.A., bill me at the bargain price of $4.24 plus 25¢ shipping and handling per book and applicable sales tax, if any*. In Canada, bill me at the bargain price of $4.99 plus 25¢ shipping and handling per book and applicable taxes**. That's the complete price and a savings of at least 10% off the cover prices—what a great deal! I understand that accepting the 2 free books and gift places me under no obligation ever to buy any books. I can always return a shipment and cancel at any time. Even if I never buy another book from Harlequin, the 2 free books and gift are mine to keep forever.

181 HDN DZ7N
381 HDN DZ7P

Name	(PLEASE PRINT)
Address	Apt.#
City	State/Prov. Zip/Postal Code

Not valid to current Harlequin Intrigue® subscribers.

Want to try two free books from another series?
Call 1-800-873-8635 or visit www.morefreebooks.com.

* Terms and prices subject to change without notice. Sales tax applicable in N.Y.
** Canadian residents will be charged applicable provincial taxes and GST.
All orders subject to approval. Offer limited to one per household.
® are registered trademarks owned and used by the trademark owner and or its licensee.

INT04R   ©2004 Harlequin Enterprises Limited

HQN™

We *are* romance™

Don't miss out on the return of a steamy classic
from *New York Times* bestselling author

CARLY
PHILLIPS

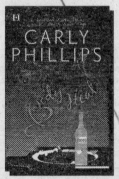

Massage therapist Brianne Nelson has fantasized about sexy,
injured detective Jake Lowell since they first met. And thanks to
his wealthy sister, Brianne is about to become Jake's personal
massage therapist for the next month! Only, Jake isn't in any
hurry to return to the police force just yet...not until he finds
the man responsible for his injuries; but in the meantime, he's
going to enjoy all the therapy he can get....

Body Heat

When wildest fantasies become a wilder reality...
available in stores in January.
www.HQNBooks.com

PHCP143